Radford Public Library
30 West Main Street
Radford, VA 24141
www.radford.va.us/library

P9-CPZ-869

Radford Public Library
30 West Main Street
Radford, VA 24141
www.radford.va.us/library

For Kafka

Copyright © 2008 by Clare Jarrett

All rights reserved. No part of this book may be reproduced,
transmitted, or stored in an information retrieval system in any
form or by any means, graphic, electronic, or mechanical,
including photocopying, taping, and recording, without prior
written permission from the publisher.

First U.S. edition 2008

Library of Congress Cataloging-in-Publication Data is available.

Library of Congress Catalog Card Number pending

ISBN 978-0-7636-3660-9

10 9 8 7 6 5 4 3 2 1

Printed in China
MAR 2 8 2008
This book was typeset in BodonAntT.
The illustrations were done in pencil
with paper collage.

Candlewick Press
2067 Massachusetts Avenue
Cambridge, Massachusetts 02140

visit us at www.candlewick.com

Arabella Miller's Tiny Caterpillar

Clare Jarrett

CANDLEWICK PRESS
CAMBRIDGE, MASSACHUSETTS

Radford Public Library
30 West Main Street
Radford, VA 24141
www.radford.va.us/library

Little Arabella Miller

met a tiny caterpillar.

One day when she was climbing trees,

she found him crawling on her sleeve.

She said, "Hello, Caterpillar,

my name's Arabella Miller."

*L*ittle Arabella Miller
carried stripy Caterpillar
through the garden with great care
and settled in her favorite chair.
She said, "Tiny caterpillar's
safe with Arabella Miller."

Little Arabella Miller
loved her wiggly caterpillar.
First he climbed upon her mother
then upon her baby brother.
Mom said, "Arabella Miller,
put away your caterpillar."

*L*ittle Arabella Miller

made a home for Caterpillar.

She stuffed a shoe box full of flowers,

then leaves and grass. She worked for hours.

She said, "Tiny caterpillar,

stay with Arabella Miller."

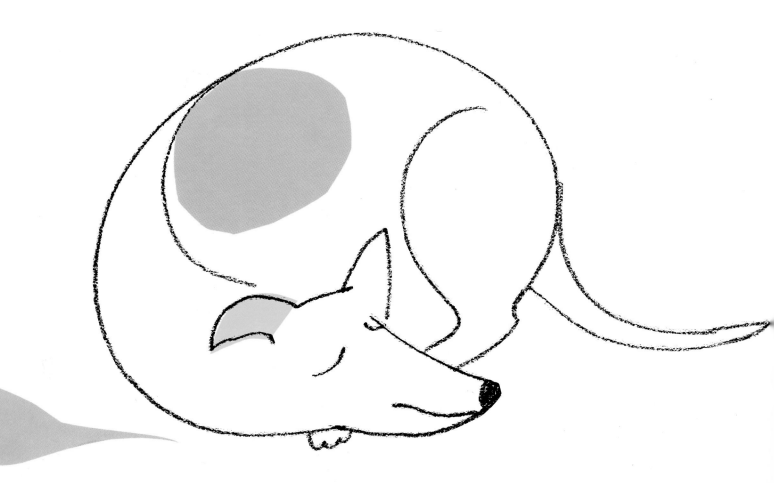

Little Arabella Miller
gathered food for Caterpillar.
Curly cabbage, crisp and crunchy,
frizzy parsley, fresh and munchy.
He mixed his meals up: first came brunch,

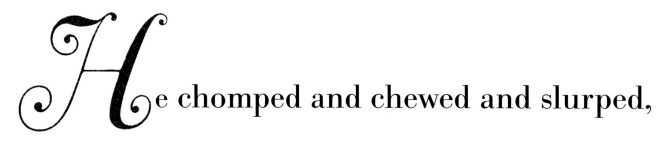

He chomped and chewed and slurped,

then *CRACK!*

His skin split all along his back.

And underneath it, big and baggy,

was a new one, soft and saggy.

He ate and ate and grew and grew,

for that's what caterpillars do.

On sunny days and in the rain,

he shed his skin time and again.

One hazy, lazy afternoon,

she watched him work and hummed a tune.

He made a shell with him inside—

the perfect, cozy place to hide.

Radford Public Library
30 West Main Street
Radford, VA 24141
www.radford.va.us/library

Weeks went by and Arabella
missed her friendly caterpillar.
She pictured him curled up in bed
inside his house upon its thread.
Every day she saw it gleaming
and wondered what he could
be dreaming.

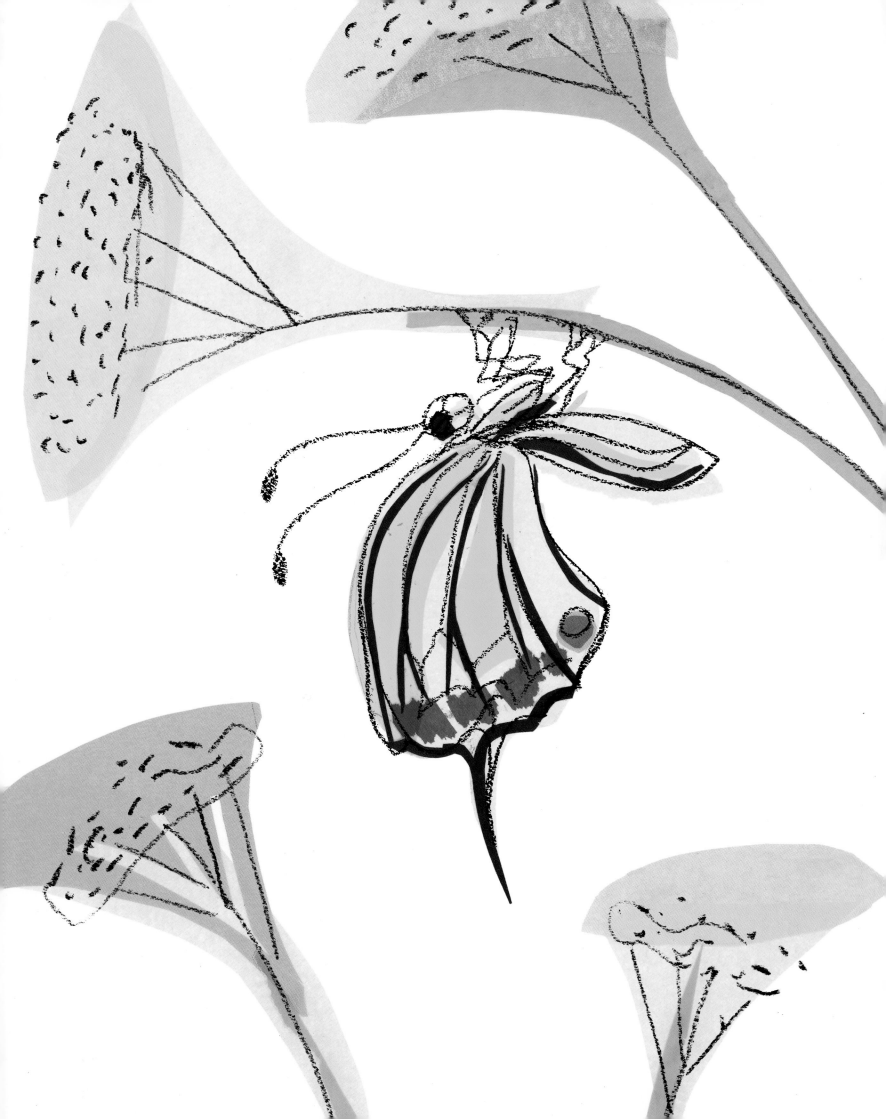

Then one day her caterpillar
puzzled Arabella Miller.

She saw him moving, poking through,

and out he came, completely new.

"Oh!" said Arabella Miller.

"You're so different, Caterpillar."

She held her breath and watched in awe

as he was changing more and more.

Bright wings unfolded, stretched to dry,

then up he floated to the sky.

"Good-bye, good-bye, away you fly, my very special butterfly!"

The Life Cycle of a Butterfly

The Egg

The female butterfly finds a plant and lays her eggs, often on the underside of the leaves. She chooses a kind of plant that her baby caterpillars will like to eat when they hatch. It takes two to three weeks for the caterpillars to develop inside the eggs.

The Caterpillar

When a caterpillar is ready to hatch, it eats a hole through the shell of the egg and wriggles out. The caterpillar's main purpose is to grow. It does this by eating constantly, shedding its skin each time it becomes too tight. The new skin underneath is larger, with room for growth. The caterpillar will take one to two months to become fully grown.

Charles Bargue

Designed by Ahmed-Chaouki Rafif
Assistant Marie-Pierre Kerbrat

© Worldwide 2003 by ACR Edition Internationale
20ter, rue de Bezons - F 92400 Courbevoie (Paris)
www.acr-edition.com

© 2003, DR
ISBN 2-86770-166-X

All rights reserved. Except for brief quotations in a review, this book, or any part thereof, may not be reproduced, stored in or introduced into a retrieval system, or transmitted, in any form or by any means, electronic, mechanical, photocopying, recording or otherwise, without the prior written permission of the publisher.

Printed and bound in France by Mame

The copyright on the photos of the 196 plates of the *Drawing Course* is held by the Musée Goupil of Bordeaux, which has given its permission for the plates to be enlarged by laser printers for educational purposes only—that is, as models for copying in classrooms or private ateliers or studios. Other pictorial material in the book may still be covered by copyright protection, and should not be reproduced.

NC
593
.B37
2003

Gerald M. Ackerman
with the collaboration of
Graydon Parrish

CHARLES BARGUE

with the collaboration of Jean-Léon Gérôme

Drawing Course

ACR Edition

DAHESH MUSEUM OF ART

This book accompanies the exhibition
Charles Bargue: The Art of Drawing
at the Dahesh Museum of Art, New York,
on view November 25, 2003 – February 8, 2004.

Visit the Dahesh Museum of Art
at 580 Madison Avenue
(in midtown Manhattan between 56th and 57th Streets),
New York, N.Y. 10022,
or visit www.daheshmuseum.org

The Dahesh Museum of Art is the only institution in the United States devoted to collecting, exhibiting, and interpreting works by Europe's academically trained artists of the 19th and early 20th centuries. The Dahesh serves a diverse audience by placing these artists in the broader context of 19th-century visual culture, and by offering a fresh appraisal of the role academies played in reinvigorating the classical ideals of beauty, humanism, and skill.

Drawing 7.
Study for *The Opinion of the Model. (Étude pour L'Avis du modèle.)*
The Walters Art Museum, Baltimore, Maryland
24.8 x 16.5 cm.
(9.75 x 6.5 in.)

CONTENTS

PREFACE AND ACKNOWLEDGMENTS

This book is dedicated to Daniel Graves for several good reasons, the most important being that he was the instigator, facilitator, and mentor for the book. From the beginnings of our friendship—some thirty years old—we talked about republishing the Bargue-Gérôme *Drawing Course*. The only complete set known to us at the time was in the National Art Library, Victoria and Albert Museum, London. Eventually both Mark Walker, the late and lamented scholar of Bouguereau, and Daniel separately photographed the plates of the *Drawing Course*, and prints from their negatives were soon circulating among a small group of artists. I enumerated to Daniel the difficulties in doing a new edition: the course had no text, and although it was self-evident that these were beautiful drawings—inspiring and exemplary models that any figurative artist would prize and want to copy—I as an art historian and not a trained artist found it hard to imagine my writing an explanation of the plates and their use.

After Daniel and Charles Cecil had opened their atelier in Florence, Daniel was able to make me the following offer: "Come to Florence and study in our atelier. I can't make an artist out of you, but I can teach you how to draw, and I can help you write the commentary for the plates." My first semester at the school was in 1983. Right off the bat I was given a plumb line, an easel, a cast of a foot in a shadow box, and was shown the rudiments of the sight-size technique. I was soon confronted by a model, whom I approached with my plumb line and chalk and the bit of experience I had gained in drawing the foot. Both Daniel and Charles—to whom I owe infinite thanks—treated me seriously as a "prospective artist." Both of them enjoyed the fact that I had had no previous training and consequently had little to unlearn. Each day they looked at my work, discussed it with me, criticized it, encouraged me, and pushed me along to the next step. It was a type of personal instruction I had never experienced and, sad to say, had never practiced in my teaching career. I was in a room with a dozen other students, and they, too, helped me with

technical matters of the most elementary sort—for instance, how to sharpen my chalk, or how to place my easel. The moments of silence and discussion among the students were equally inspiring. By all accounts a hardened art historian and theoretician, I was suddenly being initiated into how artists worked, thought, and *saw*. Following my initiation period, Daniel and Charles spent several evenings going over the plates of the *Drawing Course* with me. I made notations on one of the first portable computers. The notes I took then became the foundation of the commentaries in this book. So, Dan, here is your book. Charles, I hope you find it useful, too. You may both find it difficult to recognize your own words through the multitudinous revisions of the text, but it is their spirit and your teachings about how to look at the drawings that animate most of the text.

The writing of several books already under way prevented my immediate return to Florence and my resumption of the study of drawing. Nonetheless, I continued to draw in studio classes in the schools where I taught in the United States, and I also drew —most informally—with several groups of professional artists in Los Angeles, who patiently accepted my amateur standing while I learned more about their working habits. My gratitude here to sculptors John Frame and Judy Debrowsky, whose studios served as the sites for these weekly meetings.

In 1996 I went back to Florence, and for five years thereafter I spent a winter or spring semester at the Florence Academy. I gave several lectures—usually on great academic masters—and continued as a student, drawing *académies* in the mornings and working from casts or copying Bargue drawings in the afternoon. At the academy I was aided by many splendid artists who daily, in turn, criticized my work—Charles Weed, Maureen Hyde, Simona Dolci, Kevin Gorges, Angelo Ramirez Sanchez, Andrea Smith, among others—all of whom were patient, aware of my intentions and abilities, as well as my limitations. The ideas, methods, and sometimes even the very words of these teachers have worked their way into this book. I borrowed shamelessly:

from Kevin Gorges's discussions about what one learned from copying master drawings; from Charles Weed's critiques about the underlying reasons for using certain techniques; from the precise and thoughtful instructions of Simona Dolci and Maureen Hyde about the necessity of self-criticism and "getting it right." Among my student companions, a special acknowledgment must be given to Polly Liu, who always knew how to help out in a pinch.

These ideas, comments, and suggestions were all augmented and revised by me to give the text a consistency of voice and method. Here I was helped by my assistant, Graydon Parrish, an artist of great learning and intelligence, who regularly gave up months of his valuable studio time to sit beside me and go over every paragraph of the book. He contributed whole passages to the technical sections as well as drawing illustrations for the appendix; he constantly checked or questioned my vocabulary and helped to consolidate my various notes for the plates. We worked very closely, and he criticized and helped with all parts of the book. We often disagreed but, needless to say, our friendship has survived intact.

Many artists among my friends were interested in the project; a small number—Jon Swihart, Kevin Gorges, Peter Bougie, Tom Knechtel, and Wes Christensen—read the manuscript in its penultimate stage and offered intelligent criticism. Many other artists, eager to see the *Drawing Course* published and to give it to their students, have encouraged me through the years. I thank them all. My friends in Minneapolis—especially Annette Lesueur and Peter Bougie—sustained and encouraged me during the long travail.

I was also aided by my academic colleagues, dealers, and collectors. My colleague Frances Pohl carefully read through the final draft. The most wonderful example of how art historians work together is exemplified in the section of this book on Bargue's death: documents of great importance were discovered and forwarded to me by Madeleine Beaufort and Judith Schubb in Paris and by Eric Zafran and DeCourcy E. McIntosh in the United States. In Cincinnati John Wilson did detective work into the history of the Cincinnati Art Museum for me. The London and New York staffs of the auction houses Christie's and Sotheby's were generous with their time and always responsive in locating information and illustrations for the book. The administration and staff of the Goupil Museum in Bordeaux—in particular Hélène Lafont-Couturier and Pierrre-Lin Renié—were of crucial importance in terms of the physical production of the book. They supplied illustrations and information I requested at a pestiferous rate and arranged for the photographing of the plates of the *Drawing Course* from the two complete sets owned by the museum. Sylvie Aubenas and her staff at the Bibliothèque nationale in Paris found photographs of lost paintings by Bargue in obscure locations within the library. The staffs at the Huntington Library in San Marino and the Getty Research Center in Los Angeles, California, were especially helpful; in particular, I want to thank Linda Zechler at the first institution and Mark Henderson at the second. To the countless other librarians, registrars, curators, and collectors who in one way or another added to the information, richness, and accuracy of this book I extend my thanks and gratitude for your cheerful assistance. Curators at museums in England and the United States have done valiant work for me. The staff of the Dahesh Museum of Art—associate director Michael Fahlund, curator Stephen Edidin, associate curator Roger Diederen, and curatorial research assistant Frank Verpoorten—has provided unflagging assistance and advice both as colleagues and good friends. Last but not least, Monsieur and Madame Ahmed Rafif, my publishers, have given me the wonderful support and leeway that I have enjoyed for twenty years. It was Monsieur Rafif's genial and generous idea to add the catalogue of Bargue's paintings to this edition of the *Drawing Course*. Above all, thanks to my partner, Leonard Simon, for his patience throughout the writing and production of another book.

THE HISTORY OF THE *DRAWING COURSE*

INTRODUCTION

The Bargue-Gérôme *Drawing Course (Cours de dessin),* reproduced here in its entirety, is a famous and fabled publication of the late nineteenth century. Divided into three parts, it contains 197 loose-leaf lithographic plates of precise drawings after casts, master drawings, and male models, all arranged in a somewhat progressive degree of difficulty.[1] The course was designed to prepare beginning art students copying these plates to draw from nature, that is, from objects, both natural and man-made, in the real world. Like the curriculum of the nineteenth-century École des Beaux-Arts in Paris, whose ideals it shared, it was designed so that the student using it could eventually choose to render nature in both idealistic and realistic fashions. When the *Drawing Course* was published in the late 1860s, it was still generally assumed that the imitation of nature was the principal goal of the artist, and that the most important subject for the artist was the human body. The expression of the subject depicted had not yet been replaced by self-expression.

Despite being both rare and arcane today, the Bargue-Gérôme *Drawing Course* is one of the most significant documents of the last great flowering of figure painting in western art, which took place in the late nineteenth century. The present complete new edition will serve to instruct contemporary students in figure drawing, to present an important nineteenth-century document to historians, and to edify the general art-loving public, collectors, and amateurs.

The plates in the *Drawing Course* are *modèles,* which in English would be translated as "good examples to copy." The course follows the established routine in nineteenth-century art schools by beginning with the copying of plaster casts, proceeding to master drawings, and finishing with nude male models *(académies).* Since this tripartite division of activities was taken for granted in the curricula of the time, the plates were issued without instructions. Relying on the expertise of contemporary teachers and practitioners of academic figure drawing, the present editors have tried to indicate how these plates might be taught in classes and used by individual students today. Throughout, every attempt has been made to explain nineteenth-century drawing theory and practice.

The present book also introduces the figure of Charles Bargue (1826/27–1883), a lithographer and painter known now only to a small group of connoisseurs, collectors, and art students. An attempt has been made to clear his life of legend and to write a biography based upon the scant surviving evidence. His painted œuvre is small, and only about fifty titles have been recorded. Of those, only half have been located, most of which are in private collections. His *Drawing Course* is known to only a few through stray and scattered surviving sheets and from the hitherto only known complete set of the *Drawing Course* in the National Art Library, Victoria and Albert Museum, London. In 1991 two further complete sets were made public as a result of the founding of the Musée Goupil in Bordeaux. The plates reproduced in this book were selected from these two sets.[2] To make the introduction to Bargue more complete, an illustrated and annotated listing of all his known paintings has been included as well.

The first two sections of the *Drawing Course* were intended for use in the French schools of design, or commercial and decorative art schools. It was believed that in order to produce articles of commerce and industry that could compete on the international market, designers of utilitarian objects would benefit from knowing the guiding principles of good taste. (This was the argument in the brochure issued by Goupil & Cie to advertise the course *On Models for Drawing* [*Des modèles de dessin*]; see appendix 1 for an English translation of the text). Good taste, or *le grand goût,* was based on classical form, which was defined by the rarefied style of antique statuary. The combination of good taste and the study of nature resulted in *le beau idéal*—the rendering of nature in its most perfect manifestation—sometimes referred to more specifically as *la belle nature.*

The third section on drawing after live models, by contrast, was issued for use in art academies. Drawing after live models was discouraged or even prohibited in European and American schools of design, that is, in schools of commercial or applied arts, and was only seldom and reluctantly included in their curricula; it was strongly felt in the artistic establishment that commercial artists should not be encouraged to develop aspirations or pretensions beyond their perceived abilities.[3] The *académies* of the third part are examples of how the Neoclassicism of the early-nineteenth-century academy was revised by the new interests of the Realist movement. The Realists did not generalize their figures; personal traits—even ugly ones—are observed and recorded. Bargue's presentation of the male nude, although realistic, is always graceful and often noble.

The course sold well for at least three decades, including several large printings for various institutions in England as well as France. Individual plates were still sold by Goupil & Cie and its various successors until the dissolution of the firm in 1911. The lithographs were evidently worn out by use; some older art schools still have a few surviving relics of the set, usually framed and hung on the studio walls as examples of nineteenth-century assiduity.

The teaching of traditional academic practices almost died out between 1880 and 1950, as the number of academically trained instructors gradually diminished. This decline was concurrent with a shift in emphasis from an objective imitation of nature to a subjective reaction to the world, or even to the abstract qualities of art itself. This was a major revolution in art theory. Since antiquity Aristotle's definition of art as mimesis, or the imitation of nature, had dominated Western thought and practice. Before the 1880s "expression" meant the emotion or meaning conveyed by the subject—the person or thing depicted—not the emotional state of the artist, as in today's "self-expression."

The *Drawing Course* reveals what the last generations of traditionally trained representational artists were taught to copy and admire. Scholars investigating artists trained between the Franco-Prussian War and World War I will find that this book helps them understand the training and early work of their subjects. It is well known, for example, that Vincent van Gogh worked independently through the course more than once,[4] and that Picasso copied Bargue plates at the Barcelona Academy.[5] Many early drawings by artists of this generation thought to be drawn from life may, in fact, be copies after the models in the Bargue-Gérôme *Drawing Course*.

Today most art schools have dispensed with teaching drawing after plaster casts as an integral part of learning how to draw; and the modern life class differs greatly from the academic life class. Whereas the earlier training emphasized accuracy, solidity, and finish, modern instruction emphasizes gesture and self-expression, which often results in a nonacademic exaggeration of forms. Earlier the model held one pose for many hours, even weeks; modern life-drawing poses are very short; an hour is considered in many studios to be a long pose.

Many modern teachers and practitioners believe high finish is mechanical and inimical to self-expression. Furthermore, the modern teaching of anatomy is cursory. Modern drawing classes neglect the organic structure and unity of the model.[6] Students in drawing classes are allowed to draw approximate sections of bodies and to accept multiple test lines and accidents without correcting or erasing them. A persistent modern view holds that there are no mistakes in a work of art. The only criterion is the artist's intention.

By contrast, a good academic drawing—today as in the nineteenth century—should be accurate and finished, concerned with organic unity, and devoid of superfluous details. Careful academic practices not only develop patience but also train the student to see mistakes and correct them. In addition, academic theory urges the student to make continuous reference to nature in order to avoid excessive personal expression or mannerisms *(maniera)*. The human figure is viewed and painted with respect, without detachment or a sardonic air of superiority on the part of the artist. The academic tradition exalts the human body.

Public Controversy Over Teaching Materials

The catalyst of the Bargue-Gérôme *Drawing Course* was an official controversy about how best to teach drawing to French students of design and industry. A Parisian exhibition of student work in 1865 by the Central Union of Applied Arts (Union centrale des Beaux-Arts appliqués) caused much consternation. Eight thousand drawings and sculptures by students from the art departments of 239 public educational institutions had been put on display; officials and critics were united in decrying the exhibits as very poor in quality. Since early drawing education in the industrial and decorative art schools consisted mainly of copying after prints or casts, the general conclusion was that they had been given poor models.

At the exhibition's awards ceremony the sculptor Eugène Guillaume (1822–1905), director of the École des Beaux-Arts, verbalized his colleagues' dissatisfaction: "The main ingredient of art is taste. On this account, we are afflicted by the weakness of the models that are called upon to develop it. To place before the eyes of beginners in our schools examples devoid of all ennobling sentiments,[7] to have copied engravings and lithographs of a false style, of incorrect drawing, of schematic method—this amounts to the corruption of the taste of the nation; it makes the development of vocations impossible. These fundamentals of [art] instruction must be rigorously reformed."[8]

Ernest Chesneau (1833–1890), an art critic who became an inspector of fine arts in 1869, delved further into the problem in a series of articles published in *Le Consitutionnel*. Although he, too, expressed his unhappiness and dissatisfaction with the works on display, he saw a silver lining:

> [T]he great benefit of this exhibition will be its having opened the most obstinately closed eyes; of forcing the opinion of a few to become the general opinion; of leading, we hope, to a complete reorganization of the teaching of drawing. A reform as radical as this, I can't deny, is very difficult to achieve, but it has become absolutely necessary after the lamentable spectacle that offered us—under the pretext of drawing—a run of over a thousand meters . . . of everything that black and white together could create of inept, ridiculous, and poverty-stricken forms, deprived, with practically no exceptions, not only of any of the feelings of art but also distant from any resemblance, from any shadow of the foundations of the science of drawing: accuracy, life, beauty. . . . The lack of models! that is the dominant cry among the complaints provoked by the examination of the exhibition. . . .[9]

As an official reaction to the complaints of Guillaume, Chesneau, and others, the Ministre de l'Éducation Publique formed a committee to review available models.

Goupil Proposes a Solution

The demand for better models presented an opportunity that the publishing house of Goupil & Cie could not ignore. In 1868 it published a handsome twelve-page brochure in small quarto entitled *On Models for Drawing (Des modèles de dessin)*. With the self-righteous tone of an official government proclamation, the brochure pompously advertised the Bargue-Gérôme *Drawing Course,* which was already in print, more than half the plates having been released:

> All the known models and pattern books were passed in review [by a commission specifically appointed for this purpose]; but these models, for the most part, were exactly those that M. Guillaume had just denounced as corrupters of taste. . . .
> Thus it was left to individual initiative to solve the problem. Men of taste and learning applied themselves and a certain number of good models have been published. . . . The Maison Goupil could not remain a stranger to an effort having as its object the response to such a high degree of contemporary concern; it, too, set to work, and with the aid of some practical men it has designed a program whose execution has been entrusted to some distinguished artists. . . .
> Monsieur Charles Bargue, with the association of Monsieur Gérôme, Member of the Institute, was put in charge of the models for drawing the figure.
> In the choice and execution of these models no concessions were made to the pretty[10] or to the pleasant; their severity will doubtlessly discourage false vocations; they will certainly repulse those who think of drawing as an accessory study, a pleasant pastime; thus, it is not to such students that these are offered, but to those who seriously wish to be artists. [11]

The *Drawing Course* was not unique; there were many others on the market.[12] Around 1860, for example, Bernard-Romain Julien (1802–1871) had published his own course.[13] It was designed for use in the public schools of France, a fact it proudly declared on the title page. It parallels the Bargue-Gérôme course by beginning with details of the face and proceeding to full views of antique statuary. The plates are in a refined, linear, Neoclassical style, yet they might have been the very models against which Chesneau and the committee had reacted. It is hard to see the beautiful Julien plates as "debased," but their elaborately stylized refinement might have made them impractical models for the teaching of basic drawing skills.

Julien's drawing of a head, possibly a Diana (fig. 1), would be bewildering to a beginning student, and the schematic view to the right would not be very helpful. The delineation of the profile between the forehead and nose is subtle, with almost invisible modulations. The hair is complex and would discourage a novice. Furthermore, the dexterous cross-hatching could only be achieved with years of practice. The frontal, diffused lighting supports the clarity of the Neoclassical style but offers no indication of the underlying structure of the head, something needed by students with little experience of anatomy. Bargue, on the other hand, offered clues on how to manage the essential forms of the head and espoused a method to make long, modulated lines easier to manage by abstracting complicated curvilinear outlines into straight lines and angles.

Another Julien plate (fig. 2) depicts the head of the Roman empress Faustina, after a cast also used by Bargue, albeit viewed from another angle (plate I, 43). The Julien drawing omits the back of the head. The lack of a complete outline could lead to errors in the placement of the interior

Fig. 1.
B.-R. Julien. *Classical
Head. (Tête classique.)*
Lithograph. 47 x 28 cm.
(18.5 x 11 in.)

COURS PRÉPARATOIRE
Suivant le Programme adopté par le Gouvernement
pour l'Enseignement du Dessin dans les Lycées.
Autographié par Julien.

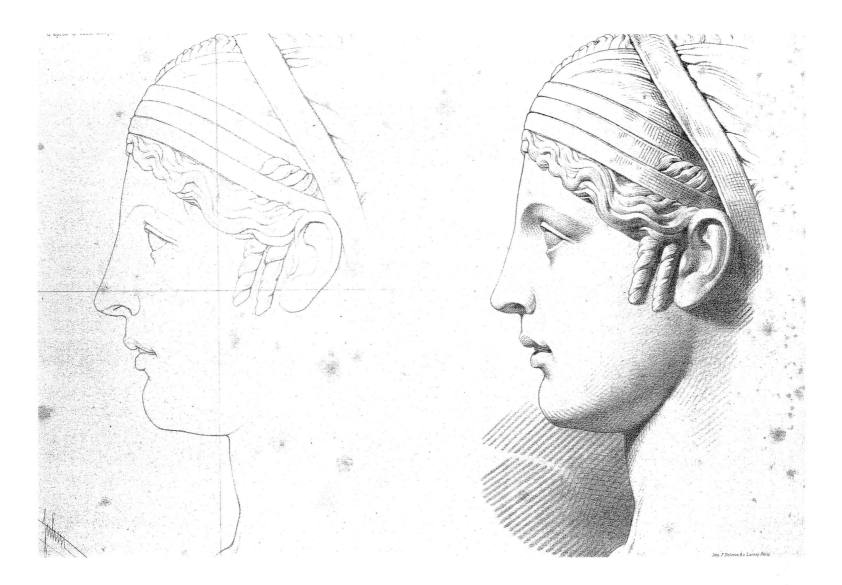

features. (Bargue depicts the entire cast first as a simple outline of points, lines, and angles, making it something measurable.) Julien has drawn the profile of the nose with a straight line, and the hair has been reduced to the demarcation of simplified shadows, with just a few lines. Bargue profits from direct, focused overhead lighting, giving a sense of presence to the figure and revealing the sitter's age. Julien's penchant for frontal lighting underplays the structure and character of his models.

A direct comparison of the *Homer (Homère)* by Julien[14] (fig. 3) and the one by Bargue (fig. 4) more clearly reveals the different approaches of the two courses. In both the drawing is excellent, tight and accurate. However, the proliferation of hatching in Julien's example confuses the relationships of the various volumes of the face. Bargue works tonally, logically progressing from light to dark. The result is a greater range of value from black to white, providing more drama, unity, and volume. It's almost as if Julien were emphasizing the decorative aspects of the antique bust as opposed to Bargue's stress on the sculptural qualities.

Fig. 2.
B.-R. Julien. *Faustina. (Faustine.)* Lithograph.
47 x 28 cm. (18.5 x 11 in.)

The Organization of the *Drawing Course*

In the Goupil catalogue of 1868 the *Drawing Course* was announced as *Models and Selected Works for the Teaching of the Arts of Design and for Their Application to Industry (Modèles et ouvrages spéciaux pour l'enseignement des arts du dessin et pour leur application à l'industrie)*. The first part was already in print; the second part, *Models after Masters of All Periods and All Schools (Modèles d'après les maîtres de toutes les époques et de toutes les écoles)* was in progress.

The first part, *Models after Casts (Modèles d'après la bosse),*[15] consisted of seventy plates and was described as "in itself a basic and [systematically] progressive course with the purpose of giving the student the capacity to draw a complete academic figure." The publishers were proud that "hardly had the first plates of the [first part of the] course been finished when the city of Paris ordered a special printing for the city schools, and in England the course was adapted by the numerous [educational] institutions supervised by the South Kensington Museum (now the Victoria and Albert Museum)." In many instances the Bargue-Gérôme course must have replaced the Julien course.

The brochure vaunts the selection of drawings for the second part: "These models were intended to develop in the soul of the students a feeling and taste for the beautiful, through familiarizing them with creations of a pure and noble style as well as with healthy and vigorous transcriptions of nature" (see appendix 1). It would be completed in 1870 as a set of sixty lithographs by Bargue after renowned old and modern masters.

The third part, *Charcoal Exercises in Preparation for Drawing the Male Academic Nude (Exercices au fusain pour préparer à l'étude de l'académie d'après nature)*, contained sixty plates and was completed in 1873. It was not mentioned in the brochure of 1868, and when it was published, it had only Bargue's name on the

Fig. 3.
B.-R. Julien. *Homer. (Homère.)* Lithograph.
45 x 33 cm. (17.75 x 13 in.)
Bibliothèque nationale, Paris.

Fig. 4.
Charles Bargue. *Homer. (Homère.)* Detail of plate I, 54.

frontispiece, without a mention of Gérôme (fig. 5).[16] This was the case because almost all of the subjects are original figure drawings by Bargue. Moreover, as was postulated earlier, the inclusion of drawings of nude males to be copied was a logical step after the first two volumes but presumably was not originally thought of as part of the course. Part III was likely disassociated from the first two volumes since it was intended for use in the fine arts schools instead of industrial and decorative arts schools. Possibly Gérôme's role as a collaborator on the project may have expired after the first two editions, or perhaps Gérôme simply respected Bargue's growing prowess and generously delegated the task to his colleague.

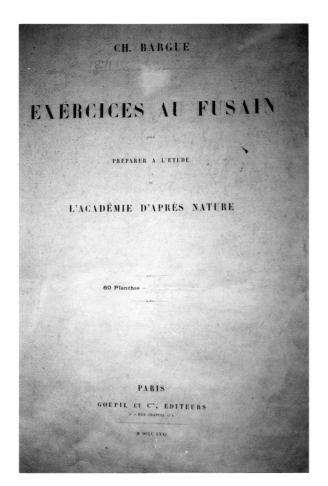

Fig. 5.
Title page of the *Drawing Course,* part III: Chalk Exercises.
(Page de titre du Cours de dessin. III: Exercices au fusain.)

PART I: DRAWING AFTER CASTS (*MODÈLES D'APRÈS LA BOSSE*)

INTRODUCTION

The first section, *Models after Casts (Modèles d'après la bosse)*, teaches the student how to systematically draw after casts by offering a collection of plates depicting casts of both partial and complete male and female bodies. Most of the casts are after famous ancient sculptures, but a few are taken directly from life.[17] They represent a selection that was duplicated, at least in part, in the collections of most European and American art schools.

There are several advantages to using casts as drawing models. Their immobility permits extended study of a single view or pose; and since they are usually white or painted in a light color, they provide an easier reading of the values of light and shadow on their surfaces. Moreover, the opinion has long persisted that copying casts of ancient sculpture develops good taste. One of the major goals of this course was to teach such elevated taste *(le grand goût)*, the proper selection from among the features and accidents of nature. Antiquity has long held the reputation for having gleaned the ideal human form from among the idiosyncrasies of individual physiognomies and bodies. The resulting classical style was for many centuries almost synonymous with good taste, and its goal was the depiction of *la belle nature*, the representation of natural forms in their purest and most beautiful manifestations, without flaws or accidents.[18] The style is recognized, indeed, defined by clarity, continuity of outline, geometric simplification of shapes, and the rhythmic ordering of forms.

In practice, the classical style sustains the integrity of each individual part of a form while containing the part in a larger, unified whole. The Greek temple facade, for example, presents a unified composition in which the parts are clearly separable and identifiable: the pediment; the entablature; the columns with their abacus, capital, shaft, and base; and the platform. Each part is independent in the exactness of its shape and the precision of its finish, yet each element is still a necessary part of a harmonious whole—that is, taken together they form a column that, in turn, is a part of the facade. Precision, assurance, clarity of form, the independence and interdependence of the parts: these traits make even a fragment of a Greek statue—a foot, a hand, a head, a limbless torso—an admirable, unified object in itself, while still alluding to the harmony of the lost whole.

Until recently art critics and historians chose the most idealizing period of Greek art as the high point of ancient art and named it the classical period (450–400 B.C.). Even so, the works of the sculptors (Myron, Phidias, Polykleitos) and the major painters of the day (Apollodorus of Athens, Zeuxis of Herakleia, Timanthes and Parrhasios) were known only from descriptions in literary sources and copies. Moreover, the few known copies of the paintings are particularly debased. This choice of one period as representative of ancient art ignores the energetic, inventive, and lengthy stylistic evolution of Greek and Roman sculpture, which expressed a variety of mental and spiritual states over a period spanning more than a thousand years,

Fig. 6.
J.-A.-D. Ingres. *Achilles Receiving the Ambassadors of Agamemnon. (Les Ambassadeurs d'Agamemnon.)* 1801.
Oil on canvas. 110 x 155 cm. (43.25 x 61 in.)
École Nationale Supérieure des Beaux-Arts, Paris.

maintaining high quality while continuing to use the classical style—which was long past its period of dominance—for certain purposes, such as giving dignity to portrayals of gods or statesmen.[19] For centuries critics ignored the production of preclassical statuary as "primitive," and decried the postclassical production as "decadent." *Le grand goût,* based on the art of the classical period (and of the major masters of the Italian High Renaissance), was thought of as the model for representational art. This classical ideal dominated art theory and teaching until it was challenged by the Realist movement of the mid-nineteenth century. After 1850 a new generation of students caught up in the principles of Realism rebelled against the practice of drawing after casts because they believed the classical conventions practiced in ancient sculpture prevented them from seeing nature accurately. For example, the young American painter Thomas Eakins (1844–1916) was a student in Gérôme's atelier at the École des Beaux-Arts in Paris during the 1860s. The students drew from life and then after casts, alternating every three weeks. Already a stubborn American Realist at eighteen, Eakins stayed home during the weeks devoted to drawing after casts.[20]

Two fine paintings, one by Jean-Auguste-Dominique Ingres entitled *Achilles Receiving the Ambassadors of Agamemnon (Les Ambassadeurs d'Agamemnon)* (fig. 6) and the other by the American master Thomas P. Anshutz, a student of Eakins, entitled *The Ironworkers' Noontime (La Pause de midi des ouvriers métallurgistes)* (fig. 7) clearly demonstrate the differences between the Neoclassicism at the start of the nineteenth century and the Academic Realism of the second half of the century. Both feature a row of masculine bodies—albeit a bit less nude in the Anshutz—all with varied features in assorted traditional studio poses. Ingres sets out a sample set of classical types: the youthful Apollonian hero Achilles; the younger Praxitilian Patrocolus; the slender, Mercurial Ulysses; and the Herculean Ajax. All are adaptations of classical statuary in Rome or Naples, and each represents one of the ages of man (the set is completed by the melancholic, brooding, elderly Briseus in the middle ground and the children playing in the distance).

The poses used by Anshutz are based on common studio poses. The underlying classicism is somewhat disguised by the nonidealized portrait heads, individualized bodies, and the recording of specific accidental traits (such as the sunburn patterns). Whereas Ingres uses a general light with just enough shadowing to model his figures, Anshutz imitates the sunlight of high noon, with resulting strong shadows, which, however, do not distort the forms. Nonetheless, both stick to the classical tradition of a frieze of figures united by their rhythmic placement and movement across the picture plane. Ingres's characters exist in the timeless world of mythology; Anshutz's figures are placed in a specific modern context, a factory yard. Thus, despite their differences, the two paintings are strongly related, demonstrating that Academic Realists retained, albeit latently, many of the interests, habits, and practices of Classicism.

The use of casts in the teaching of drawing gradually diminished until, by the 1920s, it was hardly practiced. By the 1950s even the once strict practice of drawing after live models had become merely a freehand event, without direction or criticism, and certainly without system or method.[21] The result was a decline in the quality of objective painting even by artists who wanted to maintain traditional standards.

Throughout the twentieth century the grand cast collections in the academies and art schools, which had been assembled with such effort and cost for over a century, were sold, given away, destroyed, or left to languish in corridors, subject to student pranks and mutilation.

Against the history of these changes, the Bargue-Gérôme *Drawing Course* can be seen as an attempt to balance contemporary Realism with the practices of classical Idealism. The authors intended to teach a method of drawing the human figure from nature with *good taste,* to instill in their students a practice based on careful selection, simplification, and a knowledge of the structure of the human figure. The method taught was newly informed with the excitement of the

Fig. 7.
Thomas Anshutz. *The Ironworkers'
Noontime. (La Pause de midi des ouvriers
métallurgistes.)* 1880–81. Oil on canvas.
43.5 x 61 cm. (17 x 24 in.)
Fine Arts Museums of San Francisco. (Gift
of Mr. and Mrs. John D. Rockefeller 3rd,
1979-7-4).

Realist movement of the mid-nineteenth century, and for a while—even against the incoming tide of modernism—the combination supported the creation of great modern history and genre paintings.[22]

The abandonment of the study of the classical ideal in the last quarter of the nineteenth century was a serious break in an established yet vital artistic tradition. After all, Western art is an artificial activity that became self-conscious in antiquity and again in the Italian Renaissance, each time articulating an intellectual, apologetic theory of art that continued to influence the creation and teaching of painting over the centuries. The twentieth-century break in this developed tradition is problematic for young, contemporary artists who may not be attracted by the many schools and movements of modernism but are instead drawn to the imitation of nature. Without access to the rich lore and methods of humanist figure painting, they find themselves untrained and underequipped for many of the technical problems that confront them as Realists. Without help, today's young Realist artists may end up uncritically copying superficial appearances, randomly selecting from nature, and unwittingly producing clumsy and incoherent figures.

Practical Matters: Using the Plates as Models to Copy

The Schemata or Plans

Most of the plates in part I of the Bargue-Gérôme *Drawing Course* contain two images: a finished drawing of a cast beside a linear schema. The schema, usually to the left, is a guide on how to accurately simplify the optical contour *(mise en trait)* of the cast next to it before starting on the actual depiction of the cast. The schema suggests a useful set of reference lines and sometimes a geometric configuration, around which it would be easy to organize the contours of one's own drawing (see, for example, the triangle drawn around and through the foot in plate I, 5). (The diagrams themselves should not be copied exactly but should be used as guides on how to begin a drawing.) Furthermore, the course presents only generalized rules on procedure; there seems to be no basic underlying formula. However, you should develop a working procedure of your own with reference to examples provided by the course. At the end of part I, when copying the last highly finished plates without a model schemata, you will have to rely on the experience gained from drawing the earlier examples.

The actual drawings after casts were probably done by several—even many—artists from Gérôme's circle of students and friends. We know the name of just one, Lecomte du Nouÿ (1842–1923; see "The *Drawing Course*" section of the Bargue biography in the present study), and we can safely venture the name of another, Hippolyte Flandrin (1809–1864; see comment to plate I, 70). Bargue copied their drawings on stone for printing as lithographs. The accompanying schemata all exhibit the same penchant for the use of angles, clarity in execution, and simplification of contours; it seems safe to assume that Bargue drew the schemata for the drawings as he copied the finished models on stone; they represent the unifying method of part I. However, there are a few plates where the schemata are less clear (for instance, plate I, 42) and schematized without a specific underlying method. The eyes in plate I, 1, for instance, are not organized around an unvarying point where the plumb line and the horizontal cross each other—say, the pupil—or the inner corner of the eye; instead the crossing point seems to have been chosen at random. In contrast, the other Bargue schemata are clear in purpose, skillfully organized, and based on carefully chosen angle points.

This chapter introduces and defines some terms that will be used in describing a systematic procedure for copying the model drawings. There are, of course, other methods, and if you are copying the Bargue drawings under supervision, the teacher or drawing master may suggest alternative procedures.

Start with the first drawing, work your way through the rest in sequence, or skip ahead judiciously based on your increased skill or the permission of your instructor. You will quickly note that each subdivision of part I ends with a challenging, highly finished drawing; the section on legs, for instance, ends with the fully modeled drawing of the legs of Michelangelo's *Dying Slave* (plate I, 30).

You will soon come to appreciate the skill that produced these plates, as well as their exceptional refinement. Even if you do not understand what you are copying, continue to work with accuracy. Sometimes you will not know exactly what a line or a shadow describes until you have correctly rendered it. By grasping Bargue's achievement, you will raise your own power of observation and simplification.

Materials

The lithographs were made after charcoal drawings and were intended to be copied in charcoal. You should use this medium if you have adequate command of the technique. Use natural kiln-dried vine charcoal in sticks, and reserve charcoal pencils for finishing (the binder used in them makes their lines difficult to erase). Only charcoal can equal the intensity of the blacks in the reproductions, and vine charcoal erases easily. However, you should not use it as a beginner without instruction; the use of charcoal presents too many difficulties to solve by yourself.

If you are a beginner, or if you prefer pencil, you should have a selection of well-sharpened grades—2H through B2 (remember that pencils softer than HB are difficult to use without producing slick, shiny surfaces)—and a good, kneadable eraser. Pencil cannot achieve the same density of darkness as in the plates. Any attempt to produce similar shadows with pencil will result in a multitude of loose flecks of carbon that will repeatedly spoil other areas of your drawing. Strive instead for overall lighter shadows and relatively lighter halftones.

Some of the more detailed plates need to be enlarged before you can copy them. Use a good color laser printer to have them magnified two or three times. The original plate size is 60 x 46 centimeters (24 x 18 inches). In their present size, you might not be able to see or copy many of the fine details, especially if you are working in charcoal. Regardless of the drawing medium used, you need high-grade, well-sized paper with a slight tooth and a surface that can take much erasure. Seek the advice of your art-supply dealer or artists you know. Inferior materials will lead to frustration and keep you from finishing the drawing accurately and neatly.

Drawing Terms

A *point* is a dot or mark without dimensions on a drawing surface. A *line* is a mark generated by extending a point (dot) between two points on a flat surface. Two lines that intersect or join form an *angle*. Points, lines, and angles constitute the basic elements for constructing the *contour* or *outline (mise en trait)*, the visual outer shape of an object.

Basically, drawing is the act of choosing critical elements from nature and recording them on paper while preserving their relationships. As you study the relationships of points, lines, and angles observed in nature, ask yourself: Is one point higher or lower than the other? Is one line longer or shorter than another? Is one angle more or less acute or obtuse than another? Asking these questions and making such comparisons will enable you to analyze and record the shape of the Bargue cast drawings or of any other object.

One of the goals of the course is to teach you to estimate distances, angles, and relationships with your eye. Some students use a pencil, a knitting needle, a taut piece of string, or a plumb line[23]—held with outstretched, locked arms and one eye closed—in order to more accurately measure the distances between certain points on the model and on their paper. This practice requires that you always look at the drawing or object from exactly the same unvarying position (see appendix 2). Some students also use a ruler or an angle with a protractor, which may save hours of frustration. However, you should train your eye to estimate these distances without recourse to tools.

Step 1: Make your drawing the same size as the plate you are using. This will facilitate direct comparison with the model. Then begin each drawing by locating the extreme points on the cast: the highest point, the lowest one, and those to the left and the right. Complex poses with extended arms, feet, and joints may require another dot or two to circumscribe. Make approximate marks for these four points on the paper. When joined by contour lines, they will form an irregular rectangle or shape that contains the basic shape of the cast and fixes the overall proportions. You will develop a more concise contour of the subject within this rectangle by measuring more angle points on the contour of the subject and placing them on the drawing, using your rectangle as a guide.

Step 2: As an organizational tool, draw a vertical reference line (hereafter referred to as a plumb line except in cases where the term might be ambiguous) on the paper by either copying the one from the schema or from the highest point of the cast. This line not only shows how the peak of the cast relates to the lowest point but also reveals how interior points for features inside the outline relate to each other. Since many of your initial calculations will be approximate, the plumb line becomes an invaluable empirical device. Additional vertical reference lines can assist in the understanding and drawing of complex areas.

Step 3: See which interior points the plumb line crosses on the plate and mark them on your drawing. For example, on plate I, 43 (Faustina) *(Faustine)* the plumb line intersects the top of the head and crosses through the left brow and the top of the eye. It then passes closely by the left nostril, conveniently touches the left corner of the mouth, but misses the bottom of the cast. From this line one concludes that the inward corner of the left eye relates directly to the left corner of the mouth. This is the type of observation about internal relationships that one should continually make as the drawing progresses.

Step 4: After establishing the verticals, examine the horizontals. For example, the right extremity of plate I, 43 occurs near the hairline overhanging the projection of the nose. The line drawn horizontally across the brow indicates that the width between the plumb line and the ear on the left is much greater than the distance from the same line to the edge of the right brow. Judge by sight the distances from the central plumb line to other points or angles on the contour and inside the cast; then mark their positions in your drawing. When you are drawing an entire figure and are looking at the head or feet from your standing position, do not move your head up or down, just the eyes. Failure to hold the head steady often results in elongated legs.

Step 5: Your drawing should now resemble plotted points on a graph, locating the heights and widths of the contours and interior features. Observe the angles that would be formed if the lines were connected; then join them with reference to the Bargue schema. Since the junctures of the plumb line and horizontal reference lines form right (ninety-degree) angles, use them to judge the relative degree of other angles. If the angles appear too acute or obtuse, study the finished model and correct them. Break curved lines into a series of two or more straight lines. For example, in plate I, 43 two straight lines describe the upper right brow, but seven straight lines plot the complexities of the ear. The Bargue plates offer many examples of how to abstract a complex contour into straight lines. Occasionally slightly curved lines are used instead of straight ones.

However, almost all curves can be reduced to straight lines that cross at the apex. Breaking up curves into straight lines enables you to ascertain the exact inflection point and amplitude of the curve. When you draw curves unaided, they tend to become arcs. Moreover, when drawing an arc it is hard to know when to stop.

Noting anatomical landmarks can be helpful at the outset in order to accurately draw the outline and establish the proportions. For example, the indentation on the right side of the nose and the pit of the neck are indicated within the outlines on plate I, 43. Likewise marks are made for some interior forms of the ear. These notations will vary from one cast to another. Looking up unfamiliar areas or parts in anatomy books and learning their names will help clarify your thinking.

Step 6: The next step is drawing the boundaries of the shadows. At this point your copy should appear relatively close to the preliminary schema or—if the plate has three steps—the second one. In plate I, 34 (Dante) *(Dante)*, the division between shadow and light is indicated with a line. For the most part, the shadow line is a generalization of the shadow's complex meandering across the cast, so do not make it emphatic. Squinting at the model will help in discovering this dividing line between light and shadow, for it will consolidate the dark masses. So will looking at it in a black mirror.[24] Do not outline the halftones (sometimes referred to as half-tints, from the French *demi-teinte*).

To repeat, begin each cast drawing by determining the most important points and general angles (with the aid of a plumb line or some other tool). Do not attempt to transcribe curves; average them with a series of straight lines. Concentrate on the large forms while ignoring small ones. Continually examine and correct the outline; anticipate the next set of more complex points, straight lines, and angles before attempting any modeling.

Values and Modeling

In art theory and practice, the term *value* refers to the relative lightness or darkness of an area exposed to light (some writers substitute *tone* for *value*). It can also be used to describe the absolute brightness of an object (seen or imagined as being without shadow or reflection on its surface). This even value is sometimes called the *local value* of the object. For example, a gray object has a darker local value than a white one.

In nature, values reveal the geometry of an object in relation to a light source. For instance, each side of a cube will have a different value because each has a different spatial orientation to the light source, a different amount of received light, and—to the viewer—a unique perspective. Similarly, the values will be affected by the kind of light hitting it (direct, diffused, or reflected) and by the strength of that light source (bright or dim). These distinctions all present difficult problems for the artist.

In drawing, the transcription of the relative values of an object is called *modeling*. There are three techniques for modeling: stumping *(estomper)*, veiling *(grainer)*, and hatching *(hacher)*. Stumping is the rubbing of the drawing medium into the paper, usually with the pointed end of a paper tightly rolled into a stick, called a stump *(estompe)*. Due to its cleanliness and precision, the stump is preferable to the fingertip. Stumping produces a soft, atmospheric effect.

The second technique, veiling, involves the drawing of faint lines with the pencil or charcoal tip lightly over the paper's grain. This technique alters the value in a very subtle manner; the effect may appear much like translucent veils or glazes. Veiling is useful when modeling delicate forms in the light and where the curvature is gradual.

Hatching, the third method, is the building up of dark value by means of thin parallel lines; when these lines cross each other at angles, it is called cross-hatching. This is essentially an engraver's technique. Some purists who want all the effects in a drawing to be the product of pure line favor hatching over stumping. Hatching can strengthen the modeling achieved by stumping and veiling. Moreover, hatching adds linear direction when drawn axially and helps to create the illusion of foreshortening when drawn transversely in perspective.

Procedure for Modeling

Step 1: The same rule—work from the general to the specific—applies to modeling as well as to line drawing. Begin with the large, dark, generalized shadow; fill it in evenly while referring to the finished drawing. You may schematize the boundaries in your drawing, but remember that the edge of a shadow is seldom abrupt; still, an area is either in light or in shadow and this difference must be made clear. Once added, shadows give the illusion of sculptural relief.

In modeling the shadows, Bargue downplayed reflected light, which in nature would flood the shadows of an actual white plaster cast. The simple shadows were most likely maintained by using a controlled, direct light and by placing the cast in a shadow box, a three-sided open box, lined with black paper or cloth, which diminishes reflected light (see glossary and section entitled "Excursus: Shadow Boxes" in appendix 2; see also fig. 44.[25])

Shadows record the effects of light and give the illusion of a shape turning in space. A focused light source, with a fairly small aperture (like a spotlight) emphasizes form and casts a shadow that starts out sharp-edged but becomes diffuse as it moves away from the object casting it. A general light, such as that produced outside at noon on a cloudy day, would reduce the shadows to grayish halftones. Classical taste emphasizes clarity of form over showy light effects; as a classicist, Bargue used light to reveal rather than obscure form.

Step 2: After drawing the shadows, analyze the value[26] of the halftones and place them in the drawing. (A halftone is any variant of value between light and dark—say, white and black. There are usually several halftones, of graduated value, in a drawing.) In the early stages of the course, the finished drawings are separated into three values: one for the shadow, another for the halftone area, and the white of the paper for the lights. Both the main halftone area and the shadows are clearly indicated. However, the transition from the halftones to the light areas requires care. Notice that the halftones can appear quite dark next to the lights and be mistaken for shadow. On a scale of values from 1 to 9, where 9 is the value of the paper and 1 is the darkest mark that the pencil or charcoal can make, the halftones on a white cast are around values 5 and 6. The average shadow is around 4, which is a little darker than the value of the halftones.

Step 3: After the darkest, major shadow has been filled in, the halftones are blended into the shadow and gradated toward the light areas. This can be extended to complete the modeling by the recording of every value. Plate I, 56 (Male Torso, back view) *(Torse d'homme, vu de dos)* illustrates the gradual lightening of values from the shadow into the halftones and from the halftones into the light, as well as the delicate transitions within the light itself. Here, too, the halftones and lighter values describe complex forms, as along the border of the scapula and around the dimples near the sacrum. Pay attention to the degree of lightness and darkness represented in the finished cast drawing. Each value relates to the other values yet holds its place within the total effect.

Notice the values of the halftones from area to area along the main shadow. Where the curvature of form is more acute, there are few halftones; a gentle curve produces more. Despite the range of values used in the modeling of the torso, Bargue presented a simplification of values and forms without a confusing proliferation of detail. Such control is a hallmark of the classical style.

Step 4: In general, as the course progresses, the finished drawings grow more complex and contain areas that may appear impossible to copy, especially if you were to work from the plates in the book rather than from enlargements. Resolve a complicated area by analyzing its essential structure. For example, divide the multitudinous curls of a Roman noblewoman into recognizable yet simplified masses or shapes. Squint at the values to obfuscate distractions and to average the values into discernable areas. Get a fresh view by looking at both your drawing and the model in a mirror: backward, upside down, or even sideways. Each step completed will make you aware of the next passage to work on.

Finishing the Drawing

Finish requires time and patience. However, as you gradually become aware of how much you have learned by being careful and accurate, your patience and enthusiasm will increase. Ask for criticism from knowledgeable peers. Study your drawing; it is essential that you learn to see and correct your errors yourself. You could also make a tracing of your drawing and then lay it on top of the plate. Analyze what went wrong, especially if you are working alone. Be strict with yourself. A drawing can be stopped at any time, as long as there are no errors in it.

Remember that the academic artists of the nineteenth century whom you are learning to emulate in this course thought that finish denoted professionalism, that it indicated an orderly mind and represented the complete development of the artist's idea. It was not uncommon for an artist to spend months or even years to complete a work. Accept the fact that classical drawing skills develop slowly and plan to use as much time as needed—hours, days, or even months—to achieve a respectable finish.

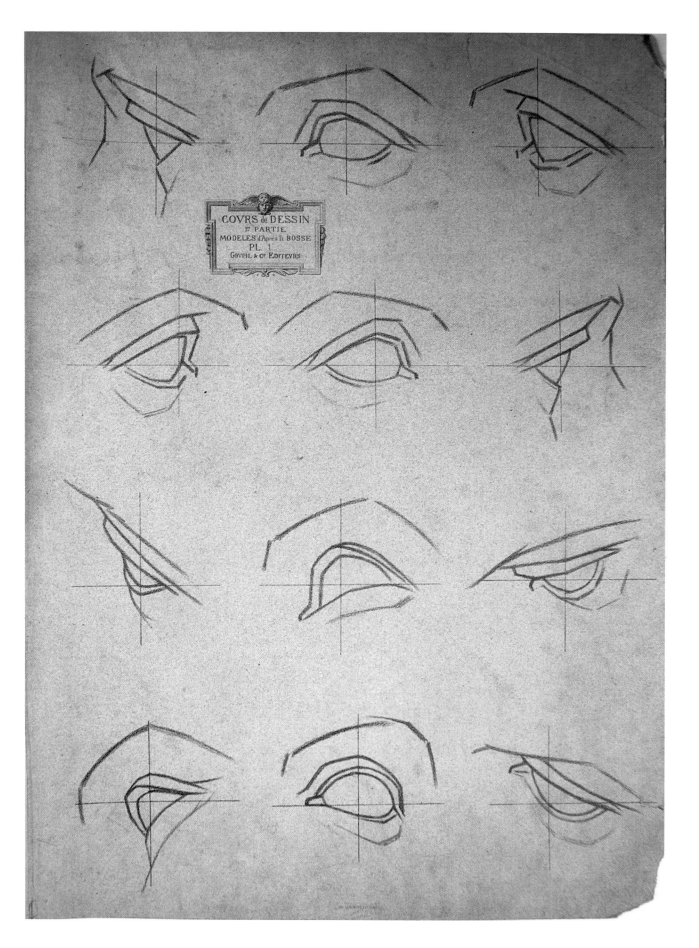

Plate I, 1

COVRS de DESSIN
1.ͤ PARTIE.
MODELES d'Aprés la BOSSE
PL. 2
GOVPIL & C.ͤ EDITEVRS

Plate I, 2

Plate I, 3

Plate I, 4

31

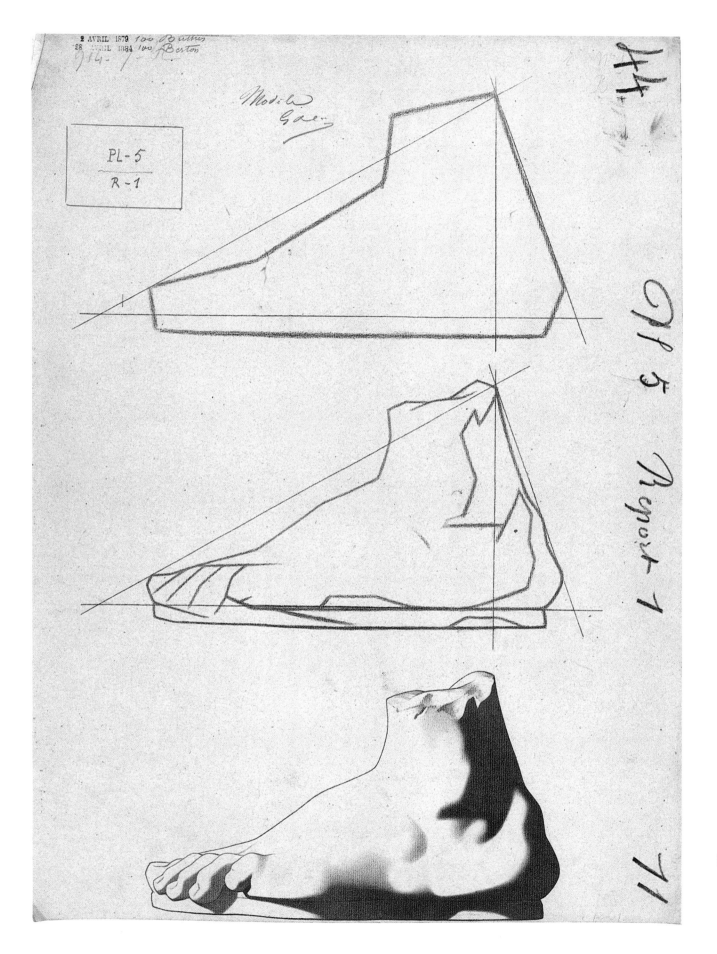

Plate I, 5

32

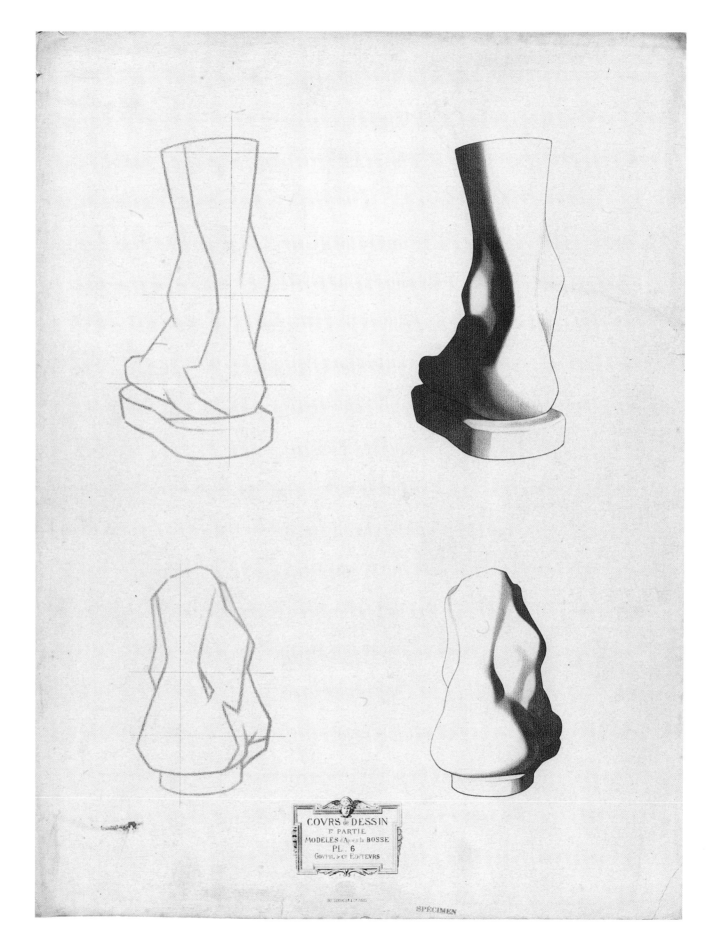

Plate I, 6

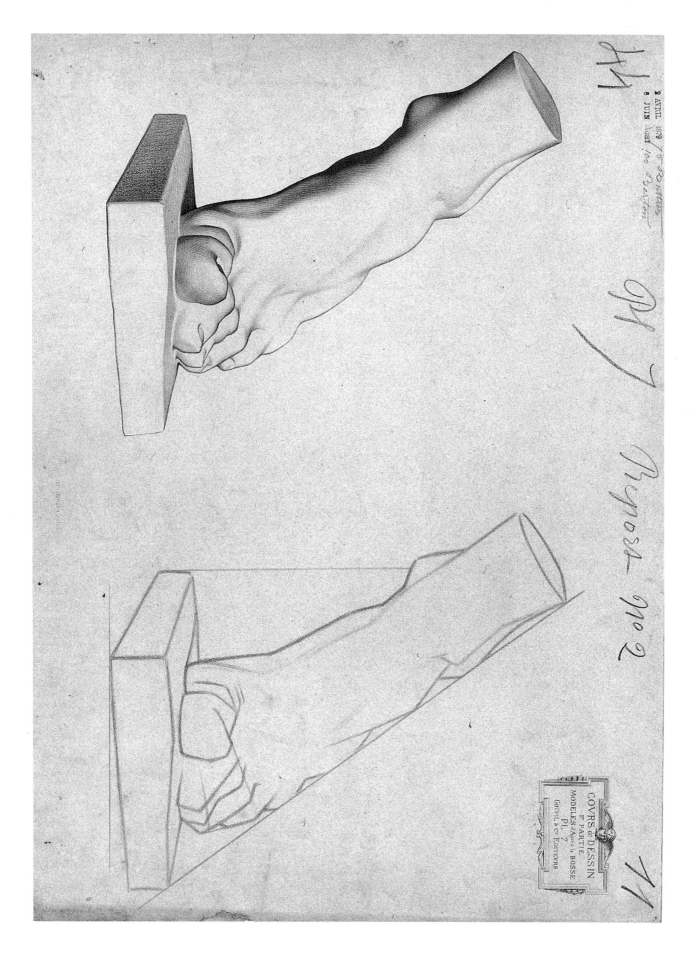

Plate I, 7

34

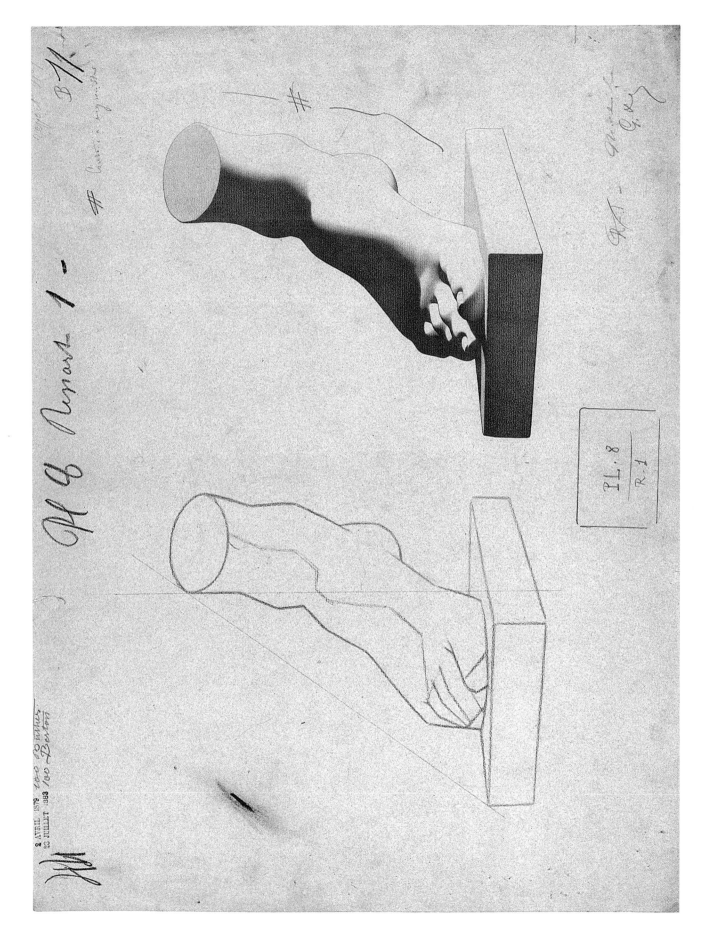

Plate I, 8

35

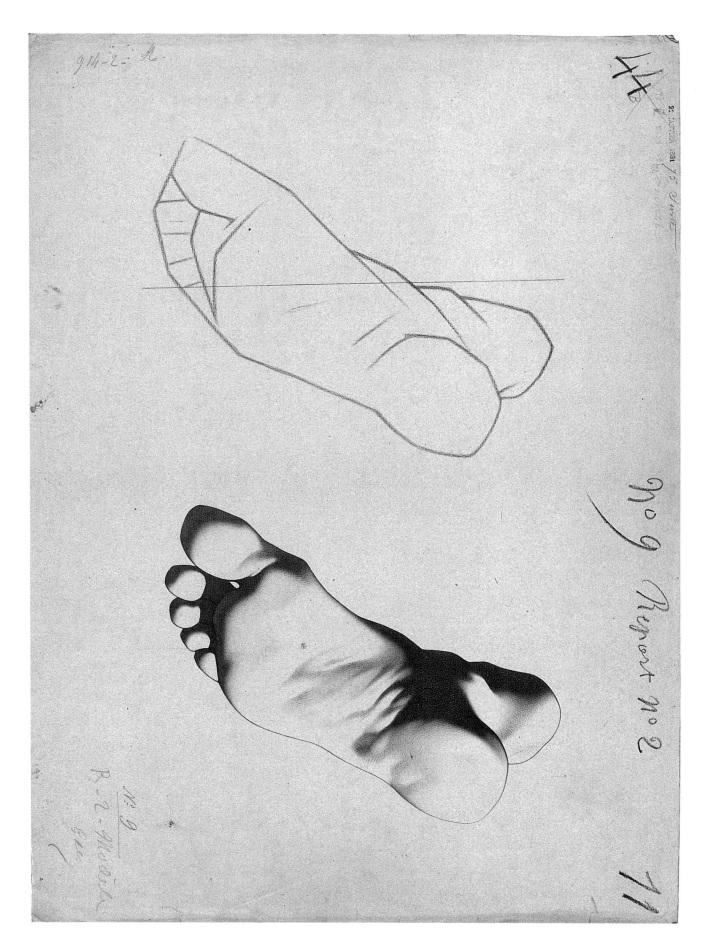

Plate I, 9

36

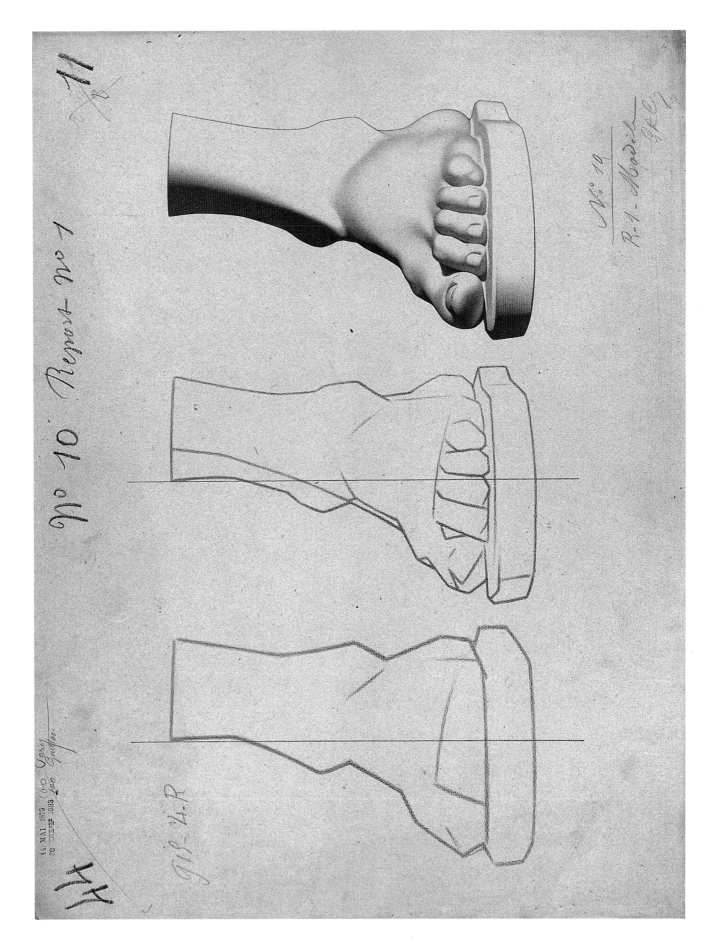

Plate I, 10

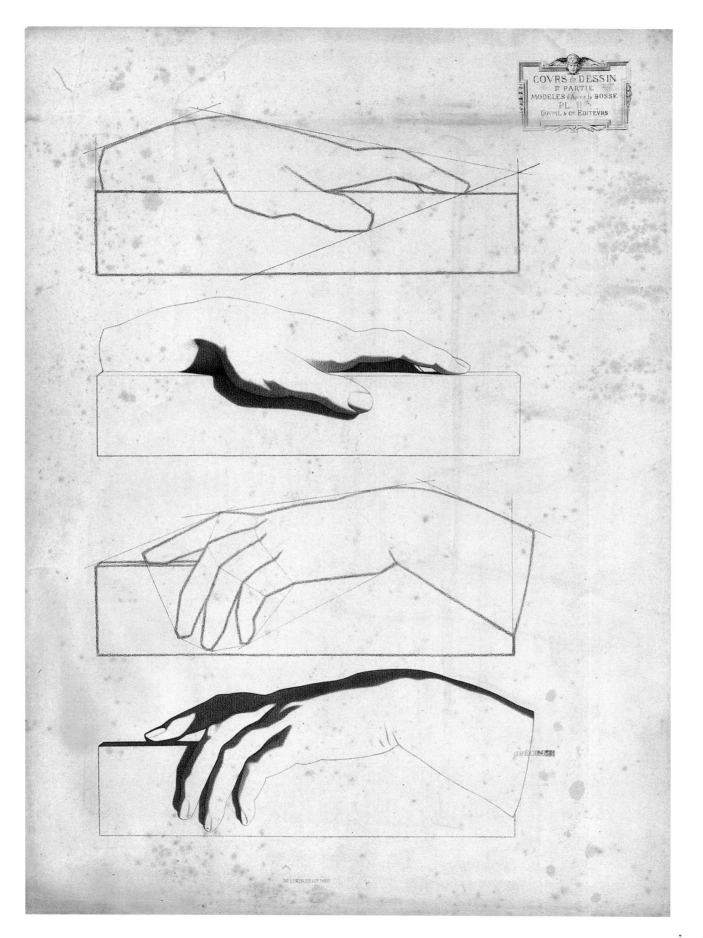

COVRS de DESSIN
I.ᵉ PARTIE
MODELES d'Apres la BOSSE
PL. 11
GOVPIL & Cᵉ EDITEVRS

Plate I, 11

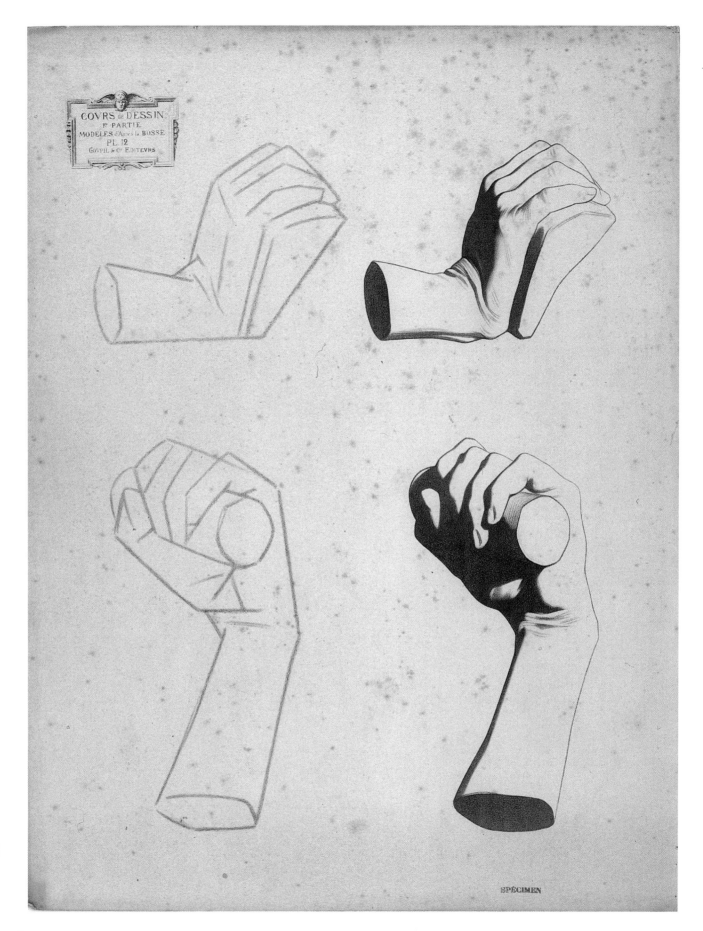

Plate I, 12

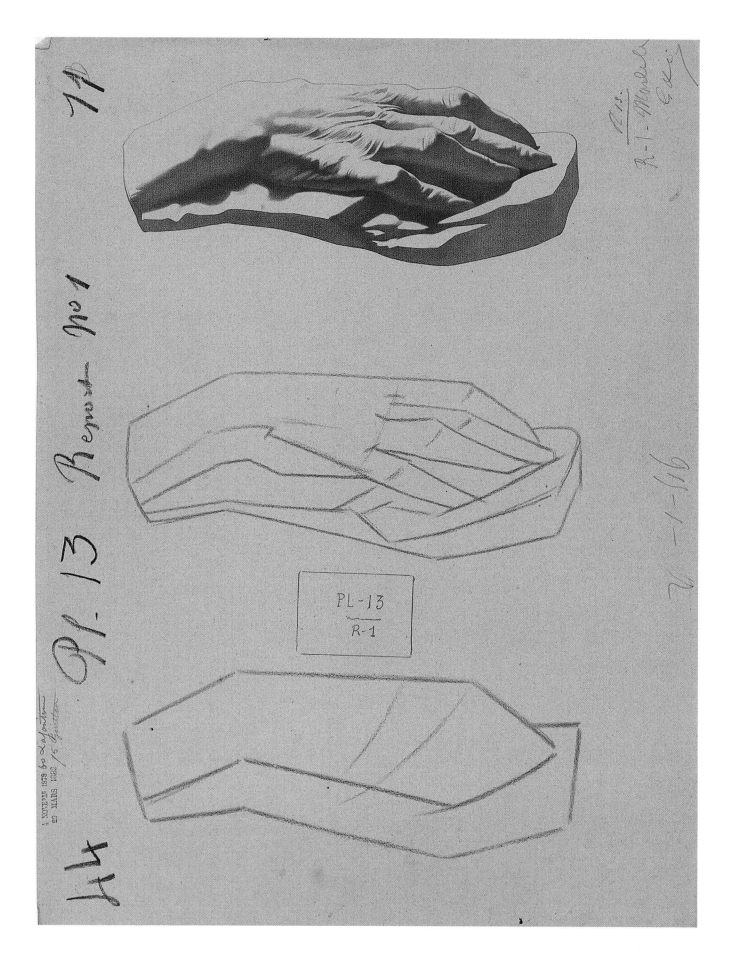

Plate I, 13

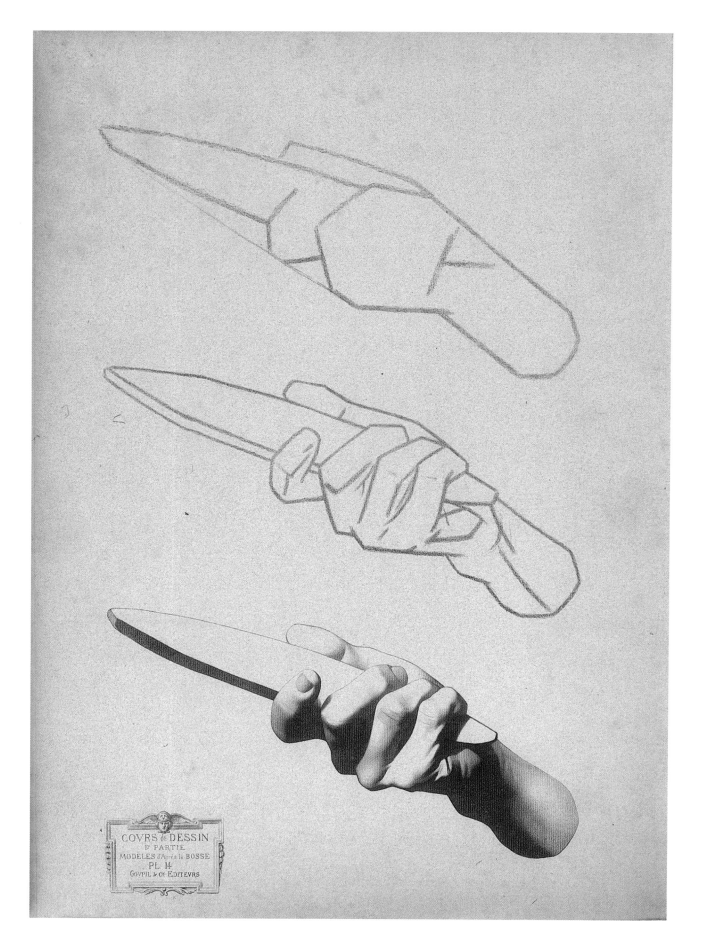

Plate I, 14

COVRS de DESSIN
1.º PARTIE
MODELES d'Après la BOSSE
PL 14
GOVPIL & C.ª ÉDITEVRS

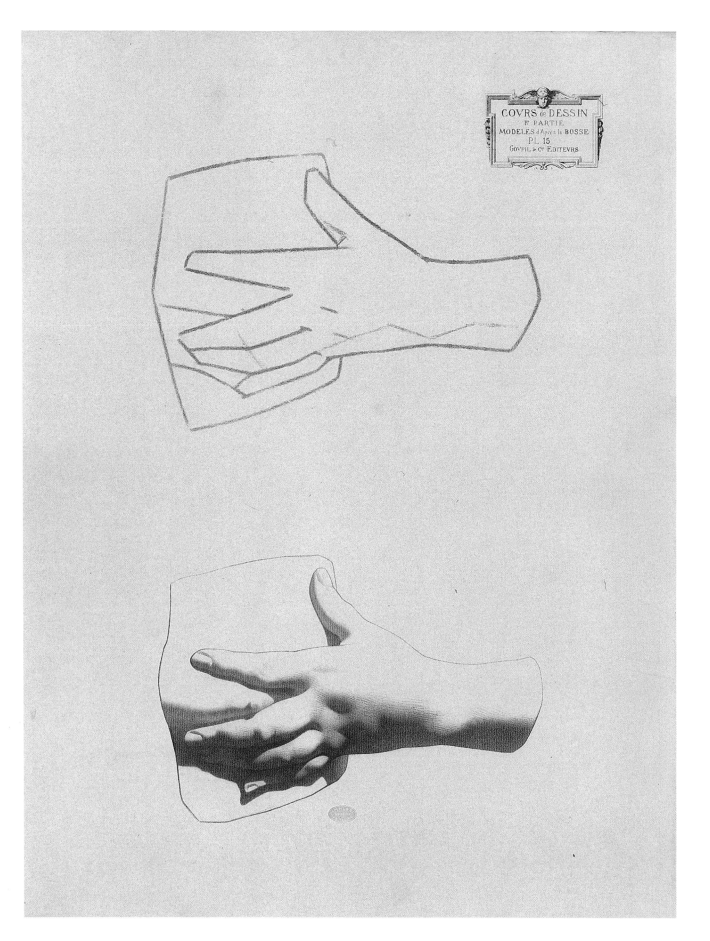

COVRS de DESSIN
I.ᵉ PARTIE
MODELES d'Après la BOSSE
P.L. 15
GOVPIL & Cⁱᵉ EDITEVRS

Plate I, 15

42

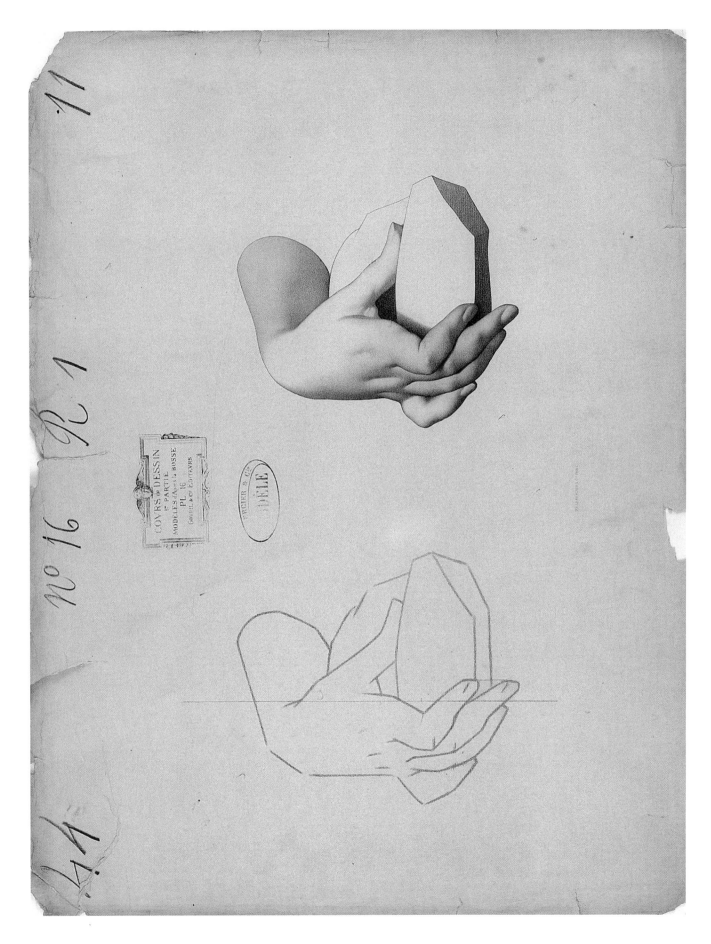

Plate I, 16

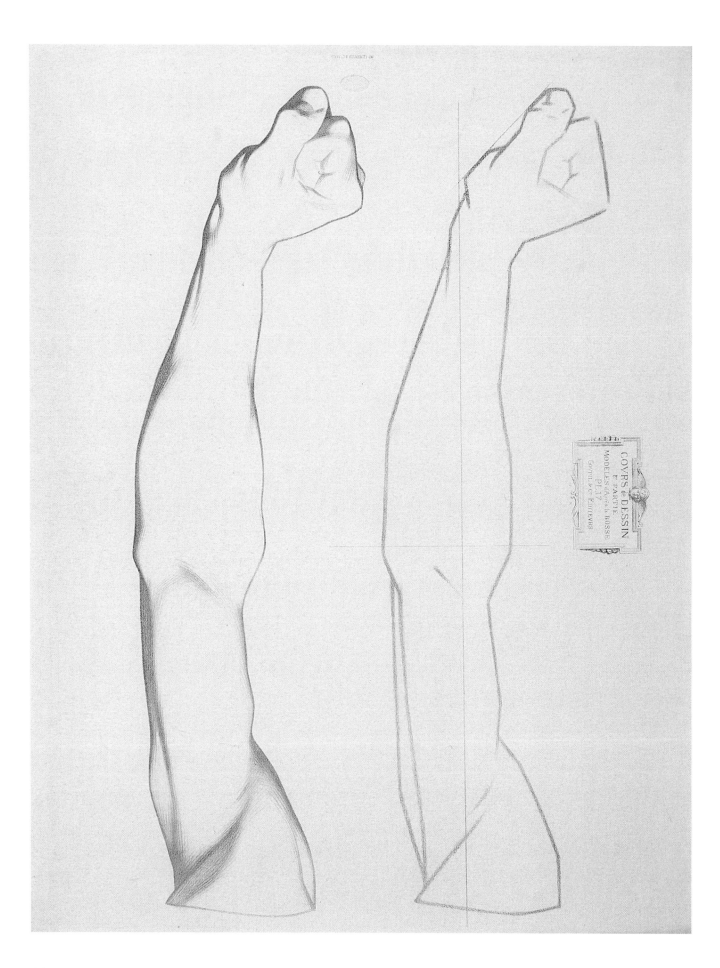

Plate I, 17

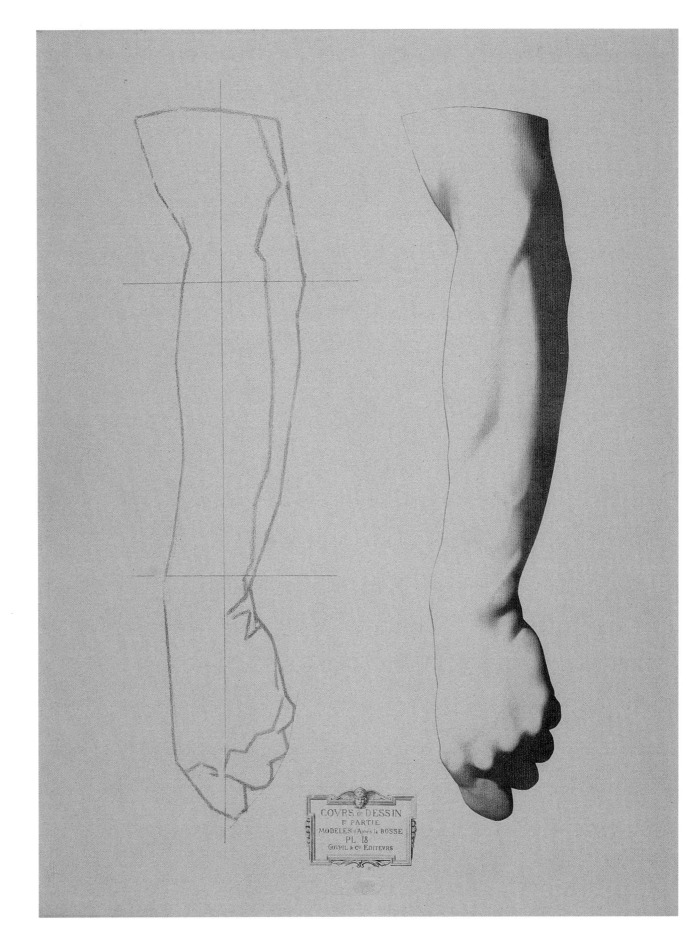

Plate I, 18

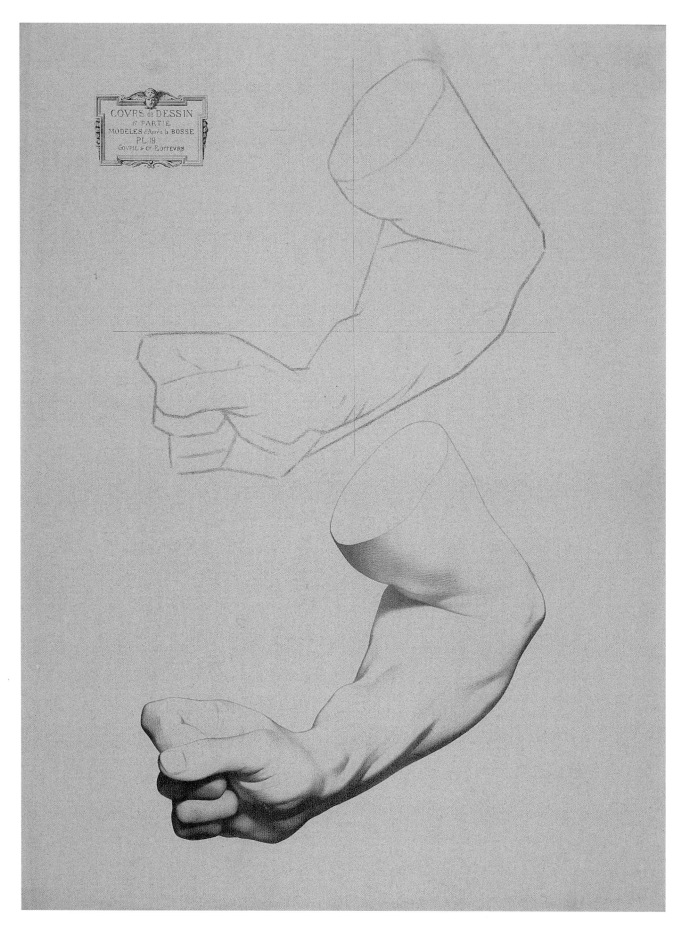

COVRS de DESSIN
1ᵉ PARTIE
MODELES d'Après la BOSSE
PL.19
GOVPIL & Cⁱᵉ EDITEVRS

Plate I, 19

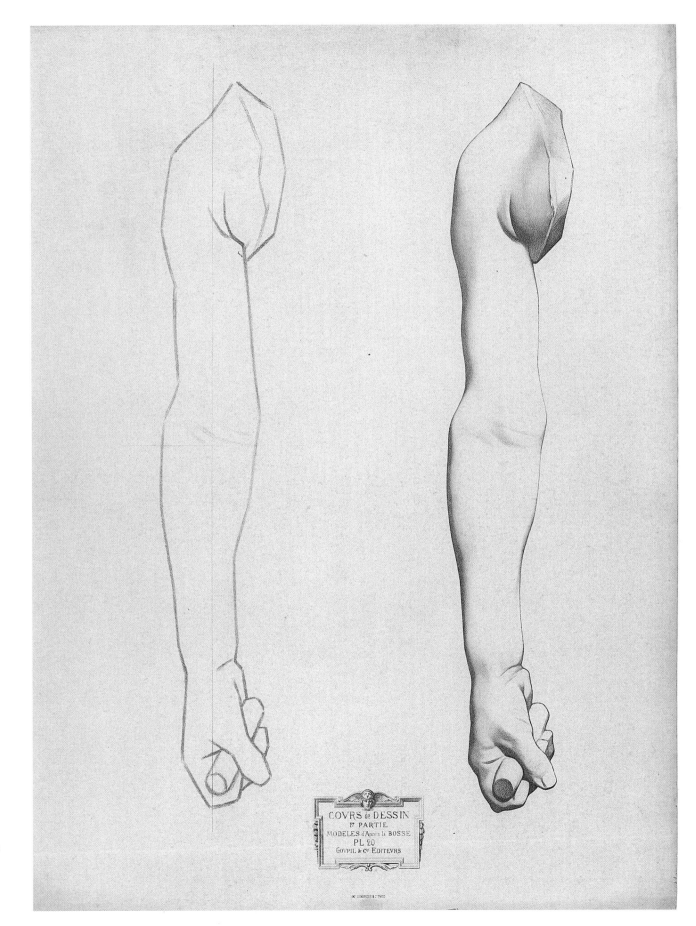

Plate I, 20

COVRS de DESSIN
Iᵉ PARTIE
MODELES d'Après la BOSSE
PL 20
GOVPIL & Cⁱᵉ EDITEVRS

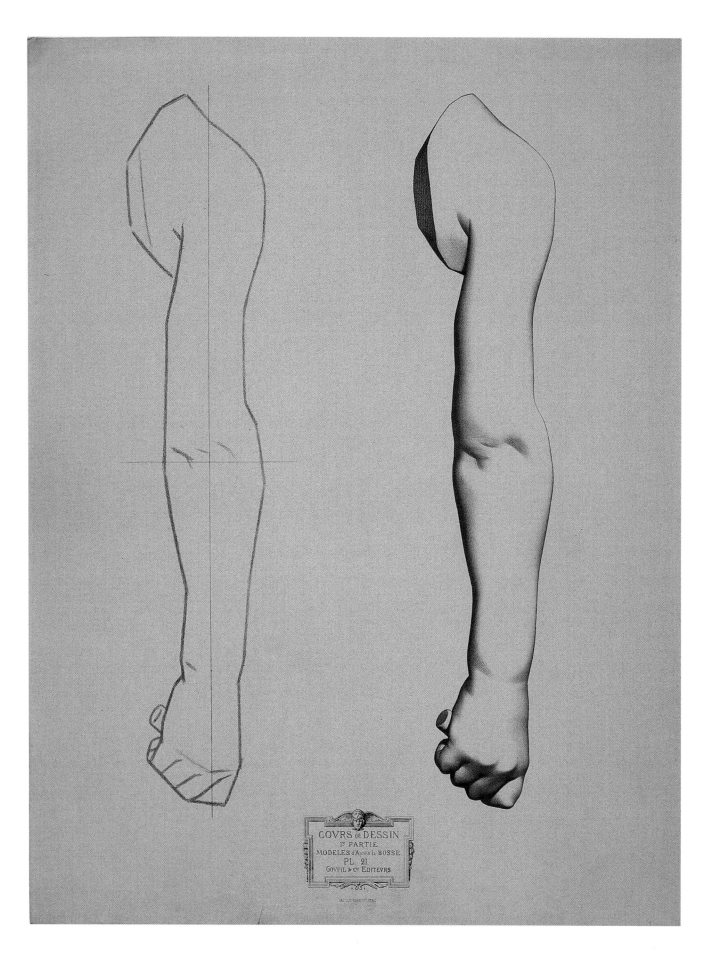

COVRS de DESSIN
Ⅰᵉ PARTIE
MODELES d'Après la BOSSE
PL. 21
GOVPIL & Cⁱᵉ EDITEVRS

Plate I, 21

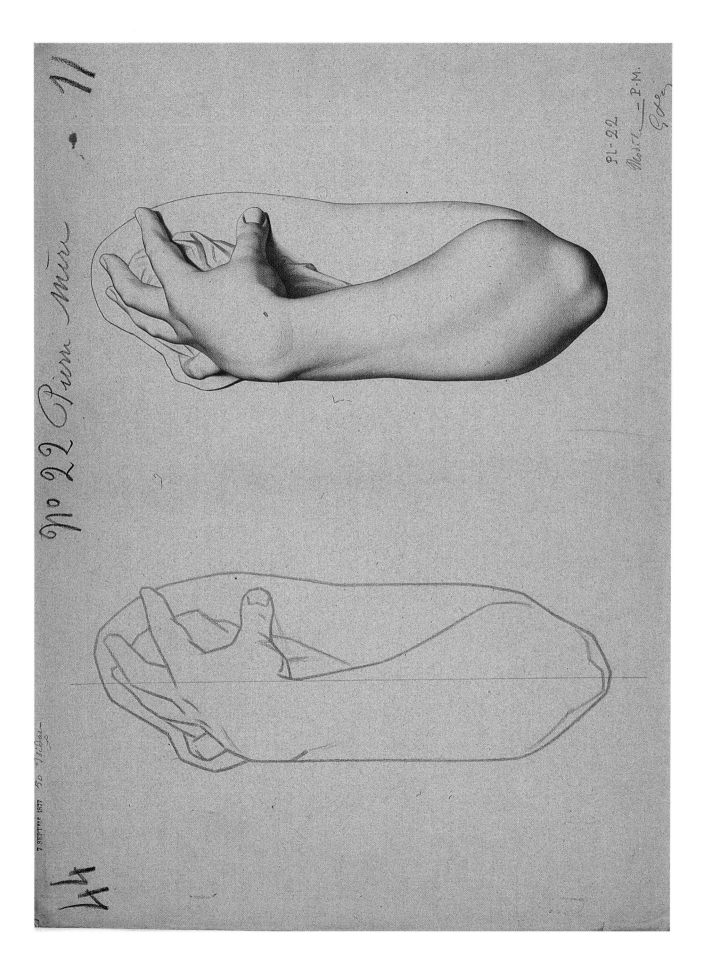

Plate I, 22

49

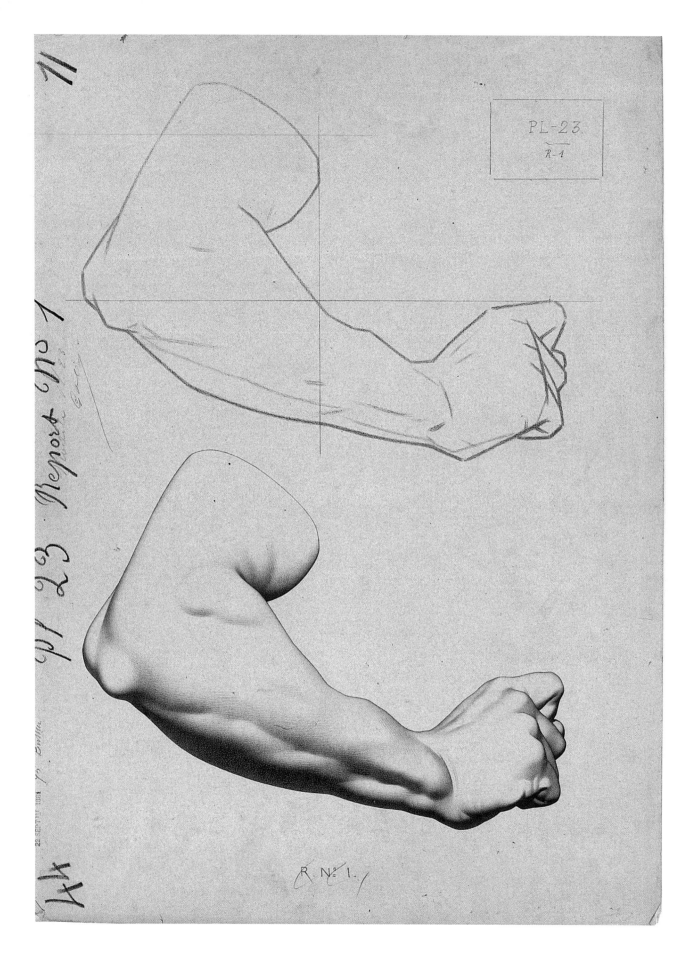

PL-23.
R-1

Plate I, 23

50

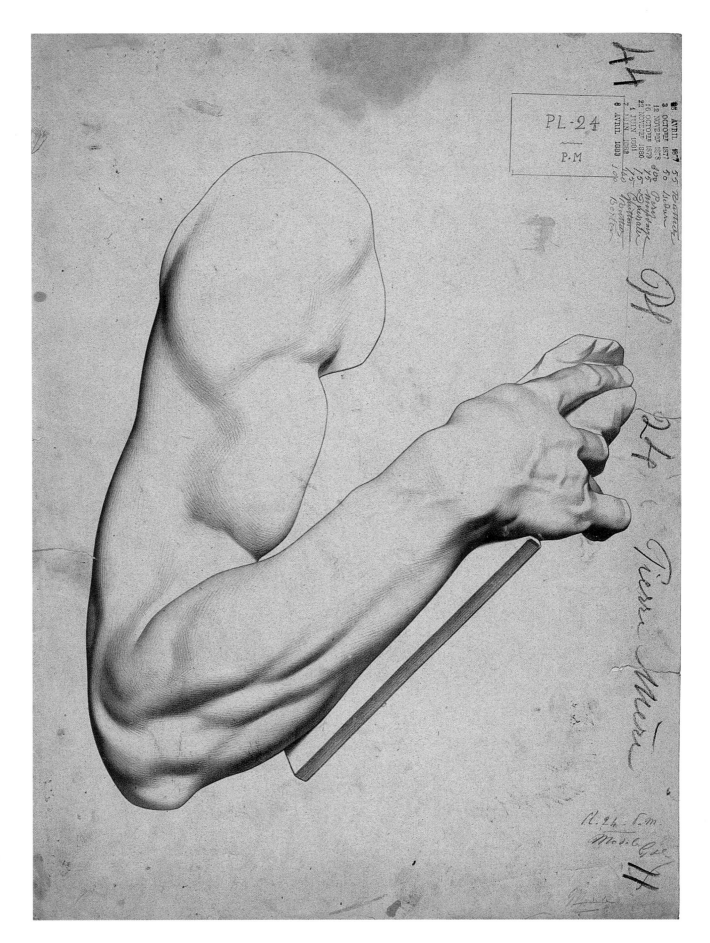

Plate I, 24

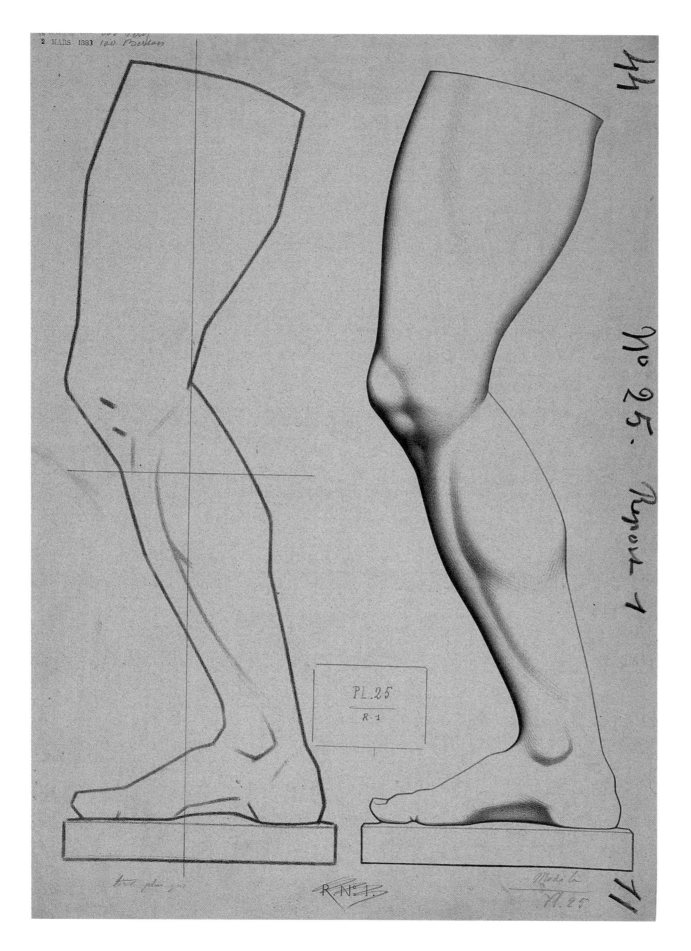

Plate I, 25

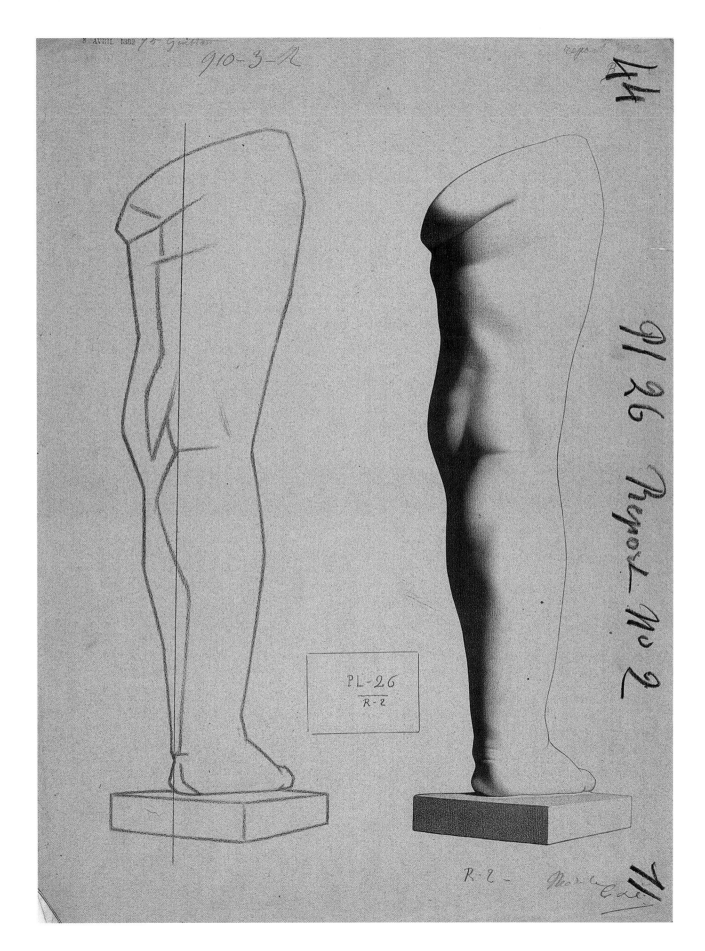

Plate I, 26

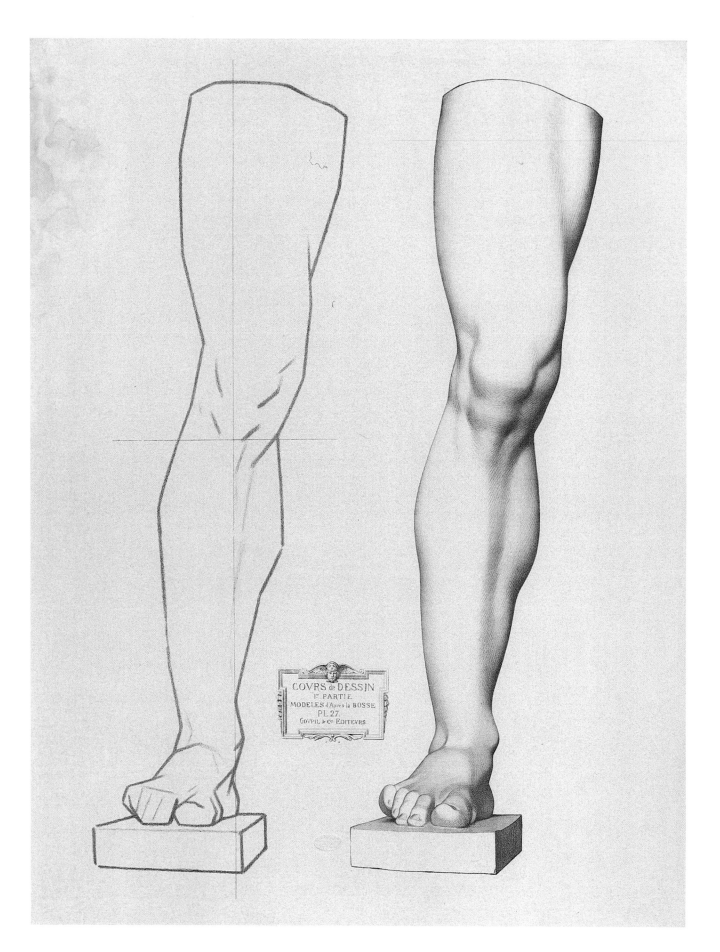

COVRS de DESSIN
I.ͤ PARTIE
MODELES d'Après la BOSSE
PL. 27.
GOVPIL & Cⁱᵉ EDITEVRS.

Plate I, 27

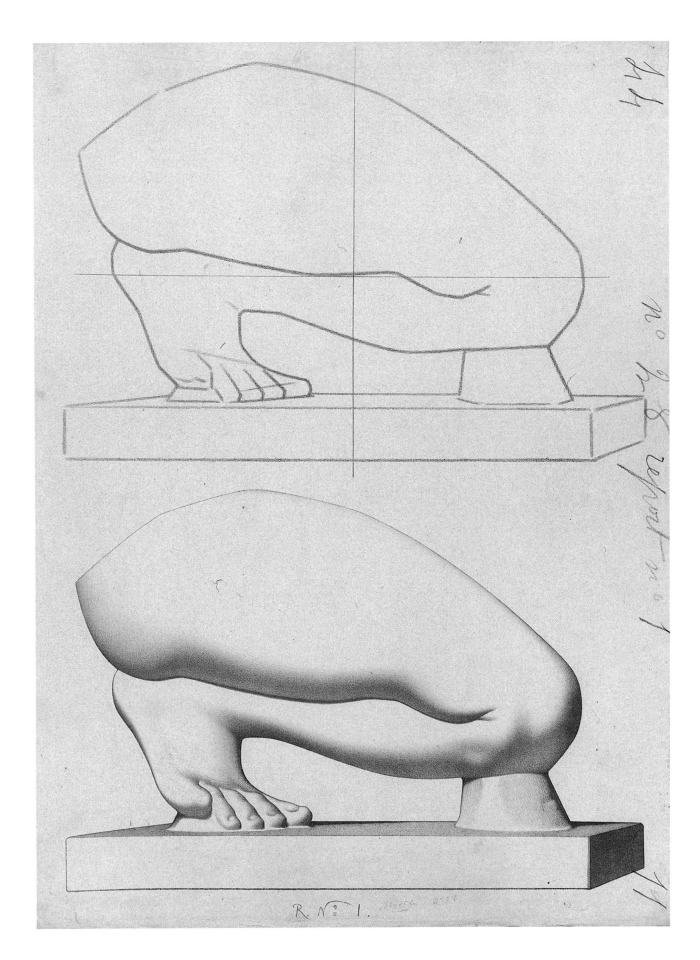

Plate I, 28

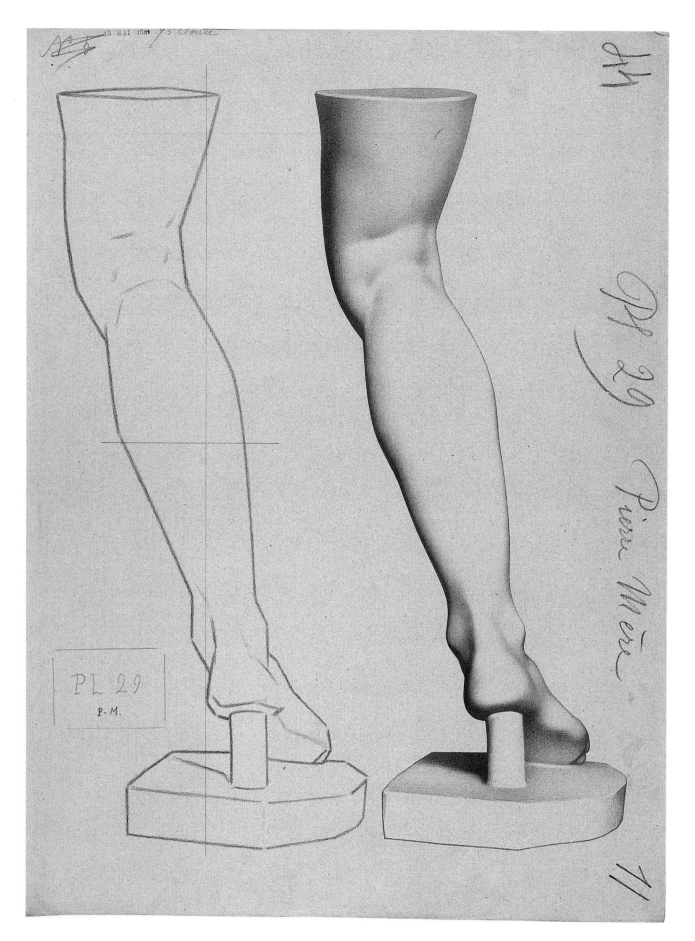

Plate I, 29

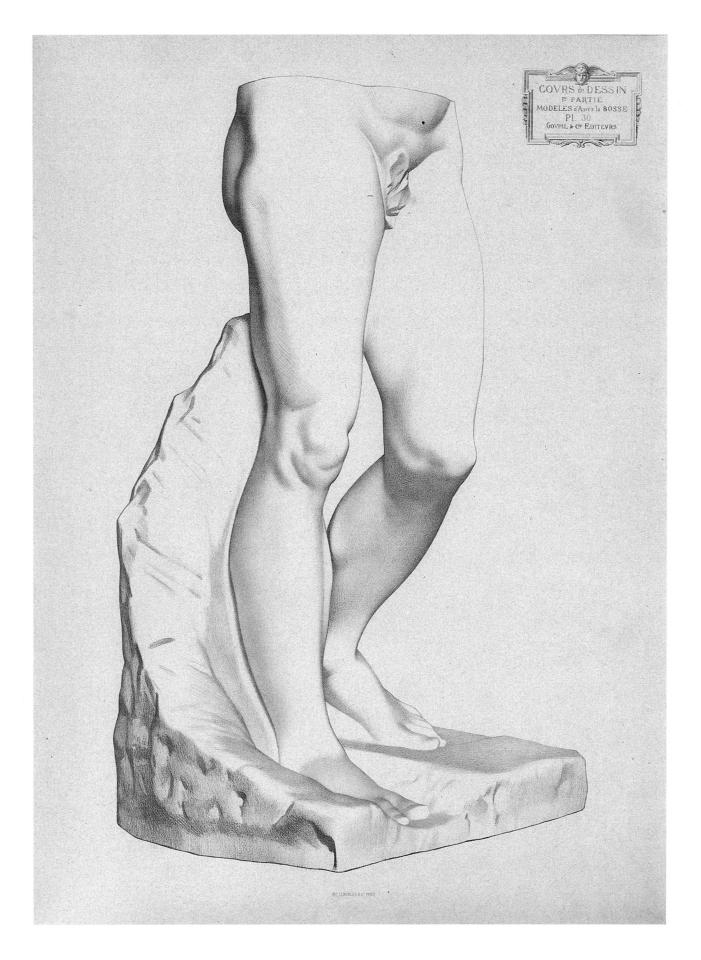

Plate I, 30

Plate I, 31

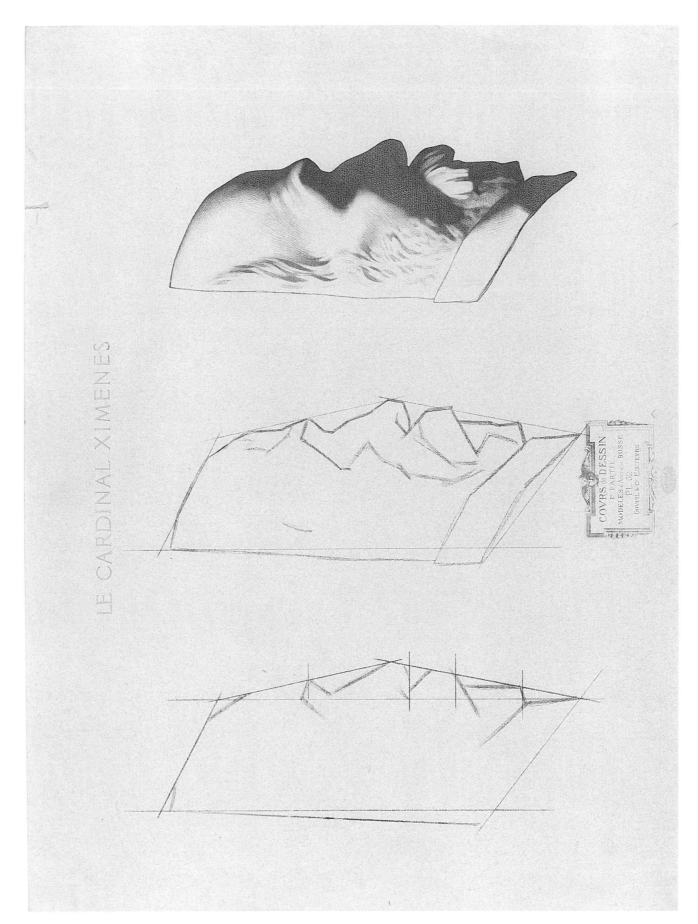

LE CARDINAL XIMENES

Plate I, 32

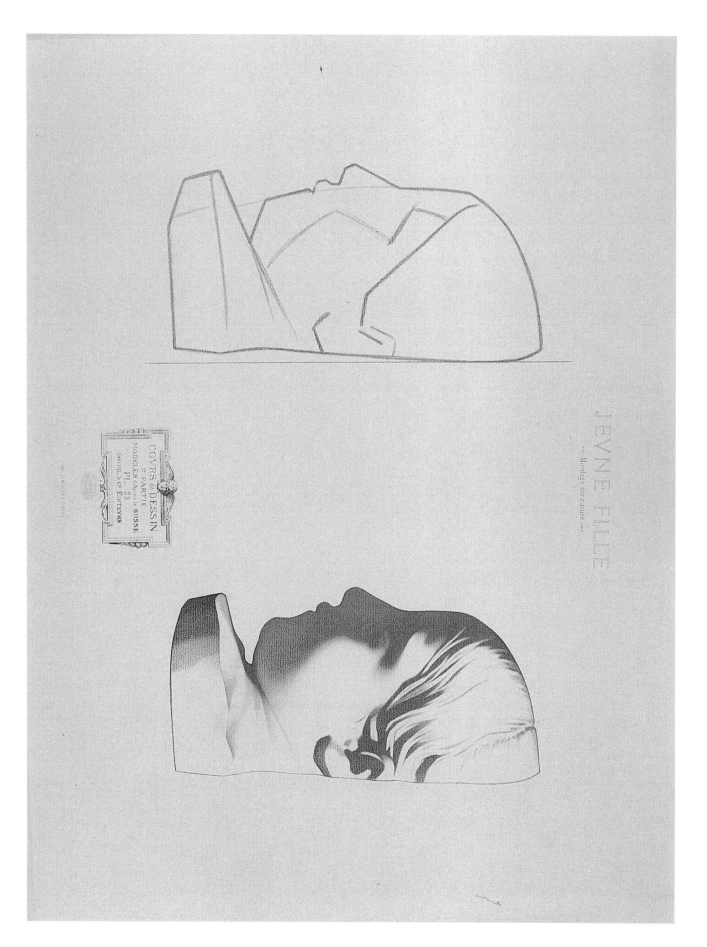

JEVNE FILLE

Moulage sur nature

COVRS de DESSIN
1ère PARTIE
MODELES d'APRÈS la BOSSE
PL. 33
GOVPIL & Cie ÉDITEVRS

Plate I, 33

Plate I, 34

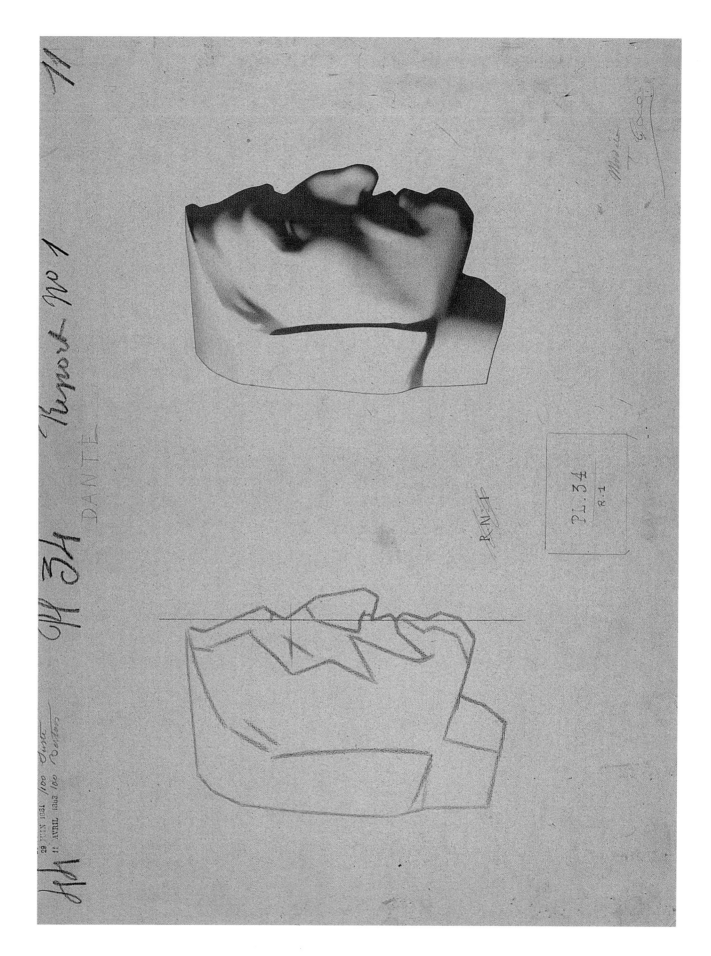

61

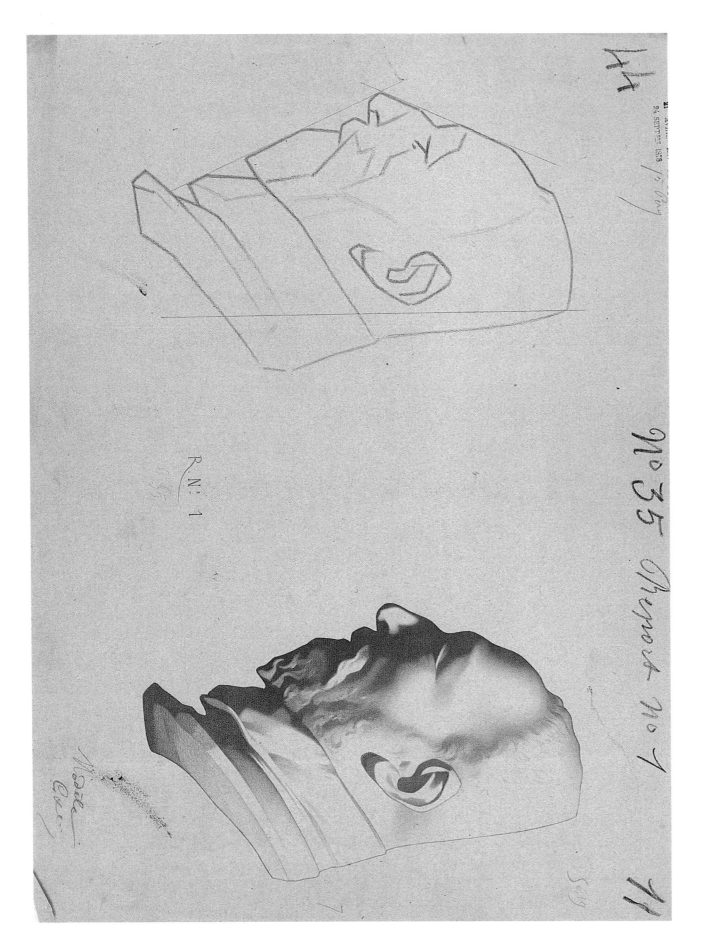

Plate I, 35

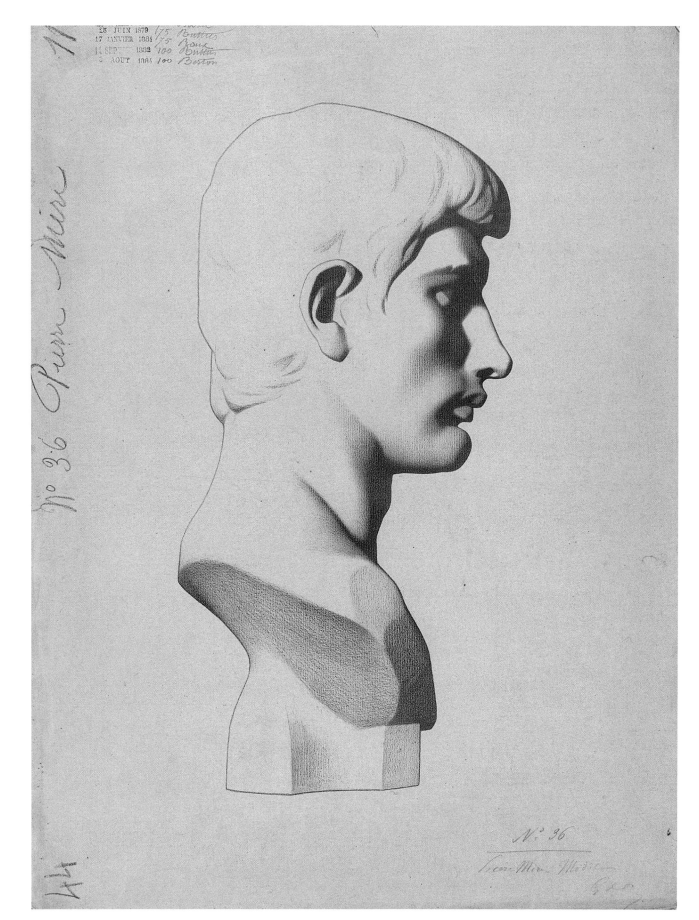

Plate I, 36

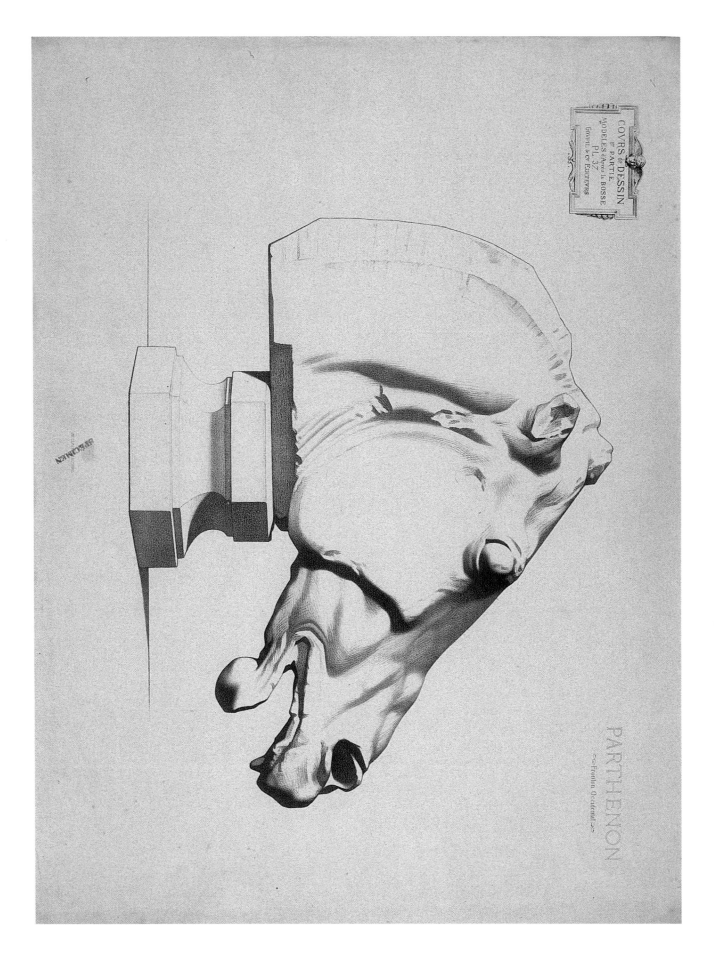

COVRS de DESSIN
1e PARTIE
MODELES d'Après la BOSSE
PL. 37
Goupil & Cie Éditeurs

PARTHENON
Fronton Occidental

Plate I, 37

64

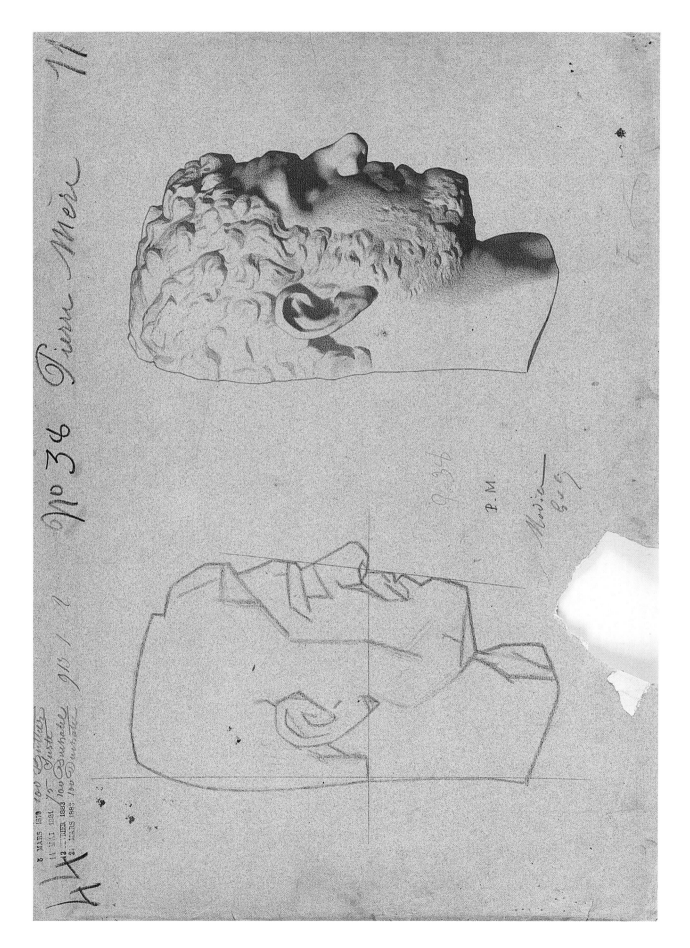

Plate I, 38

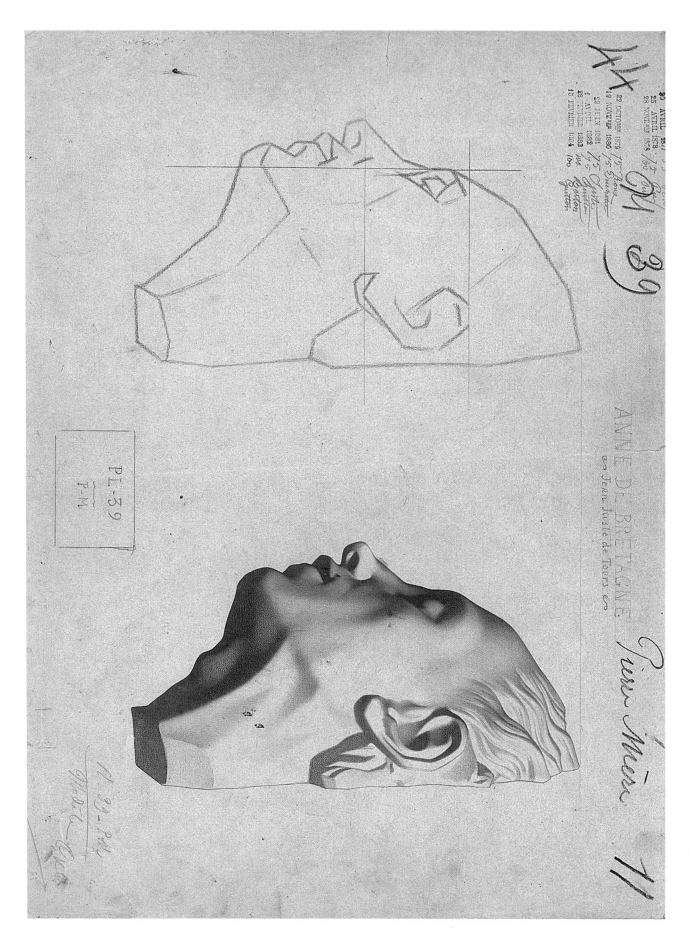

Plate I, 39

66

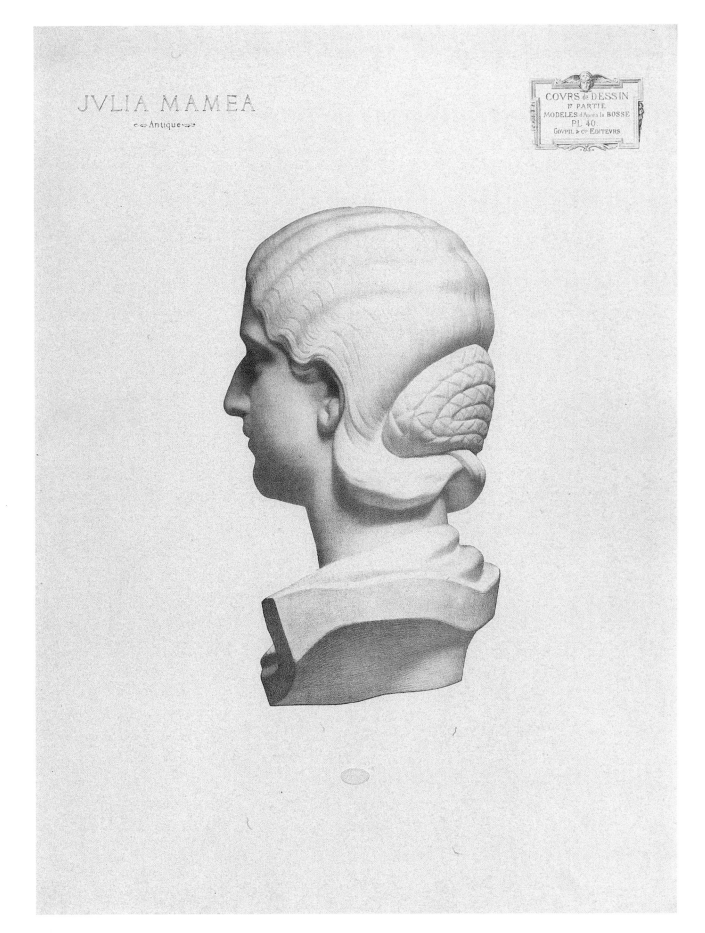

JVLIA MAMEA

Antique

COVRS de DESSIN
Iᵉ PARTIE
MODELES d'Après la BOSSE
PL. 40.
GOVPIL & Cⁱᵉ EDITEVRS

Plate I, 40

Plate I, 41

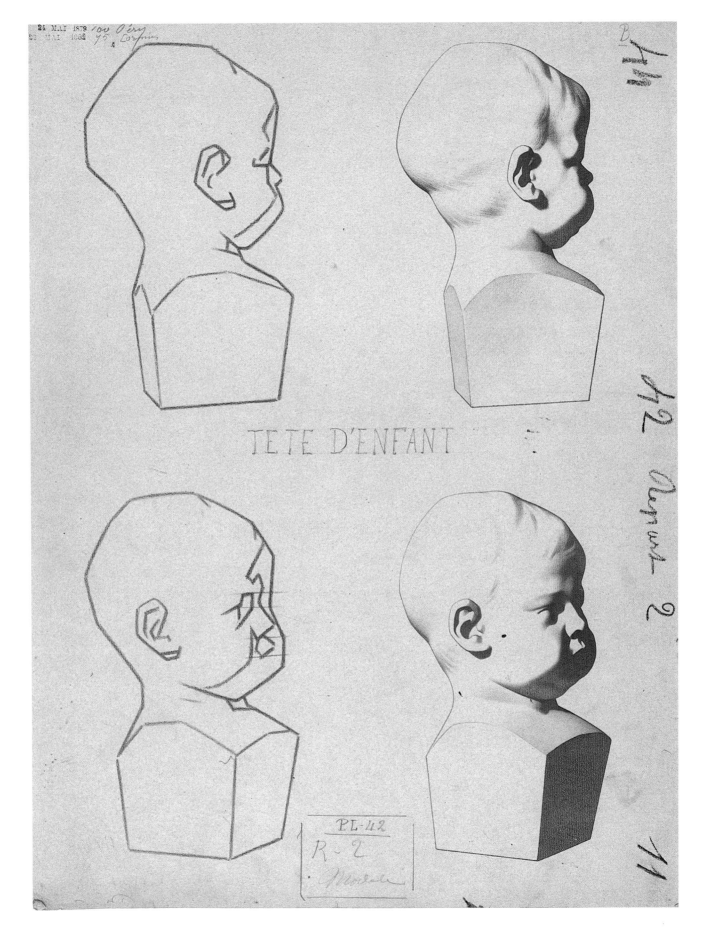

TETE D'ENFANT

Plate I, 42

69

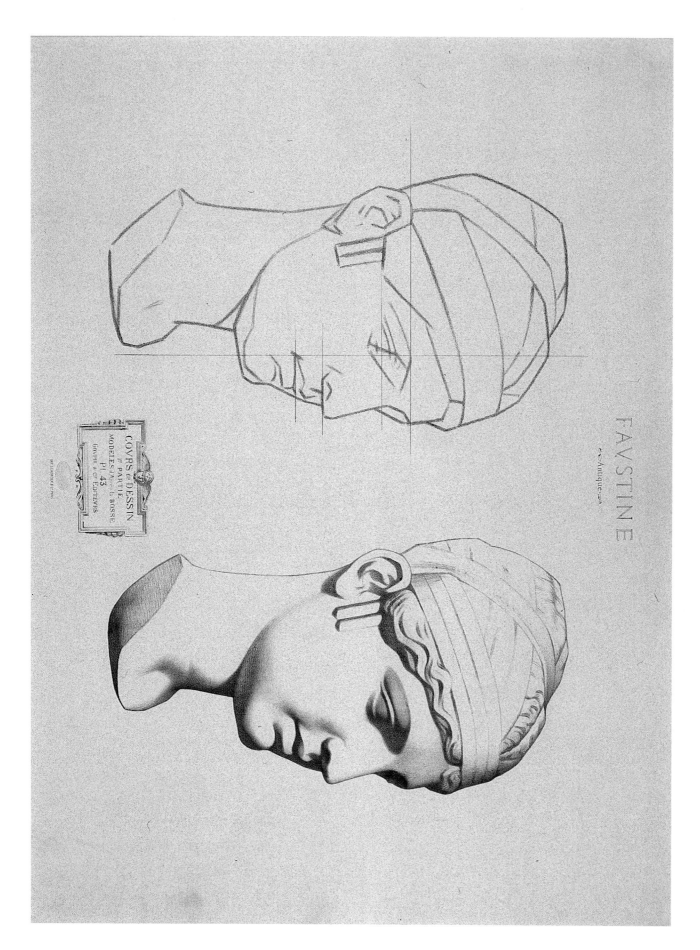

FAVSTINE

Antiques

COVRS de DESSIN
II.ᵉ PARTIE
MODELES d'après la BOSSE
Pl. 43
GIHAVT & Cⁱᵉ ÉDITEVRS

Plate I, 43

PSYCHE DE NAPLES

Antique

COVRS de DESSIN
I.ᵉ PARTIE
MODELES d'Après la BOSSE
PL 44
GOVPIL & Cⁱᵉ EDITEVRS

IMP. LEMERCIER & Cⁱᵉ PARIS.

Plate I, 44

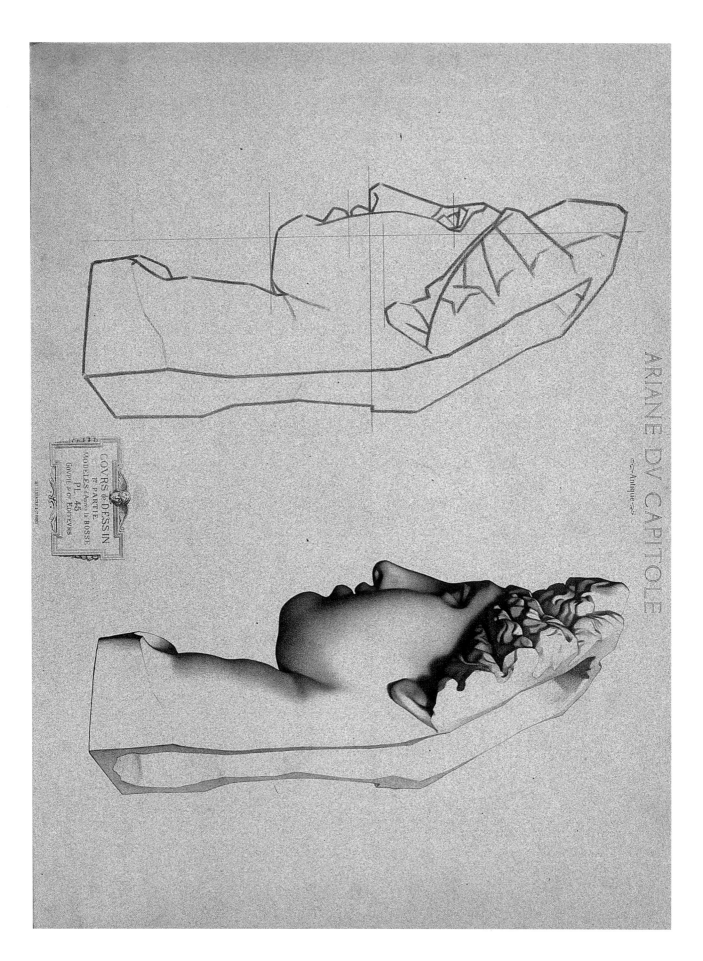

ARIANE DV CAPITOLE

Antique

COVRS de DESSIN
1.re PARTIE
MODELES d'apres le BOSSE
PL. 45
GOVPIL & C.ie EDITEVRS

Plate I, 45

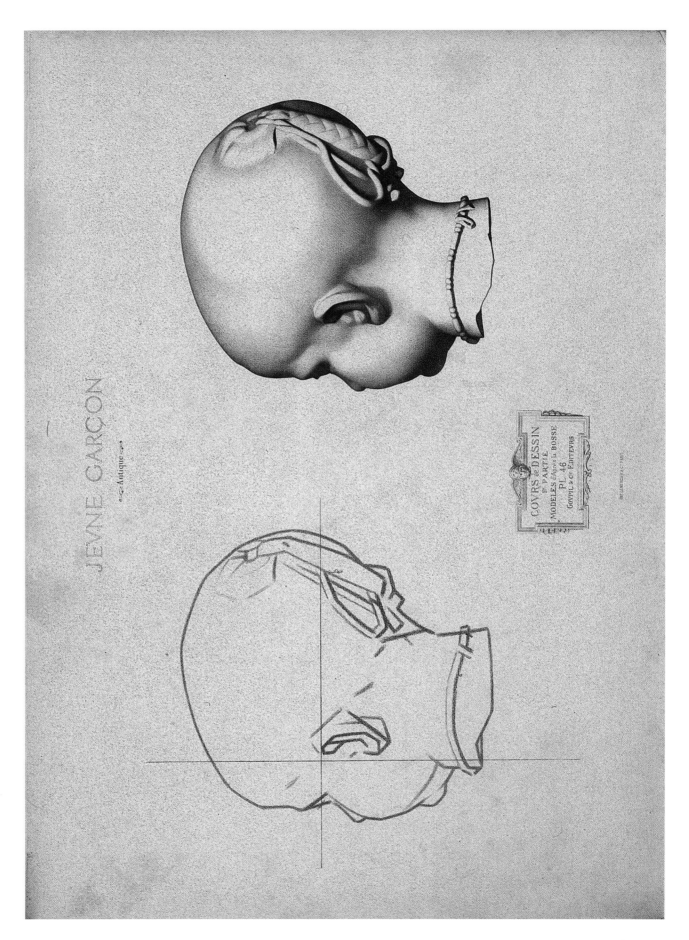

Plate I, 46

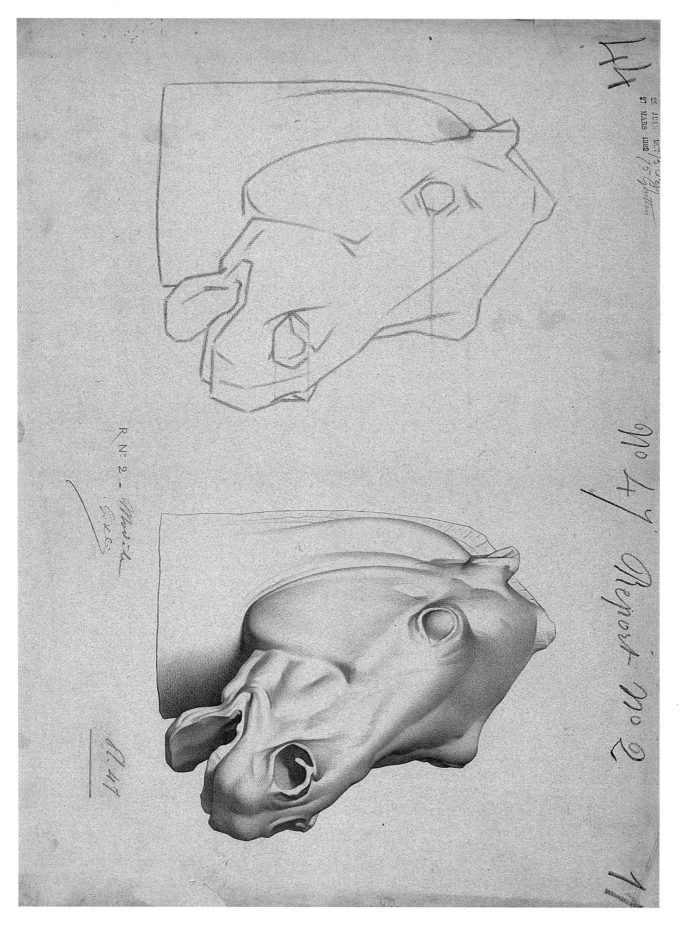

Plate I, 47

74

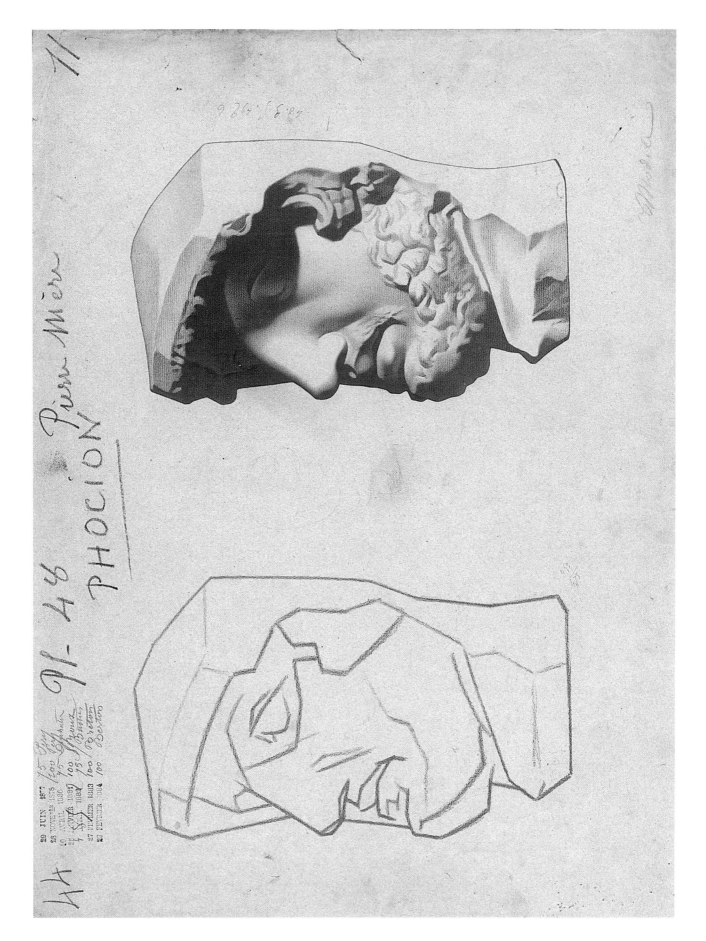

Plate I, 48

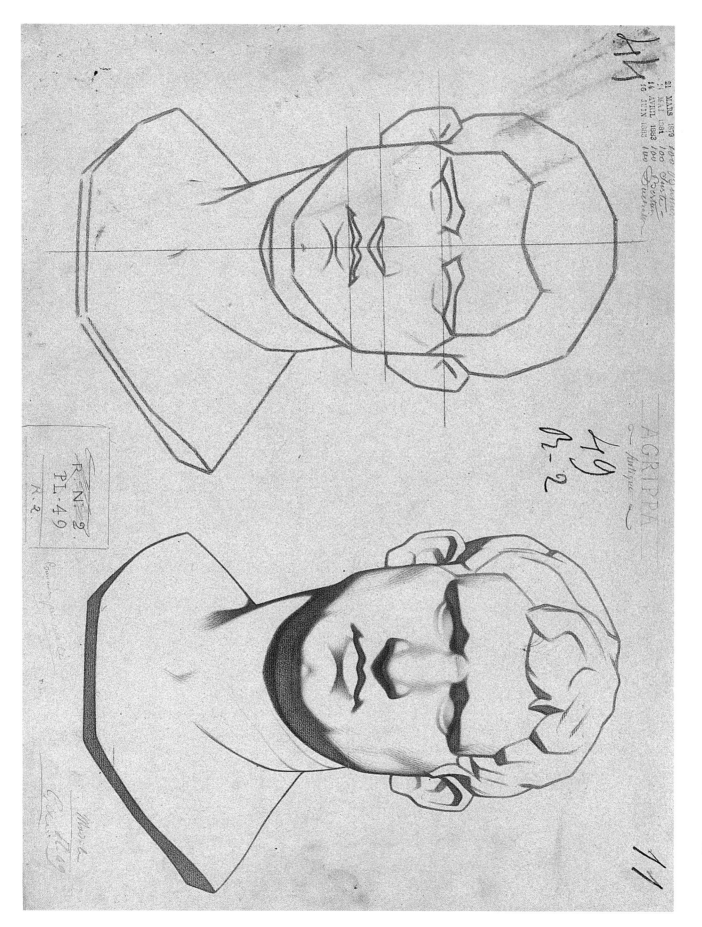

Plate I, 49

76

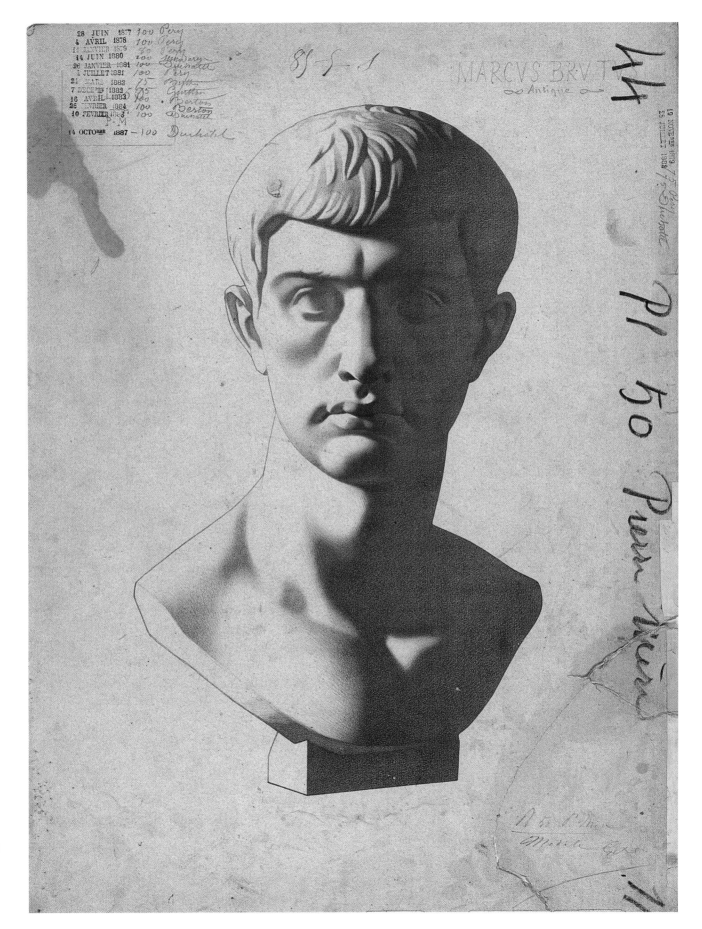

Plate I, 50

JVPITER TROPHONIVS

Antique

COVRS de DESSIN
1.ᵉ PARTIE
MODELES d'après la BOSSE
PL. 51
GOVPIL & C.ᵉ EDITEVRS

SPECIMEN

Plate I, 51

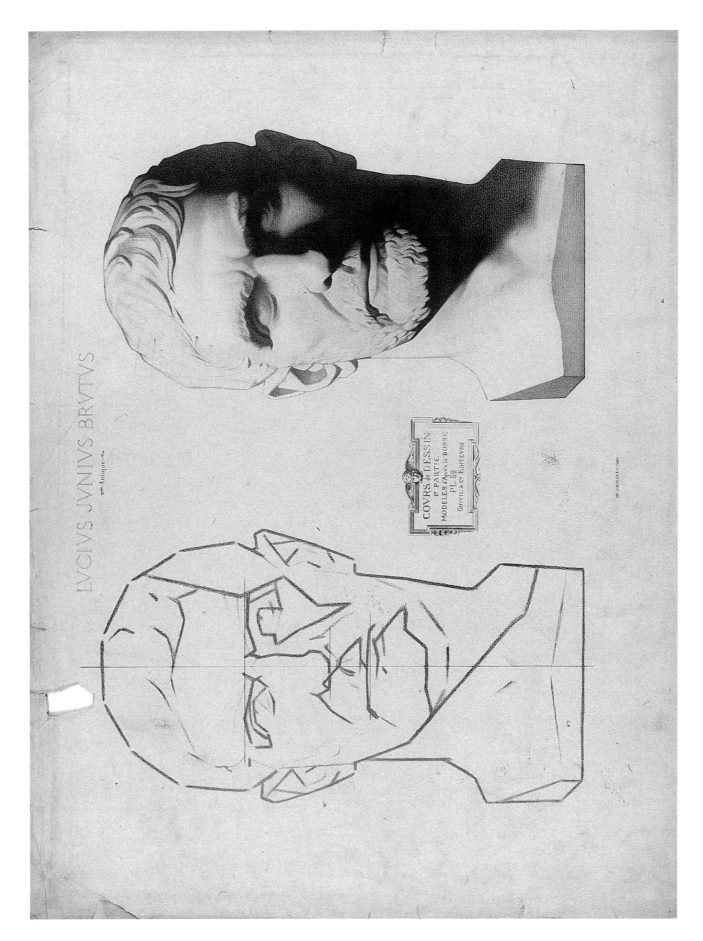

LVCIVS JVNIVS BRVTVS

Antique

COVRS de DESS IN
I.e PARTIE
MODELES d'Apr à la BOSSE
PL 59
GOVPIL & C.e ÉDITEVRS

Plate I, 52

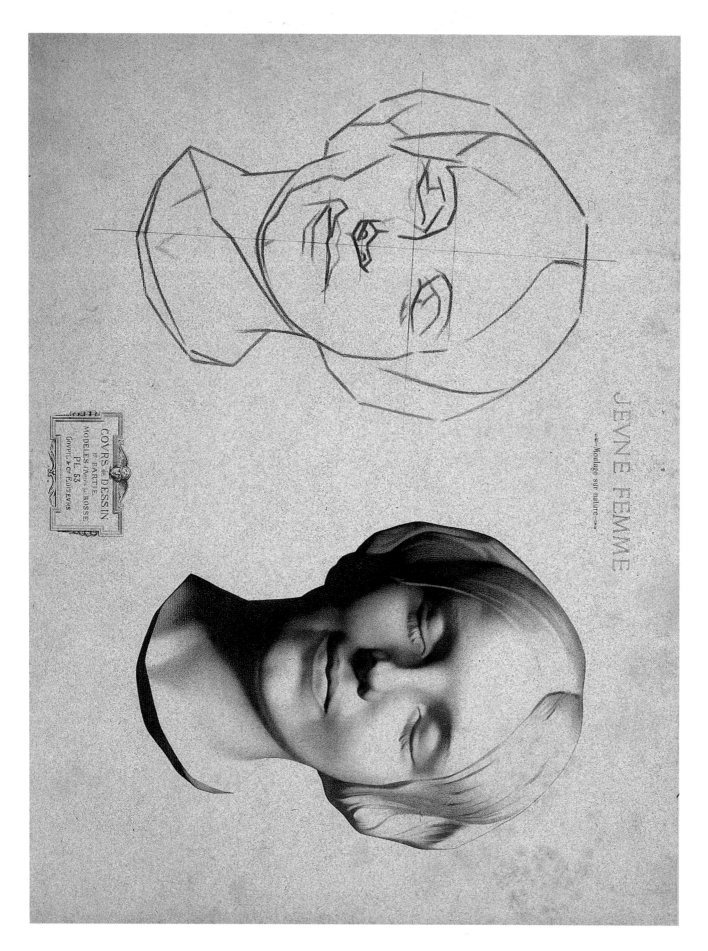

JEVNE FEMME

Moulage sur nature

COVRS de DESSIN
1ᵉ PARTIE
MODELES d'Après la BOSSE
PL. 53
GOVPIL & Cⁱᵉ EDITEVRS

Plate I, 53

80

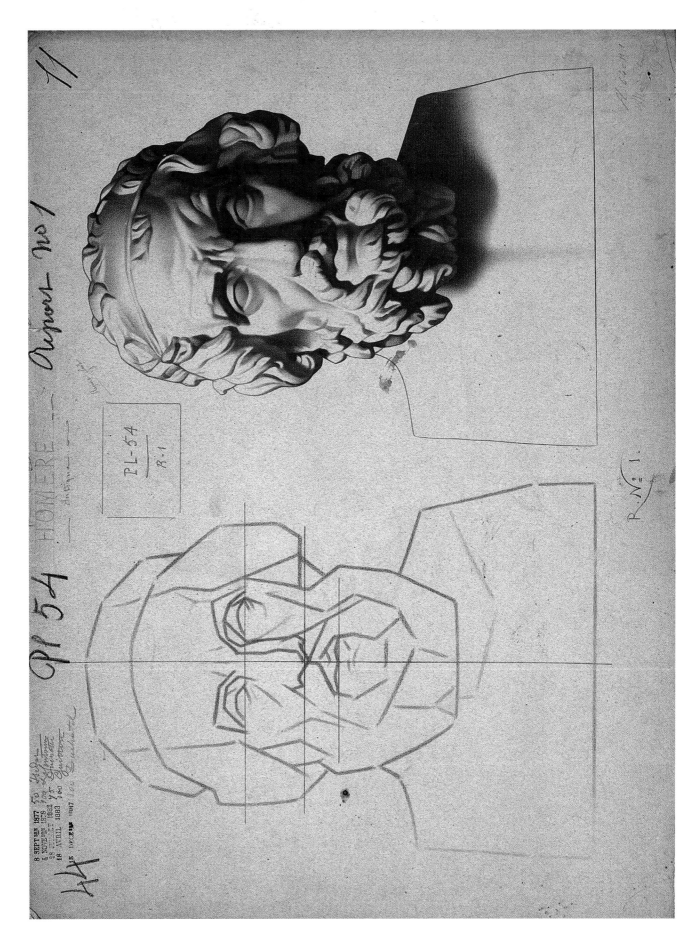

Plate I, 54

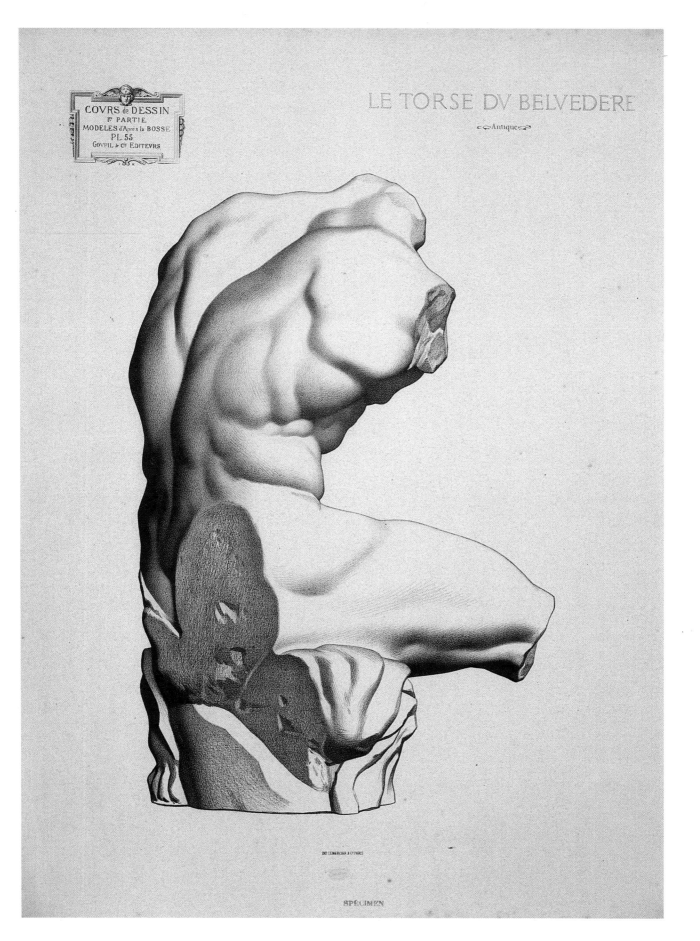

Antique

COVRS de DESSIN
I.ᵉ PARTIE
MODELES d'Après la BOSSE
PL 55
GOVPIL & Cⁱᵉ EDITEVRS

SPECIMEN

Plate I, 55

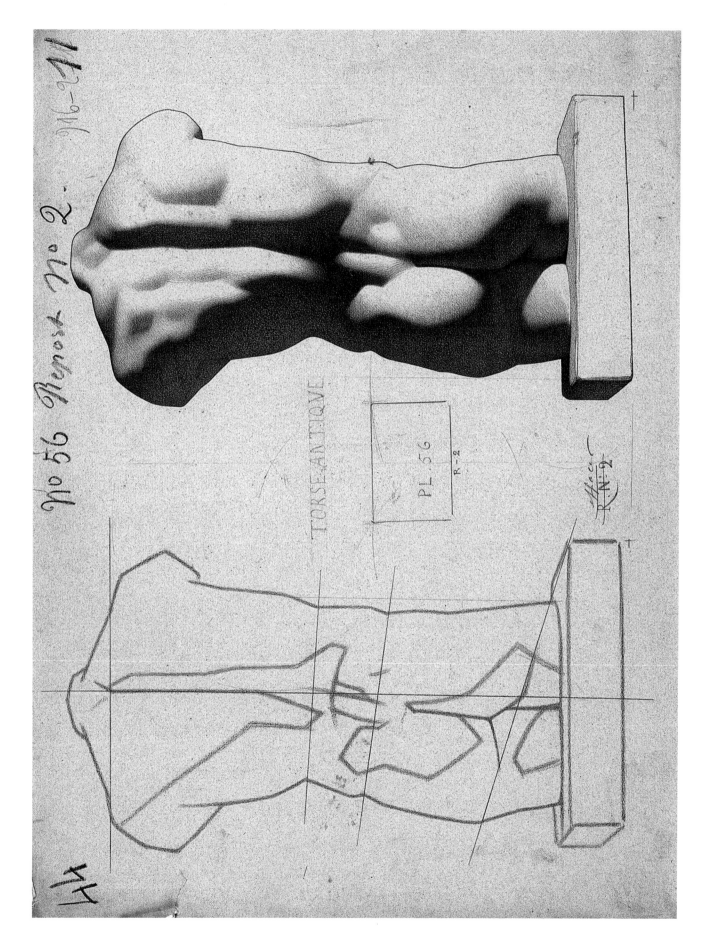

Plate I, 56

Plate I, 57

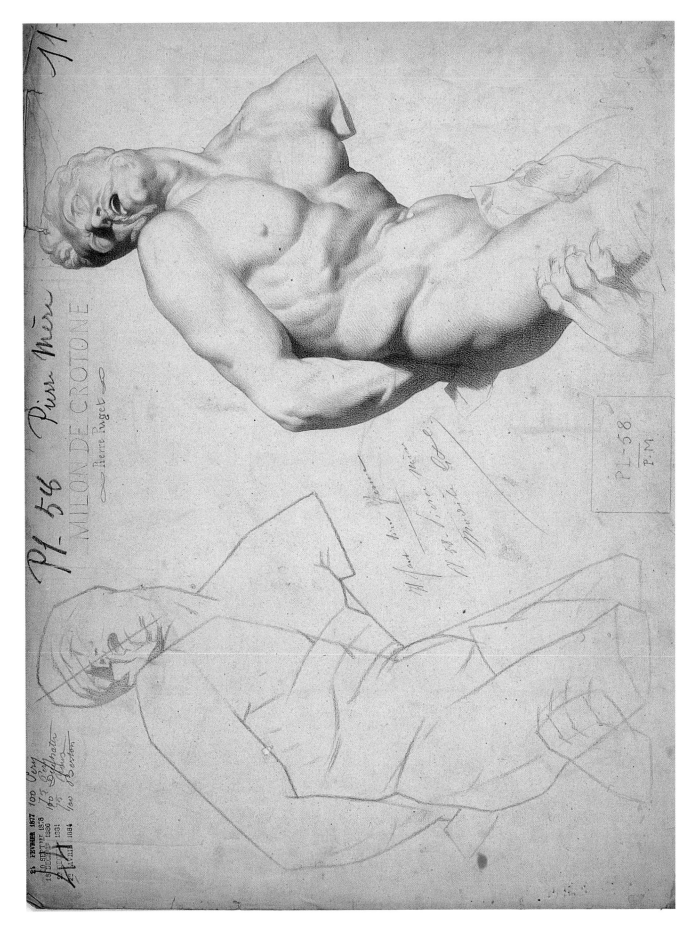

Plate I, 58

Plate I, 59

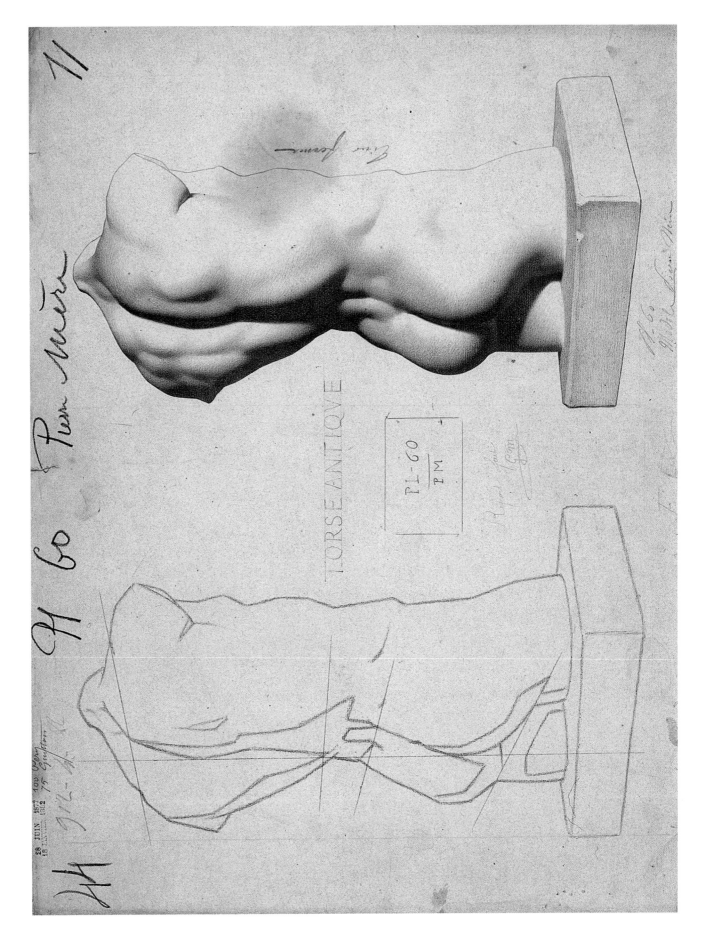

Plate I, 60

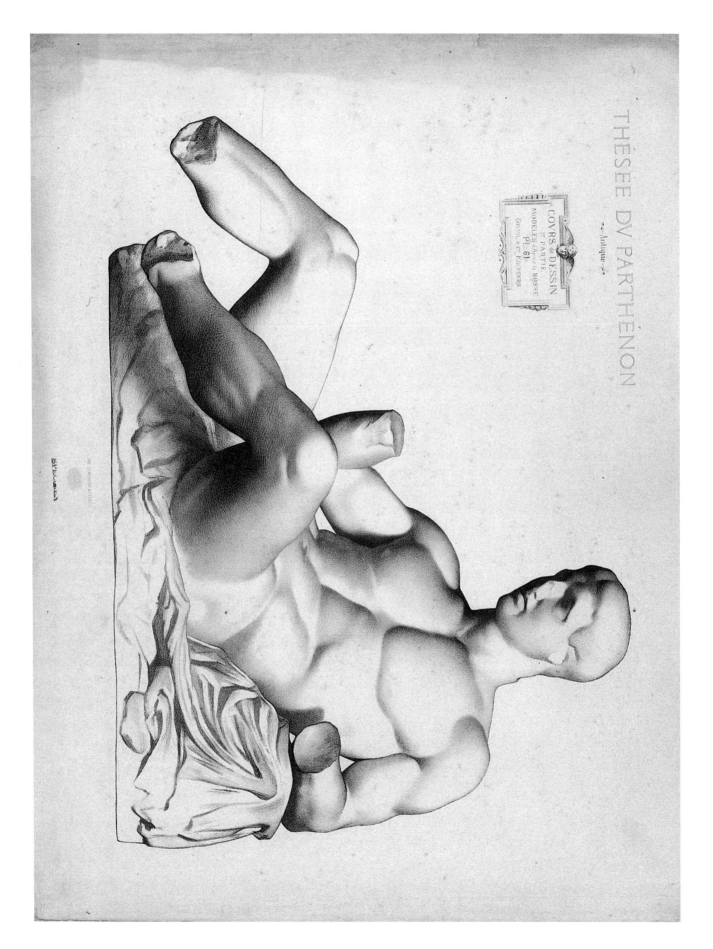

THÉSÉE DV PARTHÉNON

Antique

COVRS DE DESSIN
1.ᵉ PARTIE
MODÉLES D'APRÈS LE BOSSE
PL. 61
GOVPIL & C.ᵉ ÉDITEVRS

Plate I, 61

Plate I, 62

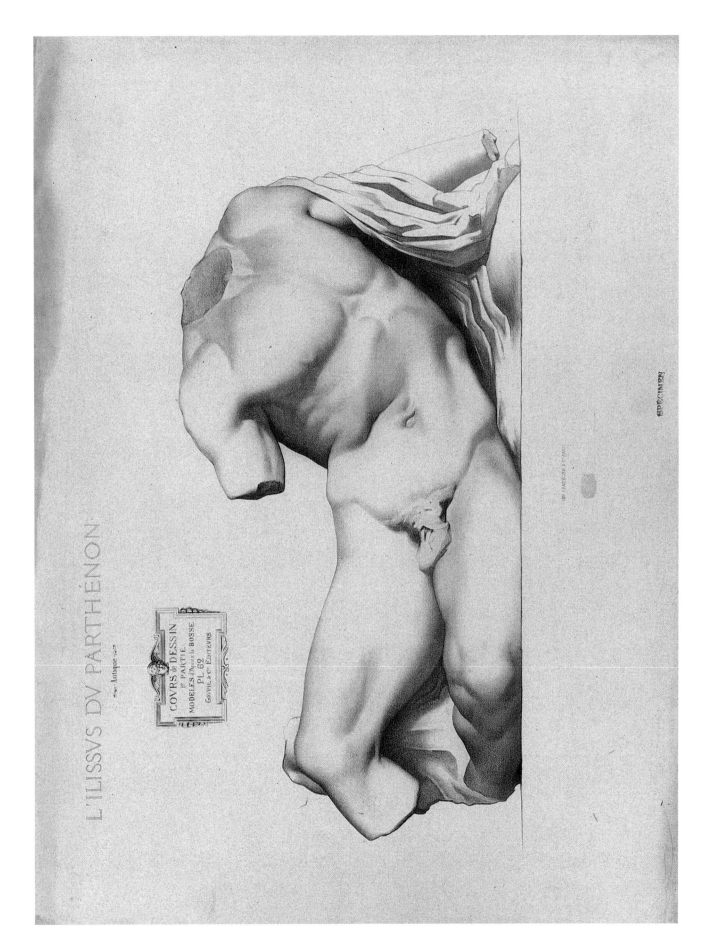

L'ILISSVS DV PARTHÉNON.
Antique

COVRS de DESSIN
2e PARTIE.
MODELES d'après la BOSSE
PL. 62
GOVPIL & cie ÉDITEVRS

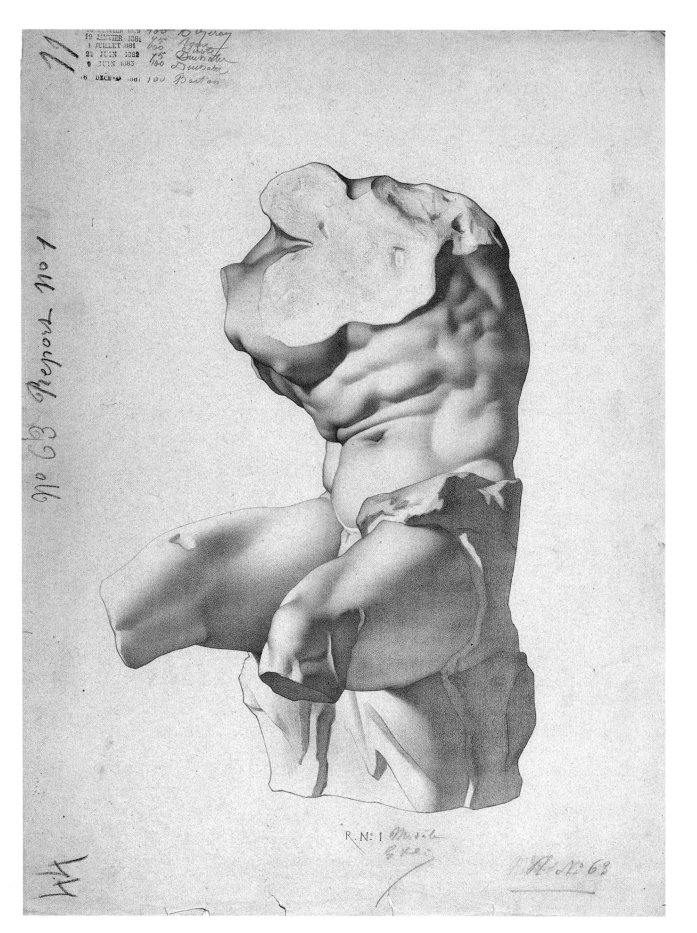

Plate I, 63

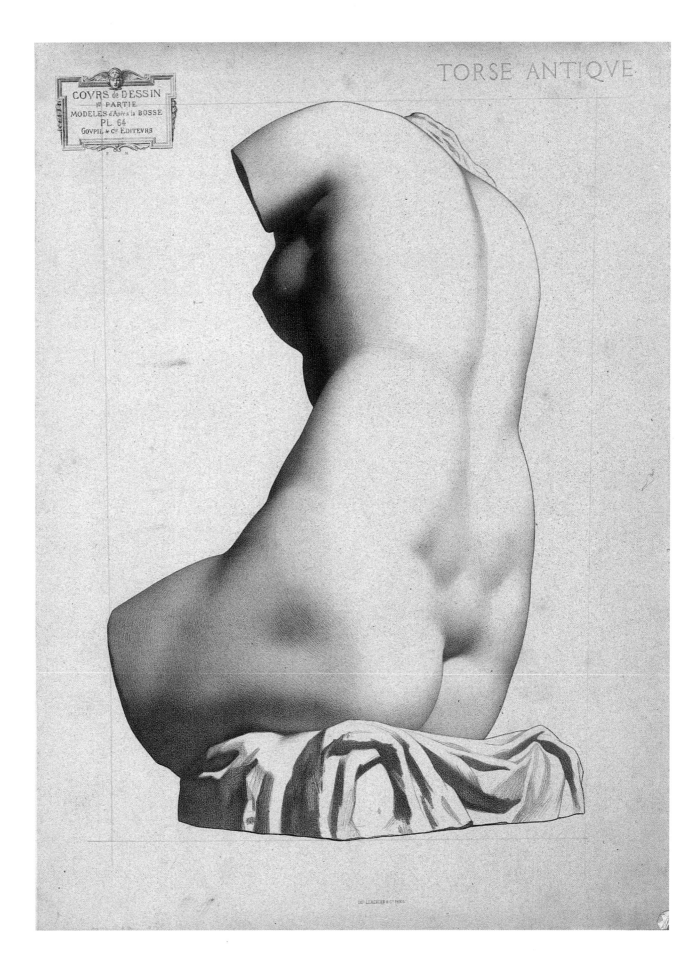

COVRS de DESSIN
1re PARTIE
MODELES d'Après la BOSSE
PL. 64
GOVPIL & Cie EDITEVRS

Plate I, 64

Plate I, 65

Plate I, 66

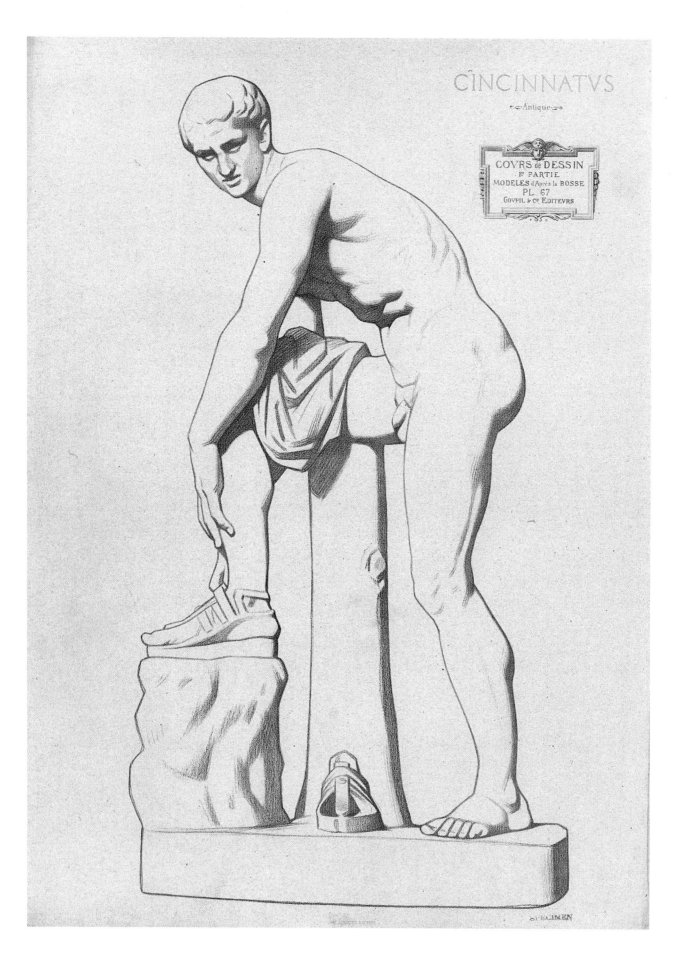

CINCINNATVS

Antique

COVRS de DESSIN
I.ᵉ PARTIE
MODELES d'Après la BOSSE
PL. 67
GOVPIL & Cⁱᵉ EDITEVRS

Plate I, 67

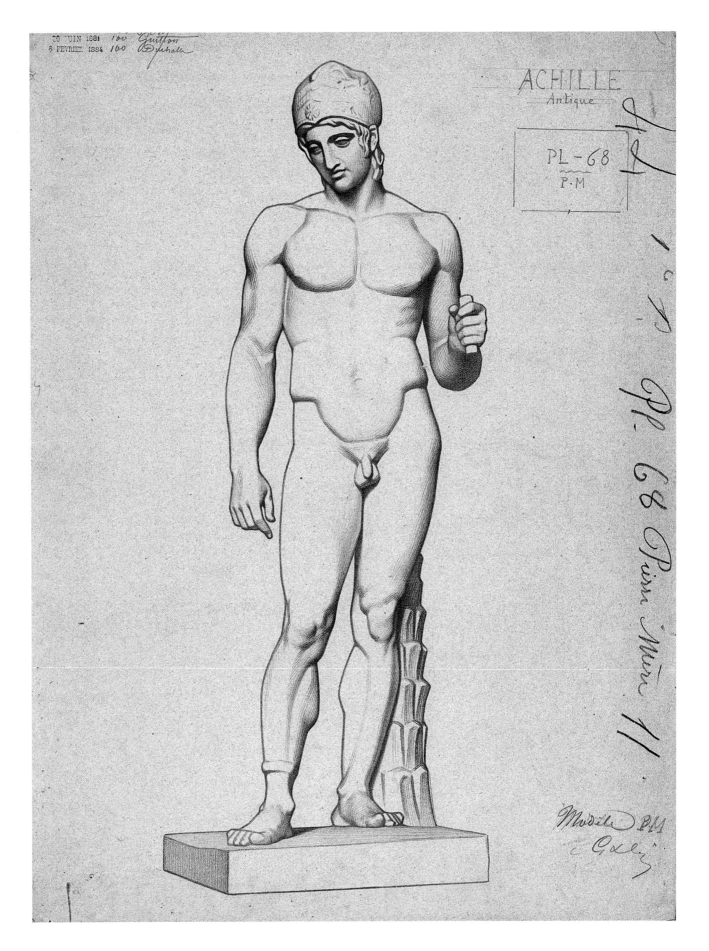

Plate I, 68

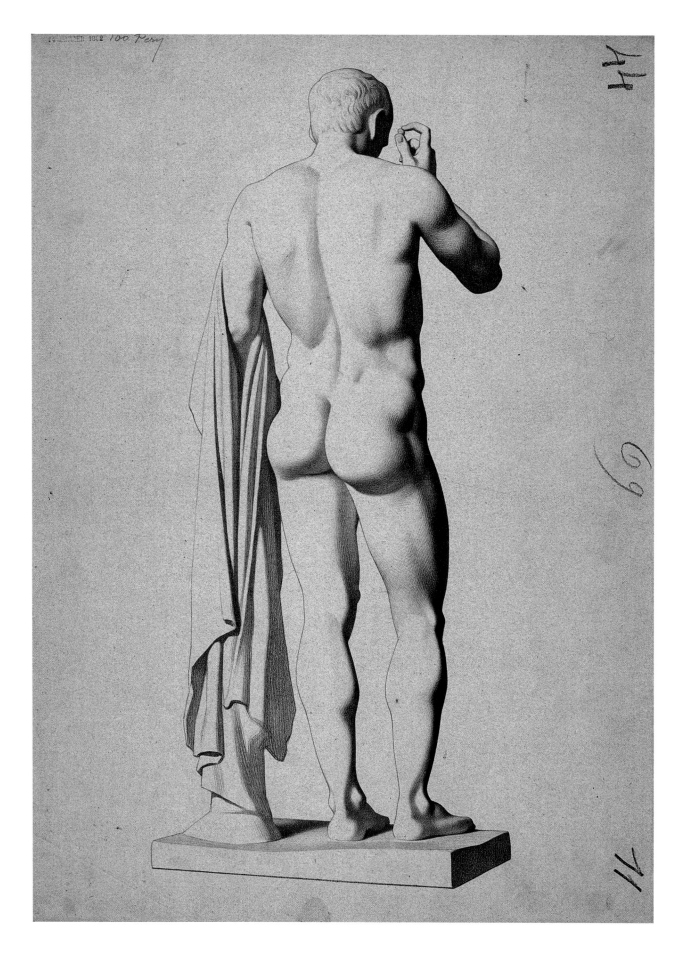

Plate I, 69

Plate I, 70

NOTES ON THE PLATES

PARTS OF THE HEAD.
(FRAGMENTS DE TÊTES.)

Plate I, 1. Eyes.
(Yeux.)

An old Neoplatonic premise has students starting their study of the human physiognomy with the eye, "the mirror of the soul." Even in the early 1600s, in Odoardo Fialette's engraved drawing course entitled *The True Method and Rules for Drawing All the Parts and Members of the Human Body* (*Il vera moda et ordine per disignare tuttia le parti et membra del corpo humano;* Venice, 1608), the first plate is similar to this one. Eyes exist in a complex anatomical setting that appears to change with any slight turning of the head; they are difficult to reduce to two-dimensional form. These models will teach you to simplify the organization of the eye and its surrounding structures.

First draw the plumb line and the horizontal on your drawing paper. Notice the organization of the angles of the other lines around these two as you copy them. Begin with simple lines—no shadows, no details; put down nothing that will detract from the essential. This will help you approach the eye in its more complex, natural setting.

Plate I, 2. Mouths.
(Bouches.)

Eight simplified schemata are paired with finished mouths viewed from different angles. These models treat the mouth as a unit that includes the nose and the chin; the student is taught to see the mouth integrated in the surrounding organic structure of the face, continually varying in shape and relationships as the view changes.

The refined version has been developed around the near straights of the schema, without following them exactly. Without the careful control supplied by the guidelines, the proportions would probably go awry. In the foreshortened views, the line cuts through the center. You are meant to get used to drawing foreshortened views right from the start.

These models are idealized views of nature, taken from classical sculpture; the simplification of nature has already been done for you twice: first by antiquity and again by Bargue.

Plate I, 3. Noses.
(Nez.)

The models are classical, some highly idealized. Just as the mouth was considered as an organic part of a face, the nose is here seen in its proper relationship to the eyes and mouth in profile. Several ways of organizing the profile are suggested.

The profile to the left is of Dante Alighieri, the great Italian poet (see plate I, 34), and the profile to the far right is that of Caracalla, the ill-famed Roman emperor (see plate I, 38 and fig.15). In the center is an idealized Apollo type. While studying the course, you are meant to build up a repertoire of human types and a consciousness of the specific traits that denote age and character. The head of Dante is plotted with a single horizontal line through the plumb line; the other schemata contain two or more. In most cases the plumb line goes through the upper corner of the eye. This placement helps to correctly measure the distance between the eye and the nose.

Plate I, 4. Ears.
(Oreilles.)

Ears are complicated, so this is an important plate that you should copy repeatedly until you can draw ears correctly from nature. Look at the finished drawings, and ask how you yourself would plot the main lines.

This plate introduces a new type of shadow called *hatching,* the building up of shadows with parallel lines. The value of an area is established by just a few lines crossing it. Even when they are somewhat spread apart, many lines together can produce a shadow. Density may be further increased by *cross-hatching,* that is, by crossing the first set of parallel lines with another set. Neatness and regularity of stroke are important in cross-hatching.

Note: It would help to look up the ear in an encyclopedia or an anatomy book to learn the names of the different features (such as the helix, the ante-helix, the concha and the tragus). Knowing the anatomical terminology will help your vision and memory by enabling you to verbalize what you see.

FEET.
(PIEDS.)

Plate I, 5. Profile of a foot.
(Pieds de profil.)

This plate codifies the successive steps of the method promoted in the course. First, a schematic diagram, supported by a plumb line, encloses the subject. A large triangle has been abstracted from the perceived shape of the foot. The points were plotted—perhaps with the aid of a tool—by measuring locations and distances with the eye. The base of the triangle plots the bottom of the foot; the other sides of the triangle establish the perimeter of the cast; one goes along the back of the foot to the heel, the other to the top of the big toe.

In the second drawing, after the accuracy of the straight lines had been checked, the outline was further refined, realizing the shape of the foot. Add the shadow line for the main, dark value (squinting will help you see the shadows more distinctly, as would viewing the drawings in a black mirror [see glossary]).

In the third drawing the shape and shadows are refined. After further checking the outline for accuracy, the shadows were filled in with an even value, either by stumping or cross-hatching. At this stage, if the plotting of points was not accurate, there will not be room here and there for all the parts of the foot. If the plotting has been accurate, a three-dimensional effect will be produced as soon as the shadows are added. After the shadows are filled in, check your outlines again. Do not be surprised if you have to make revisions to both shadows and outline. After these corrections, gently soften the merging of the shadows and the lights.

Plate I, 6. Heels.
(Pieds, talons.)

Two sets of heels are viewed from the left and from the right. Each set includes a suggested schema of two transversals, or horizontal construction lines, on the plumb or vertical reference line that in theory have been drawn from nature, that is, from studying an actual cast. Study the finished drawing until you can understand the logical placement of the plumb line and the transversals. Then, after corrections have been made and the outlines have been refined, fill in the shadows and make necessary adjustments. These casts are from Greek or Roman statuary, which means the foot has already been idealized and simplified.

Plate I, 7. The foot of the gladiator.
(Pied du Gladiateur.)

This is the foot of what was once one of the most admired of ancient sculptures, now known as the Borghese Warrior (see fig. 8) (The work was long held to be the depiction of a gladiator. We know now that gladiators wore heavy armor; the nudity here glorifies the soldier.) It is signed by Agasias, son of Dositheos of Ephesus, and is now in the Louvre Museum in Paris. Plaster casts of the statue were in virtually every academy of art in Europe and the Americas. Discovered around 1611, the statue was in the Borghese collection in Rome until 1808, when it was bought by Napoleon Bonaparte and shipped to Paris. It has been postulated that the subject shows a foot soldier attacking a mounted enemy. He holds up his (lost) shield to ward off blows from above, while at the same time trying to wound his adversary's steed in the stomach. We are looking at his back left leg; the weight of the lunge is on his advanced right leg. The statue is intact except for the loss of the metal sword and the shield.

In the drawing the movement of the foot is elegantly articulated, as in the spreading of the toes. After you have carefully measured and transcribed the triangle of the schema, ask yourself if you could use some horizontal transversals. Plot the angles of contact on the right side of the foot with great care; every point and every angle must be accurate.

Fig. 8.
Agasias of Ephesus. *The Borghese Warrior* (or *The Borghese Gladiator*).
(Le Guerrier Borghese, ou Le Gladiateur Borghèse.)
Marble. 199 cm. (6 ft. 6 in.)
Louvre Museum, Paris.
Thought to be a copy of a Greek bronze from the school of Lysippus, fourth century B.C.

Plate I, 8. The foot of the Medici Venus.
(Pied de la Vénus de Médicis.)

This is the right foot of the much-restored statue of Venus, which for centuries has been in the Rotunda of the Uffizi Gallery in Florence, Italy (see figs. 9 and 10). This marble, signed by Cleomenes, son of Apollodorus, is probably a copy of a Greek work in bronze. It was considered the epitome of female beauty well into the nineteenth century. The arms are restorations, probably of the early Renaissance. To understand its former fame, look beyond the polished surface to the balance of the pose, which runs through all the limbs, as well as the rhythmical interrelations of the masses and the proportions (the latter are better seen from the rear).

The exquisite foot rises gracefully onto the toes in a movement that evokes a response in every part of the body as the weight shifts to the left foot. You will be given the whole leg as a model in plate I, 29.

The drawing is the most refined encountered thus far, with gentle transitions from the shadows to the lighter areas. Several important areas of halftones must be added after the basic shadow has been established. Make sure your schematic drawing is accurate. Note how judiciously Bargue has simplified the two sides of the foot and the toes.

Fig. 9.
The Medici Venus.
(La Vénus de Médicis.)
First century A.D., probably a
copy of a fourth-century B.C.
Greek original.
Marble. 153 cm. (5 ft.)
Uffizi Gallery, Florence.

Fig. 10.
The Medici Venus, rear view.
(La Vénus de Médicis,
vue de dos.)

Plate I, 9. The sole of the foot.
(Plante de pied.)

This foot seems drawn from nature or after a suspended cast taken from nature. There is only one vertical organizational line, the indispensable plumb line. Depending upon the size of the model and your drawing, you might want to carefully add a transversal construction line or two. The lesson here is in seeing large shapes and blocking them out.

Note: The heel, the big toe, and the plane of the foot are summarily yet clearly outlined. Bargue leaves some shadow lines for you to develop. Squint or use a black mirror to better view the shapes of the shadows.

Plate I, 10. The foot of Germanicus.
(Pied du Germanicus.)

The statue, in the Louvre Museum in Paris (see fig. 11), is signed by Cleomenes, son of Cleomenes, Athenian, and was carved during the reign of Augustus ca. 20 B.C. For several centuries the statue was identified as Germanicus, nephew of Emperor Augustus; for a while it was taken to be a youthful portrait of Augustus: Octavius the Orator, Assimilated to Mercury, that is, with a body type (thin and dry) and a pose usually associated with Mercury, the god of commerce and cleverness (he is thought to be throwing a die). Now it is labeled Honorary Funeral Statue of Marcellus, Nephew and first Son-in-law of Augustus. At any rate, it is a genuine ancient work of the Augustan period. You will see two views of a leg of Germanicus in plates I, 25 and 27, and a full rear view in plate I, 69. The *massier* (or student supervisor) of Gérôme's atelier reported to Charles Moreau-Vauthier that, when the atelier first opened in 1864, "during our first week of work the model in Gérôme's studio was an antiquity, Germanicus."

To refresh your memory and technique, Bargue has here given you two preliminary steps: a simple blocking out around a single plumb or reference line; then more detailed schema with shadow lines and clearly planned work spaces for the individual toes. It will still take some study, measurement, and observation to refine the drawing and to fill in the shadows and the halftones.

HANDS.
(MAINS.)

Plate I, 11. Hands in profile.
(Mains de profil.)

This plate gives both an inside and an outside view of a hand resting on a block. The view from the inside or thumb side uses the margins of the block as organizational lines, along with several very useful diagonals, the lower one showing the relationship of the ends of the fingers. Study the diagonals; discern their sense before doing your own. Although shadows are referred to, no shadow line is given; that is the next step. Note the difference between the shadows on the lower part of the fingers and that on the block; the former is built up by tight cross-hatching, the latter is filled in solidly. The cross-hatching describes some reflected light on the hand.

The view from the outside has the fingers pleasingly arranged. (You should always be aware of the decorative possibilities of finger arrangement; when viewing depictions by other artists, always study how they pose hands and fingers.)

Here the schemata have two functions: they help you copy the drawing and show you how to look for organizing lines on other casts you may study.

Plotting lines connect the ends of the fingers and the joints. Do not memorize this schema; such patterns are individual and do not apply to different hands. Because of the irregular shapes of fingers, shadows are an important part of their modeling. Here they set up a dramatic pattern.

Plate I, 12. A Closed hand and a leaning hand.
(Main fermée et main appuyée.)

Turn the sheet clockwise to copy these drawings; the leaning hand is pushing down on a ledge. The preliminary drawings for both views have strong, simplified outlines. The upper part of the hand is just a single line; the back another, although the wrist will protrude beyond it. Bargue wants you to be general yet still precise in the beginning.

Plate 1, 13. Hand of Voltaire.
(Main de Voltaire.)

The French sculptor Jean-Antoine Houdon (1741–1828) was working on his life-sized statue of the seated Voltaire (1694–1778) when the aged philosopher died. It is known that Houdon made a death mask of Voltaire; he may have made this mold of Voltaire's hand at the same time. However, it does not seem to match either hand of the finished statue, of which there are three marble versions (at the Comédie Française in Paris, at the State Hermitage Museum in Saint Petersburg, and at the Musée Fabre in Montpellier).

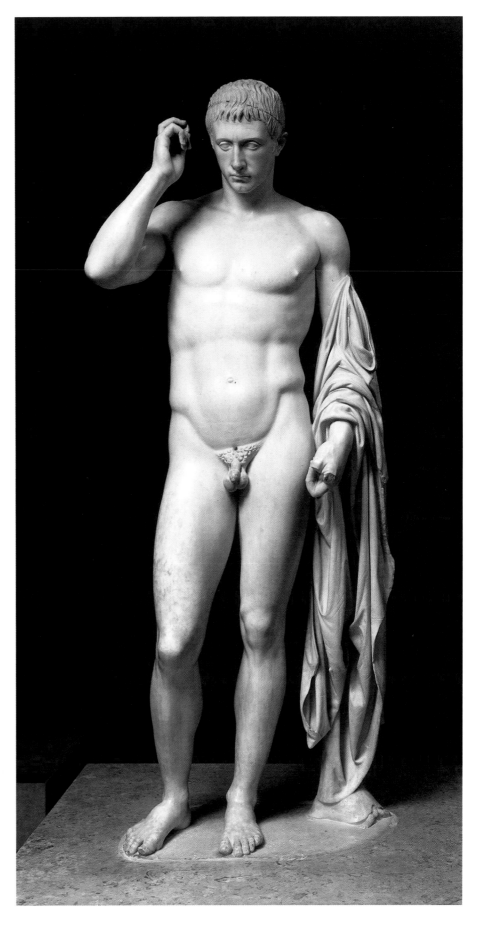

Fig. 11.
Germanicus (Honorary Funeral Statue of Marcellus, Nephew and first Son-in-law of Augustus.)
(Germanicus [Statue honorifique et funéraire de Marcellus, neveu d'Auguste].) ca. 20 B.C.
Marble. 180 cm. (71 in.)
Louvre Museum, Paris.

Step 1 is a simplification of the form to a few lines, a geometrical shape without complications, a freehand joining of measured points. Bargue wants you to be concise in your first apprehension and sketching of the form; he really wants you to see the organizing straight lines. Does the simplification of the front part of the support help you in any way? Bargue eliminates the middle point of the support in the hope that you will learn a lesson in finding the smaller change of direction relative to the two greater changes.

Step 2 fills in the fingers and the knuckles, clarifies the base, and adds a major shadow line on the base. You must supply the shadow lines for the fingers.

Step 3 reveals the form through the contrast of light and shadow and a few reflected lights at the bottoms of the fingers.

Accuracy is important throughout; otherwise all the details cannot be correctly fitted in.

Plate I, 14. Hand holding a whetstone.
(Main de faucheur.)

This is a very elegant drawing; it demonstrates the structure and grace of the hand in action.

The first outline contains a set of angles at the bottom along an external diagonal. The fingers are seen as a unit, with an indication of the forefinger. Study the general shape at first.

The second stage plots the fingers and refines the outline. Some shadow outlines are indicated, and some internal anatomical notations are sketched in.

During the final stage you should refine the contours and develop the internal forms concurrently. Be accurate in both contours and internal forms. Check the contours again after the shadows are in; you may now see some parts that need correction.

Plate I, 15. Hand of a woman pressing her breast.
(Main d'une femme pressant son sein.)

This is a very delicate hand, slightly plump, with dimples—indentions—instead of protrusions over the knuckles, an effect also seen in the hands of babies.

In *Step 1* the fingers are outlined with straights, although they curve. At first curves are best seen as simple straight lines.

Plate I, 16. Hand of a woman holding a stone.
(Main de femme.)

This final, linear handling is a delicate presentation of all five fingers of the hand without any complicated details or obtrusive shadows. It is a classical hand, clear and complete in outline, simplified, beautiful, without blemishes or the distortions of perspective. (Bargue has been training your taste along with your descriptive skills.)

ARMS.
(BRAS.)

Plate I, 17. Arm of a man, horizontal position.
(Bras d'homme, horizontal.)

This new set of plates starts out with a simple outline drawing; a flat, frontal light minimizes the internal anatomical features, with much of the anatomy expressed through contour alone. Because the fist is pulled back, the muscles of the forearm (in particular, the extensor muscles of the forearm) are tightened, and the triceps of the upper arm are flexed. (A knowledge of anatomy and its terminology will help you recognize, identify, and understand what you see; as a consequence, you will avoid making mistakes in drawing.)

Plate I, 18. Arm of a man, vertical position.
(Bras d'homme, vertical.)

The plumb line is through the center, down to the central knuckle. The upper horizontal is through the olecranon process of the elbow, and the bottom horizontal is through the lower external head of the ulna. A curve organizes the knuckles. A shadow line runs the length of the arm; it is strong in the preliminary drawing and very careful in the characterization of form through contour in the finished drawing.

Note how the line of the right profile is precisely modulated; every muscle and bone is indicated with great subtlety. Bargue teaches you to see and express form through contour.

Plate I, 19. Flexed forearm of a man, interior view.
(Bras d'homme, ployé, intérieur.)

The plumb line and the transversal cross in the center of the drawing; this helps divide the arm into easily manageable sections. The forearm is strongly foreshortened; the preliminary drawing makes this clear. In the finished drawing the overlappings (prepared for in the preliminary drawing) aid in the understanding of foreshortening. The contours of the finished drawing give a sense of breadth and fullness.

Plate I, 20. Child's arm, interior view.
(Bras d'enfant, intérieur.)

The horizontal crosses the central plumb line in the fold of the elbow. The contours of the finished drawing are more accurate than in the schema.

Plate I, 21. Child's arm, exterior view.
(Bras d'enfant, extérieur.)

This is the same arm as in the previous plate (probably the model was a life cast), this time seen from behind. The same coordinates are used again.

Plate I, 22. Woman's arm, bent [while pressing a piece of drapery to her shoulder].
(Bras de femme, ployé.)

The preliminary drawing has only a plumb line through the center. The outside contours are reduced to straight lines; be careful in plotting these, especially on the right side, which has few internal features to help. As you finish the right side, break it down into angles and turn it into curves.

For the first time this example is fully modeled. Take care with the delicate modeling across the ulna furrow (beginning at the elbow). Be sure the plotting of the fingers is accurate in your drawing. Measure and check until you are sure they are right before you start to refine them. With so many points and angles, continually check for errors; they will undoubtedly occur. The charm of the drawing depends upon the rhythm of the fingers and the shadows, as well as upon the veil of shading across the arm.

Plate I, 23. Man's arm, bent.
(Bras d'homme, ployé, extérieur.)

This is the same arm, with the forearm in tension, as in plate 19, this time seen from the outside (externally). This view avoids the foreshortening in plate 19. As in that plate, a single horizontal line crosses the plumb line, breaking the arm into three parts. The shadow line of the lower arm is indicated in the preliminary drawing, while that of the inner elbow is not.

Plate I, 24. Arm of *Moses*, by Michelangelo.
(Bras du Moïse de Michel-Ange.)

Michelangelo's statue of Moses, carved between 1513 and 1516, is in the Church of San Pietro in Vincoli in Rome (see fig. 12).

The strong right arm of Moses holds the Tablet of the Laws in its hand. The drawing is both intricate in its modeling and in its anatomical structure. Take your time. If the contours are not right, the muscles will not fit in their proper places. Continue to compare your work with the model.

LEGS.
(JAMBES.)

Plate I, 25. Leg of Germanicus in profile.
(Jambe du Germanicus, profil.)

A view of the limb of the judiciously proportioned statue in the Louvre Museum in Paris, now identified as *Marcellus, the Nephew of Augustus*. This is the play leg, the free or non-weight-bearing leg of a body in *contrapposto* (an Italian term for the turning of the body on its own axis); here the right leg, the support leg, bears the weight of the body. (See fig. 11 for a photo of the Roman marble.)

Plate I, 26. Child's leg, rear view.
(Jambe d'enfant.)

This is the leg of a robust child aged three or four years. The plumb line is very close to the shadow line. In a young child fat predominates over muscle. Even for soft, rounded forms Bargue uses straight lines.

Plate I, 27. Leg of Germanicus, front view.
(Jambe du Germanicus, face.)

To better understand the posture of the leg, compare this plate with the previous side view of the leg in plate I, 25. This is the play leg (as opposed to the support leg); it is bent at the knee, so both the upper and lower halves of the leg are seen with some foreshortening and the muscles of the leg are taut. The middle of the knee is positioned over the inner angle; the plumb line does not go through the center of the lower leg. The main feature is the clarified articulation of the knee and the foot, simplified in the tradition of ancient Greek statuary. Many artists who learn this foot seem never to need another. Very Greek is the furrow on the medial (inner) side of the tibia (shinbone). Another Grecian feature is the fullness of the muscles of the calf, the gastrocnemius (upper calf muscle) and the soleus (lower calf muscle). Note the rhythm of the toes: the big toe is separated from the other toes, which are seen together as a unit. Study the modeling on the periphery of each side; they describe halftones, shadows as well as the silhouette. Here an anatomy book would be useful in helping you identify the anatomical parts indicated by the lines. You must learn

Fig. 12.
Michelangelo, *Moses.*
(Moïse.) 1513–16.
Marble.
Height 235 cm. (7 ft. 8.5 in.)
San Pietro in Vincoli, Rome.

to distinguish what you know (about anatomy) from what you see on the surface. To draw intelligently requires that you recognize what you see as well as getting the form or shape right. However, do not add anatomical features that you do not see; they will only distract from clarity of form.

Plate I, 28. Leg of the Crouching Venus.
(Jambe de la Vénus accroupie.)

This Crouching Venus, a popular bronze statue once thought to have been cast in the mid-third century B.C., was traditionally attributed to an otherwise obscure ancient sculptor named Doidalses.

This is the leg and thigh of one of the many preserved (but still usually damaged) ancient marble copies of the lost bronze. The goddess is at her bath; the upper part shows her wringing the water out of her long hair while turning her head to look at the observer. The muscles of the thigh are covered by fat, transforming the contour to an amorphous but elegant curve. Break it into straights as Bargue does. When it is hard to find a plumb line that passes through several angles, put one in the center, as here. Then a horizontal line will divide the drawing into manageable parts.

Plate I, 29. Leg of the Venus de Medici.
(Jambe de la Vénus de Médicis.)

This is the play leg of the famous Venus in the Uffizi Gallery whose elegant foot we have already studied (see plate I, 8). Again a plumb line is simply put through the center. The preliminary drawing shows you how to abstract the angles in drawing the contours. Using a tool—your plumb line or a steel knitting needle—will help you locate the most important angles in the Bargue drawing. Be accurate when putting down the points. Check constantly. The lightness and grace in this leg will help you appreciate and understand the reputation of this statue. (See figs. 9 and 10 for photos of the antique marble.)

Plate I, 30. Legs of the *Dying Slave*, by Michelangelo.
(Jambes de l'Esclave mourant de Michel-Ange.)

The cast is from the lower part of a statue meant to decorate the three-storied tomb of Julius II, which was planned by Michelangelo for the crossing of Saint Peter's in the Vatican. The tomb was never finished as planned, and the statue (ca. 1513) came into French possession under François I and is now in the Louvre Museum in Paris. An abbreviated version of the tomb is now in San Pietro in Vincoli in Rome, which encases the famous *Moses* by Michelangelo (see plate I, 24 and fig. 12).

The statue is thought to have a Neoplatonic meaning, the leather band around the chest being read as the bondage of the senses that keeps the struggling soul from flying to heaven and experiencing pure truths.

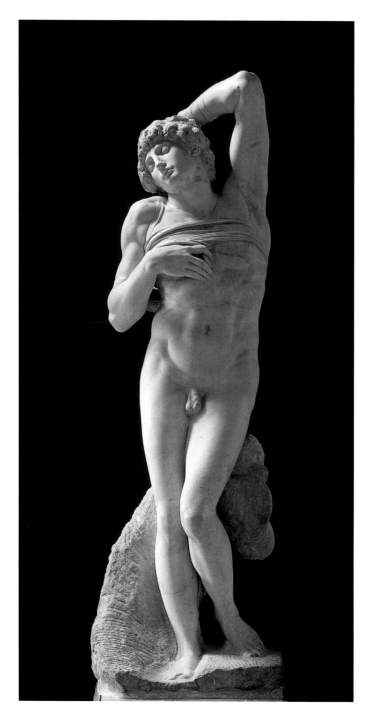

Fig. 13.
Michelangelo. *The Dying Slave* (or *The Prisoner*).
(*L'Esclave mourant. Le Captif.*) ca. 1513.
Marble. Height 235 cm. (7 ft. 8.5 in.)
Louvre Museum, Paris.

This beautiful plate is meant to be the climax of your leg studies; it features the legs in all their complexity, from the pelvis to the feet. The two legs show the contrast of the play leg and the support leg; the finished drawing is fully modeled.

HEADS IN PROFILE.
(TÊTES DE PROFIL.)

Plate I, 31. Nero as a child.
(Néron, enfant.)

The head is a cast from a full, standing figure (now in the Louvre Museum in Paris) of the future emperor as a schoolboy (ca. 45 A.D.) The portrayal of people in profile is an ancient tradition that has survived into modern times. It was used by the Greeks—and is still used by modern artists—for portraits on coinage and memorials. The clarity of the view makes it useful where identification should be easy, while adding dignity to the subject.

Step 1 is not an easy one; it would be even more difficult working from life. The sparseness of detail (as in the hair) demonstrates how little detail is needed for verisimilitude.

Plate I, 32. Cardinal Jiménez.
(Le cardinal Ximénès.)

Cardinal Jiménez de Cisneros (1436–1517?) was the grand inquisitor of Castile. His features are extraordinarily complex; consequently *Step 1* is highly analytical. Bargue suggests how one may analyze the angles of the features from a plumb line through the face, which is transversed by four horizontals. A second plumb line down the back of the cast is drawn to keep one aware that the back of the mask is not a perpendicular. The plumb line enables you to locate the outside points and angles. *Step 2* is exemplary: the correction of the outline goes hand in hand with the recording of the shadow line. In *Step 3* the full shadow is strong, without halftones. The few halftones on the face describe textures. Note the simplified and unified areas of halftones in the beard.

Plate I, 33. Young girl. Life cast.
(Jeune fille. Moulage sur nature.)

Casts made from living subjects were used in nineteenth-century studios, just as they are today. (See fig. 14, which shows an artist and his assistant making a cast of a model's leg; see also plate I, 21.) Bargue has placed the plumb line down the back of the cast and drawn a curved line to organize the profile. This is quite similar to plate I, 31.

Plate I, 34. Dante.
(Dante.)

This is based on the purported death mask of the great poet in the Palazzo Vecchio in Florence, which is now believed to be a later concoction made after several fourteenth-century portraits of Dante, and even they are of disputed authenticity. Even so, the formidable nose can still be seen among the citizens of contemporary Florence. Neither the schema nor the finished drawing is particularly elegant. Perhaps this is a preexisting drawing by another hand, interleaved among the cast plates because Dante was such a popular subject for artists in the nineteenth century.

The procedure is similar to that for the profiles above. Despite the seeming irregularity of the face, five important points are crossed by the plumb line.

The lesson to be learned here is: do not be dismayed by irregular heads.

Plate I, 35. *The Cardinal de Birague*, by Germain Pilon.
(Le cardinal de Birague, de Germain Pilon.)

Germain Pilon (1537–1590), the most notable of French Renaissance sculptors, is represented by a figure from his famous tomb for Cardinal René de Birague (1510–1583), completed between 1575 and 1590. The statue of the kneeling prelate is now in the Louvre Museum in Paris. Cardinal Birague was one of the instigators of the Saint Bartholomew's Day massacre.

In *Step 1* Bargue captures the character of the model with the sure placement of his first angles and lines, a splendid drawing in itself. The plumb line is from the highest point down the back; this line permits the placing of the point of the nose. The two diagonals, up and down from the nose, organize the rest of the face. The shadow line is more indicative than descriptive. In *Step 2* the outline is refined and the shadow is filled in—a full, flat shadow without internal modeling. There are many halftones describing details of the anatomy and costume.

Plate I, 36. Marcus Brutus.
(Marcus Brutus.)

Marcus Junius Brutus (85–42 B.C.) was the adopted son of Julius Caesar but nevertheless figured among the conspirators who assassinated the dictator and thus—following Shakespeare—earned the most famous reproach in western history. The work was felt important enough to be included twice (see plate I, 50 for a frontal view), both times as full plates without a schematic first step. Do your own schema.

Plate I, 37. Head of a horse, Parthenon.
(Tête de cheval, Parthénon.)

Although this horse is identified on the plate as coming from the west pediment *(fronton occidental)* of the Parthenon in Athens (448–433 B.C.), it is actually from the east pediment. This sculpture is one of the so-called Elgin Marbles, the remnants of the Parthenon sculptures in the British Museum in London since 1816. All the sculptures of the Parthenon are traditionally attributed to the sculptor Phidias, who supervised the sculptural program of the two pediments of the temple and sculpted the giant statue of Athena that graced the interior. Casts of the "Phidian horse" spread quickly into the art academies of Europe and the Americas, where it became the prime model for the horse despite or perhaps because of its strong idealization. The idealization certainly fits Bargue's taste. Knowledge of the horse's anatomy was essential to artists before the invention of the automobile made their presence rare in cities. A more difficult, foreshortened view of the horse's head is the subject of plate 1, 47.

Plate I, 38. Caracalla.
(Caracalla.)

This is a famous Roman portrait bust of a Roman emperor who ruled in the early third century A.D. It exists in several versions, most of them of high quality, as would be expected of works from an imperial workshop. The version in the Louvre Museum in Paris has a chipped nose, so this cast may be from another version—most likely the famous one in the Farnese collection at the National Archeological Museum in Naples. The version at the Metropolitan Museum of Art in New York (see fig. 15) is an example of how a good workshop could maintain high quality through a number of versions, all based on a plaster or clay model of the emperor. The model—perhaps made from life or from studies of Caracalla—stayed in the workshop and, like a photographic negative of a famous twentieth-century politician or celebrity, was used over and over as a model for portraits of the emperor. Imperial portraits were displayed throughout the Roman Empire in public places and buildings—particularly in law

Fig. 14.
Édouard Dantan.
Taking a Cast from Nature.
(Le Moulage sur nature.)
1887.
Oil on canvas.
165 x 131.5 cm.
(5 ft. 5 in. x 4 ft. 3.75 in.)
Göteborgs Konstmuseum.

courts, where they were symbols of the emperor's authority and supported the authority of the rulings and judgments of the courts. The presence of portraits of the head of state in courtrooms is still in evidence today. Caracalla ruled as emperor from A.D. 210 to 217; his reign, although short, was not a happy one. The personal power expressed by the portrait borders on brutality.

In the schema, the plumb line is through the back, with a crossing horizontal touching the ear lobe and the bottom of the nose. The plumb line was used to measure the points of the face, of which five are joined on a diagonal. The organizational lines for the head are almost abstract in some instances. You should be fairly advanced by now, both in how you see, how you make notations, and how you develop them. Note the abrupt change in values from the nose to the cheek; the light values of the nose complete an arc of bright values from the crown of the head and across the brow; the lighting for this cast drawing was carefully set up to produce this dramatic effect. Pay attention to the fact that these are not all areas of pure whites but also lightly veiled ones. You should save this veiling for the last stages of the drawing. The finished drawing is a good lesson in how to simplify hair; several halftones are used.

Plate I, 39. *Anne of Brittany*, by Giovanni Giusti.
(*Anne de Bretagne, de Jean Juste de Tours.*)

This is the head of a recumbent tomb figure, a *gisante,* as sculptures of the dead lying on their tombs are called. It is from the famous tomb of Louis XII in the Cathedral of Saint-Denis in Paris, the burial place of French royalty. Anne of Brittany, who died in 1531, lies next to her husband, the king.

An Italian about whom little is known, Giovanni Giusti (active 1515-22) brought Italian Renaissance style and techniques to France, where he was called Jean-Juste de Tours. The astonishing realism of this *dead* head, however, is far from the idealism we expect in Italian art of the sixteenth century.

It is easier to draw this cast as if she were standing up, but then you will not understand the sag of the cheeks, the collapse of the neck, or the fall of the hair. Remember that you are looking at her as if you were standing near her chest, so that you see the underside of her chin; this view moves her ear up. The construction lines of *Step 1* are simple, clear, and very important. The one horizontal organizes the face.

Note: It is absolutely necessary to get all the angles of the profile between the chin and brow accurately or the anatomical details of the face—mostly defined by shadows and halftones—will never fit in.

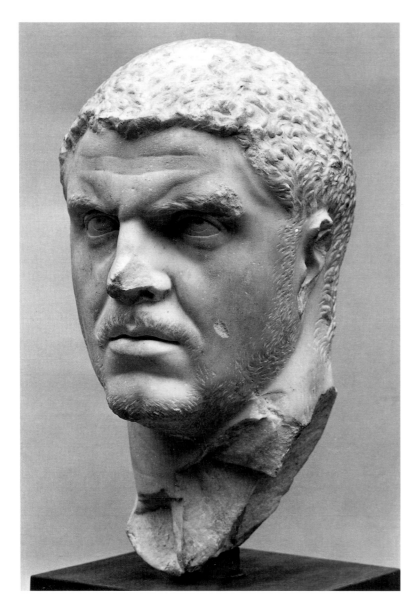

Fig. 15.
Caracalla. (Caracalla.)
Marble. 36.2 cm. (14.25 in.) Third century A.D.
The Metropolitan Museum of Art, New York
(Samuel D. Lee Fund, 1940.)

Plate I, 40. Julia Mammaea.
(Julia Mamea.)

A Roman bust (third century A.D.) in the Capitoline Museum in Rome. This is the final example in the set of profiles even though the view is not quite a perfect or pure profile. It is finished and fully modeled but nonetheless simplified in its forms.

HEADS IN THREE-QUARTER VIEWS.
(TÊTES DE TROIS QUARTS.)

Plate I, 41. The Capitoline Ariadne.
(Ariane du Capitole.)

The head alone has been cast from a full-standing figure in the Capitoline Museum in Rome. The identification of the subject as the mythical Ariadne and the attribution of the statue as after an original by Praxiteles (Greek, fourth century B.C.) are no longer accepted. It is now thought to be a statue of the god Dionysius (Bacchus), a somewhat androgynous deity.

This view is just off-profile, with three-quarters of the area in shadow. The shadow lines in the schematic drawing are masterful but by necessity approximate. Only by simplification can you see the larger aspects of the angles without getting lost in details.

Plate I, 42. *Children*, by François Flamand.
(Enfants, de François Flamand.)

Flamand was probably a Flemish sculptor active in France during the seventeenth or eighteenth centuries. The plotting lines of the baby's face are not very pretty in either schema, nor are the shadow patterns of the finished work. The plate is useful nonetheless for what it teaches about the proportions of a baby's head.

Plate I, 43. Faustina.
(Faustine.)

Two Roman empresses are named Faustina, and both lived during the second century A.D. The first was the wife of Antonious Pius and the second was the wife of Marcus Aurelius—both exemplary emperors.

Step 1 is a good example of how to schematize a model with a few construction lines. The plumb line goes through a corner of the eye and of the mouth and is a good reference line that will show you where to start each day. The longest horizontal is a good one, over ear and eyebrows. Subsidiary angles can be easily developed for the eye, the bottom of the nose, the bottom of the mouth, and so forth. The finished drawing has maintained simplicity in form and observation.

Plate I, 44. The Psyche of Naples.
(Psyché de Naples.)

This work is now commonly referred to as the Psyche of Capua and dates from the first century B.C. It is in the National Archeological Museum in Naples. This is another head cast from a full standing figure that has a well-preserved surface.

This is a highly finished example for which you must devise your own first step schema. Shadows dominate the piece, covering more than half the work. Note the sophistication in the reflected lights visible in the shadows, which are produced by careful cross-hatching on the neck. This was probably meant to be the last model of this set.

Plate I, 45. The Capitoline Ariadne.
(Ariane du Capitole.)

See the comments to plate I, 41. An unusual view, we are looking over the shoulder of the figure.

In *Step 1* an excellently placed plumb line locates five basic points and sets the intersection of the horizontal under the nose. Construct to the right and left on the horizontal. The hair is carefully plotted. In *Step 2* there is not much strong shadow but considerable halftone modeling on the lower jaw and neck. A view of a turned head with diminished or lost features is called a lost profile *(profil perdu)*. Avoid the tendency to turn it into a profile by paying attention to the accurate placement of the features.

Plate I, 46. Young boy.
(Jeune garçon.)

This is another lost profile. The shadow accentuates the profile. This presents an occasion to study the shape of the skull and a strongly foreshortened ear.

Plate I, 47. Head of a horse.
(Tête de cheval.)

Although the plate inscription describes this Greek sculpture (448–433 B.C.) as coming from the west pediment *(fronton occidental)* of the Parthenon in Athens, it is actually from the east pediment. The lithograph by Bargue is after a drawing by Lecomte de Nouÿ. The original Greek marble is in the British Museum in London. This cast is in a very difficult position for a drawing. *Step 1* is a demonstration of how to break down the head of the horse into angles. Horizontal lines relate features across the form. Be careful with the curved lines of the jaw.

Plate I, 48. Phocion.
(Phocion.)

Phocion was a Greek general and statesman of the early fourth century B.C. This is a head cast from a full-length, standing statue in the Vatican Museums in Vatican City. The top of his head is flat because the Phrygian cap he wears has not been cast except for the rim.

Step 1 is without plumb line or horizontals. You may draw in some if you wish since you have developed your own method by now. The schema shows the breakdown into angles and straights. The shadow line is indicated in most places. Reflected lights reveal forms in the shaded areas; in such cases the values may vary quite a bit. Save these areas of reflected light until last and bring them out of the shadow with an eraser. Be careful not to exaggerate them. This is a lesson in complex lighting.

Note: To plot the curls in the beard, work from large groups to smaller shapes and finally to details.

HEADS IN FRONTAL VIEWS.
(TÊTES DE FACE.)

Plate I, 49. Agrippa.
(Agrippa.)

This plate is after a cast of a famous Roman sculpture of the first century B.C., now in the Louvre Museum in Paris. Marcus Vipinius Agrippa (62–23 B.C.) was the chief administrator under the Roman emperor Augustus. His foresight, reliability, and efficiency are conveyed by the severity of the portrait. A man of about forty, he is lighted from a direct overhead source that creates a symmetrical pattern of shadows under the projecting forms. The finished drawing shows how the human form can be simplified and still retain its integrity. Underneath it all is the stolid Roman fondness for heavy forms.

In *Step 1* the plumb line through the middle divides the face into two halves. The horizontals are easily chosen through the corners of the eyes, nose, and mouth. These guidelines plot the corners of the shadow patterns as well. The shadows, in turn, describe the basic features of the face with minimal use of halftones. In *Step 2* the forms are clarified by a few halftones around the nose, under the chin and mouth, and on the cheeks.

Plate I, 50. Marcus Brutus.
(Marcus Brutus.)

See the commentary to plate I, 36 to learn about the statue and the subject.

Step 1 is not illustrated here since you know the step from the previous plate of Agrippa. The shadow line is clear from head to neck, the result of a controlled, single light source. In *Step 2,* or finishing stage, note that the cast shadows (especially on the nose and chin) transpose gradually to half lights, an effect to be carefully imitated employing skills already nurtured. The darkest values are at the center of the head.

Plate I, 51. Jupiter Trophonius.
(Jupiter Trophonius.)

Stylistically this is a complex piece. It is a depiction of the Roman god Jupiter (Greek Zeus) in the early classical or severe style prevalent in Greece around 500 B.C. A Greek or Roman sculptor from a later era carved the piece. All the stylized features are arranged in strict symmetrical patterns, but they are softened by more naturalistic conventions. The strong idealism or classicism of the depiction attracted Bargue and Gérôme. The title of Trophonius relates Jupiter to an oracular Greek god whose ritual site was in Boetia, one of the republics of ancient Greece.

Plate I, 52. Lucius Junius Brutus.
(Lucius Junius Brutus.)

This drawing is based on a cast ultimately derived from a fourth-century B.C. bronze bust in the Capitoline Museum in Rome (see fig. 16). This sculpture of an unidentified Roman has long been associated with Brutus, a legendary hero of the sixth century B.C. famous for killing Tarquinius, the tyrannical king of Rome (who had raped Brutus's sister, Lucretia). This opened the way for the founding of the Roman republic, which lasted until Octavius declared himself Caesar Augustus, emperor of the Roman Empire, in 27 B.C. Brutus's regicide made him a hero during the French Revolution. Casts of the bust, known as the Capitoline Brutus, were in academies and ateliers throughout France and Europe beginning in the early nineteenth century.

Fig. 16 .
The Capitoline Brutus.
(Brutus du Capitole.)
Bronze. ca. 325 B.C.
Head, antique bronze.
32 cm. (12.5 in.)
Capitoline Museum, Rome.

The direction of the light (as from a high window to one side) is similar to that of the other Brutus (see plate I, 50). The light, entering at a forty-five-degree angle, illuminates three-quarters of the face, leaving one side in shadow; an ideal light for revealing form. In *Step 1*, as in the other frontal portraits, the plumb line goes through the center of the face. The horizontals pass through the brows, the base of the nose, and the mouth. The shadow line is clear from head to neck—one line—again the result of a single light source. In *Step 2* be careful with the transitions from shadow through halftones to light. The shadows start out solid, and become gradually more diffuse as they progress toward the light. There are few details of the hair in the shadow pattern.

Plate I, 53. Young woman. Life cast. *(Jeune femme. Moulage sur nature.)*

On life casts, see the commentary to plate I, 33 and note 17.

Step 1: Note that the central axis is not a plumb line; it is aligned with the slight tilt of the head. The two horizontal guidelines that frame the eyes are perpendicular to the axis line. These horizontals are perpendicular to a central axis that is not perpendicular but is aligned with the tip of the head. Another set goes through the nose and mouth. The light is more than a three-quarter light. *Step 2* is highly modeled, with many halftones and smooth transitions between shadows and halftones. Note that the nostrils depicted in the first step are lost here; they were used there to aid in the construction of the nose. The gradations from light to dark on the left side of the face are darker than those on the right, showing both the direction of the light and the pattern it makes across the face.

Note: It is a convention in posing women to use bright frontal lighting, which produces rounded forms and minimizes shadows.

Plate I, 54. Homer. *(Homère.)*

This beautiful bust (Greek, first century B.C.) is not an actual portrait of the mythical Greek poet of the eighth century B.C., but rather an idealized invention of the Hellenistic period. It was very popular in antiquity; several marble versions have survived (for a good example, see fig. 17). Because Homer was so revered in the nineteenth century, casts of the bust were in most ateliers and

Fig. 17.
Homer. (Homère.)
Marble. 41 cm. (16 in.) First century B.C.
Helen Lillie Pierce Fund, Museum of Fine Arts, Boston.

117

sculpture collections. It was used as the model for almost all nineteenth-century paintings depicting the fabled poet, as exemplified by Ingres's *The Apotheosis of Homer (L'Apothéose d'Homère)* (1827) in the Louvre Museum in Paris and Bouguereau's *Homer and His Guide (Homère et son guide)* (1874) in the Milwaukee Art Museum, Wisconsin.

As the last in the series of head studies, this is fully developed in exemplary fashion. *Step 1* shows the placement of the plumb line through the middle of the face and the three horizontals through the features. The forms in the schema are blocked out in an angular fashion, showing the location or work space for the features rather than the actual forms. In *Step 2* the fully modeled head is described with a limited range of values. Begin modeling your drawing with only two or three values. As the forms become more accurate, so will your description of subtle values. Working this way can help you relate smaller value changes to the larger patterns of light in the drawing.

TORSOS.
(TORSES.)

Plate I, 55. The Belvedere Torso, rear view.
(Le torse du Belvédère, vu de dos.)

This statue (ca. 50 B.C.) is signed Apollonius son of Nestor, Athenian, and is in the Museo Pio-Clementino, Vatican Museums, Vatican City.

Despite being devoid of arms, lower legs, feet, part of the chest, as well as part of its buttocks (cut away to make it fit into a fountain niche), this statue has been famous since its rediscovery in the early 1400s. Acquired by a pope after 1506, the statue was put on display in the Belvedere courtyard of the Vatican (hence the name); now it is kept inside the museum, just off the courtyard. A favorite of Michelangelo, it was the inspiration for his superhuman male bodies. The torso is in a traditional pose for the resting Hercules (and consequently of other melancholic types like Saturn and Samson), but recently it has been suggested that the subject is Ajax resting, depressed after his fit of madness. Casts are fairly common, for the work is greatly admired down to this day (see fig. 18 and plate I, 63).

Ancient practice seems to have had a different physical type for each of the four humors, the basis of both ancient medicine and psychology: Jupiter was the sanguine type, Mars the choleric type, Neptune the phlegmatic type, and Hercules and Saturn the melancholic type. (The sixteenth-century Milanese writer Gian Paolo Lomazzo added a choleric-melancholic type to accommodate Apollo.) In the late Renaissance this system of humors was sometimes used to aid in the comprehension of a history painting, that is, the painter would paint—and the reader could interpret—the reactions of the participants in a scene according to their recognizable physical types or temperaments. You need not learn this system, but you should be aware of the individual traits of these idealized types when you copy ancient works and study them. (It might interest you to know that the popular types of astrological personalities or temperaments—the signs—are ultimately based on the four humors and their combinations.)

Most of the casts presented from now on are fully modeled and lack a suggested schema. The schemata that are provided (see plates I, 56, 58, 60) should be studied first to get an idea of how to approach such complex figures.

The illumination of the Belvedere Torso from above emphasizes the halftones across the muscles. *Step 1:* Choose a plumb line, locate good points for the verticals, and trace in the diagonals that define the Bargue lines (the straight lines that connect the major points and provide

Fig. 18.
The Belvedere Torso.
(Le Torse du Belvédère.)
Marble. 159 cm (5 ft. 6.25 in.)
Signed by Apollonius, son of
Nestor, ca. 50 B.C.
Museo Pio-Clementino,
Vatican Museums,
Vatican City.

the first outline of the figure). Delineate in straight lines the position of the spinal cord. These lines will need to be refined in coordination with the development of the outline.

Plate I, 56. Male torso, back view.
(Torse d'homme, vu de dos.)

This torso is the remnant of a full standing figure, probably an athlete or political hero. Stylistically it is in the tradition of the fifth-century B.C. Greek master Polykleitos, a sculptor who wrote a book on the proportions of the human body. This book is known only by its title and a few references to its contents in other ancient writings. Polykleitos was the sculptor of the famous *Doryphorus,* or *Spearbearer,* a lost bronze (ca. 450 B.C.) now known only through a small series of Roman marble copies in various museums (the best is in the National Archeological Museum in Naples). The Polykleitan male is elegantly proportioned, with clearly outlined, tense muscle forms that are simplified geometrically. This type became the ideal for the male body in antiquity and again in modern times (see plates I, 61 and I, 68).

Step 1: The plumb line follows the spine along the shadow edge down to the lumbar, where it becomes independent in its descent but still passes through some good angles. It is probably the most useful reference line that you can find. The top horizontal is through the outside point of the left deltoid and the inner angle of the right deltoid. There is no horizontal for the bottom, but one should be supplied to remind you that the front lines of the base are not precisely horizontal. Plot the points for the other transversals carefully. Trace in the movement of the *contrapposto* (see glossary) through the center of the body, down the spinal cord, while finding points for the transversals. The outline should be like that in the schema: all straight lines, with every important angle included. The shadow demarcation is very simple and is all done in straight lines. *Step 2:* Two values of halftones supplement the shadows. There is some reflected light in large areas of the shadow. A very dark line has been drawn in the division of the buttocks. Straight lines in the small of the back invigorate the pose.

Plate I, 57. Female torso, three-quarter view.
(Torse de femme, vu de trois quarts.)

This unidentified torso is probably of a bathing Venus, similar to the type developed by Praxiteles in the fourth century B.C. No schema is given, so you are to develop it according to established practice. Try to maintain the simplicity of the finish, with its marginal shadows, restricted halftones, and large, clear areas.

Plate I, 58. *Milo of Crotone,* by Pierre Puget.
(Milon de Crotone, de Pierre Puget.)

This is the most renowned statue by Pierre Puget (1620-1694), the most famous French sculptor during the reign of Louis XIV. It was sculpted between 1672 and 1679. By choosing an ancient hero as the subject of his sculpture, Puget meant to rival the sculptors of antiquity, and its inclusion here means that the editors thought he had succeeded. This is a partial cast of the complete work in the Louvre Museum in Paris (see fig. 19).

Milo of Crotone was a famous Greek athlete of the sixth century B.C. While chopping firewood, his hand got caught in a log that he was attempting to split with his bare hands; trapped, he was helpless when a pack of wolves emerged from the woods and attacked him. Despite the specifications of ancient texts—which Puget certainly knew—a lion has been substituted for the wolves, perhaps to give Milo a less ignoble death and to associate the athlete with Hercules.

Fig. 19.
Pierre Puget.
Milo of Crotone.
(Milon de Crotone.)
Between 1672 and 1679.
Marble. Height 270 cm.
(8 ft. 10.25 in.)
Louvre Museum, Paris.

Step 1: The schema is a beautiful drawing by itself, clear and dramatic. It lacks a plumb line; instead, a central line follows the *contrapposto* of the body. Be careful as you establish the foreshortening of the eyes, brow, pectorals, and abdominal muscles. Bargue continues to block in outsized shapes with long, straight lines that sometimes cover up anatomical details. He has put in some shadows in the head to help with the foreshortening of the nose—a good procedure for difficult constructions. *Step 2:* The lighting is frontal; as a result, most anatomical details are described by faint halftones. The darkest tone is found just inside the shadow edge between the halftone and the shadow. Note the meandering nature of the darkest part; it follows the shadow edge and describes the rise and fall of the musculature.

Plate I, 59. The Vatican Amazon, draped.
(Amazone du Vatican, drapée.)

The identification of this torso in the Vatican Museums, Vatican City, as an Amazon is no longer accepted; the work is a variant of the Hellenistic type sometimes described as a "Diana with Mantle Draped as a Sash," a type of statue extant in many ancient examples. For us it is a splendid, well-preserved or well-restored model of ancient drapery. Work with the drapery as you did earlier with hair: divide it into segments, the folds into groups; let the longer lines describe the rhythmic fall of the folds.

Plate I, 60. Male torso, three-quarter view.
(Torse d'homme, vu de trois quarts.)

This is the same Polykleitan torso as in plate I, 56, with the illumination from the same direction. The dramatic difference between the views demonstrates that any cast has multiple views for drawing exercises. Note that the plumb line has changed. The verticals, although similar, do not reinforce the anatomical structure as effectively as they did in the first drawing, although the shift of the *contrapposto* is well described. The rarified beauty of the outline in *Step 2* contrasts dramatically with the modeled shadows of the back, which, in turn, contrast with the unified lights.

Plate I, 61. Theseus.
(Thésée.)

This is an original Greek work from the east pediment of the Parthenon (447-432 B.C.), now in the British Museum in London. The figure is sometimes identified as Dionysus. Both this and the next statue were parts of greater compositions with a unifying story, tucked into a triangular temple pediment high above the public that viewed it. This great fragment sat on the shelf of the pediment down through the millennia, somewhat protected from the weather by the projecting cornice overhead. The statue was dismounted and brought to London by Lord Elgin in 1803, where it immediately became a standard for the portrayal of the human body and was traditionally accepted as by the hand of the fabled sculptor Phidias, who actually was the supervisor of the pedimental sculpture.

Bargue made his lithograph after a drawing by Lecomte du Nouÿ (see note 58). He has ignored the roughness of the long-exposed surface, while at the same time neglecting to restore the parts detached by war and vandalism (see fig. 20). However, the stains on the marble were not evident on the cast from which the plate was drawn. This is a good mid-fifth-century body, clear in its proportions and geometrically simplified in its anatomical forms. The musculature is emphasized; it is firm, not relaxed, although it is slightly more supple than the Achilles of plate I, 68.

This is the first reclining figure in the course. You are presented with a finished cast drawing, with overhead lighting. The central line of the statue is based on a half circle: up the right thigh, along the

Fig. 20.
Theseus. (Thésée.) 447–432 B.C.
Marble. Over life size.
British Museum, London.

linea alba—the visible line through the center of the torso that separates the body into symmetrical halves, from the pit of the neck, between the pectorals, through the center of the abdomen and the navel, down to the groin—through abdomen and chest, and up through the neck and head. Here you can see both the usefulness as well as the beauty of Greek geometrical simplification. Refined Greek taste is seen in the general idealization: the body surfaces are simplified; the muscles are clear-edged and do not overlap. These are characteristics of the good taste that Gérôme and Bargue have been trying to teach you plate by plate.

In schematizing the drawing, erect verticals that divide the body into logical, workable sections. Find one or more plumb lines; work out the schematic lines between important points, and so forth.

Plate I, 62. Ilissos.
(L'Ilissus.)

The original Greek sculpture from the west pediment of the Parthenon in Athens (447–432 B.C.) is in the British Museum in London.

The time period given for the pediments is between the making of the contracts for both pediments and the last payment. The west pediment is usually considered to have been started after the east pediment, by artists of the next generation. Although still idealized, Ilissos is more naturalistic than Theseus. The fifth century was a period of rapid stylistic development in Greek sculpture. As with the Theseus, the composition is based on a subtle circle. The muscles are not all taut and firm, as in the Theseus, but relaxed, moving away from the geometrical confines of the earlier sculpture and covered by a pliable skin. Under the right knee, a tendon cuts across two forms. (There are no tendons in the Theseus statue.) Your study of the leg of plate I, 27 has prepared you for the left knee of Ilissos. To build a schema, start with a plumb line through the head. Building a triangle with the extremities as points (as in plate I, 5 of the foot) might be helpful. Other vertical reference lines crossing through the triangle might help you determine additional angles.

Plate I, 63. The Belvedere Torso, front view.
(Le torse du Belvédère, vu de face.)

This lithograph by Bargue is after a drawing by Lecomte du Nouÿ (see note 58).

Look at the schema for Puget's *Milo of Crotone* (plate I, 58) for guidance. Find the plumb line and the organizing verticals. Then plot out the straight schematic lines. Check and recheck for accuracy: you have many details to put inside the outline, so it must be accurate for them all to fit intelligently. The light from above left emphasizes the halftones of the muscles, and every bit of the surface is modeled. This is a very elaborate drawing. In fact, all the drawings at the end of the first part of the *Drawing Course* are very polished and highly finished, so do not rush them.

Plate I, 64. Female torso, rear view.
(Torse de femme, vu de dos.)

This seated Venus is again of the Praxitilean type, with large hips and thighs, geometric breasts like hemispheres, and areas of fat not yet rejected by modern standards for feminine pulchritude. Look at the schema for *Male torso, rear view* (plate I, 60) to aid you in copying this drawing.

COMPLETE FIGURES.
(ENSEMBLES.)

Plate I, 65. Knight.
(Cavalier.)

Plate I, 66. Two knights.
(Deux cavaliers.)

These two reliefs come from the Parthenon frieze in Athens; both are *in situ* in the frieze on the west end. When finished, the frieze extended some 160 meters (406 feet) around all four sides of the building; it was placed high up, under the protecting roof of the porch. Great portions of the frieze have survived: one fragment is in the Louvre Museum in Paris; many sections are in the British Museum in London; other panels are in the Acropolis Museum in Athens; and—miraculously—some 30 meters are still in place on the building. Casts of the frieze exist in many art schools and academies, most likely having survived the twentieth-century neglect and destruction of casts because they hung out of the way, high up on the wall, or perhaps—one would like to think—because they were still admired. These are your first models of complete figures. As reliefs, they allow you to concentrate on the outlines and to study the subtle yet critical modeling. This is also a lesson in drawing the complete Phidian horse, with a head even more simplified than the horses's head from the east pediment (see plates I, 37 and I, 47). Organize your drapery around the directional lines describing movement in the drapery and the specific points where it hangs and drops in simple folds.

Plate I, 67. Cincinnatus.
(Cincinnatus.)

The subject of the statue, now identified as *Mercury Tying His Sandal (Hermès rattachant sa sandale)*, is attributed to the School of Lysippus (ca. 330 B.C.; see fig. 21); the depiction of the thinking process through facial expression is thought to be an innovation of Lysippus, the great Greek sculptor of the fourth century B.C. This statue, which exists in two incomplete marble versions—the most famous of which is in the Louvre Museum in Paris—was probably a bronze of the late fourth century B.C. cast during the Hellenistic age, when sculptors were experimenting with movement and its effects on bodily structure. The statue was long interpreted by earlier scholars (who loved attaching stories to statuary) as the proverbially patriotic Cincinnatus (a Roman leader of the late sixth century B.C.) putting on his sandals after he has been told that he has been elected counsel of

Fig. 21.
Cincinnatus (or Mercury Tying His Sandal).
(Cincinnatus ou Hermès rattachant sa sandale.)
Marble. 154 cm (60.5 in.)
After a Greek original from the school of Lysippus, fourth century B.C.
Louvre Museum, Paris.

125

Rome and prepares to leave his farm for Rome to serve his country. It could just as easily be Hermes (Mercury) preparing for a flight, although the sandals are not winged (in any event, they are modern restorations), or it might be an athlete looking up to acknowledge a call as he prepares to enter the arena. The identification with Mercury is useful because the mercurial type of body is muscular but not buffed, sinewy rather than massive, and his frame is elongated and agile. Carefully note which muscles are tense and which relaxed.

Plate I, 68. Achilles.
(Achille.)

Now referred to as the Ares Borghese (ca. 430 B.C.), the statue is in the Louvre Museum in Paris (see fig. 22). In this perfect young male all the parts of the body we have studied separately are harmoniously integrated. Earlier archeologists dramatized the statue by seeing in it the image of Achilles, the greatest of the warriors of Greek legend. It is now identified as Ares (Mars), the god of war. This is a great example of post-Phidian Greek sculpture, showing the attributes of style assigned to Skopas and Polykleitos, still surviving on the Parthenon in the figure of Theseus (plate I, 61). The presence of the palm tree–like support is evidence that the marble was copied from a bronze (where one could have simply strengthened the walls of the leg to make it strong enough to stand). The original was probably carrying a bronze spear, an artifact now lost and here indicated by a plug. The muscles are clear and geometrically simplified in their boundaries (no overlappings), and the distortions are minor. If you have already drawn a thigh from a muscular model, you will recognize the accomplishment in the simplification of the figure's upper legs. A memorable trait seems to be the groin line, intact from the lower edge of one lateral oblique to the other. But note the grace added to this otherwise somewhat dehumanized—if still erotic—body by an almost mysterious movement through the body engendered by the curve of the *contrapposto* stance.

Plate I, 69. Germanicus.
(Germanicus.)

This statue is now identified as Marcellus, nephew of Augustus (ca. 20 B.C.). It is signed "Cleomenes, son of Cleomenes." The original Roman statue is now in the Louvre Museum in Paris. We have already studied the left foot (plate I, 10) and the right leg (plates I, 25 and I, 27). This is a rear view of a perfect man in the Greek style of the late fifth century B.C. The work is more supple in form and more complex in its musculature than the *Achilles* of the previous plate. We are given only the rear view to copy, although we have studied the right leg and the

Fig. 22.
Achilles (Ares Borghese). (Achille ou Arès Borghèse.)
ca. 430 B.C.
Marble. 212 cm. (6 ft. 11. 25 in.)
Louvre Museum, Paris.

left foot. Probably both Bargue and Gérôme thought that the individualized portrait head was incongruous with the idealized body (see fig. 11). The drapery support might indicate that the marble was copied from a bronze (which would not have needed such a support), but by the end of the first century B.C., when this work was sculpted, such supports may have become a standard accessory to marble originals.

The small support between the figure's right thumb and forefinger was probably meant to guard against breakage (perhaps at one time it was tinted black). This did not discourage earlier archeologists from seeing it as a die and interpreting the statue as "Mercury Casting a Die," a common iconographic motif for the god.

Plate I, 70. Saint Martha.
(Sainte Marthe.)

This unlocated statue, in the Late Gothic French style, was carved around 1500. Bargue made the plate after a study of the statue by Hippolyte Flandrin (1809–1864), several of whose drawings are reproduced in the second part of the *Drawing Course*.

Around 1500 the medieval Gothic style persisted in France, as it did in most of Europe. It is hard for us to realize that in the first part of the fifteenth century the Italian Renaissance was still a minority movement in a few cities of Italy. French Late Gothic sculpture nevertheless had some of the intellectual traits of the Italian style, including better anatomical proportions (even under the drapery) and more naturalistic drapery; its folds were designed according to the weight of the fabric and not moved by a decoratively expressed spiritual power that obscured the body underneath, as in earlier Gothic sculpture. This courtly Late Gothic style, often called "détente style," was the perfect model for the French Neo-Gothic movement of the early 1800s.

Flandrin made this study of the statue for his celebrated frieze in the Neoclassical church of Saint-Vincent-de-Paul in Paris. He worked on the commission between 1848 and 1853. Saint Martha, clearly labeled, stands to the left side of the choir, the thirteenth figure from the altar. Her costume and attributes are the same; her gesture, however, is changed and the fall of her drapery has been simplified.[27]

Saint Martha appears in the Gospel of Luke (10:38–41); she is a diligent housekeeper in contrast to her more intellectual sister Mary. The two come to represent the *active* and the *contemplative* lives. In Jacopo da Voragine's *Golden Legend,* a compendium of saints' lives from the twelfth century, Saint Martha accompanies her brother, Saint Lazarus, on a mission to France. There she kills a dragon in Tarascon with holy water. Here she holds the handle of a broken aspergillum, an instrument for spreading holy water, and a vessel for the liquid—or perhaps it is just a water bucket symbolizing her domestic activities.

Saint Martha is entered into the course as a drapery model, perhaps to counter the seemingly realistic but highly agitated and stylized drapery of the *Diana* (The Vatican Amazon of plate I, 59.)[28] Compared to the drapery of the *Diana,* this sober drapery obscures body parts, with gravity controlling its decorative role. Be aware of how the *contrapposto* affects the posture of the shoulders, hips, and legs; look for the points from which the drapery hangs. The right shoulder forms just such a hanging point for drapery, which falls over the transverse sash down to the foot of the play leg. The high breasts are also hanging points. Because there is so much detail to organize, the shadows must be mapped out carefully; otherwise the details will not fit in correctly.

PART II: COPYING MASTER DRAWINGS (MODÈLES D'APRÈS LES MAÎTRES)

INTRODUCTION

The drawings in part II were selected both for their aesthetic value—as lessons in good taste—and for their demonstration of specific techniques that can be learned in practice. Even though copying works by other artists might appear contrary to the modern stress on originality, centuries of the practice have proven it to be a good learning experience.

Under the guild system that existed prior to the French Revolution, apprentices regularly copied drawings, studies, and iconographic models, as well as travel notations, from the portfolios of their masters. They thus absorbed the style of their masters while at the same time forming a personal repertoire of useful subjects and poses. The results are apparent in the similarity of style and continuity of iconography passed from, say, Robert Campin to his student Rogier van der Weyden, from Perugino to Raphael, or, for that matter, from Gérôme to Bargue.

For the master in charge of a workshop, the apprentice system had a beneficial result: his students, having absorbed his personal style through copying, could assist on all of his projects without noticeable differences in execution.[29]

During their *Wanderjahre*—a two-year period of wandering between taking their master's examination and being able to set up an independent studio—young artists sketched compositions and figures from public or easily accessible monuments, as well as from the portfolios of the masters under whom they served temporarily as assistants.

Bargue did not make all his lithographs directly from the original drawings. He made most of his plates from copies drawn by artists who were chosen by Gérôme from among his colleagues and students. The copyists either visited the collections where the drawings were conserved or they worked after photographs. The Holbeins, for example, are mostly kept in Basel and London, so it is unlikely that many of the lithographs were made after the originals. Probably only the lithographs after contemporary French masters were copied from originals; this would have been an easy matter for Gérôme and Bargue to arrange either from among the circle of Gérôme's artist friends and students or from the artists of Goupil's coterie of painters.

Consequently, it is difficult to look at the set of plates as an example of nineteenth-century taste without some qualifications. This is a selection with didactic purposes chosen by Academic Realists. Nonacademic and optical Realists (such as the Impressionists) might have made a different selection. It is also strange that one drawing (plate II, 6) attributed to Agnolo Gaddi, a trecento or Gothic master, is included. It has since then been reattributed to a quattrocento master.[30] This drawing was probably chosen—like the inclusion of Hippolyte Flandrin's neo-gothic drawing of Saint Martha in the first part (plate I, 70)—as a sop to the new fashion for the *primitifs,* as the Gothic masters were then called. Some critics think that Hans Holbein the Younger—whose works are amply represented in the second part—was popular with the Realists for his "primitive" or "naïve" qualities.[31]

More surprising is the fact that the academician Jean-Auguste-Dominique Ingres, one of the greatest of all draftsmen, and an older contemporary of Bargue and Gérôme, is represented by only one figure (plate II, 33) drawn after a highly finished (and famous) oil study for a painting.[32] (The author of the Goupil brochure announcing the *Drawing Course* described the drawings after painted figures included among the plates of drawings in part II as "interpretations of achieved works.")[33]

As a draftsman Ingres had developed a wondrously extravagant personal style. He had a fondness for fluid, curvaceous outlines and was cavalier in his disregard of anatomy—traits that could have displeased Gérôme. It is easier to understand the exclusion of Delacroix and Rembrandt, despite the fact that they were both draftsmen greatly beloved and admired in the late nineteenth century. Delacroix would have been left out because his loose, expressive but not always accurate or descriptive line was alien to the academic style. Rembrandt's chiaroscuro was imitated by Bargue (see painting no. 33). His inimitable drawing style, however, was too advanced for young artists to imitate and was probably thought to be beyond the Academic Realists' goal of precision. Rembrandt was nonetheless the favorite painter of Gérôme, who thought the old master's sincerity compensated for his loose and often "incorrect" drawing. All in all, the sixty-seven plates comprising part II must be considered a didactic collection supporting late nineteenth-century academic principles, with a few plates included under pressure from Goupil, who either wanted to exploit plates already made or to include some that would have a good sales potential in and of themselves.

It is not surprising that Bargue was more at home copying the works of his contemporaries, especially the works of modern masters of his own school: Gérôme; the students of Gérôme; Gérôme's teachers Charles Gleyre (1808–1874) and Paul Delaroche (1797–1856); and other academics and Academic Realists who worked for Goupil. The authenticity of these works, as well as their sympathy with the principles of the *Drawing Course,* make them the most edifying of the drawings. A selection of those drawings possessing the highest quality appear as full-page illustrations, with expanded notes to aid those students wishing to copy master drawings.

Realism, Idealism, and Academic Drawing

It is popularly thought that a major trait of Realism is the minute recording of surface detail. This may be true of some artists and some schools (such as those influenced by John Ruskin in England and the United States). Such a practice, however, can often become a compulsive, automatic, and even brainless activity. The description of minute details is not, in fact, a trait of every Realist style. The practice of Academic Realist drawing is selective in its creation of the illusion of reality. The academic draftsman simplifies and even omits surface detail in order to amplify the effects of light and shadow, the illusion of volume, and the character of the subject. Furthermore, many drawings have specific purposes: preparatory drawings, studies, idea sketches, compositional sketches, and so forth. In fact, very few drawings are ends in themselves; they may be intended as preparation for a painting or a sculpture and might contain a notation of light effects, a study of anatomy, of balance, the movement of drapery, or the fleeting expression of a face.

In drawing, you will be continually balancing the details of nature against your specific purpose. To put it more abstractly, visual facts in themselves are of interest, but they only have meaning when intelligently organized, criticized, and judged.

Developed details are not, then, a necessary feature of all styles of Realism, just as forms and shapes are not always experienced visually as comprehensible wholes in the natural world. We all know how often a trompe l'oeil effect fools us in our daily lives. The popular works of the French Impressionists are good demonstrations of the optical Realism concurrent with the tactile values of Academic Realism. In optical or impressionistic painting, human figures often have outlines obscured by other objects or shadows. Furthermore, organic unity and structure are hidden by clothes, obfuscated by shade, and distorted by direct sunlight. Optical Realists will often pursue the distortion of forms by light and shadow; seldom will they try to correct them.

Academic Realists will organize these optical distortions within a clarified, logical structure, recognizing them while minimizing their disintegrating effect. A norm of clarity and of unity is sought. Consequently, a clear outline is required, as is a good balance of light and dark areas to produce volume and three-dimensional shape. Poses are carefully chosen so that all parts of the body are seen and understood. There is an avoidance of distortion and ugliness. First and foremost, there is the presentation of a unit, recognizable as a body, a person, *an organic unity* without distracting details. These are major features, even principles, of the basic academic style. The drawing style taught in the *Drawing Course* is a compromise between the intellectual, generalizing qualities of Idealism and the visual accuracy and specificity of Realism. This compromise avoids both the tendency toward oversimplification of line and form common in idealistic practice and the uncertain and distorted forms recorded by optical Realists, as well as the depiction of ugliness accepted by doctrinaire Realists. Academic Realists treat the human body with respect and honor its integrity; they give the human body a sense of dignity and autonomy.[34] Their figures think for themselves, and their motions are the result of self-conscious thought. Academic Realism is essentially a humanistic style, based primarily on an interest in human beings, their actions, their reactions, and their fate.

The drawings in the second part of the *Drawing Course* were selected as didactic models primarily for their developed sense of unity, simplicity, and effectiveness. There are, of course, other didactic purposes underlying the selections. Like the models of casts, the model drawings were also selected for their variety of techniques and views. Furthermore, Gérôme and Bargue are giving you models of good, selective taste ("le grand goût"), a taste formed by studying specific examples of ancient and High Renaissance art. Good classical taste is basically a matter of combining beautiful features selected from nature with an ideal of human perfection. Underlying this taste is both an ideal of simplification geared toward clear geometrical shapes in planes and outlines and an abhorrence of distortion.

Copying these drawings should give you intimate contact with an absorbed, digested, and projected classical taste, as well as with a variety of personal styles and idiosyncratic ways of seeing, absorbing, organizing, and recording visual information. The academic concerns do not hinder, squelch, or make impossible a personal style, as the drawings in this part demonstrate.

Look carefully at the following three portraits: lithographs based on works by Filippino Lippi (1457–1504) (plate II, 12), Gleyre (plate II, 13), and Gérôme (plate II, 14). These drawings demonstrate both the consistency of academic conventions and the variety of expression and personal styles possible within them. Each is clear in outline, simple in procedure, and restrained in details; in all three the illusion of three-dimensional form is achieved with these simple means. Filippino's young man looks at us with an expression of intense thought, underscored by deep shadow covering one side of his face. Gleyre's Omphale is clearly meant to be beautiful; her face is round, with delicate, varied changes of value. Gérôme—who was one of Gleyre's students—was a master of solid, firm form; his bodies are neither mysterious nor delicate but rather forthrightly present. With little or no unobtrusive detail, his young Arab is presented as solidly present, self-contained, and handsome. The solidity of form is maintained through the clarity of the outline and the incredible simplicity of the shading. The shadows are minimal, consisting of areas slightly darkened by lines. Although there is careful description in the turban, the outline of the face, and the ear, these details are not ends in themselves; the structural unity of the head still dominates the drawing.

After practicing this short exercise in the comparison of drawing styles, we must congratulate Bargue in getting the different character or personal style of each of these drawings into the lithograph. Our awe increases when we look at one more drawing (plate II, 23) entitled *A Roman Woman (Femme romaine)* after a drawing of Adolphe-William Bouguereau (1825–1905). It is a wonder, displaying a marvelous balance between the observation of a realist and the ideals of a classicist. Bouguereau is more concerned with anatomy than some of the other masters. The bony appearance of her nose, the sunken eyes and cheeks, and the thickness of her neck are qualities he describes so accurately that it places the woman in her late forties, at not quite overripe maturity. The outline is elegantly, sensitively drawn by means of a line that continually changes its thickness or emphasis as it gives sensitivity to the nose and lips, strength to the chin, and fullness to the neck. The hair is complex without being detailed. In this drawing Bouguereau is an absolute master of the Academic Realist drawing technique, a mixture of observation, knowledge, and ideals.

Practical Matters

On Choosing a Master Drawing to Copy: The Benefits of Copying

When you choose a model to copy, there is something about the drawing that attracts you. What is it? What entices you? Why do you think it matches your level of ability?

Once you choose a drawing as a model, you are going to have a long, intense period of intimacy with a realized, perhaps great, work. You will more or less memorize it in the concentration of copying, as well as learning the techniques or solutions the artist employed. This experience will mean more to you after you have been drawing from nature for a while and consciously or subconsciously recognize some of the problems of drawing from nature.

You might have chosen the drawing for the image, in which case you can copy it in any medium that seems appropriate. Or you may want to copy it for the techniques used, in which case you should use the same materials as the artist did. At first you might be concerned with the shape or outer contours. You might want to copy a drawing for solutions to problems that you have already experienced—for instance, the transitions at the edges of shadows or the overlapping lines of the outline that enter a form to become anatomical features. Gradually you should choose more challenging drawings.

Some passages may not make sense at all until you succeed in copying them exactly and they take shape on your paper. Some distinctions will only become visible as you copy, such as the variety of shades and forms, of light and shadow. The techniques or the solutions may be absorbed without your consciously knowing it through the intensity of the experience of careful copying. That does not mean you should copy slavishly and brainlessly; always keep your mind engaged in the act of transcribing.

What you and the artist are trying to do is produce an illusion, a convincing imitation of nature. These drawings all teach the effectiveness of simplicity and economy—how even a few elements are enough to create the illusion of three-dimensional shape on a flat surface. This is an achievement even in a copy. Finally you will witness a mystery: a series of lines abstracted from nature and recorded carefully suddenly assume shape, depth, and character—with an aura of beauty.

Getting Down to Copying

Putting your drawing board on an easel, with your model and a piece of drawing paper alongside each other is a good way to copy. Attach the papers with white tape you can get at an art-supply house (masking tape will leave a sticky, dirty residue and may be hard to remove). Make sure the easel is upright (check with your plumb line); this will give you a view of the model without perspectival distortions. You can judge the shape and seek out the salient outline points and transfer them to the paper in several ways. You can proceed as you did for your cast drawings, using your held-out plumb line to create vertical reference lines and to estimate distances. As part of this process you are simultaneously learning how to use tools to ascertain measurements and how to use your eye to estimate them. Eventually it is the eye that has to do the judging, so use your eye from the beginning; it will gradually take over more and more of the measuring and estimating from your tools. However, the tools—very useful at the beginning—will remain useful in laying out the shape of objects, checking your measurements, finding concordances of distances, and solving technical problems. No matter how good your eye is, do not abandon the measuring tools; knowing how to use them is part of your craft as an artist.

Since working with shadows will mean getting values right in your copy, it would help to draw a scale of appropriate values at the bottom of your drawing, from the lightest to the darkest, to use as a guide.

As you did with the cast drawings, develop the outlines of the larger forms first; put in the linear shapes and refine them; work on the shadows next, starting with the largest, darkest shadow; leave the halftones till last. Remember, you want the outlines of the forms and shadows to be exact before you fill in the details. Some areas you may not understand until you get them down correctly; so study the special and subtle effects before you attempt them. How does the master handle the edges? How does he use his materials? Are the shadows hatched, stumped, or veiled? Does he vary the strength of his line? Is the type classical, idealized, realistic, general? Is something happening in the picture? What? Can you capture the same projection of thought and movement in your transcription? Copying a drawing should be an act of concentration, just like working from a live model. There is a tendency when copying to flatten out shapes. The artist was probably working from a three-dimensional form; you, as a copyist, are working from a flat image, and this fact usually reveals itself in the copy. Carefully study how the artist achieved a sense of form and space in his drawing.

A Note About the Drawings by Hans Holbein the Younger

The drawings by Hans Holbein the Younger in the selection of old master drawings are mainly from the Royal Library at Windsor Castle, England, and the Kunstmuseum in Basel, Switzerland. Despite the fact that they are in a location or milieu in which they were created (Holbein lived and worked in both Basel and London)—which is reassuring with respect to their good condition—one must remember that these drawings are all over 450 years old. Although the Windsor Castle drawings were executed in the English court, they were not made permanent parts of the royal collection until around 1675. Before that time they passed through several English collections, bound together in a book. In 1727 Queen Caroline had the drawings taken out of the book and framed. During the early years of the reign of George III, they were rebound as two volumes, where they remained until they were again separately matted. The matting was removed in the 1970s—the glue was affecting the drawings—and they are now mounted between acrylic sheets. Of course, as a result of all this they have suffered physical damage: the charcoal has rubbed off in various places, stains acquired, and the outlines reinforced in charcoal and silverpoint at various times by various hands. Some lines are faint, but most of them are still legible and compelling.[35]

The lithographs after Holbein by Bargue are not precise facsimiles of the drawings but rather "interpretations." The old retouched and restored drawings have been freshened up and made whole again in the lithographs. Faded lines have been strengthened and coloring has either been ignored or interpreted in lines. The lithographs were meant to be good models to copy, as well as good prints to frame and display for aesthetic enjoyment. The drawings that Bargue used as models seem to have been executed by several different artists, which explains why they vary in quality. Nonetheless, most are satisfactory lithographs. Whether Goupil's artists copied the actual drawings in the two collections or worked from photographs is not known. To facilitate your own comparison between the originals and the lithographs, two Holbein drawings from the Kunstmuseum in Basel have been reproduced in large format and in color for you to compare with the lithographs by Bargue; compare plate II, 67, of *Bürgermeister Jakob Meyer* with fig. 24; and plate II, 10 of *Anna Meyer* with fig. 23.

Plate II, 1

Plate II, 2

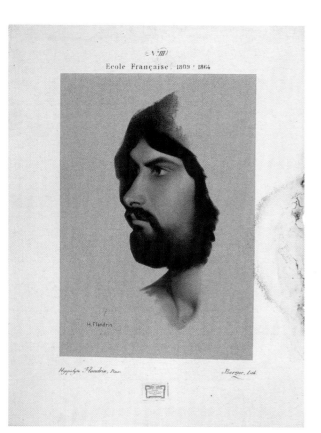

Plate II, 3

Plate II, 4

Plate II, 5

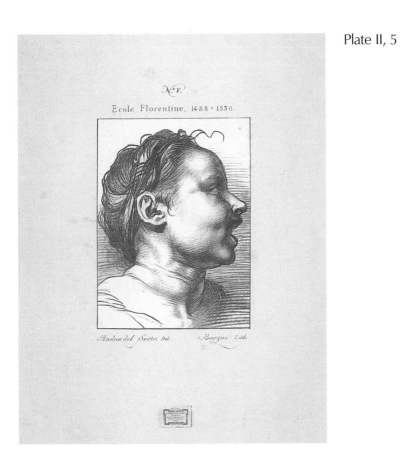

Plate II, 6

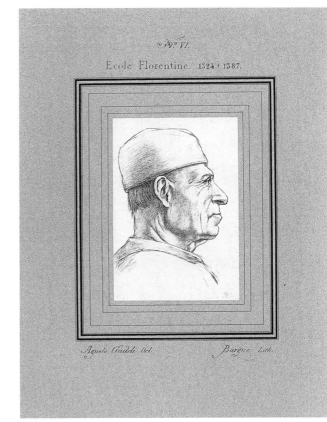

Plate II, 7

Plate II, 8

135

Plate II, 7

Plate II, 10

Plate II, 9

Plate II, 10

Plate II, 11

Plate II, 12

138

Plate II, 13

Plate II, 14

Plate II, 15

Plate II, 16

Plate II, 12

Plate II, 13

Plate II, 14

142

N.º XV

Ecole Française

1809 – 1864

Hippolyte Flandrin del
Bargue lith.

Plate II, 15

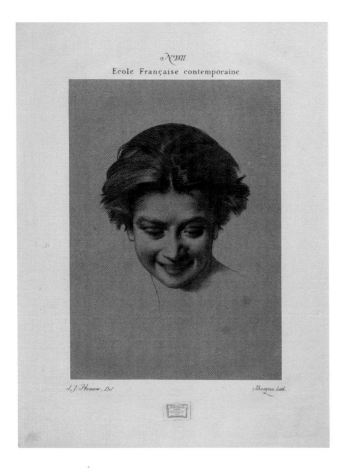

Plate II, 17

Plate II, 18

Plate II, 19

Plate II, 20

144

Plate II, 21

Plate II, 22

Plate II, 23

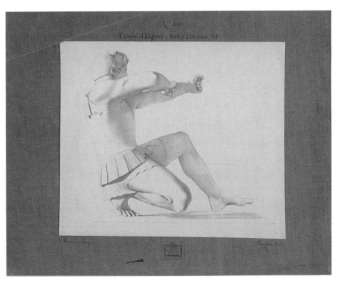

Plate II, 24

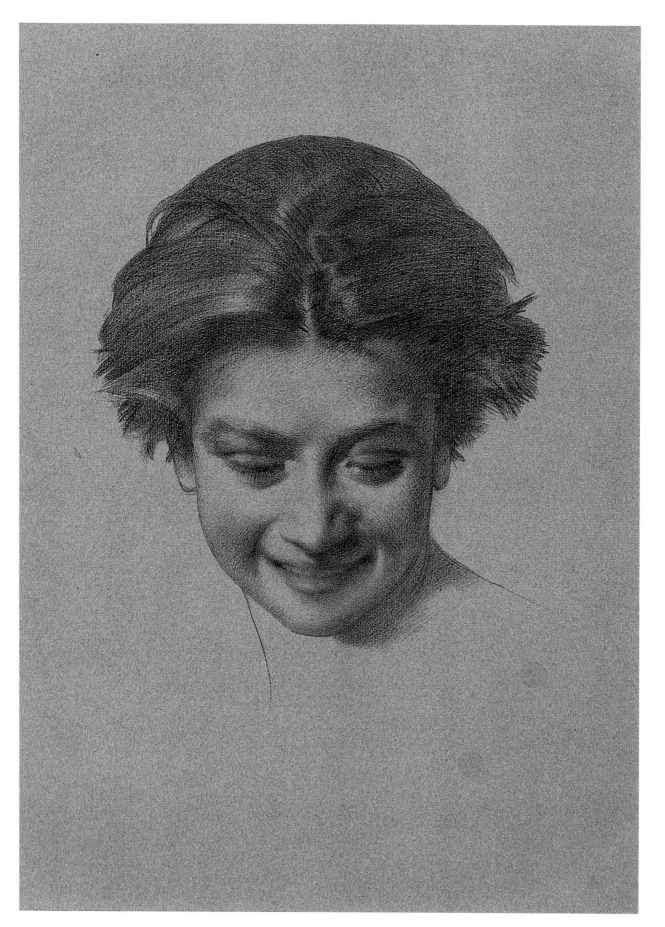

Plate II, 17

Plate II, 18

148

Plate II, 23

149

Plate II, 25

Plate II, 26

Plate II, 27

Plate II, 28

Plate II, 29

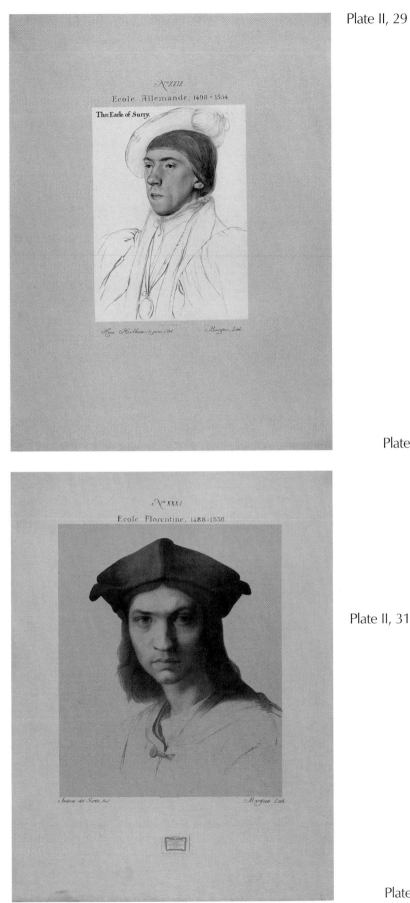

Plate II, 30

Plate II, 31

Plate II, 32

N° LVI

École Française

1809 † 1864

Hippolyte Flandrin, pr.
Bargue, lith.

SPÉCIMEN

Plate II, 25

153

Plate II, 31

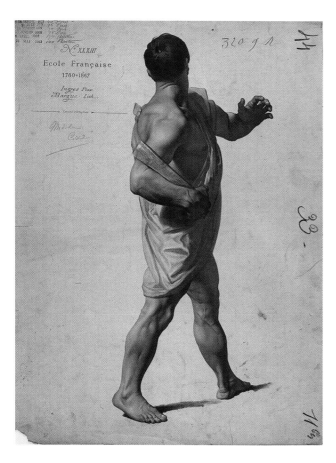

Plate II, 33

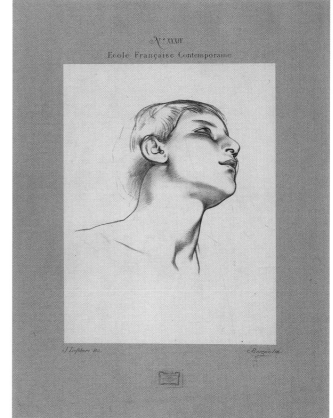

Plate II, 34

Plate II, 35

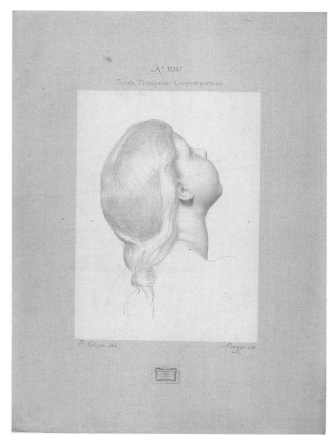

Plate II, 36

Plate II, 37

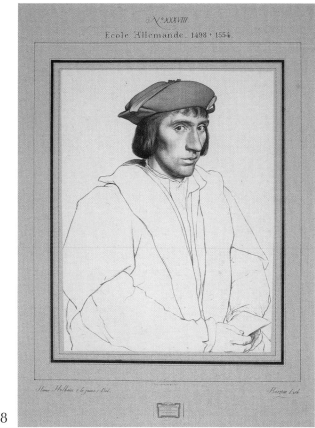

Plate II, 38

Plate II, 39

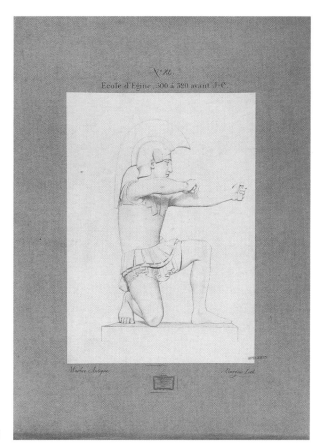

Plate II, 40

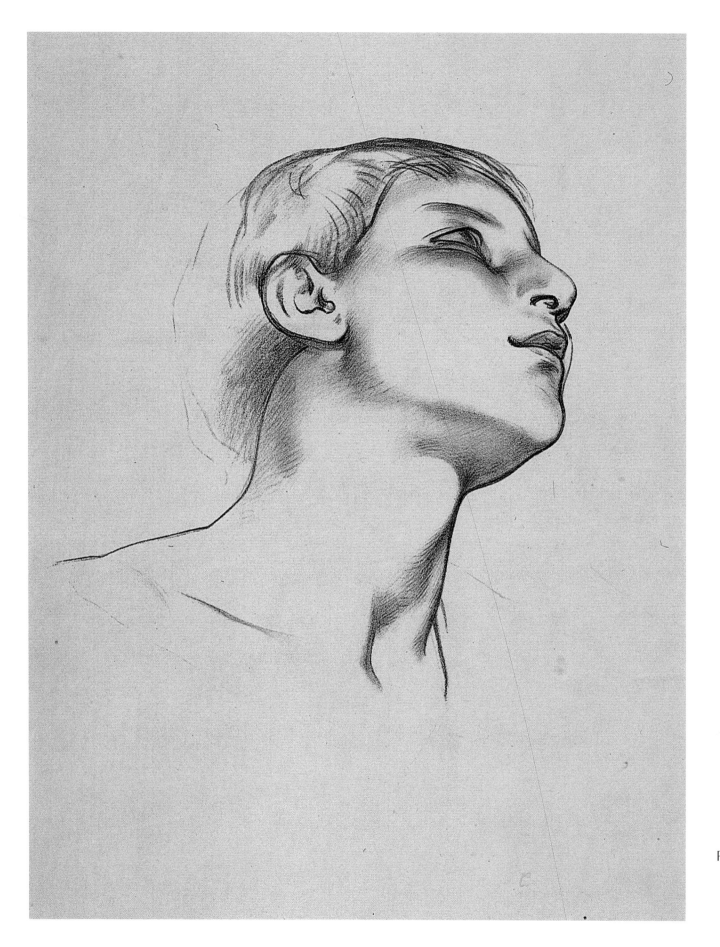

Plate II, 34

Plate II, 35

Plate II, 41

Plate II, 42

Plate II, 43

Plate II, 44

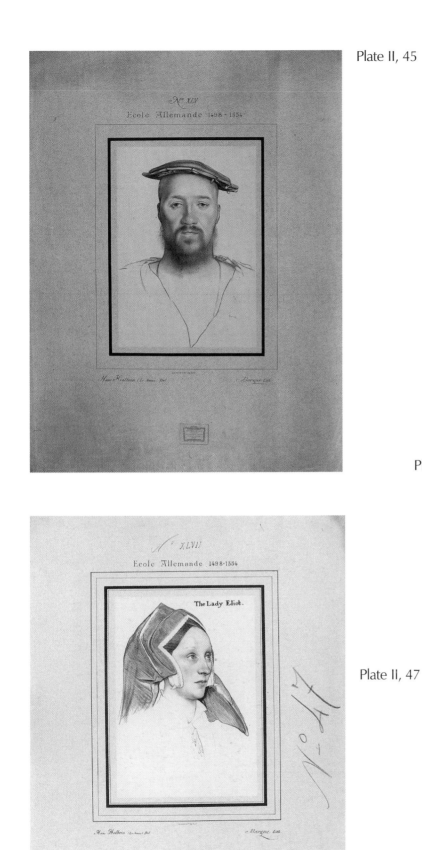

Plate II, 45

Plate II, 46

Plate II, 47

Plate II, 48

Plate II, 49

Plate II, 50

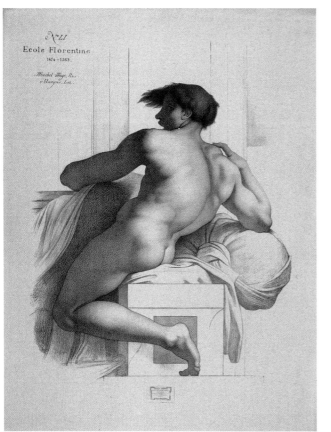

Plate II, 51

Plate II, 52

Plate II, 53

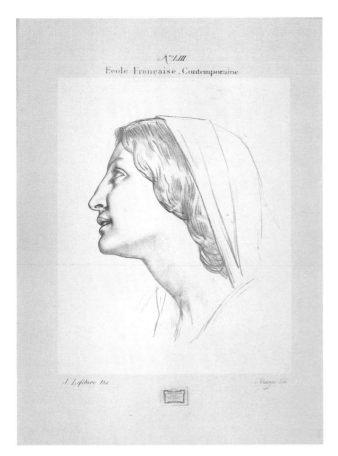

Plate II, 54

Plate II, 55

Plate II, 56

Plate II, 52

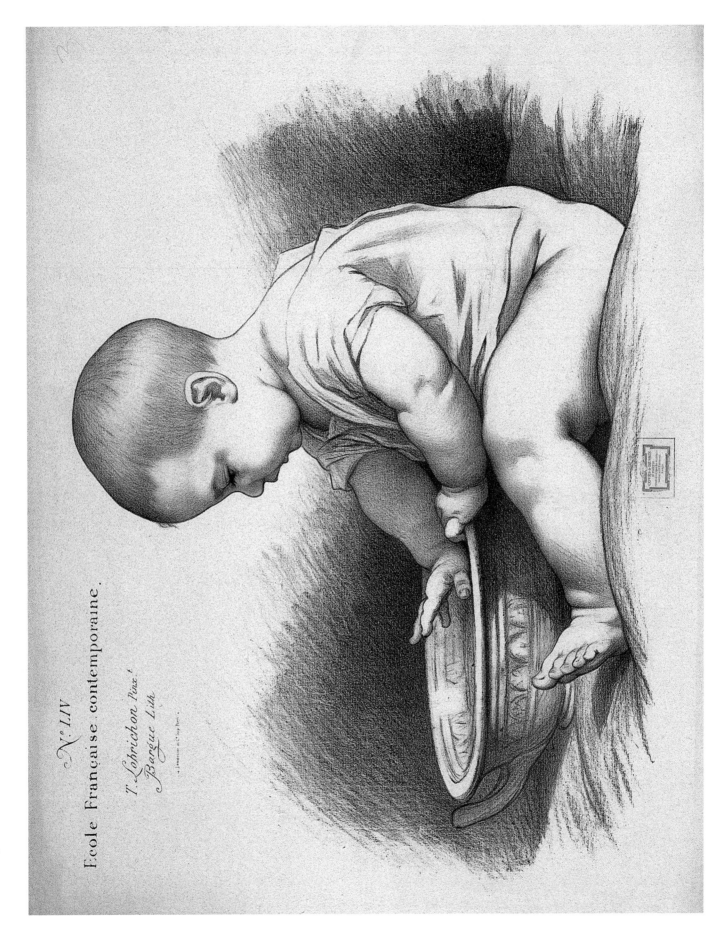

N.º LIV
Ecole Française contemporaine.

T. Lobrichon Pinx.t
Barque Lith.

Imprimerie et C.ie Imp Paris.

Plate II, 54

163

Plate II, 57

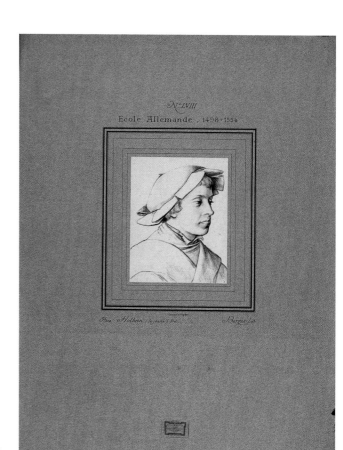

Plate II, 58

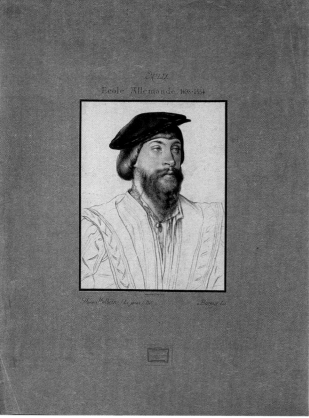

Plate II, 59

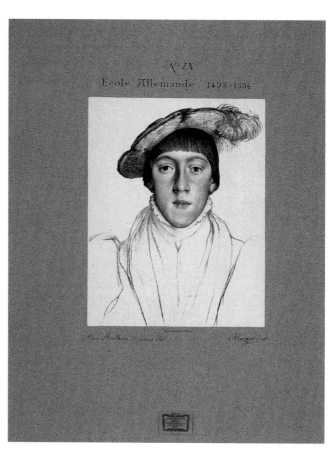

Plate II, 60

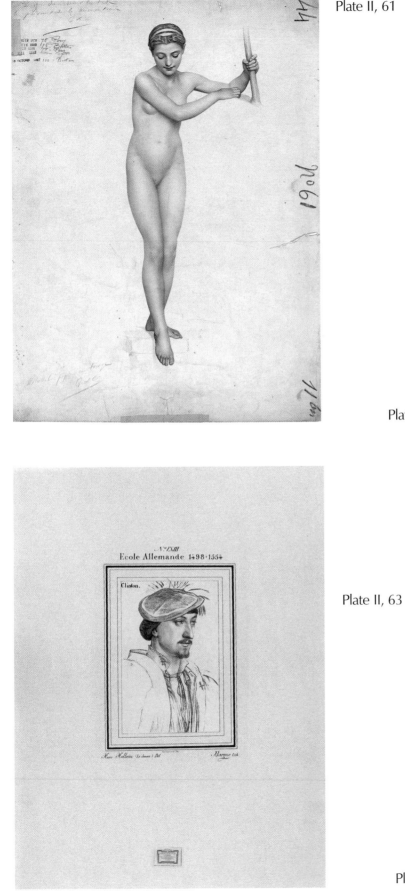

Plate II, 61

Plate II, 62

Plate II, 63

Plate II, 64

Plate II, 67

Plate II, 65

Plate II, 66

Plate II, 67

Notes on the Plates

Although all the lithographs in part II are reproduced, not all are recommended for copying. Those thought to be the best models for beginning students are reproduced as full-page illustrations and are accompanied by technical notes. The others are reproduced as quarter-page illustrations.

Plate II, 1. Michelangelo (1475–1564), *Angel Blowing a Trumpet.* *(Ange sonnant de la trompette.)* Sistine Chapel, Vatican City

This drawing is an "interpretation" of a famous figure in the grand fresco *The Last Judgment* (1536-1542) in the Sistine Chapel in the Vatican.

Plate II, 2. Hippolyte Flandrin (1809–1864), *Study of a Woman.* *(Étude de femme.)* Whereabouts unknown

Flandrin, a student of Ingres, was most famous for his decorations of churches and palaces. This is a preparatory drawing for the decorations done in 1841 for the duc de Luynes at his chateau in Dampierre.[36] See also plates II, 15 and II, 25.

Plate II, 3. Hippolyte Flandrin, *Italian Shepherd*, study. *(Pâtre italien* [tête d'étude].*)* Whereabouts unknown

Plate II, 4. Jean-Léon Gérôme (1824–1904), *Head of a Fellah*, three-quarter view. *(Tête de fellah, vue de trois quarts.)* Private collection

See the comments to plate II, 14.

Plate II, 5. Andrea del Sarto (1486–1530), *Head of a Child.* *(Tête d'enfant.)* Louvre Museum, Paris

This is a drawing for a figure in the painting *Caritas,* painted in Paris in 1518. The painting is also in the Louvre Museum in Paris. See also comments to plate II, 31.

Plate II, 6. Agnolo Gaddi (1345–1396), *Portrait of a Man.* *(Portrait d'homme.)* British Museum, London

The drawing has the attribution to Agnolo Gaddi inscribed on the verso. It was attributed to Masaccio by Johann David Passavant (1833) and to Domenico Ghirlandaio by Bernard Berenson (1938), an attribution retained to this day.

Plate II, 7. Léon Bonnat (1833–1922), *Young Roman*, study. *(Jeune Romain* [tête d'étude].*)* Bonnat Museum, Bayonne

Bonnat was a good friend of Gérôme and accompanied him on excursions (on safari) in Egypt and Palestine on several occasions. A portrait painter noted for the illusionistic qualities of his realism, Bonnat was also a famous collector of master drawings; his collection is now in the Bonnat Museum in Bayonne.

Vigorous cross-hatching establishes the hair, showing both its growth pattern and its general planes. The roundness of the globe of the eye is described by careful construction of its darkest parts as well as by the placing of a few accents that follow the form. The subtle structure of the children's heads taxes any artist's knowledge of anatomy because the surface does not reveal the body structure.

Fig. 23.
Hans Holbein the Younger.
The Daughter of Jakob Meyer. (La Fille de Jacques Meyer.) 1525.
Black and colored chalks. Light green wash background on paper.
39 x 37.2 cm.
(15.5 x 14.75 in.)
Öffentliche Kunstsammlung Basel, Kupferstichkabinett.
Compare plate II, 10.

Plate II, 8. Hans Holbein the Younger (1497–1543), *Gentleman from the Court of Henry VIII*.
(Gentilhomme de la cour de Henri VIII.) Collection of Her Majesty the Queen, Royal Library, Windsor Castle

Hans Holbein the Younger was born in Augsburg, where he was trained by his father, Hans Holbein the Elder, a noted artist. He worked first in Prague and Basel. After traveling in Italy and France, he went to London, where he became court painter to Henry VIII. He sketched and painted many members of the court in a frank and objective style. His drawings are the most frequently reproduced in part II.

Plate II, 9. Hans Holbein the Younger, *Sir Nicholas Carew*.
(Sir Nicolas Carew.) Öffentliche Kunstsammlung Basel, Kupferstichkabinett

Sir Nicolas was an *écuyer,* or squire, in charge of the stables of Henry VIII.

Plate II, 10. Hans Holbein the Younger, *The Daughter of Jacques Meyer*.
(La fille de Jacques Meyer.) 1525. Öffentliche Kunstsammlung Basel, Kupferstichkabinett

This drawing of Anna Meyer is a preparatory drawing for a portrait in the Gemäldegalerie Alte Meister, Staatliche Kunstsammlungen, Dresden.

If you look ahead to the portraits by Paul Dubois (plate II, 18) and Adolphe-William Bouguereau (plate II, 23), you will see that Holbein has more carefully delineated each element—including facial features and costume—than either artist. Yet both Dubois and Bouguereau have outlined the contours of the face with great subtlety, noting the sitter's anatomy: the forehead, the brow, the cheekbone, the nose, the fullness of the cheek and of the muscles around the mouth, and the protuberance of the chin. Study each drawing. Try to understand the reason for each bump or depression of the face; refer to an anatomy book for guidance. The light is frontal but diffused. Lighter areas are modeled by veiling. Compare this drawing with the photograph of the original drawing, done in black and colored chalks against a green background (see fig. 23).

Plate II, 11. Raphael (1483–1520), *Kneeling Woman*.
(Figure de femme agenouillée.) Pinacoteca Vaticana, Vatican City

The drawing is after a figure in Raphael's oil painting, *The Transfiguration* (painted between 1517 and 1520), in the Pinacoteca Vaticana, Vatican City.

Plate II, 12. Filippino Lippi (1457–1504), *Portrait*.
(Portrait de Filippino Lippi.) Ufizzi Gallery, Florence

This is an "interpretation," that is, a drawing after a finished work, in this case a self-portrait in fresco (probably a fragment of a wall decoration). Fresco technique requires broad handling. Whereas Bonnat (see plate II, 7) had used hatching for shading, here the artist uses a sfumato—a gentle modeling by means of an overlapping, blended succession of values—in a dramatic chiaroscuro. The light on the right side reveals the fleshy roundness of the artist's parted lips. The direction of the illumination—frontal lighting slightly off to one side—causes a raking shadow and sets the mood of the portrait. A slightly agitated youth emerges from the shadowed uncertainty of adolescence.

Plate II, 13. Charles Gleyre (1808–1874), *Omphale*, study.
(Omphale [tête d'étude].*)* Whereabouts unknown

Gleyre was one of Gérôme's teachers. This is a study "from nature" for the painting *Hercules at the Feet of Omphale (Hercule aux pieds d'Omphale),* now in the Musée Cantonal des Beaux-Arts, Lausanne. William Hauptman thinks the drawing was done by Gleyre expressly for the *Drawing Course;* he also notes that Diego Rivera (1886–1957) copied this lithograph while a student in Madrid.[37]

Gleyre's interpretation of the Greek portrait style is modified by his working from life. The frontal lighting pushes most of the darker tints to the edges, emphasizing the outline. The expression is tender yet ambiguous, as is the modeling, which describes Omphale's features in a thin veil of tone.

Plate II, 14. Jean-Léon Gérôme (1824–1904), *Head of a Fellah,* profile. *(Tête de fellah, vue de profil.)* Private collection

A fellah is an Egyptian peasant. This sketch was made while traveling on safari in Egypt during the winter of 1856–57; the young man was probably a retainer. Gérôme also engraved the portrait.

Gérôme uses a device that successfully focuses our interest on the face: he finishes the features, while handling the clothing in a sketchier style. His cross-hatching is very vigorous. Gérôme was obviously attracted to the pronounced, punctuated features of the young Arab. Compare the handling of this head with Gleyre's treatment of a young girl's head in plate II, 36.

Plate II, 15. Hippolyte Flandrin, *Study of a Woman.* *(Étude de femme.)* Whereabouts unknown

This is a preparatory drawing for the decorations done in 1841 for the duc de Luynes at his chateau in Dampierre. See also comments to plates II, 2 and II, 25.

Flandrin has reserved the most pronounced modeling for the contours, an effect produced more naturally by Gleyre (see plate II, 13). These are not actual shadows but rather a darkening of light areas with cross-hatchings, the effect of frontal lighting. Like Gérôme, Flandrin has described the drapery sketchily, although not enough to disturb the classical, intellectual imitation of Greek vase painting behind the pose of the woman and her chair. Compare the idealized portrait of the woman with the cast drawing of a Roman empress (plate I, 43), the depiction of her body to Raphael's clothed figure (plates II, 11 and II, 43), and the modeling of the outstretched hand to that of the cast drawing of a woman pressing her breast with her hand (plate I, 15).

Plate II, 16. Raphael, *Self-Portrait.* *(Portrait de Raphael.)* Uffizi Gallery, Florence

This drawing is an "interpretation" after an early painting by Raphael also in the Uffizi.

Plate II, 17. Jean-Jacques Henner (1829–1905), *Laughing Boy*, study. *(Le Rieur* [tête d'étude].*)* Whereabouts unknown

Henner was famous for nudes painted in a developed chiaroscuro. His house in Paris is now the Musée national Jean-Jacques Henner.

Strongly animated heads are in the tradition both of Hellenistic sculpture and of the sculpted *têtes d'expression,* or expressive heads (that is, heads showing specific emotions) produced by students at the École des Beaux-Arts in Paris (see also *concours* in glossary). Henner combines all three methods of shading—stumping, hatching, and veiling—in this lively head. Seen from above, the hair becomes the dominant feature. The view was chosen to add movement to the figure and to support the expression on the boy's face. The hair is decorative yet still true to the values one might see in nature. The part breaks the hair up into sections that follow the growth pattern.

Plate II, 18. Paul Dubois (1829–1905), *Roman Woman.* *(Femme romaine.)* Whereabouts unknown

Dubois was an excellent sculptor whose work was influenced by Florentine quattrocento sculpture. He was a student at the École des Beaux-Arts in Paris, where even sculptors were taught to draw well.

By deliberately putting his model in profile, Dubois emphasizes the abstract and formal qualities of the picture rather than the personality of the sitter. Her features are described in halftones that contrast with the light background and further distinguish the contours. Both stumping and veiling techniques could have achieved the painterly qualities of this drawing. Whereas Gérôme suppressed most of the values of the face in his portraits of Arabs, Dubois describes every change in values—and he finishes the clothing and accessories as well.

Plate II, 19. Hans Holbein the Younger, *Sir Charles Elliot*.
(Le chevalier Charles Elliot.) Collection of Her Majesty the Queen, Royal Library, Windsor Castle

Plate II, 20. Hans Holbein the Younger, *Gentleman from the Court of Henry VIII.*
(Gentilhomme de la cour de Henri VIII.) Collection of Her Majesty the Queen, Royal Library, Windsor Castle

Plate II, 21. Michelangelo, *Study of a Man*.
(Étude d'homme.) Sistine Chapel, Vatican City

This is another "interpretation" after a figure in the *Last Judgment* fresco (1536-1542) in the Sistine Chapel. It is a lesson in foreshortening.

Plate II, 22. Auguste Toulmouche (1829–1890), *Young Woman Kissing Her Child.*
(Jeune femme embrassant son enfant.) Whereabouts unknown

Like Gérôme, Toulmouche was a student of Gleyre. He and Gérôme also belonged to the Néo-Grecs, a group of young painters of the mid-nineteenth century who painted genre scenes set in antiquity. Toulmouche soon switched to contemporary genre scenes, depicting middle-class women and their children. This pair was also used in a lost painting entitled *The Maternal Kiss (Le Baiser maternel),* which was shown at the Salon of 1857.

The lighting is frontal. Both interlocked figures are seen in profile. Toulmouche uses subtle changes in perspective to create rhythms that move forward as well as up and down.

Plate II, 23. Adolphe-William Bouguereau (1825–1905), *A Roman Woman*, study.
(Tête de femme romaine [étude].*)* Whereabouts unknown

Bouguereau was almost an exact contemporary of Gérôme. Along with Ernest Meissonier (1815–1891), they were the most famous representatives of French Academic Realism of the second half of the nineteenth century.

Bouguereau's use of loose hatch lines is closer to Gérôme's methods than to the hatching of Dubois. He probably drew this in pencil—the shadows of the hair and figure are rather light—reserving the darks for the accents in the eye, nose, mouth, and ear.

Plate II, 24. *Archer from Aegina*.
(Sagittaire Éginète.) Staatliche Antikensammlungen und Glyptothek, Munich

This is a figure (480 B.C.) from the east pediment of the Doric temple of Aphia on the island of Aegina. The lion-head cap identifies him as Hercules. In the early nineteenth century the twelve figures of the pediment were restored by the great Danish Neoclassical sculptor Bertl Thorvaldsen (1770–1884). The draftsman has chosen a view of the statue where the restorations are least evident, which includes the right forearm, the left hand, the left thigh, part of the right foot, and parts of the hem of the skirt (see also plate II, 40).

Plate II, 25. Hippolyte Flandrin, *Study of a Woman*.
(Étude de femme.) Whereabouts unknown

This is yet another drawing for the decoration of the chateau of the duc de Luynes in Dampierre; see comments to plates II, 2 and II, 15.

This drawing shows a woman drying her hair after a bath. The most remarkable feature is the continuous, unbroken line describing the left contour of the figure. Even though the character of the figure is round and voluptuous, the outline is stabilized by straight passages. Moreover, its linear, decorative quality vies with its ability to express volume. As with the other nude studies prepared for the Dampierre decorations, there is very little interior modeling. Dark accents are prominent only in the features of the face. With a little practice the student will be able to see how the drawing differs from nature, how Flandrin abstracts and flattens the figure to achieve his conception of the ideal, and which aspects of the figure he chooses to stress—such as the facial expression—and which he chooses to suppress. The simplicity of the drawing is deceptive. Flandrin's style is practiced yet truthful in its larger concepts: the muscles and morphological forms fit together, and a minimum of tones reveals these forms. The lighting is similar to the drawing of the cast of the *Achilles* (see plate I, 68).

Plate II, 26. Hans Holbein the Younger, *Citizen of Basel*.
(Bourgeoise de Bâle.) Öffentliche Kunstsammlung Basel, Kupferstichkabinett

Plate II, 27. Hans Holbein the Younger, *Anna Grisacria*.
(Anna Grisacria [Cresacre].) Collection of Her Majesty the Queen, Royal Library, Windsor Castle

Plate II, 28. Hans Holbein the Younger, *John Poines*.
(John Poines.) Collection of Her Majesty the Queen, Royal Library, Windsor Castle

Plate II, 29. Hans Holbein the Younger, *Thomas, Count of Surrey*.
(Thomas, comte de Surrey.) Collection of Her Majesty the Queen, Royal Library, Windsor Castle

The sitter is now identified as Henry Howard, earl of Surrey.

Plate II, 30. Hans Holbein the Younger, *Anne Boleyn*.
(Anne Boleyn.) Collection of Her Majesty the Queen, Royal Library, Windsor Castle

Plate II, 31. Andrea del Sarto (1486–1530), *Self-Portrait*.
(Portrait d'Andrea del Sarto.) Whereabouts unknown

This is an "interpretation," a drawing after a finished painting, *Charity*, (1486) in the Uffizi Gallery, Florence. Andrea del Sarto was one of the great masters of the Italian Renaissance, whose major works are in the Pitti Palace in Florence.

Andrea's treatment is more realistic than that of Gleyre and Flandrin. He attends to all the major forms of the face, putting them in tonally by means of stumping. The eyes are circumscribed by halftones that give clarity to the skeletal sockets. Compare this with plate II, 12.

Plate II, 32. Raphael, *Dante*.
(Portrait du Dante.) Stanze di Raffaello, Vatican City

This is a drawing after the figure of Dante in the fresco *Parnassus* located in the Stanza della Segnatura (1508–11) in the Vatican. Raphael developed his likeness from older, traditional portraits of Dante.

Plate II, 33. Jean-Auguste-Dominique Ingres (1780–1867), *A Lictor*. *(Licteur.)* Ingres Museum, Montauban

This is an "interpretation" after a famous oil sketch in the Ingres Museum in Montauban. The oil sketch was a study for a large painting entitled *The Martyrdom of Saint Symphorian (Le Martyre de saint Symphorien)* (1834) in the Cathedral of Saint Lazare, Autun.

Plate II, 34. Jules Lefebvre (1836–1912), *Head of a Child*. *(Tête d'enfant.)* Whereabouts unknown

Lefebvre was a successful academic painter, famous for his nudes, and a longtime teacher at the Académie Julian in Paris. Although he received many decorations, honors, and state commissions, he is hardly remembered today, although several of his works are still admired and reproduced.

This is a preparatory drawing for his painting *Cornelia, Mother of the Gracchi (Cornélie, mère des Gracques)*, whose present location is unknown. This is a masterful study of a foreshortened head, seen from below, as well as an example of "stopped modeling." The halftones are produced both by stumping and hatching. Thick and thin lines form the contours, which are darkest on the shaded side of the head. The neck is a cylinder that meets the shadowy underside of the chin. The mastoid muscle *(sternocleidomastoideus)* is fully described under the ear, as is its attachment to the clavicle below the lightly hatched Adam's apple.

Plate II, 35. Émile Lévy (1826–1890), *Head of a Young Italian Girl*. *(Tête de jeune fille italienne.)* Whereabouts unknown

Émile Lévy was a student of François-Édouard Picot (1786–1868) and Alexandre Denis Abel Pujol (1787–1861). Winner of a Prix de Rome in history painting in 1854, he had a long career as a history and genre painter. Since his death he has slipped into obscurity. Although a contemporary of Gérôme and Bouguereau, he adhered to the conventions of Neoclassicism and avoided the more strident traits of Realism.

To copy this, use red or sanguine conté or chalk. It might be helpful to look again at the classical profiles in plates I, 33 and I, 40. The design of the hair is especially fine in its controlled ornamentation. The contour is stressed, as in many of the drawings. The lips are parted but still planar. Although each feature of the profile is carefully articulated, there is less detail in the interior modeling, with its sfumato, diffused shadows, and nebulous halftones.

Plate II, 36. Charles Gleyre, *Head of a Young Italian Girl*. *(Tête de jeune fille italienne.)* Whereabouts unknown

On Gleyre, see comments to plate II, 13. William Hauptman has identified the subject as either a study for or after the figure in the painting *La Charmeuse* of 1878, in the Kunstmuseum Basel. He postulates that the drawing might have been commissioned by Goupil for the *Drawing Course*.[38]

Use red or sanguine chalk. This is another unusual and instructive view complicated by the plumpness—more fat than muscle—of the child. Axial and vertical hatching describe the top and lower planes of the simplified hair. The prominent ear is fully finished, as are the values of the face. Note that the ear does not distract from the beauty of the modeling along the contour of the neck and face. The integrity of the head is maintained because the ear is seen in proper value relationship to the whole. The dark values inside the ear are lighter than the dark values under the ear and chin. If the values in the ear were too dark, they would draw attention to the ear.

Plate II, 37. Adolphe-William Bouguereau, *A Pifferaro*. Study painted from life. *(Pifferaro.* [Étude peinte d'après nature].) Whereabouts unknown

A *pifferaro* was a music-playing Italian shepherd, usually equipped with a rustic bagpipe or a bassoon. (The duet for oboe and bassoon in the country dance movement of Beethoven "Pastoral" Symphony imitates the *pifferari*.) In the nineteenth century they were for hire as party entertainers and models for painters.

Plate II, 38. Hans Holbein the Younger, *Portrait of Sir John Godsalve*.
(Portrait de Sir John Godsalve.) Collection of Her Majesty the Queen, Royal Library, Windsor Castle

On Holbein, see the comments to plate II, 8. This plate is not a facsimile but rather another "interpretation" of a finished work.

The features are precise; the eyes have both upper and lower lids. The sharpness of the features differs from the two Italian portraits (plates II, 12 and II, 31). The device of a fully modeled head contrasting with a strictly linear body—although extrapolated from the finished drawing by the copyist—was nonetheless employed by Holbein in other drawings.

Plate II, 39. Hans Holbein the Younger, *Erasmus of Rotterdam*.
(Érasme.) Louvre Museum, Paris

This is a partially finished "interpretation" of Holbein's oil portrait of the great humanist scholar. The oil is also in the Louvre Museum in Paris.

Plate II, 40. *Archer from Aegina, Wearing a Helmet*.
(Sagittaire Éginète, casqué.) Staatliche Antikensammlungen und Glyptothek, Munich

This statue (480 B.C.) is a concoction of ancient and modern parts assembled and carved by Thorwaldsen to complete the damaged figure of an archer from the west pediment of the Doric temple of Aphia on the island of Aegina. Thorwaldsen was attempting to make an archer for the left side of the triangular pediment to balance the relatively lightly restored Hercules as archer from the other side of the pediment (see plate II, 24). New are parts of the helmet and its crest, the head, both forearms, the hem of the skirt, the lower part of the left leg and foot, and part of the right leg and foot. These restorations are not identified in the drawing, although they were evident *in situ* because of the differences in color of the old and new marble. Thorwaldsen's additions were removed in the 1960s, making the remains purely antique but destroying a great nineteenth-century conception of a primitive Greek warrior.

Plate II, 41. Michelangelo, *Man Pulling a Rope*.
(Homme au chapelet.) Sistine Chapel, Vatican City

This is yet another figure from Michelangelo's *Last Judgment* fresco in the Sistine Chapel in the Vatican, painted between 1536 and 1542.

Plate II, 42. Michelangelo, *Eve*.
(Ève.) Sistine Chapel, Vatican City

This figure was painted between 1508 and 1512.

Plate II, 43. Raphael, *Woman Carrying Vases*.
(Femme portant des vases.) Sistine Chapel, Vatican City

This drawing is after a famous, oft-copied figure in the fresco *Fire in the Borgo (Incendio di Borgo),* completed in 1514–17.

Plate II, 44. Raphael, *The Violinist*.
(Le joueur de violon.) Sciarra Collection, Rome

Now ascribed to Sebastiano del Piombo (1485–1547), it was much admired as a Raphael in the nineteenth century. As a student in Rome in the early 1840s, Gérôme painted a copy; perhaps he supplied the painting or a drawing as the model for the lithograph. He certainly suggested its inclusion.[39] The oil was not only admired by Gérôme but was also praised by both Bouguereau and Eugène-Emmanuel Amaury-Duval (1806–1885). Although most of the Sciarra collection was sold in 1898–99, *The Violinist* is still in the collection in Rome.

Plate II, 45. Hans Holbein the Younger, *Portrait of Brooke*.
(Portrait de Brooke.) Collection of Her Majesty the Queen, Royal Library, Windsor Castle

The sitter is George Brooke, ninth baron of Cobham.

Plate II, 46. Hans Holbein the Younger, *Portrait of a Lady*.
(Portrait de femme.) Collection of Her Majesty the Queen, Royal Library, Windsor Castle

Plate II, 47. Hans Holbein the Younger, *Portrait of Lady Elliot*.
(Portrait de lady Elliot.) Collection of Her Majesty the Queen, Royal Library, Windsor Castle

The sitter is Margaret, Lady Elliot. Her name is misspelled on the drawing.

Plate II, 48. Hans Holbein the Younger, *Portrait of William, marquess of Northampton*.
(Portrait de William, marquess de Northampton.) Collection of Her Majesty the Queen, Royal Library, Windsor Castle

The sitter is William Parr, first marquess of Northampton.

Plate II, 49. Jules Breton (1827–1905), *The Servant*.
(La servante.) Whereabouts unknown

This is a "facsimile of a drawing after nature." A contemporary of Gérôme, Pierre Puvis de Chavannes (1824–1898) and Bouguereau, Breton was a famous and prolific painter of peasant scenes.

Plate II, 50. Jean-Léon Gérôme, *The Dog of Alcibiades*.
(Le chien d'Alcibiade.) Baron Martin Museum, Gray, France

A study ("painted from nature") for Alcibiades's dog in the 1861 painting *Alcibiades in the House of Aspasia* *(Alcibiade chez Aspasie).*[40]

Plate II, 51. Michelangelo, *Man Sitting on a Sack*.
(L'homme au sac.) Sistine Chapel, Vatican City

This drawing is after a figure in a fresco (1508–12) on the ceiling of the Sistine Chapel in the Vatican. The anatomy in the original is not totally correct, and the copy compounds Michelangelo's errors. The right shoulder and arm are exaggerated in size. Michelangelo's ability, however, comes through in the rhythmical disposition of the parts, which gives the body a sense of grace and movement.

Plate II, 52. Thomas Couture (1815–1879), *Portrait of a Young Boy*.
(Portrait d'un jeune garçon.) Whereabouts unknown

Couture had a distinguished career, although several large commissions from the French government remained unfinished because of the political upheavals during his lifetime. Known primarily for his large history paintings executed in a loose, individual style, he had many students, among them Anselm Feuerbach (1829–1880), Édouard Manet (1832–1883), William Morris Hunt (1824–1879), and Puvis de Chavannes.

Couture utilizes another manner of drawing the hair; compare it to the handling of hair by Henner (plate II, 17) and by Gleyre (plate II, 36). Couture uses long strokes of the charcoal for the general direction of the growth patterns and general veiling to indicate the top and lower planes of the head. Praiseworthy skill is evident in the drawing of the foreshortened ear, in the slight toning for the depression between the nasal bone and the nasal eminence, and in the gradual shading on the left cheek. The end of the nose has a planar quality, separating it from its sides.

Plate II, 53. Jules Lefebvre, *Head of a Woman*. *(Tête de femme.)* Whereabouts unknown

On Lefebvre, see comments to plate II, 34.

Plate II, 54. Timoléon Lobrichon (1831–1914), *Study of a Baby*. *(Étude d'enfant.)* Whereabouts unknown

Lobrichon was a student of François-Édouard Picot. In the 1850s he was associated with the Néo-Grecs, a group of painters, headed by Gérôme, who composed genre scenes set in antiquity. Later he painted mothers and children in modern settings.

This complete figure will aid you in understanding the difficulties of drawing babies, where baby fat and the surface bones dominate the shape and contours of the body and limbs. Note how the hair radiates from the crown of the head. Throughout outlines are strong, even in interior forms. The technique is similar to Holbein's in plates II, 19 and II, 60.

Plate II, 55. Hans Holbein the Younger, *Portrait of N. Poyntz*. *(Portrait de N. Poyntz.)* Collection of Her Majesty the Queen, Royal Library, Windsor Castle

The sitter is Sir Nicolas Poyntz. The plate is inscribed with an added signature *N. Poines Knight*.

Plate II, 56. Hans Holbein the Younger, *Portrait of Lady Hanegham*. *(Portrait de lady Hanegham.)* Collection of Her Majesty the Queen, Royal Library, Windsor Castle

Plate II, 57. Hans Holbein the Younger, *Portrait of the Wife of Jacques Meyer*. *(Portrait de la femme de Jacques Meyer.)* Öffentliche Kunstsammlung Basel, Kupferstichkabinett

Dorothea Kannengiesser and her husband, Jakob Meyer, the mayor of Basel, were drawn twice by Holbein, and the Kunstmuseum has both sets of drawings. This is from the second set and is dated 1525–26.

Plate II, 58. Hans Holbein the Younger, *Portrait of a Young Man*. *(Portrait d'un jeune homme.)* Whereabouts unknown

The style of this drawing is very close to that of Holbein's illustrious father, Hans Holbein the Elder (ca. 1465-ca. 1524). It may be an early drawing by the younger Holbein.

Plate II, 59. Hans Holbein the Younger, *Portrait of Lord Vaux*. *(Portrait de lord Vaux.)* Collection of Her Majesty the Queen, Royal Library, Windsor Castle

The sitter is Thomas, the second Lord Vaux.

Plate II, 60. Hans Holbein the Younger, *Thomas, Count of Surrey*.
(Portrait de Thomas, comte de Surrey.) Collection of Her Majesty the Queen,
Royal Library, Windsor Castle

The sitter is now identified as Henry Howard, earl of Surrey.

Holbein's naturalistic observations vie with the almost perfect oval of the face, as if he were subordinating nature to geometry. The faintly indicated clothing contrasts with the high finish of the face; individual strokes describe individual hairs; and the features of the face are very precise. Holbein is a master of the facial structure around the eye.

Plate II, 61. Philippe Parrot (1831–1894), *Bather,* study of a young girl.
(Baigneuse. [Étude de jeune fille].*)* Whereabouts unknown

Another "interpretation" of a painting. Now almost forgotten, Parrot specialized in portraits and elegant nudes in mythological guise.

Plate II, 62. Hans Holbein the Younger, *Portrait of a Man*.
(Portrait d'homme.) Whereabouts unknown

Before Word War II this drawing was in the collection of the duke of Weimar, in Weimar, Germany. The attribution to Holbein the Younger is not certain.

Plate II, 63. Hans Holbein the Younger, *Clinton*.
(Clinton.) Collection of Her Majesty the Queen, Royal Library,
Windsor Castle

The sitter is Edward, ninth earl of Clinton. Although the drawing is located at Windsor Castle by Goupil, it cannot be found in any catalogue of the collection.

Plate II, 64. Hans Holbein the Younger, *Portrait of a Lady*.
(Portrait de femme.) Whereabouts unknown

Plate II, 65. Hans Holbein the Younger, *Portrait of a Man*.
(Portrait d'homme.) Collection of Her Majesty the Queen, Royal Library,
Windsor Castle

Plate II, 66. Hans Holbein the Younger, *Lady of the Court of Henry IV*.
(Dame de la cour de Henri IV.) Öffentliche Kunstsammlung Basel,
Kupferstichkabinett

The sitter is Lady Guildford. This is a poor rendition of a masterful drawing by Holbein.

Plate II, 67. Hans Holbein the Younger, *Portrait of a Man*.
(Portrait d'homme.) Öffentliche Kunstsammlung Basel, Kupferstichkabinett

This is a sketch (1516) for one of the two paintings on panel of Jakob Meyer and his wife, also in the Kunstmuseum Basel (see comments to plate II, 57). In an extremely efficient manner Holbein has given much attention to the features of the face—such as the slight sag of the skin around Meyer's mouth and his chin—without detracting from the simplicity of the presentation. The clothing is simply outlined. In the finished oil it is painted from life. In the original preparatory drawing (see fig. 24) Holbein used silverpoint and red chalk.

Fig. 24.
Hans Holbein the Younger.
Portrait of a Man (Jakob
Meyer). *(Portrait d'homme.
Jacob Meyer.)* 1516.
Silverpoint and red chalk
on paper.
26.9 x 19.1 cm.
(10.5 x 7.5 in.)
Öffentliche
Kunstsammlung Basel,
Kupferstichkabinett.

PART III: PREPARATION FOR DRAWING *ACADÉMIES (EXERCICES AU FUSAIN POUR PRÉPARER À L'ÉTUDE DE L'ACADÉMIE D'APRÈS NATURE)*

INTRODUCTION

I n general art-historical usage, an *académie* means a drawing or a painting of a nude model in a pose considered "noble and classic."[41] Highly finished charcoal drawings of male nudes were produced in such numbers in art academies that the institution became synonymous with its most representative product.

Female models were not used in life drawing classes at nineteenth-century academies until sometime after the middle of the century.[42] Students were expected to learn how to draw the female nude from statuary and other works of art, such as the models in the first and second parts of Bargue's *Drawing Course*. This was true even at the École des Beaux-Arts. Thus, the term *académie* in Bargue's title for the third part is the most restrictive use of the term: the seventy drawings are all of male nudes.[43]

The mastery of the nude male body was considered the most important part of the artist's repertoire, for it was taken for granted—in the persistent patriarchal worldview—that males were the most important members of society; for all practical purposes, they were also the most important characters in the historical and biblical subjects academy students were instructed to paint. Despite the fact that history paintings had gradually gone out of favor after the middle of the century—and that it had always been easier to sell a painting of a nude female than of a nude male—intense study of the male nude persisted until late in the nineteenth century. During the twentieth century the practice changed; now females are the favored models in art schools and drawing groups.

The results of the nineteenth-century practice can be seen in the works of Gérôme. In the lycée in his hometown of Vesoul there were no live models at all in any of the drawing and painting courses Gérôme took. When he left Vesoul and went to Paris in 1839, he studied in the ateliers of Delaroche and Gleyre; only the latter is known to have used female models, but Gérôme's time with Gleyre was a mere six months. Although his male nudes were, from the start of his career, both accurate and learned, it is easy to see from his early paintings that he had learned the female form by studying Greek statuary: his nude women are geometrically idealized, with taut skin over rounded forms, and with particularly firm, hemispherical breasts. Not until relatively late in his life—probably influenced by the growing severity of the standards of Realism—did Gérôme produce female nudes that seem to be drawn, painted, or sculpted from live models.

Ancient Sculpture as the Model of True Beauty: The Prevalence of Male Models

The nineteenth-century preference for male nudes as studio models had an old and embedded philosophical tradition behind it. The preference, nurtured and developed over a long period, was based on some tenets of Neoplatonism. The term covers a series of independent and different philosophical schools of thought in ancient and recent times, all sects or varieties of which were ultimately based on the dialogues of the ancient Greek philosopher Plato (427?–347 B.C.). Neoplatonism flourished, in various forms, into the seventh century A.D., when it was suppressed first by the Christians and then the Muslims as pagan, although many Neoplatonic ideas had already been assimilated by Christian theology. The interest of the humanists of the fifteenth century in ancient texts and philosophies led to a revival of Neoplatonic thought in several forms (such as philosophy, mysticism, and theurgy), branches of Neoplatonism that have influenced Western thought down through modern times. Popular astrology, for instance, is organized according to a Neoplatonic system: the planets are intermediaries between a higher, spiritual, reality and our world.

The belief by Plato that an independent, intelligible reality exists above and outside our sensible, material world is the basis of all schools of Neoplatonism. This higher reality is the realm of the truth, of values and principles that are the basis of our intellectual and moral life. The purpose of philosophy was the attainment of knowledge of these principles through study, instruction, ritual, revelation, and restraint of the senses (denial of the flesh). At the most elevated level it could result in a union of the individual soul with the highest sphere of the cosmos.

Human attainment of knowledge about the true principles was endangered by the lower emotions, which were aroused by the distracting sensory experience of the material world, or, as Christians saw it, a struggle between the spirit and the flesh. The sensory experience of this lower, material world evokes the lower emotions—lust, anger, gluttony, pride, envy, greed, sloth—which can consume our energies, weaken our judgment, and obscure the guidance of the higher principles, which already exist—instilled by God for our guidance—in our minds, thus delaying or destroying our ability to understand the true, absolute, and immutable principles or truths, such as piety, honor, obedience, justice, the Good, beauty, and so forth. To live an enlightened and blessed life, one had to free one's self from the domination of the senses, while clarifying to the point of unambiguous purity the concepts of the higher truths in our minds. Odd as it may seem, despite this antisensual argument, art—in particular the depiction of the nude human body—was seen as an aid in the pursuit of truth.

In Plato's dialogue *Phaedrus* the love for a beautiful youth is described as an aid to comprehending the higher principles of the mind. Even though love is evoked by the youth's physical beauty, the latter still provides an insight into the nature of true beauty, an insight that could lead to the knowledge of other absolute truths or principles planted by the creator in the mind but nonetheless difficult to access.[44]

It is important to stress that the path opened by physical beauty to true knowledge is also the path away from sensory or erotic entanglements. Giving in to the senses would not only debase the relationship of lovers but would further entangle them in the material world and obscure their understanding of higher principles. (Hence the popular expression "Platonic love.") Without embarrassment, this belief that falling in love could lead to spiritual enlightenments was revived by several Neoplatonists of the Italian Renaissance.[45]

The idealized male body, especially as exemplified in the sculpture of antiquity, became a paradigm of *true beauty*. This pagan association of virtue and beauty can be sensed in many ancient sculptures as well as in the works of the ardent Christian and fervent Neoplatonist, Michelangelo, as in his famous statue of *David* and his poetry.

In the eighteenth century Renaissance Neoplatonism informed the thought of Johann Joachim Winckelmann (1717–1768), the founder of archeology and a prolific writer on ancient art. While studying Greek sculpture, he decided that the beauty of the Greek depiction of male bodies was due not to idealization by Greek sculptors but rather to the perfect bodies of their models, the Greek men of antiquity. Moreover, these men were more beautiful than modern men because they were simply better people. The idea that the contemplation of natural male beauty opened the door to *la belle nature*—the pure and eternal idea of nature in the mind—and that this could lead to other higher truths remained popular into the second half of the nineteenth century.[46] Thus, through several manifestations the influence of Plato may be seen lurking beneath the exclusive use of male models in the École des Beaux-Arts until late in the nineteenth century, which is reflected in the third part of the *Drawing Course*.[47]

The ancient statuary of female nudes likewise presented women in an already idealized and ideal form. From the Renaissance on, most artists—docile, chaste, timid, or shy—used ancient statuary as models from which to learn how to pose females and how to depict their anatomy. In a pinch when dealing with a difficult pose, artists often used a male model—preferably slightly plump—to pose for a female figure; in addition to substituting a female head, they made a few bodily adjustments to feminize their drawing, such as adding breasts or thickening the hips. As the female nude began to predominate in Western art, its "rarefied beauty" and purity were praised; the simplification of natural forms through geometry, such as hemispherical breasts, represented a step toward the ideal, and hence toward moral thought.

Nonetheless, the counterargument—that viewing an image of a nude woman put the male viewer in moral peril of experiencing an erotic reaction or of harboring impure thoughts—was an important and persistent position. Thus, it was argued for centuries that both female and male nude bodies, if depicted, should be presented in an idealized manner, bereft of direct erotic stimulus. In France between 1875 and 1881 official censors inspected and approved prints and photographs of nudes before they could be put on public display or sold in shops. Despite this review, many approved prints and photos of nudes could not be displayed in shop windows. After 1881 the police were empowered to arrest those who made an offensive public display of a nude in a shop window, on a magazine or a book cover. If a trial ensued, the defense would usually argue that the nude, no matter how lasciviously depicted, was purified, with rounded, geometrical, unnatural forms—"like a sculpture"—and that the depiction was aimed at the higher consciousness and consequently was unlikely to arouse the lower emotions. The defense often won. In 1888 a lawyer defended a nude on the cover of the magazine *Le Courrier français* by pointing out that no genitalia were visible and that "the marmoreal bust with its imaginary rigidity and strength bears no trace of realism. . . . I see nothing more here than an admirably pure body, its lines powerful and chaste. . . ."[48]

Even so, students were thought to benefit in some practical sense from this philosophical preference for male nudes. Human anatomy was believed easier to grasp by observing the thinner, angular bodies of males than the fuller, rounder figures of females. It was thought easier to maintain discipline among the usually rowdy students—all male in most academies and art schools until very late in the nineteenth century—when the nude model was a male. Furthermore the teachers and administrators thought that they were protecting the morals of their students by shielding them from the power of the lower, sensual emotions that would be evoked by the depiction of a nude woman, especially one who was considered "available" (the popular assumption being that any woman who bared herself for money was of doubtful virtue). Even after the introduction of female models into the drawing classes in the mid or late nineteenth century, the general public, artists, and students often regarded and treated female models as no better than prostitutes.

Practical Matters: Copying the Drawings

As the title of this section indicates, these drawings of posed nude males are meant as preparation for drawing after live models in a studio. These exercises—the careful, exact copying of good drawings after a model—are meant to be executed in charcoal, as was the practice when drawing after a model posed in the studio. A good *académie* in charcoal should take at least fifteen hours, if not longer. Your copy should be developed and finished according to the steps in the first part (see the section entitled "Suggestions for Copying the Plates").

These *académies* are remarkable inventions of Bargue. You will come to appreciate them more and more as you work with them; your admiration will intensify when you start drawing from live models. Even so, the procedure—from schema to outline to shadows—was not Bargue's invention; it was standard practice in art schools and studios in the nineteenth century.

The drawings in this part are almost pure outline drawings, without shading or background; there are only sparse internal indications of anatomical features. Even if you are fairly advanced and sure of yourself, you should start out with the simpler, early plates, thereby making sure you grasp Bargue's procedural method.

The first two parts of the course were designed to make you see the essential elements of a figure and teach you a procedure for drawing from a model. The drawings in the third part stress structure and unity as opposed to seeing bodily parts separately. The large factors—character, pose, and proportion—are more important than surface detail. A quick perusal of the pages of the third part discloses just how little internal information Bargue puts within the outline: faces are left blank and hands and feet are often indicated by schematic lines. Furthermore, the complexities of the outline of the body are often reduced to straight lines between points, as in the first schemata for the cast drawings in the first part. Despite the fact that there is little internal musculature, the figures are both simple and successfully articulated.

As this is preparatory practice for drawing a nude from life, it is best to simulate the working conditions of drawing from a model in a studio. (In all the drawings in this part, the model is assumed to be on a platform at least 40 centimeters [16 inches] in height. This will put the eyes of a seated model about level with an artist standing at his easel—an ideal height for portraiture—and will result in the artist looking up at a standing nude.) This is best done by working with the Bargue *académie* and your drawing paper side by side or on a wall or on a straight (not angled) easel. (Students working without instructors should first carefully read appendix 2. Knowledge of sight-size practices will help students better understand many of the suggestions in the comments on the individual plates.)

At times the straight lines with which Bargue first captured the shape of certain parts of the body may seem like mannerisms, that is, traits or features reflecting a personal style; in practice these straight lines are tools that indicate the peaks of the planes on the surface of the body, which are demarcated by the protruding anatomical features under the skin. The straight lines do not retain their abstraction in the finished drawing, where they are usually rounded out to achieve a natural appearance. The schema—the resulting silhouette of connected outlines—is just the first step. And if you have worked through or from the plates in part I, you know how to proceed once you have outlined the figure. In part III only the last few drawings are finished: no shadow line has been developed and filled in and, of course, no halftones have been recorded. If you were working from a live model, you would be expected to finish the procedure, to produce a finished drawing with most of the surface modeled. Bargue teaches you to correctly draw the structure before you start adding the finishing touches, as well as how to determine the correct proportions of the outside shape of the subject; otherwise the interior features will not fit in correctly. You may continue making or checking your estimates by stepping back and measuring them at a distance; eventually you will make the measurements without a tool. Checking your drawing by comparing it with the model viewed in a hand mirror is always helpful.

With the Bargue drawing and your drawing side by side, you will soon learn to see errors. Remember, if these drawings were to be used as models for a painting, any inaccuracies would be compounded once you tried to fill in the interior. Such strictness is necessary both to teach you how to see and transcribe a human being's form correctly and to purge your own practice of any mannerisms or impreciseness that you may have already acquired.

The *Drawing Course* was published on full folio sheets, about four times as large as the reproductions in this book. If you are working in charcoal, you should take the book to a photocopy shop that has a good laser printer and have the drawing you wish to copy enlarged in color two or three times. It will be easier to see and understand Bargue's linear decisions in a larger drawing; many details would be virtually impossible to copy in a small scale, especially in charcoal. If you wish to copy directly from the book, you should work in pencil.

Some Notes on Bargue's Style

Bargue's use of straight lines seems intuitive rather than programmatic. In some complex anatomical areas (calves, knees, elbows, biceps, hands, and feet) he usually uses straight lines as a deliberate simplification. Whenever there is a lot of information to transcribe, the outlines of his forms generally tend toward straight lines. Just as often he uses a long, simple, sensuous and elegant line, slightly curved, taking in several dots. The virtuosity of these passages makes it seem as if he were performing for us, in comparison to the short, choppy units in the other passages.

The angles, both concave and convex, that change the contours of the figure imperceptibly are all based on internal anatomical features: swelling of muscles; attachments of tendons to bones; emerging surface bones; flexed muscles or fat. Emphasizing the protuberances of internal anatomical features punctuates the outline, clarifies the inner structure, and gives fullness to the contours. It takes a good knowledge of anatomy to see and articulate these features.

Bargue's abstraction of the figure involves more than the simplification of planes and outlines. Each of his figures has a singular rhythm that subordinates and subsumes the details—or, rather, unites them: each element supports the overall effect of the pose and the direction of the gestures.

Bargue uses overlapping lines to emphasize the structure of the body (as in plate III, 38). These lines assist in the foreshortening since they indicate if one form or muscle is in front of another. Bargue is particularly well versed in the construction of joints and the knee: he always indicates the patella, the protuberances of the condyles of the fibula and tibia, and the connecting tendons for the larger leg muscles that anchor themselves around the knee. Similarly, Bargue often records accented forms caused by folds in the flesh or pits like the navel, axillae, and the pit of the neck.

Bargue's indication of interior anatomy is almost calligraphic, particularly in the legs. These indications are drawn with a bit of brio. Some contours are quite refined, with Bargue recording all the expected changes in curvature (see the legs in plates III, 18, 19, and 37). Others are drawn in a more economical, "off the cuff" manner. For example, in plate III, 32 Bargue audaciously draws the outer contour of the left leg with a single sweeping arc that is interrupted only by the bend in the knee; in plate III, 41 the outer side of the right leg is a sinuous s-curve.

A Repertoire of Traditional Poses

In the many studies in part III Gérôme and Bargue have included a repertoire of traditional poses, some of which might occasionally have been useful to history or narrative painters. They were certainly useful to students at the École des Beaux-Arts in Paris, many of whom intended to compete for the Prix de Rome. A list of the recognizable poses follows.

Rhetorical poses: plates III, 10 and 37.

Allegorical figures: plates III, 28 and 40 (melancholy); plate III, 29 (grief or mourning [he could be holding an urn or a libation vessel]); plate III, 37 (prayer); plate III, 39 (grief); plate III, 47 (astonishment).

Action figures: plate III, 12 (David with his sling); plate III, 38 (an archer); plate III, 46 (a man tugging); plate III, 45 (stretching).

Famous figures: plate III, 24, Hippolyte Flandrin's *Young Man Seated on a Rock,* study (*Jeune Homme nu assis sur un rocher. Figure d'étude);* plate III, 33, after Michelangelo's *Dying Slave (L'Esclave mourant)* (fig. 13); plate II, 35, the *Dying Gaul (Gaulois mourant)* at the Capitoline Museum in Rome.

Biblical figures: plate III, 12 (David); plate III, 15 (Saint John the Baptist or a shepherd); plate III, 18 (a shepherd); plate III, 36 (Adam expulsed from Paradise); plate III, 42 *(Ecce Homo);* plate III, 44 (Abel dead, the dead Christ, or a martyr).

Traditional women's poses: plate III, 17 (examining a bird's nest); plate III, 50 (a bather).

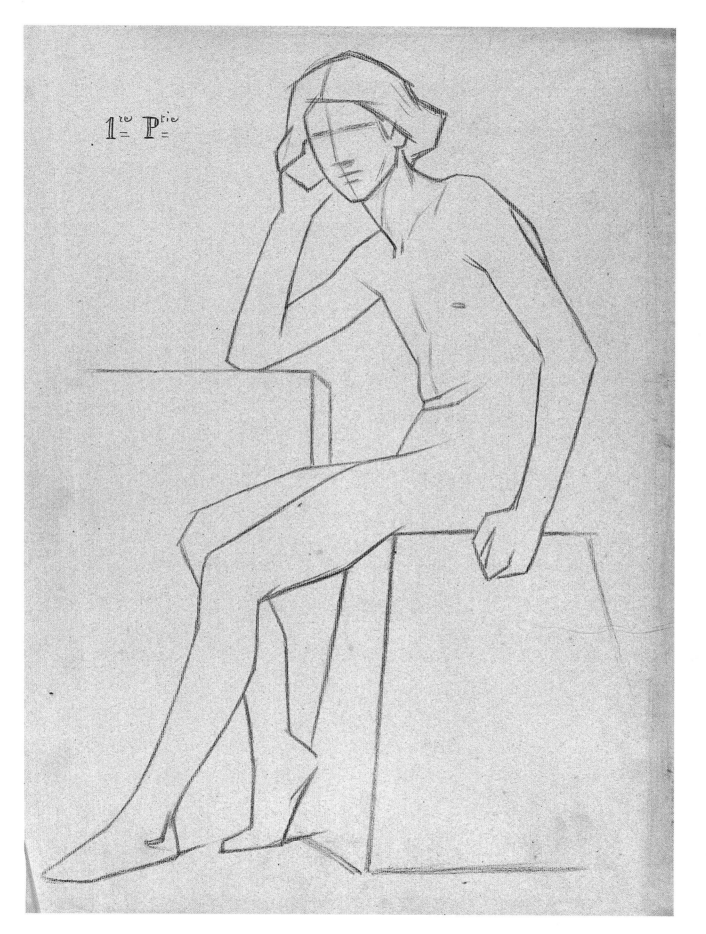

1re P^{tie}

Plate III, 1

186

Plate III, 2

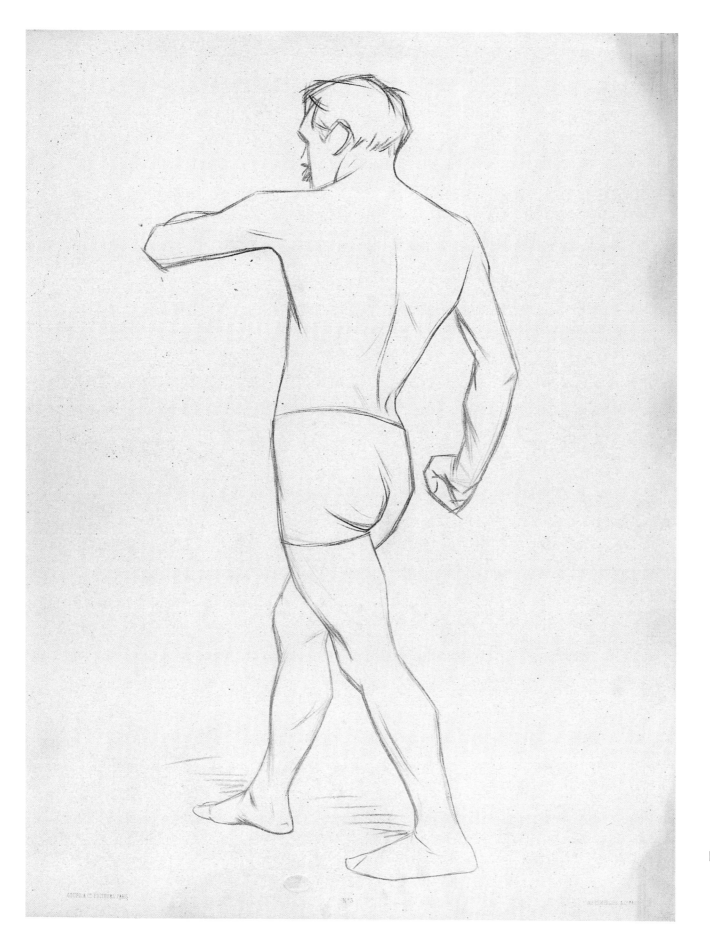

Plate III, 3

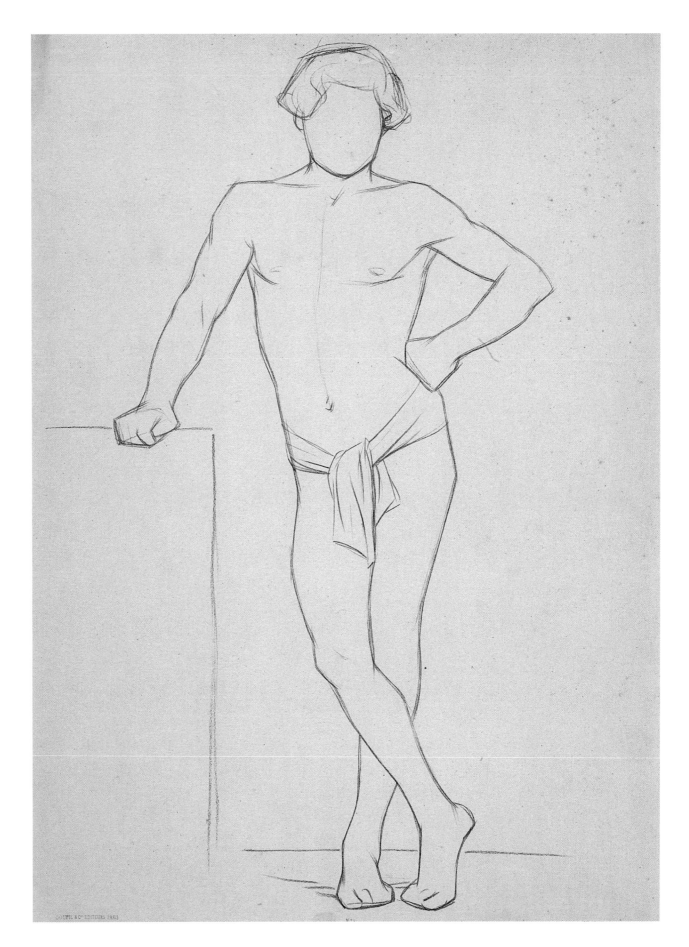

Plate III, 4

Plate III, 5

Plate III, 6

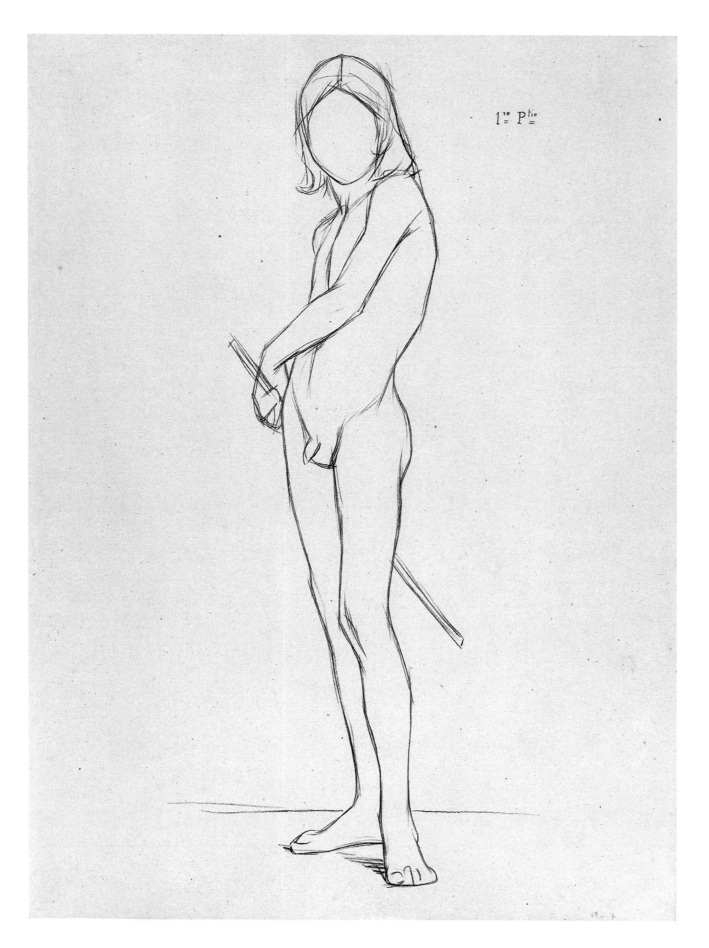

1re P^{tie}

Plate III, 7

192

Plate III, 8

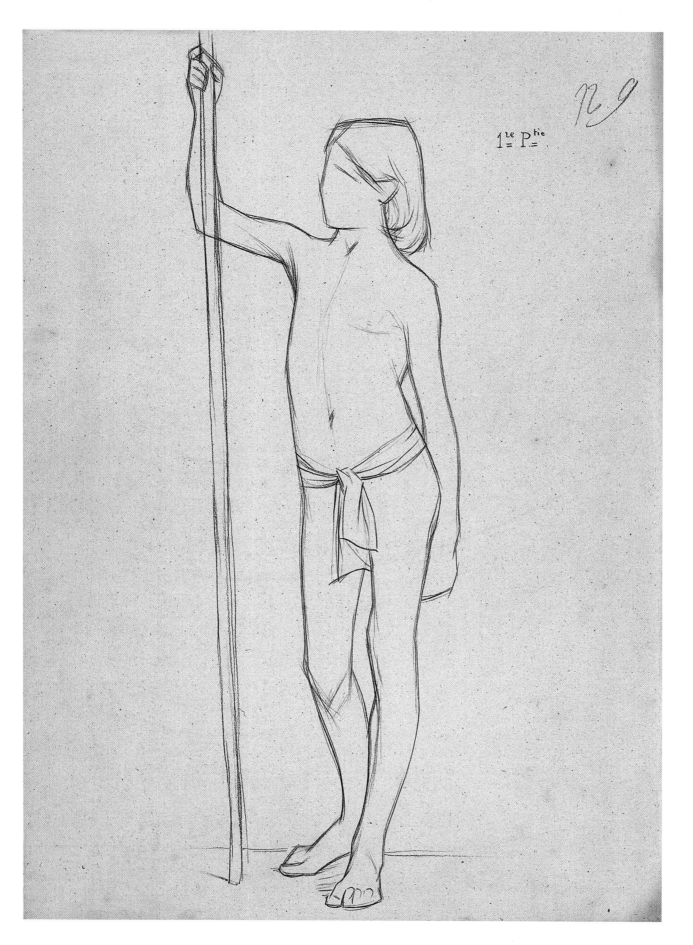

1^{le} P^{tie}.

Plate III, 9

Plate III, 10

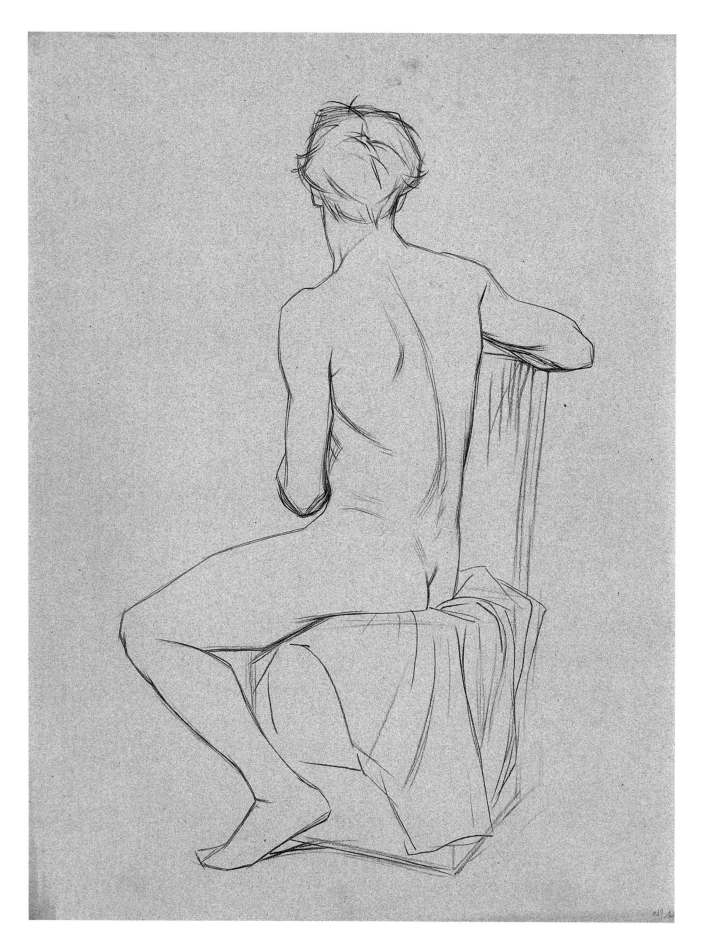

Plate III, 11

Plate III, 12

Plate III, 13

Plate III, 14

GOUPIL & C.ᵉ EDITEURS PARIS

N.º 15

IMP. LEMERCIER & C.ᵉ PARIS

Plate III, 15

Plate III, 16

Plate III, 17

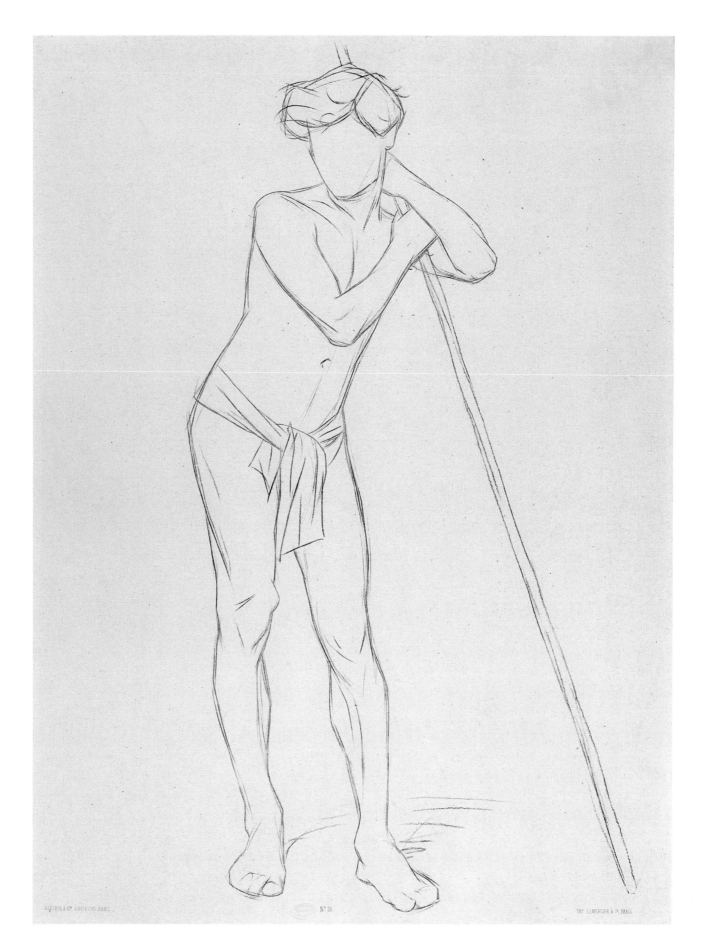

Plate III, 18

COUPIL & Cⁱᵉ EDITEURS PARIS.   N° 18   IMP. LEMERCIER & Cⁱᵉ PARIS.

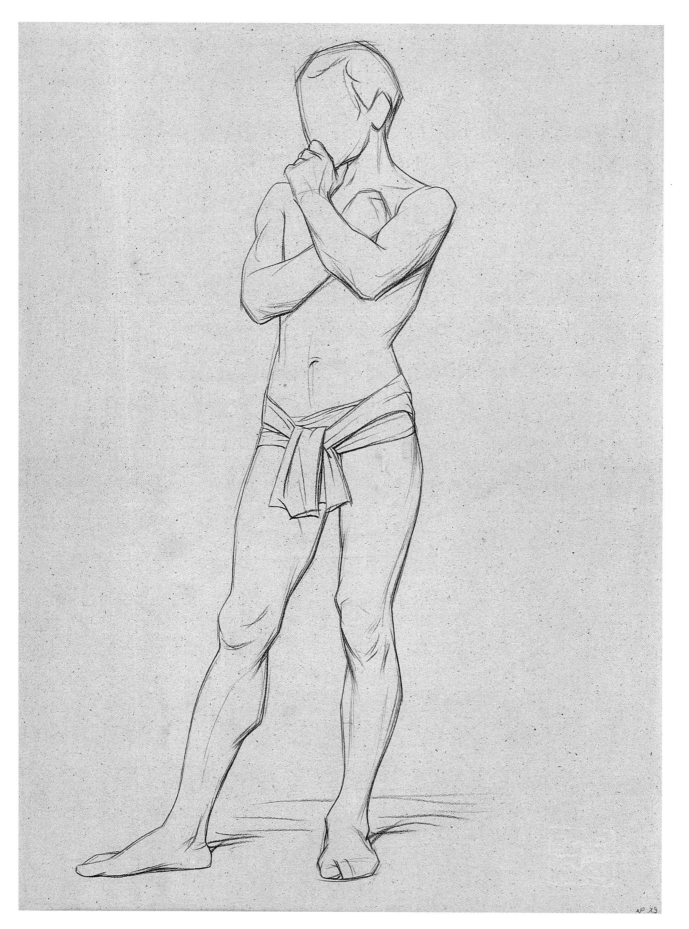

Plate III, 19

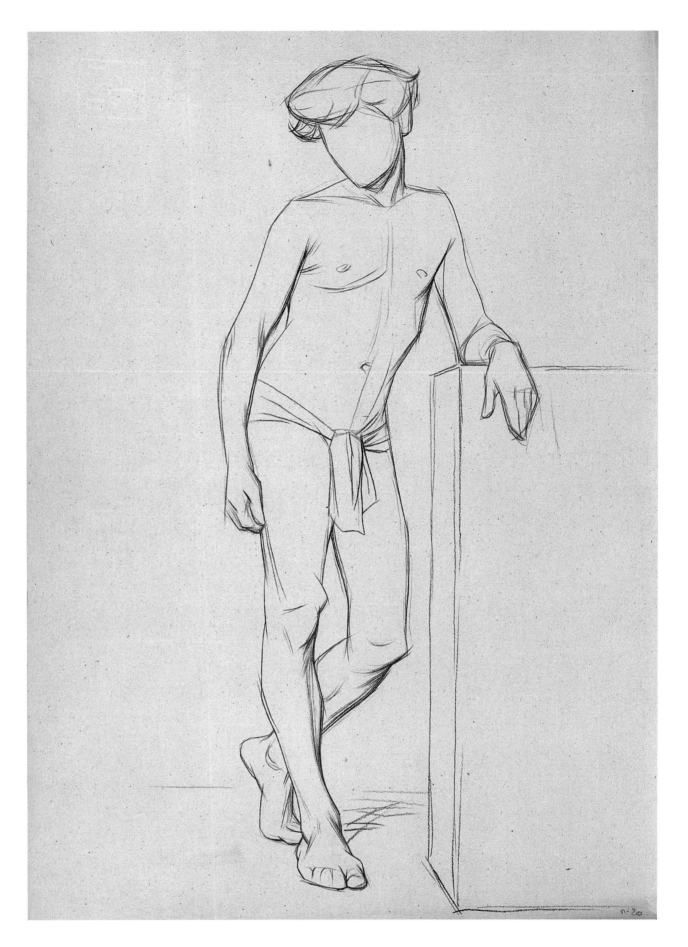

Plate III, 20

205

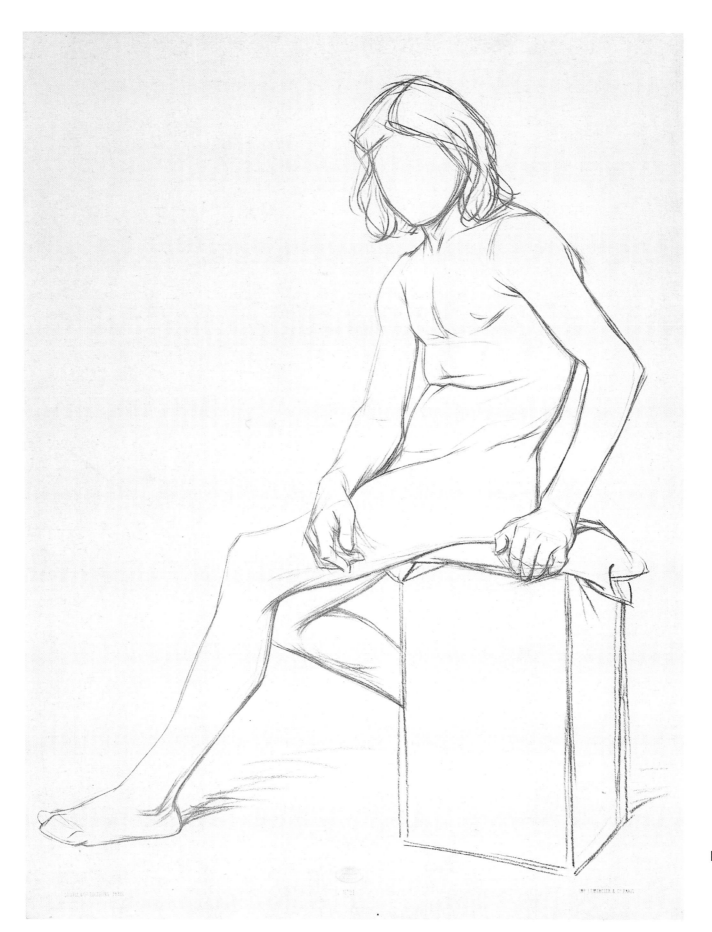

Plate III, 21

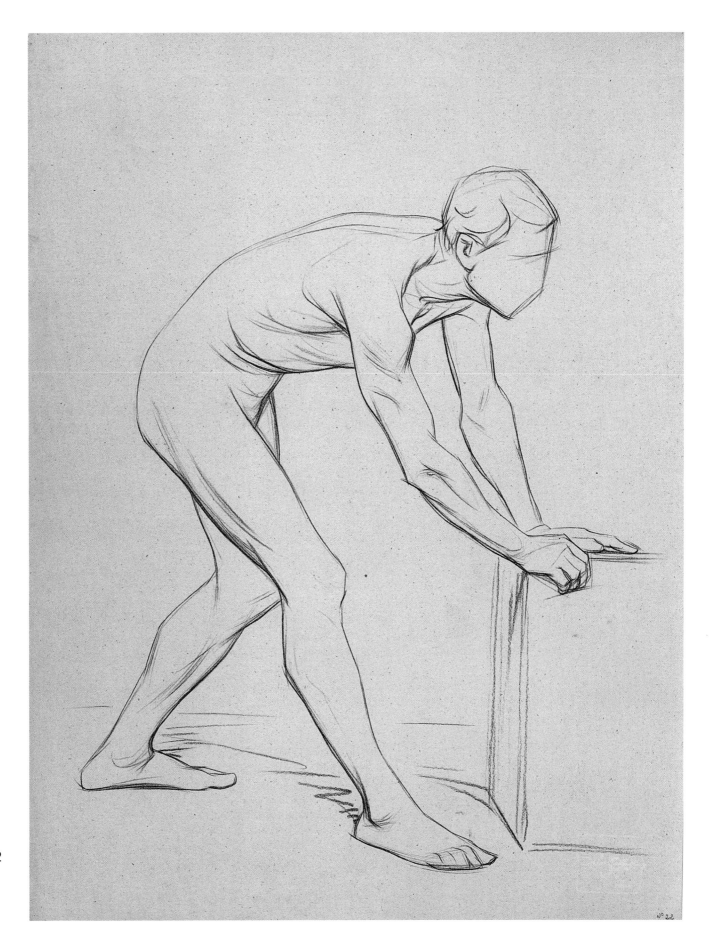

Plate III, 22

207

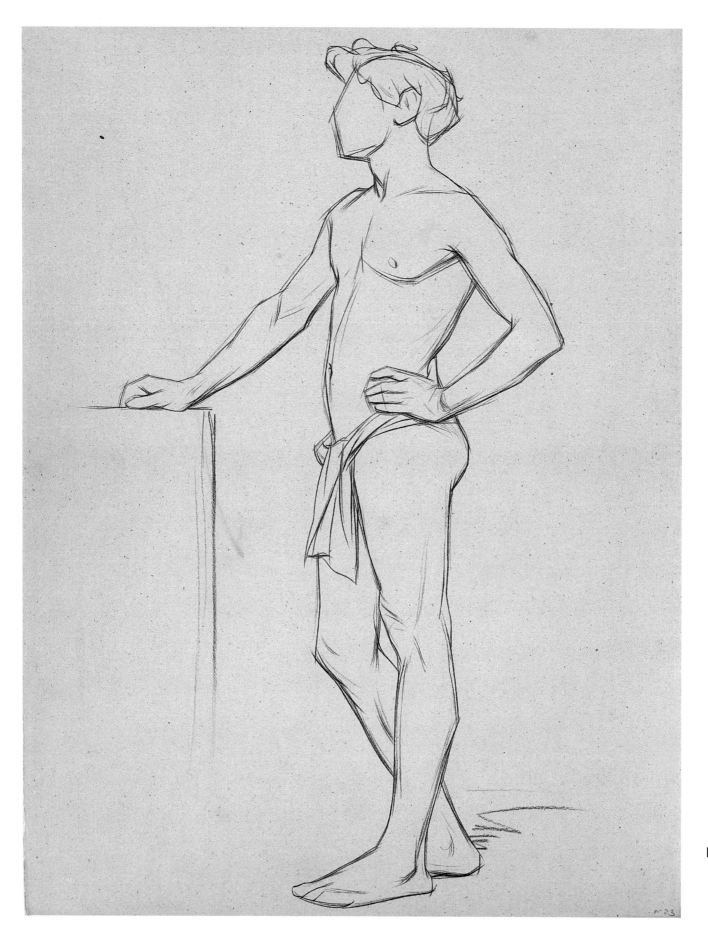

Plate III, 23

Plate III, 24

Plate III, 25

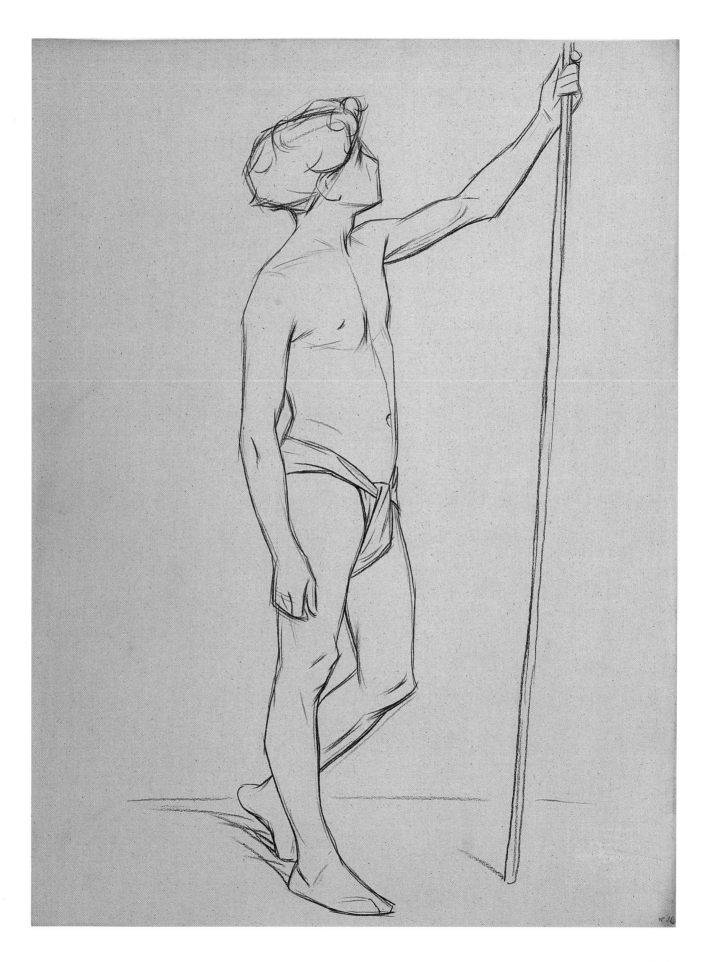

Plate III, 26

211

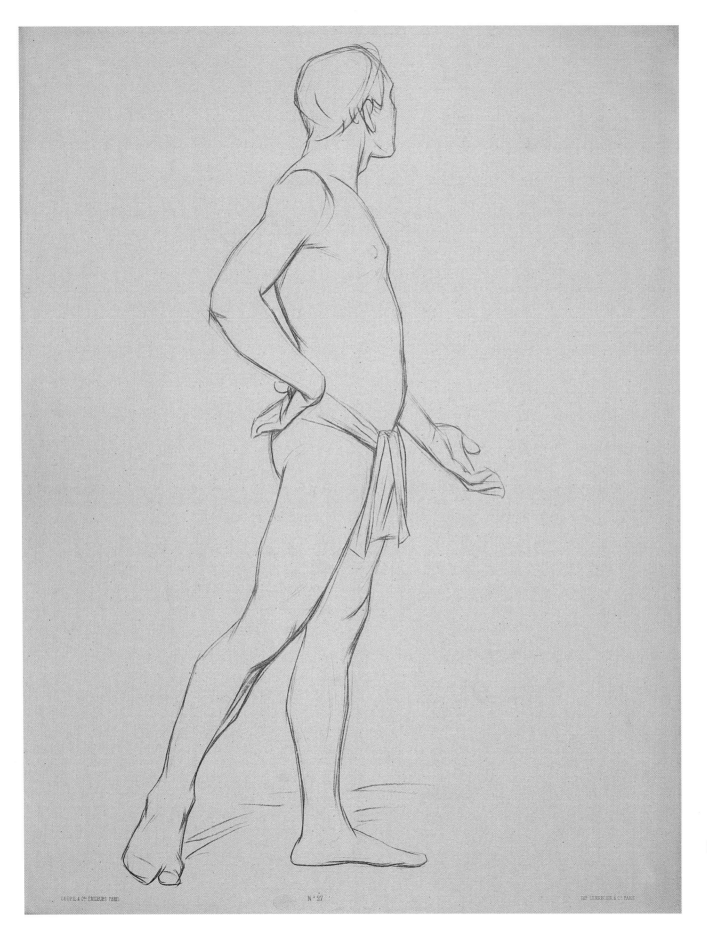

Plate III, 27

Plate III, 28

213

Plate III, 29

214

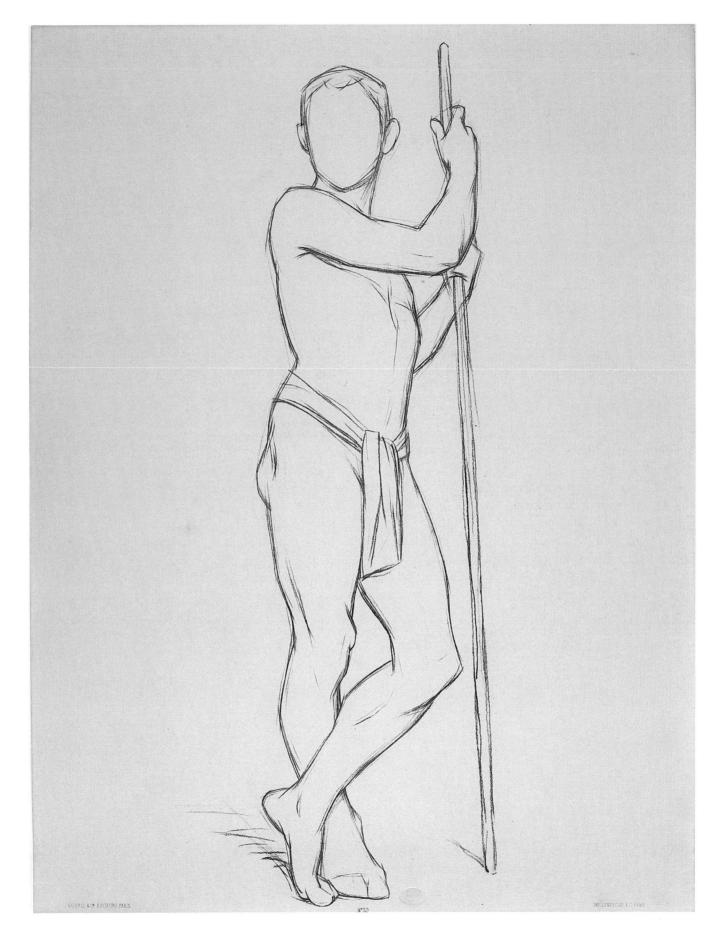

Plate III, 30

GOUPIL & Cᵉ ÉDITEURS PARIS   Nᵒ30   IMP LEMERCIER & Cᵉ PARIS

215

Plate III, 31

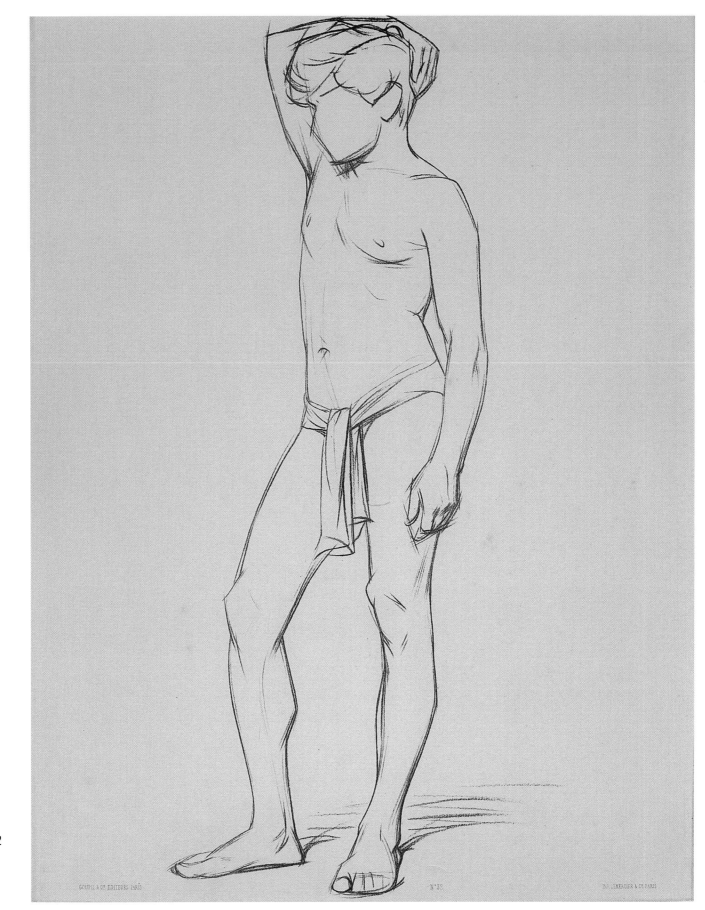

Plate III, 32

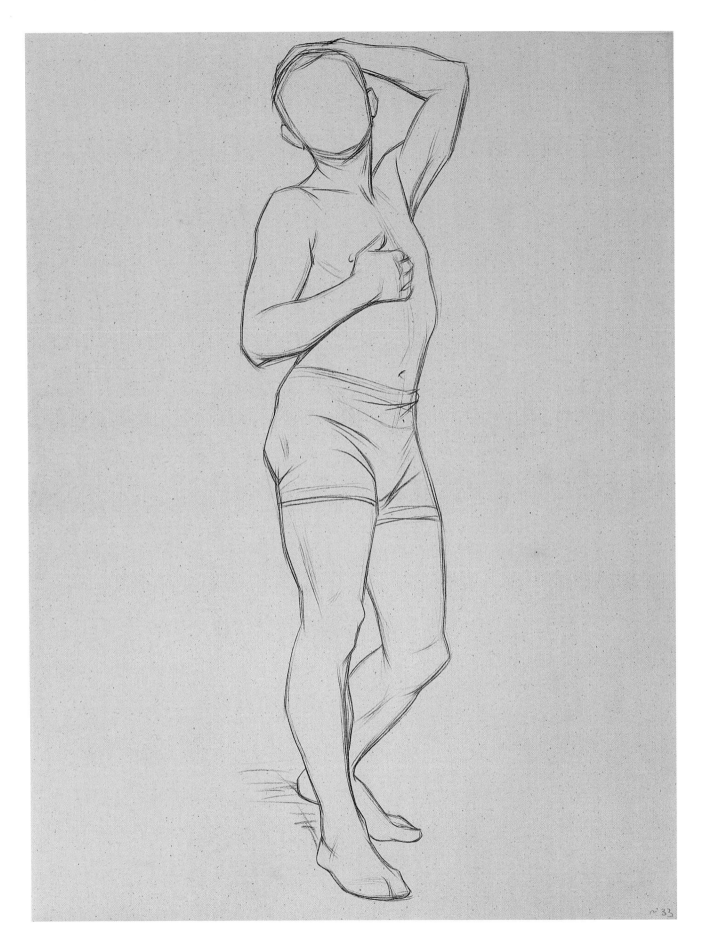

Plate III, 33

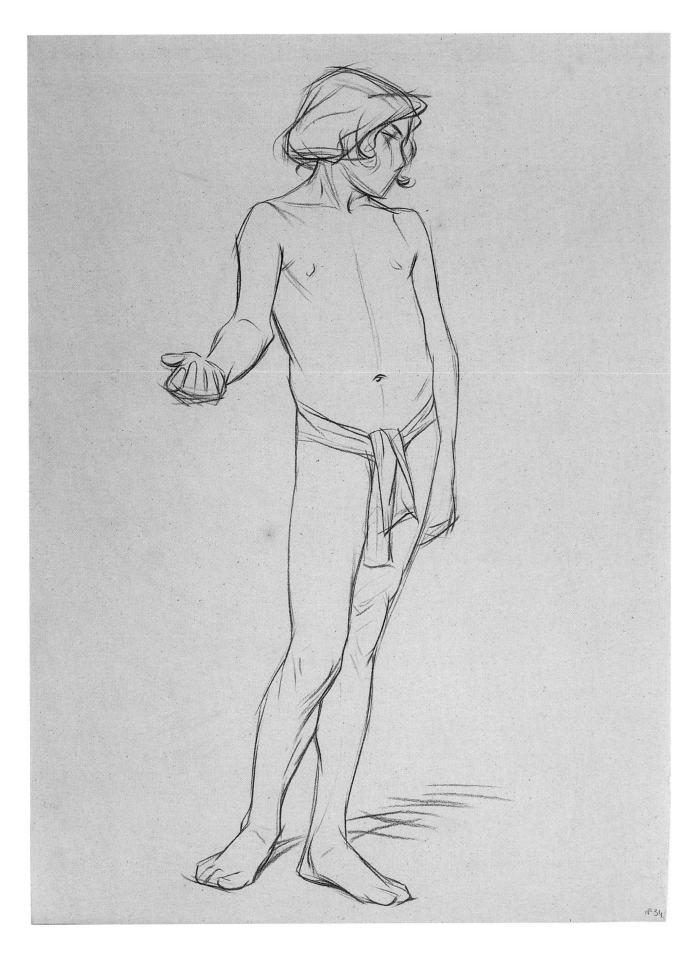

Plate III, 34

219

Plate III, 35

Plate III, 36

221

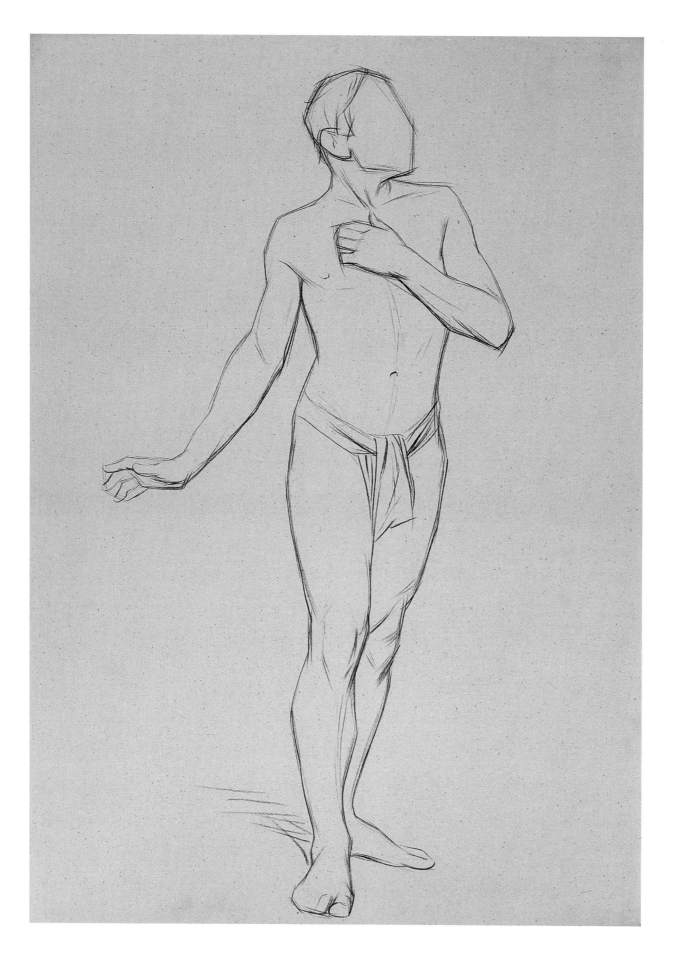

Plate III, 37

Plate III, 38

223

Plate III, 39

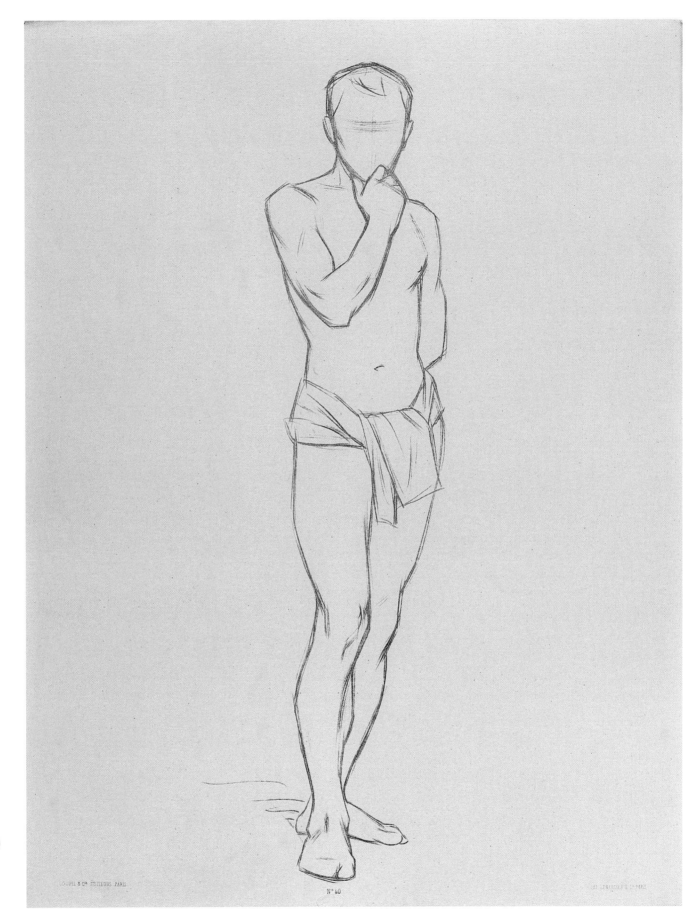

Plate III, 40

225

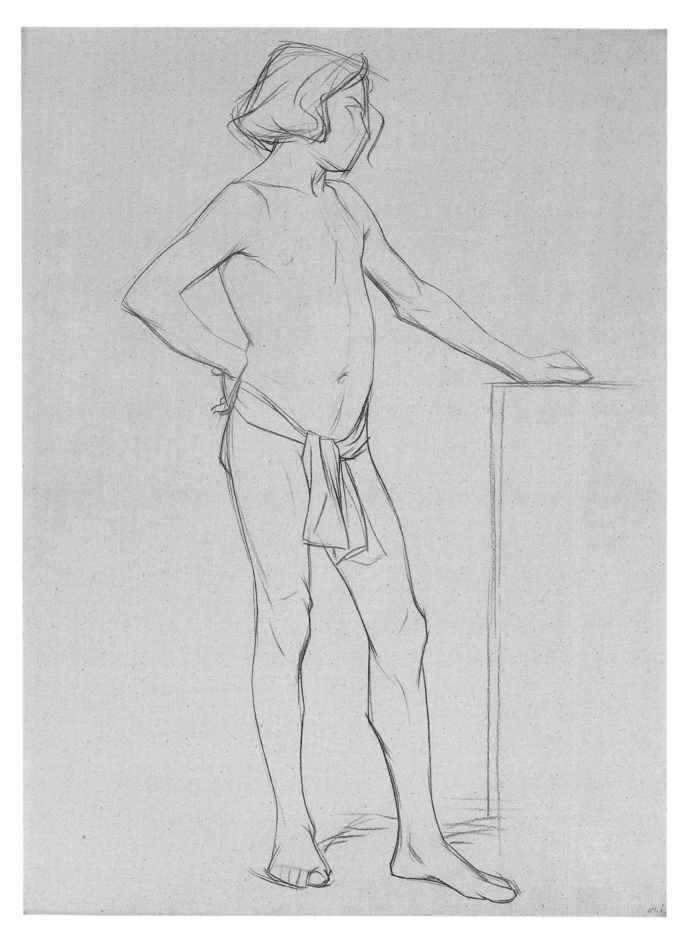

Plate III, 41

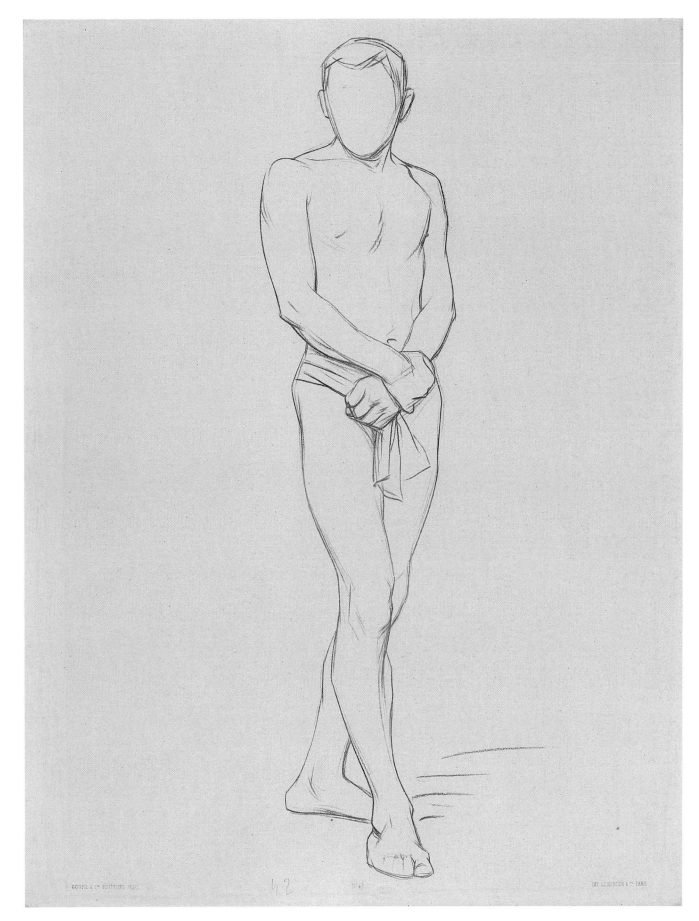

Plate III, 42

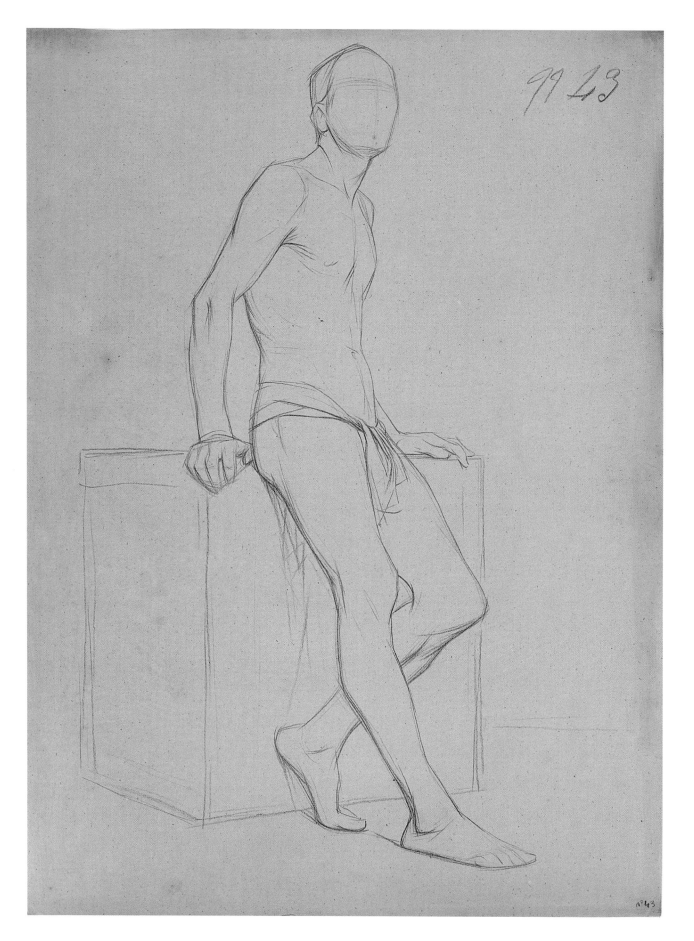

Plate III, 43

Plate III, 44

Plate III, 45

Plate III, 46

231

Plate III, 47

Plate III, 48

GOUPIL & C.ᵉ ÉDITEURS PARIS

Nº 49

IMP. LEMERCIER & C.ᵉ PARIS

Plate III, 49

234

Plate III, 50

Plate III, 51

Plate III, 52

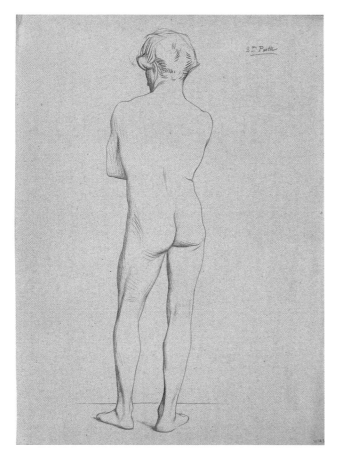

Plate III, 53

Plate III, 54

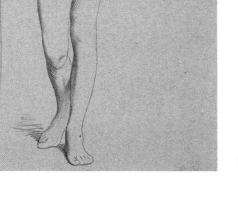

Plate III, 55

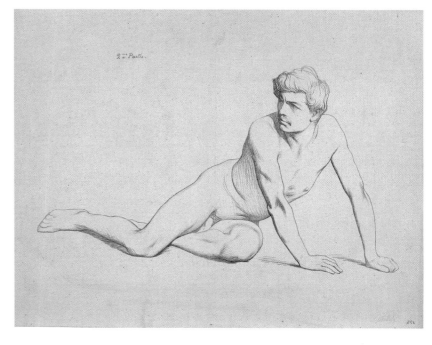

Plate III, 56

238

Plate III, 57

Plate III, 58

Plate III, 59

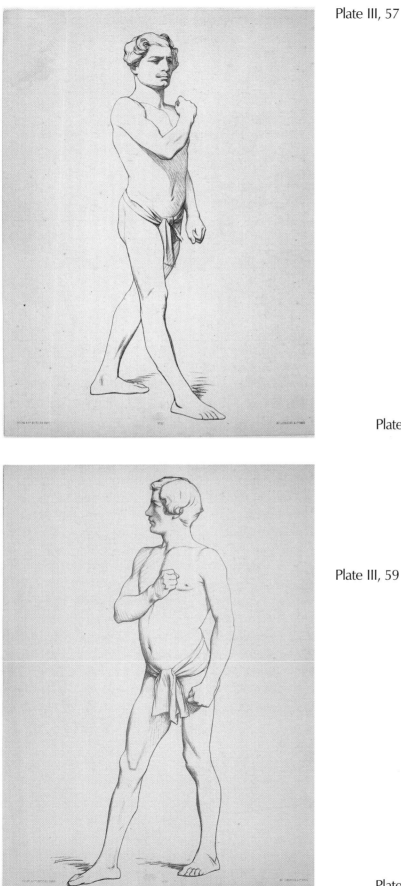

Plate III, 60

Notes on the Plates

[N.B.: The French titles used and translated are the modern inventory descriptions of the Goupil Museum. In the text "left" and "right" refer to the left and right side of the model.]

Plate III, 1. Young man, leaning on his right elbow.
(Jeune homme, accoudé sur le bras droit.)

The first drawing is the most simplified of all the figure drawings, reduced to an almost abstract figure of straight lines and angles; the emphasis is on proportion. Bargue wants you to begin the figure with straight lines right from the start. We suggest a plumb line from the bottom of the stand upon which the boy is sitting, through the margin of the stomach, and up the back of the neck. This is a popular, effective pose for a full-length portrait.

Plate III, 2. Young boy, standing while leaning on a box.
(Jeune garçon, debout accoudé à un mur.)

This is a funerary or mourning pose. The weight is divided between the feet and elbows. Pay attention to the very faint construction lines that travel between the buttocks and the upper body. *Note*: the line of the stand is an absolute vertical.

Plate III, 3. Standing man, walking, rear view.
(Homme debout, marchant, de dos.)

This drawing of a fighter is more developed than the previous two: the arms, the hair, and the shoulders are more detailed; the pose, with its many foreshortenings, is more sophisticated. In places the outline cuts into the body, following the shape of a muscle. These overlappings are one of the techniques Bargue teaches. The outer limits of the scapula are clear on his right side, while its inner limit is indicated inside the back. The bones of the elbows show through the skin. The lower part of the raised arm is drawn with two quick, overlapping lines. This is a pure outline, as if all the light were coming from the front, flattening the form. A light from a window or a lamp would cast a clear shadow across the body, as in most of the cast drawings in part I. The shadow line should be drawn first and then the shadow filled in with an even tone; the halftones may be added next. However, shadows are not recorded in most of the figure drawings of part III. I suggest a plumb line from the lower tip of the ear, through the knee, to the left toe. When drawing from nature—such as a studio model—it is best to make your first reference points from the bottom up. Although it does not make much difference when you are working from a drawing, you might start forming the habit of doing so now. With a model the position of the feet would be marked on the stand and would always be in the same place. The rest of the body will sway and move as the pose settles in. As a consequence, secure reference points taken from the feet will always be useful and assuring.

Plate III, 4. Standing young man, leaning on a box, front view.
(Jeune homme debout de face, appuyé sur un mur.)

This simple pose, with the emphasis on the outline, has only minor areas of foreshortening. There are some careful indications of anatomy in the upper body and arms. An important area is the interlocking of the model's left hand with the waist. In some areas you can guide yourself by the distances across empty spaces outside the figure, between limbs and the body (the so-called negative spaces). A good plumb line could run from the left side of his neck to the top of the little toe of the standing leg.

Plate III, 5. Standing young man leaning on a box while holding up his left arm, front view.
(Jeune homme debout, de face, appuyé sur un mur, levant le bras gauche.)

The model in this drawing was probably holding onto a pole or a rope suspended from the ceiling. There is tension in various parts of the body; pay attention to how this tension is shown and how it affects the anatomy. His right arm is very accurately foreshortened. Leaning on the box produces a tilt of the rib cage and gives an angle to the hips. An axis or medial line through the head and torso will help organize the proportions of the upper body; furthermore, the symmetrical features of the body will align themselves more or less perpendicular to the line.

Plate III, 6. Standing young man, leaning on a pole, left leg set back, side view.
(Jeune homme debout, de côté, appuyé sur un bâton, jambe gauche en arrière.)

This is a sensuous, serpentine pose with a surprising sense of movement initiated by the act of looking over the shoulder. There are broad and subtle overlappings along the back and shoulders. The plumb line can run from the right heel to the back side of the head.

Plate III, 7. Standing young man holding a pole behind himself in his left hand.
(Jeune homme debout tenant un bâton de la main gauche derrière lui.)

The young man could be pulling a sword out of a scabbard, albeit with his left hand. Concentrate on the rhythms of the muscles in the arm and legs. The plumb line runs from the part of his hair through his right foot.

Plate III, 8. Standing young man, right hand on his head, rear view.
(Jeune homme debout de dos, main droite sur la tête.)

The angles of the arms and legs are set in rhythmic response to one another. The main weight is on the left leg, although equilibrium is maintained by the right leg. The negative spaces are small but critical since they indicate that the legs are not touching. On the model's back Bargue uses predominantly straight lines to describe internal structure.

Plate III, 9. Standing young boy holding a pole, head turned toward the pole.
(Jeune garçon debout tenant un bâton, tête tournée vers le bâton.)

The only areas of pronounced foreshortening are in the legs and feet. The pole forms a safe negative space along the boy's right contour, which you can use to check your measurements and your shapes.

Plate III, 10. Standing man holding out his right hand, rear view.
(Homme debout de dos tendant la main droite.)

This could be the stance of an orator conceding a point (with his hand upturned); or it could be a repoussoir figure framing the central event of a history painting. The tension of the pose is described in several parts of the outline, particularly in the waist and thighs. The plumb line could run from the peak of the head to the inside right ankle.

Plate III, 11. Seated man, rear view.
(Homme assis de dos.)

After a popular studio pose, this is a more advanced, lifelike study. The outline is accurate, especially along the left side of the back, and the upper part of the leg. Light lines describe the medial line of the figure, and some of the internal structure. The weight of the body is emphasized by the flat line of the buttock and the bulging flesh above it.

Plate III, 12. Standing young man, right hand on left shoulder.
(Jeune homme debout, main gauche sur épaule droite.)

This could be the biblical David with his sling over his shoulder, getting ready to shift his weight forward (notice the tilt of the pelvis) for the pitch. The plumb line is from the peak of the head down. You may need vertical reference lines to assist you in plotting this narrow figure. In a free-standing pose the head is always positioned over the weight-bearing or standing leg (the other leg is sometimes referred to as the free or play leg).

Plate III, 13. Standing young boy holding a pole, legs crossed.
(Jeune garçon tenant un bâton, jambes croisées.)

The visible hand and the feet are drawn with great clarity and emphasis. Watch the proportions of the slightly foreshortened left arm. The pole steadies the model and furnishes an extra reference line from which to judge. This drawing also demonstrates that the head is usually positioned over the weight-bearing leg (although here it tilts slightly off center due to the support by the pole).

Plate III, 14. Standing young man turning his back, hands crossed behind him.
(Jeune garçon debout tournant le dos, mains croisées dans le dos.)

This could be a prisoner tied from behind. The angular outline stresses the boniness of the young body. There are obvious anatomical notations on the back, such as the scapulae, and more subtle ones on the legs, such as the tendons of the hamstring. The plumb line runs from the top of the neck to the inner right ankle.

Plate III, 15. Standing older man leaning against a stand while holding a pole.
(Vieil homme debout adossé à un mur tenant un bâton.)

The vague support—a wall or a stand—is clearly improvised; nevertheless sketch it in so that you will not forget how the weight is distributed in the stance. Observe how a faint line has organized the angles of the man's lower chest and belly. This observation relates nicely to the method taught in part I. Moreover, there are many negative spaces to help further organize the limbs. The plumb line runs from the peak of the head to the right toe.

Plate III, 16. Seated man, leaning on a wall.
(Homme assis, accoudé sur un mur.)

There are few straight lines in this splendid pose. The seated young man leans back against a table, so that all of the body recedes: the face is back, the hip forward. Study the position of the back and the upper torso. There are many good lessons in foreshortening in the drawing: one leg comes forward, the other goes back; the torso leans away from the viewer, the head is behind the shoulder; and the right arm reaches back, foreshortening the upper arm as well as the forearm.

Plate III, 17. Seated young boy, holding an object in front of him in his hands.
(Jeune garçon assis, tenant un objet devant lui dans ses mains.)

This is a moody pose, as if the boy were reading his fortune in a teacup. All the forms are lean and sinuous. His left leg, however, is in an inelegant view (a situation that often arises when models are carelessly posed and may be inevitable when many students work from the same model). Relate the right leg to the left as you draw.

Plate III, 18. Standing young man leaning on a pole.
(Jeune homme debout appuyé sur un bâton.)

This is a shepherd's pose. The young man is not so graceful as some of the other models; his legs are knobby and long. Pay attention to the articulation of the elbows and knees, which are described by Bargue with overlapping lines.

Plate III, 19. Standing young man, frontal view, with hand on chin.
(Jeune homme debout de face, main sur le menton.)

This could be either a pensive or pugilistic pose. Is he sizing up his opponent or simply dreaming? Although the model has articulated fingers, the toes are summarily indicated. The loincloth is elegant in that it does not obscure the silhouette. Part of each arm is in foreshortening. Study the marks that Bargue makes for internal features. Usually they describe the boundaries of major anatomical forms as well as the center lines of the torso. The plumb line runs from the right corner of the face to the inner ankle of the model's left foot.

Plate III, 20. Standing young boy leaning on a stand, left leg crossed behind the right leg.
(Jeune garçon debout accoudé à un mur, jambe gauche croisée derrière la droite.)

In this highly developed drawing, the arms, hair, shoulders, legs, and feet are all detailed. The pose is sophisticated; the parts of the body are arranged in interesting juxtapositions. Notice the overlapping of muscles on the legs. Carefully measure the foreshortening of the reclining upper arm. The several negative spaces can be used as guides to the shapes around them. Such sharp lines show the angles produced by the bones, whereas the softer lines show muscle and fat.

Plate III, 21. Seated young man, three-quarter view, hair somewhat long.
(Jeune homme assis, trois quarts, cheveux mi-longs.)

The slump of the torso is shown by curves, the boniness of the arms and legs by straight lines. Bargue's main interest is in the upper body, particularly in the tension of the supporting left arm. The plumb line runs from the peak of his face to the side of the box. This helps in measuring the distance from the box to the left toe, and so forth. In addition to a plumb line, extra horizontal reference lines (all perpendicular to the plumb line) would help to organize the various areas, say, through the top of the box under the buttocks and through the navel and left elbow.

Plate III, 22. Man in profile, leaning to the right.
(Homme de profil, penchant à droite.)

This is a pose with some action or movement indicated. It is a successful drawing, especially in the forms of the two arms. It is important to transcribe the negative spaces accurately. The tension between the left and right side of the contour is subtle and sensitive; small deviations in the contours may detract from the roundness of the figure. Work from side to side across the form and notice the variety of the contours. Normally a depression on one side will be paired with a swelling on the other. Again, some well-placed horizontals will help divide the figure into manageable areas.

Plate III, 23. Standing man, right hand on a stand.
(Homme debout, main droite posée sur un mur.)

In this classic pose the head tilts back with a hopeful expression. The left knee is locked to indicate support and the belly protrudes forward gently, adding grace and movement to the pose. You need horizontals here as well as a plumb line.

Plate III, 24. Man seated upon the ground, his head on his knees.
(Homme assis sur le sol, tête sur les genoux.)

The youth in this splendid drawing holds a pose similar to that in the famous painting of 1836 by Hippolyte Flandrin entitled *Young Nude Boy Seated by the Sea*, study *(Jeune homme nu assis au bord de la mer. Étude),* in the Louvre Museum in Paris. The areas of greatest interest are his right arm and hands, the vertebrae on the back of the neck, and the blocky feet. You'll need horizontals as well as a plumb line to organize your work.

Plate III, 25. Standing man, seen from behind.
(Homme debout de dos.)

A back view is always difficult because of the ever-changing morphology of bones, muscles, and fat. This is an older model, and the muscles and fat under the skin have sagged in a few places. The weight displacement is on his left leg, throwing the left hip up and the right one down. The foreshortened right foot is obscured, making it difficult to copy. You have to measure the angle of the foot from a horizontal. Bargue's attention to structure and the shift of bodily weight is as refined as his subtle notations of age. This drawing is a splendid example of the mixture of the idealist and realist interests of the Academic Realists.

Plate III, 26. Standing young man, holding a pole in his left hand while looking at it.
(Jeune garçon debout, tenant un bâton de sa main gauche et le regardant.)

This is a well-developed drawing with accurate proportions. The gesture is subtle: the boy looks up toward the pole in his left hand (as if he were admiring a banner lost to our view); he shifts his weight to the right leg, and moves his left leg back. As a result, his shoulders and hips tilt at opposing angles. Opposing angles similarly animate the fingers, which are carefully arranged on his left hand.

Plate III, 27. Standing man, in profile, holding out his open left hand.
(Homme debout de profil tendant la main gauche ouverte.)

This subtle drawing emphasizes the placing of the weight on the model's left leg. The head is clear in its turn and structure. The hand bent back by the akimbo arm is noteworthy; the other hand—held in a position that a model would find hard to maintain—seems to have given Bargue trouble. This hand appears to have been added later; its gesture is not supported by any connection with the body, which inevitably makes it look too large. Such an effect was perhaps unavoidable given this pose. The classical rule is to choose a view in which all major joints are visible.

Plate III, 28. Young man seated on a box, his right hand supporting his head.
(Jeune garçon assis sur une caisse, main droite soutenant la tête.)

Traditionally a cheek resting on the hand of a seated figure represents melancholy. The most famous examples are Dürer's 1514 engraving *Melancholia I* and Rodin's 1880 statue *The Thinker (Le Penseur).* Melancholy is one of the traditional four humors (or temperaments) that determine human physiognomy and personality. The humors were an integral part of the Neoplatonic system; even today they are embedded, albeit discreetly, in popular astrology. The emphasis is on the supporting left arm; notice the taut deltoid and scapula. Faint construction lines are visible throughout, and there are indications of the ulna and patellae. The hand is carefully blocked out to show its importance and to balance it with the foreshortened arm and hand holding up his head. Use horizontal reference lines as needed.

Plate III, 29. Young man in profile holding a ball.
(Jeune homme de profil tenant une balle.)

The figure holds a ball, putting the biceps of the arm in flexion to support the weight; the tension runs down the right side of the body through the locked knee. The far side of the body, not bearing the weight, is relaxed and lowered. The entire torso from buttock to neck is exemplary. The chest, belly, and thigh are described by a single curved line.

Plate III, 30. Standing man in three-quarter view, holding a pole with both hands, his left leg crossed over the right.
(Homme debout de trois quarts, tenant un bâton à deux mains, pied gauche croisé devant le pied droit.)

This drawing of a mature man with fairly well developed anatomy emphasizes gesture and movement. Compare him with other models, such as in plate III, 33, and note how his contours differ from the younger men. The right foot seems to be an undeveloped thought.

Plate III, 31. Seated man in profile, his hands crossed on his left knee.
(Homme assis en profil, les mains croisées sur genou gauche.)

This is an excellent example of a well-proportioned figure with judicious indications of anatomy. The negative shapes are clear and therefore helpful. The foremost leg is accurately drawn. The arms are twisted over one another. Make sure you pay attention to the rhythms in the outlines of the legs and arms by precisely placing the high and low parts of their curves, all the while comparing one side of the contour to the other. Draw the left and right sides at the same time, using the internal indications of anatomy to guide you.

Plate III, 32. Standing young man, right arm resting on his head.
(Jeune homme debout, bras droit posé sur la tête.)

When copying this model remember that the two legs are on different planes!

Plate III, 33. Standing man, right hand on his chest, left hand on his head.
(Homme debout, main droite sur le poitrine, main gauche sur la tête.)

The model imitates the pose of Michelangelo's Dying Slave (L'Esclave mourant) in the Louvre Museum in Paris (studied in plate III, 30 and shown complete in fig. 13). The view is higher than in the other drawings. Notice how the feet steady the body, as if he were standing on an incline. Be sure to maintain the character of the model's maturity throughout the drawing; his limbs are thicker and more muscular than those of a youthful body. The drawing of the right arm and of the right leg is noteworthy.

Plate III, 34. Standing young man, turning his head to the left, right hand extended.
(Jeune homme debout, tournant la tête vers la gauche, main droite tendue.)

This very exciting drawing combines the subtlety and grace of the *contrapposto* pose with an extended, foreshortened, and accurately viewed right arm. It exemplifies several qualities of a good drawing, combining an interesting pose, a legible mood, clear anatomy, and a simplified line.

Plate III, 35. Half prone man, holding himself up on his hands.
(Homme presque allongé se soutenant de ses bras.)

The pose echoes that of the famous *Dying Gaul* (ca. 190 B.C.) in the Capitoline Museum in Rome. Each arm bears weight in a different manner. The foreshortened legs must be copied exactly. Throughout, the information—external and internal—is very subtle. The boy was probably first inscribed within a triangle of construction lines, with a plumb line through one side of the head and left hand. Try to imagine such geometrical shapes around your figures as you were trained to do in the cast drawings (see comments to plate I, 5).

Plate III, 36. Standing man in profile, hiding his face in his hands.
(Homme debout de profil, se cachant le visage dans les mains.)

The pose is for Adam being expulsed from Paradise; it is a rhetorical pose, with codified gestures. It could be used for anyone in despair or grief. Throughout this section Bargue helps the student develop a repertoire of archetypal poses. Learn to distinguish their individual qualities; consider how figures can communicate meaning and emotion.

Plate III, 37. Standing man, left hand on his chest, right hand extended.
(Homme debout, main gauche sur la poitrine, main droite en arrière.)

The man strides forward, looking up as if imploring someone and putting his hand on his chest to demonstrate his sincerity. Note the grace of the extended arm and the carefully posed fingers. This pose is traditional and, although rhetorical, it is full of emotion. The fact that a pose is traditional does not mean it is worn out and useless; a good artist can infuse standard iconography with fresh expression by rethinking and experiencing the emotion, resulting in a figure that is legible and communicative.

Plate III, 38. An archer.
(Homme tirant à l'arc.)

This drawing emphasizes the archer's balance and the muscular tension throughout his body —especially in his arms and upper body—as he pulls the bowstring back.

Plate III, 39. Seated man, hiding his face in his hands.
(Homme assis, se cachant le visage dans les mains.)

The student must learn to draw the figure in a variety of poses—seated, lying down, leaning—with each position presenting specific problems. This pose is complex, containing more detailed observation than hitherto. Be careful to preserve the relationship of height and width so that the negative spaces retain their descriptive quality. Also pay attention to the breaks and overlappings in the contour.

Plate III, 40. Standing man, right hand on his chin, left hand behind his back.
(Homme debout, main droite sur le menton, main gauche dans le dos.)

Since antiquity the gesture of the hand to the chin has traditionally symbolized pensive contemplation. Among the problems that should be noted, the arms are both rather cumbersome in their foreshortening. Although the right arm is well drawn, the left elbow seems out of place. The upper torso looks small relative to the hip, legs, and head. Assume this pose and check the appearance of your arms in a mirror, or ask a friend to assume the pose for you. The rhythms of the legs are well conceived and the disposition of weight seems logical.

Plate III, 41. Standing young man, left hand resting on a stand, right hand akimbo.
(Jeune homme debout, main gauche posée sur un mur, main droite sur les reins.)

This is an assertive pose. The young boy stands alongside the box, with one hand resting on it. Between the weight of the hand on the box and the weight on his standing leg, an equilibrium is established which resounds throughout the body. The concavity of his right side emphasizes the jut of the pelvis and then quickly turns into the convexity of the buttock. A good plumb line would run down the center of his body, from the pit of his neck through his navel. Note how many straight notations have been turned into curves.

Plate III, 42. Standing young man, hands crossed over his waist.
(Jeune homme debout, mains croisées sur le ventre.)

Here is another bound prisoner, this time with his arms in front. This could also be Christ, either presented to the populace in the traditional *Ecce homo* iconography, or being baptized by John the Baptist. The drawing is a good example of anatomical articulation, particularly in the legs around the knees and calves.

Plate III, 43. Man leaning against a stand, face lifted up.
(Homme appuyé le long d'un mur, visage vers le haut.)

This is a very relaxed pose seen from a low position. The legs are strong, the fingers nicely posed and spaced, and there are great subtleties of observation in the outline of his left side, from shoulder to groin. Note the depiction of his weight-bearing right hand.

Plate III, 44. Supine young man.
(Jeune homme allongé.)

A supine young man with foreshortening effects across his whole body. This is a pose often used for the dead Christ, the dead Abel, and various martyrs. Use vertical reference lines to divide the body into manageable portions; for example, from the ends of the fingers of the right hand up through the thighs. Continue relating one part of the body to the other.

Plate III, 45. Standing man, his hands behind his head, looking up.
(Homme debout, mains derrière la tête, visage en haut.)

This is a wonderful drawing of a man stretching. The relatively low placement of the ears assists the foreshortening of the head. Muscular rhythms play throughout the body. Very light interior lines show features of the anatomy, such as the under part of the chin. On both sides you can see the insertion of the latissimus dorsi into the armpit. The left leg is seen from the medial angle, that is, from the inside, and should be much wider than the right leg, seen from the front, which it is not.

Plate III, 46. Man pulling on a rope.
(Homme tirant une corde.)

This drawing depicts a man—with a rather small head for his body—pulling on a rope. The gesture suggests that he is pulling against someone. The right pelvis has dropped and the left buttock is compressed as a result of the physical effort. The tapering of the right bicep into the forearm is precisely noted. In drawing an action, pay attention to the muscles that are working. They contract and change their forms: muscles are shorter and fuller in flexion and leaner and longer in extension.

Plate III, 47. Standing man, arms spread out.
(Homme debout, bras écartés.)

This pose could represent surprise or astonishment. This is a very developed drawing even without a face. Notice the guiding schematic lines of the hands: Bargue groups the fingers together rather than drawing them individually. This example provides an extremely good drawing lesson: you see indications of the sternum, the knees, and the ankles. Bargue does not want you to forget where the bones are. He has caught the movement of the figure in all the limbs. Note the foreshortening of the right forearm and of the left upper arm. Academies in the nineteenth century usually had ropes hanging from the ceiling to help the models maintain such poses.

Plate III, 48. Standing young man, three-quarter rear view, crossed arms.
(Jeune homme debout, trois quarts de dos, bras croisés.)

This drawing shows a bystander in pensive mood. The young man has fine legs, broad buttocks, and faintly defined shoulder muscles. From this point on the facial features are included, and the internal anatomical features are better described than in previous examples.

Plate III, 49. Man lying on his right side.
(Homme allongé sur le côté droit.)

The bearded model sleeps, lying on his side. The shape of his body is altered by gravity, not by effort. Noteworthy is the sag of the abdomen, an area that is carefully developed by Bargue.

Plate III, 50. Seated man, left profile, slightly leaning toward the right.
(Homme assis, profil gauche, légèrement penché sur la droite.)

This pose is that of a bather seated on a rock and looking out to sea or of a faun perched to watch mortals (or nymphs) at play or work. Keep in mind that he is leaning away from you: his head is behind his shoulder; the shoulder is behind the thigh.

Plate III, 51. Semi-prone man, holding himself up by his hands, the left leg turned back, head in profile.
(Homme allongé se tenant sur les avant-bras, la jambe gauche repliée, la tête de profil.)

This older man is posed like the young man in plate III, 35. The problem here is drawing an older body with some sagging forms. There is a strong sense of loose skin over the frame and musculature, which characterizes the age of the man. The anatomy is more developed; the hands are refined, as is the head. Even so, the anatomical observations do not distract from the general unity. A pedantic convention is used for the first time: the lower lines of the limbs and body are emphasized by thickening. This mannerism is more exaggerated in the next drawing. Whether this was done by Bargue or a revising editor is not known.

Plate III, 52. Supine man, a pillow under his back.
(Homme allongé, coussin sous le dos.)

A mature man is shown in a supine position in this very finished drawing. Almost all of the outline has been made firm and definite—perhaps by another hand. Supine and prone figures are hard to plot. To determine the plumb line, find a center point at the groin, equidistant from head and feet. Several additional verticals will help relate smaller features.

ACADÉMIES BY ANOTHER HAND

For some reason—perhaps the confusion of the war of 1870—Bargue did not finish all sixty plates of part III. Evidently the original intention was to conclude with a set of finished drawings, that is, drawings with firm outlines, internal notations, without organizational lines, and even with some chiaroscuro. One would love to have such a set in Bargue's hand. Unfortunately someone else—competent but without the style or grace of Bargue—drew the last eight plates, which are reproduced here, in smaller format, not as models to copy but for the historical record.

Plate III, 53. Standing man, rear view, arms crossed on chest.
(Homme de dos, debout, bras devant.)

Plate III, 54. Standing man, pushing something.
(Homme debout poussant quelque chose.)

Plate III, 55. Standing young man, right hand resting on a stand.
(Jeune garçon debout, main droite posée sur une table.)

Plate III, 56. Man seated on the ground, his hands holding his chest up, left leg folded back, head in three-quarter profile.
(Homme assis sur le sol, les deux mains soutenant son buste, la jambe gauche repliée, la tête de trois quarts à droite.)

Plate III, 57. Standing man, right hand on left shoulder.
(Homme debout, main droite sur épaule gauche.)

Plate III, 58. Standing man, his two hands joined behind his head, without a loincloth.
(Homme debout, les deux mains jointes sur la tête, sans cache-sexe.)

Plate III, 59. Standing man, three-quarter view, right hand on his heart, with a loincloth.
(Homme debout, trois quarts face, main droite sur le cœur, avec cache-sexe.)

Plate III, 60. Standing man leaning against a stand, wearing a loincloth.
(Homme debout accoudé, avec cache-sexe.)

CHARLES BARGUE, THE ARTIST

At the beginning of his career, Charles Bargue (ca. 1826/27–1883) was an accomplished lithographer but a rather lowly and prosaic inventor when it came to subject matter. The exercise of making virtually all of the 197 plates for the *Drawing Course* between 1865 and 1871 either elicited from the artist or instilled in him talents and abilities hitherto not manifested, for the lithographs shimmer with the poetry of observation and display great technical dexterity. After the publication of the *Drawing Course*, Bargue blossomed forth as an excellent painter of small, intense figures filled with the exuberant tensions of life in settings imbued with mysterious color harmonies. Between the completion of the plates for the course in 1871 and his death in 1883 as a result of a fatal stroke, he produced a small number of masterpieces.

Bargue's career as a lithographer began with the publication of *Twenty Childhood Scenes, after* [drawings by] *Henri de Montaut (1825-1890) (Vingt scènes enfantines d'après H. de Montaut,* 1847–48). The series was published by Chartrain, a Parisian publisher of popular prints.[49] Two lithographers are named: Charles Bargue and Paul Bargue. Paul was most likely a relative, perhaps an uncle or a brother. (According to the hospital records, Charles's father was named Jacques.)[50] It seems highly likely that he learned drawing and lithography within a family of professional lithographers; nothing else is known about his early artistic education.

Thus, Bargue was an artist trained outside official circles. His training as a painter was probably informal, too, but it seems to have been very good, for he possessed a solid if basic oil technique. As an unofficial artist, he left no paper trail, no files or archival documentation. For the public and for art historians, who have busied themselves with mostly famous and officially trained artists, Bargue's mysterious career points to the existence of a thriving world of talented, well-trained albeit unknown, unofficial artists hitherto neglected in studies of nineteenth-century French art.

As a painter Bargue is little known for several reasons besides the general prejudice against genre painting in the late nineteenth century, which kept his works from receiving serious consideration. His production was small: just over fifty titles or subjects are known. We know through reproductions what some thirty of these paintings actually looked like; of that number only seventeen finished works have been located. The rarity of his paintings is compounded by the fact that most of the known works are hidden away in private collections; the few that are scattered in public collections—mostly in the United States—are seldom displayed. Paintings by Bargue appear only infrequently at auction.

Bargue's Early Career

Bargue's first paintings, like the lithographs he rendered from drawings by other artists, were evidently of rather tawdry subjects, mainly low-comedy scenes. His two earliest known paintings were lithographed by H. Massard: *Caught Napping (La Partie de chat)*[51] of 1847 (painting 1), and *Addition and Subtraction (Addition et soustraction)* (painting 2). They were both published in London by Owen Baily on the Strand. The first depicts a bachelor dozing over a book while his house is being overrun by his pet cats. The second shows a prelate being cheated by his maid. In the early lithographs—aimed at popular, sentimental, and certainly not highbrow tastes—the drawing is usually routine, with just a few areas of solidity. The figures are vulgarly caricatured, with clichéd, easily recognizable expressions and gestures. There are few fresh conceptions or ideas in the paintings.

Fig. 25.
Charles Bargue. *The Generous Heart. (Le Cœur qui se donne.)* 1847.
Lithograph. 45 x 56.5 cm. (18 x 22 in.)
Cabinet des Estampes, Bibliothèque nationale, Paris.

Fig. 26.
Charles Bargue. *The Venal Heart. (Le Cœur qui se vend.)* 1847.
Lithograph. 45 x 57.5 cm. (18 x 22 in.)
Cabinet des Estampes, Bibliothèque nationale, Paris.

Fig. 27.
Charles Bargue. *Inimical but Not Blind Passions. (Passions ennemies mais non aveugles.)* 1848.
Lithograph. 36 x 28 cm. (14 x 11 in.)
Cabinet des Estampes, Bibliothèque nationale, Paris.

His earliest recorded independent publication comprised two thematically related lithographs after his own drawings—each a folio genre scene—one entitled *The Generous Heart (Le Cœur qui se donne)* and the other *The Venal Heart (Le Cœur qui se vend),* both dated 1847; they depict scenes with a simple narrative and moral lesson. Each has a developed village landscape in the background (see figs. 25 and 26). Thus, it would seem that Bargue's professional career both as a lithographer and painter started in the same year of 1847.

An 1848 caricature entitled *Inimical but Not Blind Passions (Passions ennemies mais non aveugles)* (fig. 27), which depicts Louis Philippe brooding over his loot while in exile, is Bargue's only known venture into political cartooning—and perhaps one of the last prints to lampoon the king.

Bargue's popular, easily identifiable types—the tippling cleric, the insubordinate servant, the neglectful bachelor—were part

Fig. 28.
Charles Bargue. *A Friend in a Pinch. (The "Taking" of Sebastopol, or, The Pinch of Sebastopol).*
(La Prise de Sébastopol.) 1855.
Lithograph. *63 x 47,5 cm (24.8 x 18.7 in.)*
Cabinet des Estampes, Bibliothèque nationale, Paris.

of the popular print tradition. Although they remind us of the types developed and popularized by Honoré Daumier and Cham (pseud. comte Amédée-Charles-Henry de Noé, 1819–1879), they are not accompanied by Daumier's sense of humanity; indeed, some of the subjects have hints of cruelty in them. *Caught in the Fact* [*sic*] *(Prise et surprise)* of 1851 (painting 10), the earliest known satirical print labeled "painted and lithographed by Charles Bargue," shows his comical sense to be uninventive as well as overplayed.

At best Bargue's comical compositions recall some of the stilted jokes occasionally produced by Horace Vernet (1789–1863). Compare Bargue's *A Good Friend in a Pinch (La Prise de Sébastopol),* of 1855, after his own drawing (fig. 28), with Vernet's *A Grenadier of the Guard at Elba (Un Grenadier de la garde à Elbe),* ca. 1823, a painting in the Wallace Collection in London (fig. 29). Bargue's lithograph is a rather insensitive pun on the taking of the city and the taking of a pinch of a popular brand or type of snuff. It would be nice to think that the young Bargue learned his painting technique in the exalted circle of an excellent painter like Vernet. More likely he studied Vernet's multitudinous prints as models. Most of Bargue's early print production was published by F. Sinnet, whose shop was located in the rotunda of the passage Richelieu in the center of Paris. Bargue was probably not a salaried employee in Sinnet's atelier—if Sinnet even maintained one—but was more likely a freelancer, working in his own or his family's atelier, or even renting a space in someone else's workshop. He probably got commissions wherever he could in a competitive atmosphere that did not pay very well. Although there are plates showing that he worked for other publishers, the major source of his early commissions seems to have been Sinnet.[52] In the late 1860s he started working for Goupil—probably the print publisher with the highest standards, the best distribution, and the most generous fees. Much of Bargue's employment for Sinnet involved the making of lithographs after the drawings of Henri de Montaut, who continued to furnish drawings as models for lithographs, most of which may charitably be described as "cute," such as the series of mothers and children dating from 1852 (figs. 30 and 31).

He was evidently a good copyist. In studying the early lithographs Bargue did after other artists, one gets the impression that the mediocre, conventional figures in the lithographs were probably just as good as the models in the drawings supplied to him. His figures did not improve as quickly as his lithographic technique, which became increasingly more masterful. The earliest drawings that he copied were of children or pretty girls with large eyes and hair centrally parted over broad foreheads *à la mode anglaise*. The figures were placed against the unembellished white ground of the paper, without borders, with few accessories, and a few landscape or interior elements—in short, inexpensive, sentimental prints. His own earliest lithographic subjects—those he drew after his own drawings or paintings—were more ambitious, with the comic scenes often in fully worked out interiors. Thus, judging from the evidence before 1860 of lithographs of Bargue's lost paintings, his subject matter was, for the most part, cheap, vulgar, and—when meant to be comic—banal. Just a handful of the prints of the *Les Sylphides* series rise to some distinction.

It is most surprising, then, that the paintings of his last decade are of a consummate skill and sophistication. Bargue eventually became one of the most refined painters of his time. How this change from banal to exquisite taste came about in two decades can only be faintly surmised from the few known facts about his career and the evidence of the lithographs and the few paintings that I have managed to locate.

Fig. 29.
Horace Vernet. *A Grenadier of the Guard at Elba.*
(Un Grenadier de la garde à Elbe.) 1823.
Oil on canvas. 64.7 x 54.8 cm. (25.5 x 21.5 in.)
The Wallace Collection, London.

From Craftsman to Artist: Bargue's Early Development

Bargue's skills as a lithographer were evidently recognized early, for in 1850 he was given an important commission by Sinnet in partnership with Ernest Gambart, the famous Belgian dealer, who would become the distributor in London. This commission was for a series entitled *Les Sylphides*, which consisted of twenty plates after compositions either drawn or painted by Bargue (see Bargue's paintings 3–9, 14–16).

Each large quarto print depicts a park or country landscape with two large nudes (see fig. 32). The poses are coy and naïvely erotic yet never actually lascivious despite some traditional sexual iconography. The drawing of the figures, while not amateurish, is rather mediocre and routine, without the solidity of the nudes of the academic painters published as lithographs by Goupil & Cie, the most fashionable of the print publishers. Even so, the poses are often inventive as well as provocative, and the erotic appeal cannot be denied. The backgrounds of woods or parks (shrubs and trees), water (fountains, ponds), and garden accessories (an occasional stone fountain or a statue) are excellent. Bargue exploits a

Fig. 30.
Charles Bargue, lithographer, after H. de Montaut.
Supplication. 1852.
Lithograph. 44 x 32.5 cm. (17.5 x 12.75 in.)
Cabinet des Estampes, Bibliothèque nationale, Paris.

Fig. 31.
Charles Bargue, after H. de Montaut.
The Spoiled Child. (Le Petit Gâté.) 1852.
Lithograph. 44 x 32.5 cm. (17.5 x 12.75 in.)
Cabinet des Estampes, Bibliothèque nationale, Paris.

great range of textures and values; occasionally patches of light filtered by the foliage fall gracefully and delicately on the bodies of the nudes and across the backgrounds. The first series of twenty prints was successful enough for a second series to be started, which was described on the title page as "a collection of graceful subjects taken from nature to serve in the study of the female form" ("une collection des sujets gracieux d'après nature pour servir à l'étude de la femme"). An informative frontispiece could be put in a print shop window, whereas the sheets of the nudes could not; the description was meant to indicate to potential purchasers that the subjects were enjoyable nudes as well as models for artists to copy. We do not know if the second series progressed beyond the three known prints, but they did show a great improvement in figure drawing compared to the nudes of the first series (see fig. 33), although one should not believe the claim that the figures were all drawn from nature, especially since the heads were popular types and often look superimposed (see paintings 14–16). Of great interest is the fact that ten of the known sheets carry the inscription "Painted and lithographed by Charles Bargue" ("Peint et lithographié par Charles Bargue"). None of these paintings has been found.

Bargue continued working for Sinnet—probably as an independent contractor—until at least 1855, lithographing many extensive series drawn by a number of popular print artists. These series were often open-ended, accumulating new numbers as long as the public would buy them. The production of the first series of *Les Sylphides,* for instance, was spread out over half a decade. He also did lithographs of his own subjects in two colors.

The earliest prints made by Bargue after his own work are dated 1851: *Caught in the Fact* [*sic*] *(Prise et surprise)* (painting 10) and *A Bachelor's Kitchen (Un Ménage de vieux garçon)* (painting 11). Despite the banality of the subject matter, the kissing husband and the maid are better drawn than any figures hitherto, and the two form a group with convincing movement; if Bargue used some other artist's group to serve as a model for his couple, he had sense enough to choose a good model. Most likely he had profited from the experience of composing two figures together in the many plates comprising *Les Sylphides*.

At the same time, the attempt to launch an original series featuring half-dressed, sexy girls lounging about in bed in various inviting postures died out after three numbers. One was entitled *May I Come In? (On attend la réponse)* (fig. 34). The other two subjects, after paintings by Bargue, were *The Last New Novel (Un Roman du cœur)* and *Castles in Spain*

Fig. 32.
Charles Bargue. *The Heart's Avowal.*
(Les Sylphides, no. 1, Les Petits Secrets.) 1850.
Lithograph. 48.5 x 30 cm. (19 x 11.75 in.)
Cabinet des Estampes, Bibliothèque nationale, Paris.

(*Châteaux en Espagne*), both now lost (see paintings 12 and 13). The lush juxtaposition of various fabric textures against soft skin, as well as jumbles of bedside accessories, show a great advance in Bargue's technical skills; he was quickly becoming a distinguished lithographer.

Inadvertently amusing is the risqué rather than pornographic cycle of lithographs in octavo by Bargue after paintings and drawings by H. de Montaut, who seemed to know where the public taste lay. The series was entitled *Rivers of the World* (1852–56). Each plate featured a native lady of uncertain virtue, dressed in a scanty version of the local costume, posing on the banks of a famous river, such as the Guadalquivier, the Danube, and the Neva. Concluding the twenty-one numbers—it evidently had a long and successful run—is *On the Banks of the Ohio (Aux bords de l'Ohio),* in which a befeathered Indian maid lies supine on the grassy bank of the river (fig. 35). Bargue's work on these prints was interspersed with commissions for several other series by other artists, along with some single prints after his own drawings. Most of this work was published by Sinnet: six scenes of mothers and children after drawings by Bargue (1852); four subjects after Bouguereau (1855); seventeen scenes of eighteenth-century life at Versailles after drawings by Montaut—with all the participants portrayed as children (1849); seven scenes of court life under Napoleon III after drawings by Montaut (1854); and numerous single prints after various masters. Bargue was kept very busy, but it is doubtful that he became rich thanks to all these commissions.

Fig. 33.
Charles Bargue. *Nature's Books*.
(Les Sylphides, no. 2, L'Oracle des bois.) 1850.
Lithograph. 48 x 30 cm. (19 x 11.75 in.)
Cabinet des Estampes, Bibliothèque nationale, Paris.

Fig. 34.
Charles Bargue. *May I Come In?*
(On attend la réponse.) 1851.
Lithograph. 27.5 x 39.5 cm.
(11 x 15.5 in.)
Cabinet des Estampes,
Bibliothèque nationale, Paris.

Fig. 35.
Charles Bargue, after H. de Montaut.
On the Banks of the Ohio.
(Aux bords de l'Ohio.) 1856.
Lithograph. 27.5 x 39.5 cm.
(11 x 15.5 in.)
Cabinet des Estampes,
Bibliothèque nationale, Paris.

Bargue and Goupil & Cie

Beginning in 1858 Bargue did occasional lithographs after works by other artists for Goupil & Cie, probably as a freelancer. The artists whose works he copied for Goupil were better and more accomplished—both in their range of subject matter and professional abilities—than those who had hitherto furnished him with models. His 1860 lithograph after Auguste Toulmouche's (1829–1890) *A House of Cards (Le Château de cartes)*, a lost painting (fig. 36), is a good example. Toulmouche, a successful genre painter who belonged to Gérôme's old circle of Néo-Grec painters, was one of Goupil's regular artists. English readers will recognize the iconography as dependent upon Augustus Egg's (1816–1863) work entitled *Past and Present, I* (Tate Britain), a painting early (1858) and famous enough to have served as the inspiration for Toulmouche. The woman, seated by the dining room table, dreamily plays at building card castles while her children look on in dismay. She is contemplating an adulterous affair; their future is in danger. Bargue's control of space, tonal values, figures, and textures is splendid; he seems to have been inspired by his model, one so much more satisfactory intellectually and aesthetically than the admittedly unsophisticated and weaker models supplied by Montaut. This intimate contact with upper-class taste was an education for the artist. For Goupil he also did a number of large portraits, suitable for framing, of notables after Paul Delaroche (1797–1856), such as a splendid Marie Antoinette (fig. 37).

A series of equestrian subjects after models by the famous animal painter Alfred de Dreux (1810–1860) was undertaken for Goupil in 1861. These complex compositions both honed and exploited Bargue's skills; their success no doubt gave him a reputation as a lithographer among Goupil's customers (fig. 38).

Fig. 36.
Charles Bargue, after Auguste Toulmouche. *A House of Cards.*
(Le Château de cartes.) 1860.
Lithograph. 39.4 x 50.6 cm.
(15.5 x 20.25 in.)
Goupil Museum, Bordeaux.

In 1862 Bargue lithographed two boudoir scenes for Goupil—*The Dancing Slippers (Les Souliers de bal)* (fig. 39) and *The Empty Cage (L'Oiseau envolé)*—after Charles Chaplin (1825–1891) that exactly fitted his inclinations and talents: scenes of partially undressed young ladies in well-curtained chambers. Chaplin's nudes have a delicate sensuous quality far superior to Bargue's own inventions; the erotic quality was heightened by the sense of a private space being invaded. The prints are excellent. Finally Bargue's skill with nudes and drapery are in perfect balance.

The work done for Goupil not only gave Bargue informal training and furthered his intellectual aspirations but also brought him into direct contact with famous contemporary artists whose works were sold by the firm, including Gérôme. One could easily imagine that Toulmouche or de Dreux, both readily available in Paris, more or less looked over Bargue's shoulder as he worked, and most likely the artists themselves personally approved the proofs.

The first painting by Bargue of which we have a photographic reproduction is a small oval 1860 portrait in grisaille of Napoleon III entitled *Sa Majesté, l'Empereur des Français* (painting 17). The portrait, in turn, is a copy done with astounding but neat exactitude by Bargue, probably after a photograph. The grisaille, in turn, was reproduced as a photograph and sold by Goupil. The portrait was the first painting by Bargue accepted for sale by Goupil, and there is a sad story connected to it. After the portrait was photographed, the firm had it framed for forty-one francs forty centimes. No patriot stepped up to purchase it, and after three years in stock it was put up for sale at the *Hôtel des Ventes*. There it was sold for the price of the frame. It has not been heard of since.

Fig. 37.
Charles Bargue, after Paul Delaroche. *Marie Antoinette.
(Marie Antoinette.)* 1858.
Lithograph. 80.5 x 56 cm. (31.75 x 22 in.)
Cabinet des Estampes, Bibliothèque nationale, Paris.

Fig. 38.
Charles Bargue, after Alfred de Dreux. *Fording the Stream.*
(Le Passage du Gué.) 1861.
Lithograph. 57 x 81.5 cm. (22.5 x 31.75 in.)
Cabinet des Estampes, Bibliothèque nationale, Paris.

Fig. 39.
Charles Bargue, after Charles Chaplin. *The Dancing Slippers.*
(Les Souliers de bal.) 1862.
Lithograph. 63 x 47 cm. (24.75 x 19 in.)
Cabinet des Estampes, Bibliothèque nationale, Paris.

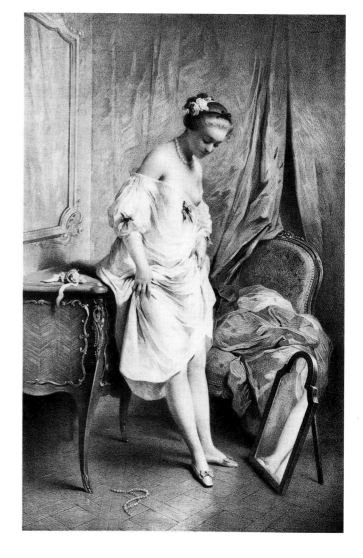

Goupil's Reductions

Goupil & Cie evidently kept on call a group of talented younger painters to make "reductions" on demand of popular paintings by the great contemporary names on its roster.[53] *Reduction* is an ambiguous term that evades the accepted nomenclature of repetition, replica (both by the artist) and copy (by another hand). These reductions appear to have been supervised by the master concerned; they also seem to have been produced after the originals with the aid of the original preparatory drawings and sketches. For instance, there are several known reductions of Gérôme's painting *The Cock Fight (Combat de coqs)*, the large version of which was shown at the Salon of 1847 (it is now in the Musée d'Orsay in Paris). Although they are all very precisely drawn and slavishly detailed, they are just not fine enough in the detail to equal Gérôme's practice; thus, they must all have been done by copyists.[54] The common dissatisfaction with the ubiquitous versions of Ary Sheffer's (1795–1858) *Francesca da Rimini* and with the equally common reductions of Delaroche's more popular paintings is probably due to their being reductions—that is, to their having been painted by other hands.[55]

The practice of producing reductions for sale is not so reprehensible as it might at first seem. Painting in oil using the nineteenth-century academic technique was painstaking and slow, which limited the income of popular masters, who could turn out only so much work. Since the abolition of the guild system and, with it, the apprentice system during the French Revolution, artists no longer maintained the large workshops that masters before 1800 had considered normal; for the most part they worked, single-handedly, or with one paid assistant; if they were teachers, they could rely on occasional help from their better students. Bouguereau did most of his own reductions until the early 1870s, when he turned almost all of the commissions for reductions over to talented assistants.

It seems highly likely that Charles Bargue was among those painters of occasional reductions. According to the Goupil stock books, in 1863 he was paid three hundred francs for a copy of a pastel by Chaplin entitled *Lady with Pigeons (Tenue aux pigeons)*. The copy could be of any of a number of compositions by Chaplin, who produced many full- and half-length figures of beautiful women amusing themselves with birds of various sizes and species. A reduction of Gérôme's *Prisoner (Le Prisonnier)* was painted in 1863. It is of very high quality and was long taken for a replica by Gérôme's own hand. When it is compared to other Gérômes (as was possible during the Gérôme exhibition held in Dayton, Ohio, in 1972), there is a telltale flatness about the figures, a trait usually indicative of a copy. However, in all its details the work is so fine that it might be the work of Bargue. One of several reductions of *The Cock Fight* was sold by Goupil in 1868—when Bargue and Gérôme were preparing the publication of the *Drawing Course*. Gérôme's American biographer Fanny Field Hering recounts that while visiting Gérôme in the mid-1880s, she heard him include Bargue in a discussion of his "beloved students."[56] Nonetheless, Bargue was never recorded in Gérôme's atelier at the École des Beaux-Arts. He may have been promoted, so to speak, from being Gérôme's copyist to being his assistant and thence to being his pupil—almost like an old-fashioned studio apprenticeship, albeit outside the official track.

The *Drawing Course*

The quality of Bargue's lithographic work was certainly appreciated in the Goupil circle of painters and printmakers, which of course included Gérôme. At some point in the mid-1860s he received the commission to be the lithographer for the *Drawing Course*. It was probably a cooperative affair, Gérôme choosing the casts and drawings to be used as models in the first two volumes of the course, as well as the artists who made the drawings for the lithographer to work from. A biography of Gérôme's student Lecomte du Nouÿ (1842–1923) was published in 1906. It contains a chronological list of the artist's paintings, which for the year 1865 mentions "seven drawings after the antique for the Goupil Course (Gérôme, director)," as well as a drawing after Antonello de Messina (1430–1479) for the course, which was not used in the *Drawing Course*.[57] Based on other sources, Roger Diederen has identified several of the drawings by Lecomte du Nouÿ in the first part of the *Drawing Course*.[58] Thus, the earliest starting point for the course would be 1864 or 1865.

Making the plates seemed to occupy Bargue on a full-time basis, for no other lithographic works other than a portrait of Marshal Bazaine *(Le Maréchal Bazaine)* (fig. 40) drawn and lithographed by Bargue are known to have been created during the years 1865–70 (the *Maréchal Bazaine* is the last recorded single lithograph). It is a folio sheet, a large, elegant work meant for framing. Bazaine first proved himself a hero in the capture of Sebastopol during the Crimean War and again at the Battle of Solferino during the Italian campaign, but he played a duplicitous role in the Franco-Prussian War of 1870, for which he was tried and condemned.

The lithographic plates for the three parts of the *Drawing Course* were most likely finished before the war started; the third part of the course appeared in 1871. Where and how Bargue spent the war years is not known. He probably holed up somewhere outside Paris and painted, for we know of at least four completed paintings dated 1871. They show a remarkable improvement professionally over the last known painting, the 1860 grisaille portrait of Napoleon III (painting 17). The portrait was painted from a photograph, whereas *The Smoker (Breton fumant)* (painting 18), *Seated Negro [The Sentinel] (Nègre assis)* (painting 21), and *A Footman Sleeping (Valet de pied, dormant)* (painting 23) are all painted from models. In terms of both conception and skill they represent a complete break from the unsophisticated paintings known only from lithographs of the 1850s. The single figures are evidence of what Bargue had learned since he started his association with Goupil. As a friend and student of Gérôme he had picked up technical and artistic sophistication; and as the lithographer of the almost two hundred plates for the *Drawing Course* he had received an intense and advanced education in figure drawing. He was, in effect, the first graduate of the *Drawing Course*.

Fig. 40.
Charles Bargue. *Marshal Bazaine.*
(Le Maréchal Bazaine.) 1867.
Lithograph. 81 x 56 cm. (31.75 x 22 in.)
Cabinet des Estampes, Bibliothèque nationale, Paris.

Bargue's Work During the 1870s

The Smoker (Breton fumant), the least successful of the several known paintings dating from 1871, is nonetheless astonishing as a miniature. The composition is simple. The figure is placed in the center of the panel in a valiant attempt to make the tension of the stance—locked knees, bent neck, extended arms as he lights his pipe—perceptible through the heavy costume, which consists of a pair of full-cut, wrinkled pantaloons and a heavy wool peasant jacket. The detail—as in the folds of the trousers—is minuscule. It is the first recorded painting by Bargue in the Goupil stock books since the entry for the small portrait of Napoleon III over a decade earlier. *The Smoker (Breton fumant)* was sold at auction in 1998 together with an oil study entitled *Seated Breton* (painting 19). Each was described as "a study for *Les Vendéens,*" an unknown composition either lost or never executed. The seated peasant wears the same costume as the standing smoker. Even though the painting is not so fine, the sense of volume and space are more convincing.

What must be the last of the paintings of 1871 is *A Footman Sleeping (Valet de pied, dormant)* in the Metropolitan Museum of Art in New York (painting 23). It represents such an advance over the smoking Breton peasant as to be astounding: the footman does not stand before the background but is integrated into it without the benefit of a strong chiaroscuro. He sits uncomfortably on a wooden bench and has fallen asleep, either out of fatigue or boredom. His livery, the contortions of the patterns of the fabrics, and the wrinkles in his coat and his stockings are all elaborately described. Beside the carved bench is a book beladen, leather-covered chair with brass studs. An elaborate bronze brazier is crowded in between the chair and bench. The hat and gloves of the footman appear to have been carelessly dropped, with one landing on the bench and the other on the floor. All these details are painted in the bravura technique of someone overjoyed at his ability to draw and paint anything he sees and confident that he can depict space and atmosphere correctly. The most splendid feature of the composition is the solidity of the forms: the physical body of the footman sensed under his uniform; his strongly modeled head, full arm, and legs—despite the humor implicit in the depiction of his cheap stockings and shoes—are all extraordinary. The sturdy figure of the footman is ensconced in a marvelous row of solid furniture and accessories, a strong form rhythmically aligned with several others. There is, sadly, a technical error in the wainscoting between the bench and the chair: Bargue has evidently used some slow-drying medium in the underpainting that has induced a *craquelure anglaise,* that is, cracks surrounding large islands of paint. He evidently learned his lesson from this canvas, for the defect does not occur again in Bargue's works.

Since painting *The Smoker* Bargue has done some serious thinking—or profited from conversations with better-trained artists. He has raised all his standards in drawing, color, and composition. As for content, the simple situations he chooses are an improvement over the vulgar jokes and halfhearted eroticism of his earlier paintings. The ideals of the contemporary Realist movement liberated him, allowing him to do what he did best, namely, paint what he saw before him: costumed models posing in a studio.

A Possible Voyage to the Near East: Bargue's First Orientalist Paintings

Drawing 1.
Arabs Observed at a Distance.
(*Feuille d'études de figures arabes.*)
Private collection
Pencil on paper. 16 x 17.4 cm.
(6.25 x 6.75 in.) "Vente Bargue" stamp.
Provenance: Bargue sale, Paris,
31 May 1883; Hazlitt, Gooden & Fox,
Nineteenth-Century French Drawings
(London, 1977), no. 56; Robert
Isaacson Collection.
The immediacy and probable
employment of sight-size technique
suggests that this drawing was made on
the spot during an unrecorded trip to
North Africa by Bargue. This may be the
only evidence for such a trip except,
perhaps, for drawings 2 and 18.

Bargue probably made an undocumented visit to North Africa—either Egypt or Algeria—sometime in the early 1870s, probably in the winter of 1871–72. Between 29 June and 10 October 1871 he sold five paintings to Goupil. Not until 10 March 1872 is another sale registered in the Goupil stock books—a gap of five months—so Bargue had money enough and time for a trip to North Africa during the best season.

The first two paintings he sold to Goupil upon returning were Orientalist subjects. The first, *Seated Negro* (*Nègre assis*) (painting 21) was sold to Goupil on 16 April 1872. Although it is dated 1872, my instinct is to date it 1871, between *The Smoker* (*Breton fumant*) and *A Footman Sleeping* (*Valet de pied, dormant*). All the poses smack of the studio, and some of the accessories are borrowed from Gérôme. Furthermore, the *Seated Negro* does not reflect someone having experienced the light of North Africa. My supposition is that upon returning to Paris in 1872 he picked up, finished, and dated this painting, which had been left behind either as an unfinished or unsatisfactory work, and took it to Goupil for some quick cash. [59]

There exists in a private collection a drawing of several rows of Arabs seen from a distance in a market or some open place. They seem drawn from life (although there is the slight possibility that they were copied from someone else's sketches) (drawing 1). However, the supposition of a visit to North Africa is supported by another drawing of an Arab seated on the ground who looks as if he had been drawn incommodiously *in situ,* while the artist stood above him, and not in a studio, where the model would have been raised on a stand (drawing 2). These conditions were met for the finished version of *The Sentinel* (*Une Sentinelle*) (painting 27), dated 1873, painted with patience and care back in Paris. For the first time Bargue demonstrates in this work the experience of the ambient light in the narrow streets of North African cities, as well as a more intimate knowledge of how Oriental fabrics reflect and absorb that special light, how they glow softly in the shade. He could have learned about Oriental fabrics and finery from Gérôme's costume collection, but he would not have learned about the more subtle refinements of near-equatorial light from Gérôme, who did not often imitate it in his works. With few exceptions Gérôme used colors decoratively, independent of the atmosphere. The delicate, refined glow of the yellow jacket must be the result of Bargue's personal experience on location. One could also argue that Bargue was innocent of actual contact with the Orient and could have picked up his conventional Orientalism from Gérôme and other Orientalist painters.

Gérôme had gone to London during the siege of Paris in 1870–71. Within five years after his return to Paris, he made at least two trips to the Near East, one in 1871 and another in 1874. [60] Could Bargue have been with him in 1871? Or did he make a cheaper solo trip to Algiers or one in the company of other companions? Such questions arise because I have not found evidence in any of his known paintings or drawings of an encounter with the desert, with the antiquities of Egypt, or with the monumental architecture of Cairo.

Drawing 2.
Seated Arab.
(Arabe assis.)
The Art Museum,
Princeton University,
bequest of Dan
Fellows Platt, class of
1895
Pencil and
watercolor on paper.
26.6 x 19.8 cm.
(10.5 x 7.75 in.)
"Vente Bargue"
stamp. Inscription,
lower left: "dessin par
Charles Bargue"
Provenance: Bargue
sale, Paris, 31 May
1883; Dan Fellows
Platt collection;
Platt bequest to the
museum.
Notes: There
is something
haphazard about the
proportions; the view
from above and the
uncertainty of the
pose makes this seem
like a drawing made
on the spot rather
than the recording
of a studio pose.
See also drawing 18,
which also has an *in
situ* aspect.

Painting 28.
The Prayer to Allah. **Sketch**
(En adoration. Ébauche.*)*
1874
Private collection
Oil on canvas. 46 x 33 cm.
(18.5 x 13 in.)

Painting 33.
Bashi-Bazouk.
(Bachi-Bouzouk.) **1875**
The Metropolitan Museum
of Art, New York, Catharine
Lorillard Wolfe collection,
bequest of Catharine Lorillard
Wolfe, 1887.
Oil on canvas.
47.6 x 33.3 cm.
(18.25 x 13 in.)
Signed, lower right:
"BARGVE '75"

Painting 36.
A Turkish Sentinel.
(Une Sentinelle
turque.) **1877**
Museum of Fine Arts,
Boston, bequest of
Susan Cornelia Warren,
03.601
Oil on panel.
28 x 21 cm.
(11 x 8.25 in.)
Signed, lower right:
"BARGVE '77"

Painting 40.
An Oriental Coffeehouse.
(Dans un café oriental.)
1877
Private collection
Watercolor on paper.
29.8 x 21.6 cm.
(11.75 x 8.5 in.) Signed at
right, on bench:
"BARGVE '77"

A Rococo Theme: *The Artist and His Model* of 1874

The first work to be listed in the Goupil stock books after the *Seated Negro (Nègre assis)* is *The Opinion of the Model (L'Avis du modèle)* (painting 29), often referred to as *The Artist and His Model (L'Artiste et son modèle)*.[61] No paintings are known from 1873 and no other work dates from 1874. Could this fine painting have taken more than a year to prepare, or was Bargue kept busy as Gérôme's assistant? Set in an ornately decorated eighteenth-century room, the composition may have been inspired by the Rococo themes of Mariano Fortuny (1738–1874), then at the height of his popularity, or by the seventeenth-century costume pieces by Gérôme, who first exploited the era in 1864 in one of his best paintings, *Louis XIV and Molière (Louis XIV et Molière)* (in the Malden Public Library, Malden, Mass.), and subsequently in his *Jean Bart* (private collection),[62]

Fig. 41.
J.-L. Gérôme. *Rex Tibicien.
(Rex Tibicien.)* 1874. Lost.
Oil. 79 x 61 cm. (31 x 24 in.)

a painting of a fidgety and bored retired admiral unimpressed by the luxury of Versailles, a picture that might have been the inspiration for Bargue's *A Footman Sleeping*. Gérôme prepared three new Baroque scenes for the Salon of 1874, his first salon showing since the war: the lost *Rex Tibicien* (fig. 41), depicting Frederick the Great playing his flute in a Rococo room at Sans Souci; Corneille and Molière together in *A Collaboration* (private collection); and the famous painting *The Gray Eminence (L'Éminence grise)* (Museum of Fine Arts, Boston). It may be that at this time the role of Gérôme had broadened to that of mentor as well as teacher. Even so, Bargue's early pictures are more strongly related thematically to the works of Fortuny and Meissonier (1815–1891). Although the costumes, models, and accessories used by Bargue could have come from Gérôme's studio accessories, they seem mostly to be his own.

The Opinion of the Model is lost, but its image is recorded in a Goupil photograph and in a watercolored photogravure published by Goupil in 1882 (see fig. 42). A series of studies and sketches in pencil and oil for the painting have either been preserved intact or recorded in photographs (see the entry for painting 29 in the preliminary catalogue section).

Two photographs reproduce drawings of the model by Bargue once in the Alexander Young Collection (sale Christie's, London, 1 July 1910); in one drawing she is fully nude, in the other, half so. A delicate drawing of the model is in the Walters Art Museum in Baltimore, Md. (drawing 7). A succinct, quickly drawn conceptual sketch is in the

Fitzwilliam Museum in Cambridge, England (drawing 5). A full-scale *ébauche* of the work, glorious in itself, is in the National Gallery of Wales, Cardiff (painting 30). A splendid *ébauche* of the artist in his chair—in its sureness of touch and value practically a finished painting in itself—is in the collection of Mrs. Noah L. Butkin (painting 31).[63] These chance survivals of what must have been a large group of studies are evidence of how carefully Bargue prepared his subjects, in terms of both composition and color. Such studies would lead up to the cartoon, a complete drawing of the composition, ready for transfer to canvas. The cartoon for *The Opinion of the Model* (*L'Avis du modèle*) is in a private collection (drawing 6). All the properties and figures are in very clear outline, and the dimensions give a clue to the size of the lost painting. The cartoon would be transferred onto the canvas either by tracing or by using squares. Note that whereas in almost all of these preparatory versions the model is partially clothed, to varying degrees, by a piece of drapery that she has wrapped around herself—the result either of a chill or modesty—in the finished painting she is fully clothed.

Fig. 42.
Charles Bargue. *The Artist and His Model.*
(*L'Artiste et son modèle.*) after 1867.
Hand-colored photogravure issued by Goupil & Cie.
Sheet, 63 x 48 cm. (24.5 x 19 in.) Image much smaller.
Bibliothèque nationale, Paris.

Compositional Experiments

Some familiar accessories appear in three extraordinarily crowded compositions of 1877: scenes of a black Cairene merchant surrounded by antiques (paintings 38, 39 and 40). The model is seated in the studio among a collection of Oriental accessories that are spread out on the floor around him. There is no attempt to imitate the cramped, dark quarters of North African shops. In both paintings the model is wrapped in thick robes; only his face and his bony hands are visible. Both works are enticing in the wealth of objects depicted.[64] The richness of props leads one to think that the artist vacillated between his love of painting figures and his skill at painting the shapes and textures of artifacts. The clutter—the vases, bottles, lamps, and other antiques, not arranged particularly well—contrasts strongly with the austere surroundings of most of the sentinels. Obviously Bargue is experimenting with compositions of various types, switching from perspectival compositions to somewhat mannered, decorative contractions of space. (Could the richness of the proudly displayed Oriental bric-a-brac in the antique shop be the shopping haul of the purported voyage to the Near East, brought home as studio accessories?)

The crowning work in this series of complex backgrounds is a spectacular watercolor, also dated 1877, entitled *In an Oriental Coffeehouse (Dans un café oriental)* (painting 40), where the clutter has become spatial, with several layers of furnishings, one behind the other. A bench back, partitions, and screens, dropped like canvas theatrical flats, frame the cumbersomely clothed black model, who sits on a bench by a tray of coffee, lost in melancholy reverie. The long rifle is familiar, as is the ostrich-shell hookah, both accessories visible in the painting *Bashi-Bazouk (Bachi-Bouzouk)* (painting 33). The perspective is a bit confusing, particularly in the deepest plane, but this hardly matters, for this is one of the most perfect and elaborate watercolors one will ever see. The colors and textures that rise from the fabrics of the four or five visible layers of clothing are sumptuous as well as impeccably drawn. One is amazed by the problems Bargue set for himself. The splendor of his watercolor technique in this painting is sure evidence that he must have produced many other watercolors, but only one other has been recognized.[65] Quick watercolor sketches, however, are known, such as the one for *The Almeh (L'Almée)* (drawing 13).

The Artist and His Model of 1878

In 1878 an old theme, that of the artist and the model in the studio together, previously investigated in *The Opinion of the Model (L'Avis du modèle)* of 1874 (painting 29), was completely rethought for *The Artist and His Model (L'Artiste et son modèle)* (painting 43). A surviving oil sketch of the artist proves that Bargue started from scratch again and did not just flip his earlier studies for the first version. The artist now faces toward the left with the nude placed behind him. The two are comparing a nude sketched out on a canvas with a study for the figure that the painter holds in his hand. Two parrots huddle together on a bird stand whose round base creates a diagonal that leads into the canvas. The colors of their feathers—white and red, blue and orange—mimic the colors worn by the couple. The intimate snuggling of the two glorious birds also echoes the affectionate nudging of the artist and the model. The room is full of softly distributed pinks, oranges, and rich browns. A few areas of green form a triangle within the picture. The scene is nonetheless dominated by the rich apricot-orange tones of the painter's coat. The grouping is excellent and the lush, rich tonality is warm and satisfying. Bargue had found out how to combine all his talents and interests into a unified composition—a *tout ensemble*.[66]

Mosque Scenes

A series of oil sketches, *ébauches,* and one finished painting, all undated, depicting Arabs at prayer in a mosque may have been inspired by sights seen on the purported trip to North Africa, although the backgrounds are rather general and the figures look as if they were posed in a studio. They may have been intended for use in one or more large mosque interiors. Only one completed mosque scene by Bargue is known, a lost work identified as *Arabs at Prayer (En prière),*[67] and as a grisaille (painting 46). A corner of the mosque is filled with figures, in various postures of prayer, grouped between the prayer niche and a *mihrab.* The beauty of a related *ébauche* entitled *Muslims at Prayer (Musulmans prosternés)* (painting 47) is the best indication of what the scene promised in color. The grisaille may have been painted as the model for an illustration in a book or magazine. However, the number of study drawings for this picture (see drawings 14–17) seems unwarranted for a simple book or magazine illustration. Perhaps the grisaille was a copy after a finished painting now lost, which was to be used as a model by an engraver.

A Bashi-Bazouk and Some Albanians

After the animated, multifigure compositions of Muslims at prayer, it is not surprising that Bargue returned to what he knew he could do best, namely, the painting of single figures. The *Bashi-Bazouk (Bachi-Bouzouk)* of 1878, now in the Metropolitan Museum of Art in New York (painting 33), is a demonstration of his growing skill and sensibility. Several problems in the first single-figure compositions have now been solved. The figure sits more convincingly in place, with an implied energy in his posture that gives his body organic unity and, at the same time, sets the limbs in a rhythmic pattern. Furthermore, the figure sits in an atmosphere that envelops him in the space of the room. The chiaroscuro is a solemn setting for the rich colors that enliven and punctuate it.

A single figure dominates the scene. Seated, he assumes a pose that puts every part of his body in tension, which extends through and unifies the figure. Ensconced in the dark atmosphere of the room, the Arab's every limb receives and reflects different and varying values of light and shadow. The Bashi-Bazouk wears an old yellow silk jacket with long sleeve tails. In his holster belt he sports the ivory, double-handled knife, now transformed into a gun. An elegant water pipe is supported by his left hand, the two pipes crossing his body. One foot, as if keeping time to music, has lost its shoe; this elegantly foreshortened foot juts forward above the discarded shoe on the floor.[68] The colors have a deep resonance of yellow and gold—another accomplished *tout ensemble.* Bashi-Bazouks were known for their ferocity, which in painting is usually reflected in their fanciful attire. In Bargue's and Gérôme's Orient, they wear a high-domed, decorated felt hat. As irregular troops who followed the Ottoman army, they could be members of any race. Although the painting is infrequently displayed, generations of students of figure drawing have occasionally been able to marvel at the Arab's calves, one pushed out of shape by the knee it crosses, the other by the stone bench behind it—a tour de force of figure construction.

In contrast to the colorful clothing of the Bashi-Bazouks, Albanian soldiers, or Arnauts, wore white pleated skirts and the white bindings about their legs and bodies. They are generally depicted as light-skinned, thin, and usually somewhat elegant. They come from what is now modern Albania, and northern Greece; consequently they are often referred to as Greek soldiers.

Two known depictions of Albanian soldiers by Bargue, which he called sentinels, are dated 1877. A small, unfinished painting of another can safely be related to them through two drawings of a full figure and an oil study of a head that seem basic to all three. Although none of the drawings precisely matches the model for a known painting, at least five other unidentified and unlocated sentinels are listed in the Goupil stock books. Who knows how many "Arnauts" recorded in the stock books were mistakenly sold as "Bashi-Bazouks" or under the generic title of *sentinel*.

Of the three known pictures from this set, an *Albanian Soldier (Soldat albanais)* (painting 34), shown leaning against a wall while his carefully rendered dog rests nearby, is clearly dated 1877. The tight, white short pants are familiar, as are the bifurcated ivory knife handle and the silk jacket with the extended sleeves, now blue instead of yellow. (The change in color demonstrates that Bargue's mastery is based not just on precise observation but also on his control of values, which he could transpose from one color to another.) The long rifle will reappear. The handsome soldier, painted with great delicacy, has a real corporal presence, his frame articulated even under the thickest of drapery. A tracing of almost exactly the same pose, but with the head turned in, does not agree in some details with the finished painting (drawing 8). A small oil study of the model for the head of the Albanian could be used as evidence that Bargue changed heads not through improvisation but assemblage (see painting 35). Evidently Bargue's preparation for a composition was long and arduous. Especially noteworthy here are the scattered pebbles in the left foreground. They are not optical but tactile stones that one could almost pick up, so strong is Bargue's projection of solid shapes! The same model in the identical pose appears in the incorrectly titled *A Turkish Sentinel (Une Sentinelle turque)* (painting 36), in the Museum of Fine Arts in Boston. It, too, is dated 1877. This time the model wears an Arnaut skirt (perhaps borrowed from Gérôme's collection of costumes) and his hair is tucked under his cap. The jacket has changed color again. He leans against a small closet-shop built into the wall, containing a splendidly painted pile of drapery, a brass hookah, and a couple of brass pots on the ground before it.

A small, precious painting of a sentinel in a passageway somewhat similar to the background of the previous painting was left unfinished by Bargue (painting 37). It was bought from Bargue's studio after the artist had a stroke and entered a hospital, Goupil probably purchasing it from the landlord, who had commandeered the drawings left by Bargue in lieu of overdue back rent. The Greek soldier, a rather full-chested, strong-legged, mature man, stands somewhat jauntily, a sword in his right hand, the other hand akimbo, and a long rifle slung across his back. The drawing—or pose—used as a model is of a slight, somewhat coquettish adolescent (drawing 9). These paintings are all works done in the studio, with the models in the general light of a northern window and the backgrounds improvised. Since we know of several preparatory drawings and paintings that do not precisely match the drawings, we can postulate that other variants, mixing poses and models, could have been made. Some unknown "Albanian Soldiers" may still turn up.

Bargue's Final Five Years, 1878–83

As far as one can tell, in his final five years Bargue produced just a few paintings. Displaying a mastery of drawing, a richness of color, and often a complexity of composition, these last paintings demonstrate that he was about to enter the first rank of genre painters and become a worthy rival of Gérôme and Meissonier. The last finished painting, *The Chess Players (Joueurs d'échecs)* (painting 52), portrays an incident laden with psychological interest that opens up a path away from the comical anecdote—so abhorred today—of his contemporary genre painters and his own earlier work.

Anecdotal information confirms one's suspicion that the fineness of his technique and the care with which he used color and light meant that he painted very slowly and consequently—at least for most of his career—not very lucratively. His manifold preparatory studies in pencil and oil—of which we get enough of a glimpse to assure us of his conscientiousness and industry—show a generous use of models and an equally generous use of time in preparations of the most careful sort. He also had a love of accessories and costumes that undoubtedly proved a major expense for each picture even when he economized and reused some favorite properties. Despite the high prices he charged at the end of his career, he probably could not have supported himself in luxury, or even comfortably, because his working methods were so slow. In the same five years Gérôme produced about fifty paintings, perhaps with the assistance of Bargue, who consequently lessened his own productivity.[69] The actual painting of the finished canvases—so small, so detailed and accurate in drawing, so precise in the values of colors and halftones, so refined in touch, so unified in color—took much time as well. The difficulty was compounded by the small size of his canvases. It is therefore not surprising that we know of only one painting a year in the five years before his death.

Bargue's interest in Rococo settings never died out; the Rococo silk jacket continued to inspire him to the end of his life. *The Flute Player (Joueur de flûte)* (painting 51) was sold to Goupil in 1880. The flutist sits alone in the paneled music room of a Rococo palace. The room is filled with Rococo furniture, the walls are decorated with gilt Rococo boiserie, and a Chinese screen stands between a mirror and a decorated harpsichord. Sheet music lies on the parquet floor. The musician leans forward to concentrate on his playing. His silk jacket clings to his shoulders and arms, flattens into a stretched billow across his hips, and then hovers in a great display of pleats over the floor. One does not see his face, but the intensity of his playing is conveyed by his posture, his legs, and his fingers. The work is minutely detailed, but even more amazing than the precision of Bargue's brushwork is the suffusion of one dominant tonality, a harmony of whites, yellows, and golds, with the latter predominating and echoed in the gilt of the decorative woodwork, giving the composition an astounding sense of unity. Just a few small spots of crimson across the middle of the canvas extend the color chord. Even the white satin jacket is tinted with yellow so subtly that it is not immediately apparent unless one contrasts the cloak with a whiter white or really peers into the picture. Only then does one discern small areas of the cloak flooded with little pools of a thin, transparent yellow; the yellow patches are not glazes, however, and the technique used remains a mystery.

Bargue sold the oil to Goupil for 27,000 francs; Goupil sold it to J. W. Wilson of London for 40,000 francs. This is much more than twice the selling price for *The Artist and his Model* (painting 43) sold to W. H. Vanderbilt in 1878.

Two Chess Games

Bargue's acknowledged masterpiece—by those few who know his work—is *The Chess Players (Joueurs d'échecs)* (painting 52) of 1883, which was once owned by successsive generations of the Vanderbilt family and is now in a private American collection. The playing of games as a subject in painting had a long history and propounded a clear moral: game playing was a waste of time, a distraction from a pious and virtuous life. Earlier in the century Daumier had reinterpreted the theme as one of the activities of human recreation. Bargue's composition is full of the tension of competition. It is a large picture for Bargue, being quite wide. The autumn woods behind the terrace, where the men play an aggressive game of chess, is painted with superlative observation. Indeed, the wide swatch of red-orange-brown leaves positioned over the chess game sets the color tonality for the whole composition. In the center, a large, leafless tree spreads its branches in all directions, building a space within the tree, an ability matched only by the eye and hand of Adolph Menzel (1815–1905), Bargue's German contemporary.

The two players are dressed in high Rococo fashion, including, of course, the familiar silk coat worn by each. They straddle a bench as they play; one makes a triumphant move, his checkmate hand raised high over the board like a bird of prey about to pounce. The opponent is frozen in shocked astonishment. Their silk-stockinged legs convey the tensely balanced pose of each player. Leaning against a balustrade behind them, next to a tray of drinks and a tankard, a neutral but fascinated observer follows the game. The balustrade continues across the picture, forming an angle that frames a perched parrot in the act of squawking at a dog on the ground below him, cleverly underscoring the intensity of the game being played a few steps away. A servant, unconcerned and simply in attendance, leans on the parapet and gazes at the garden below. The uniform he wears is the same one worn by the sleeping footman years earlier (painting 23). The concentration of the action, the stillness of the autumnal park, the diagonals of the bench and balustrade, the horizontals of the trees, and the verticals of the two standing men and the parrot perch—all hold the composition together and unify it around a mysteriously intense psychological moment.

In *The Chess Players* Bargue has replaced the importance of telling a story with the analysis of a specific dramatic moment pregnant with underlying psychological tension, thus raising Realism above the thoughtless recording of nature. On this quiet afternoon the two players are putting such great emphasis on winning or losing that we can sense the stakes are higher than a mere bet, although we have no idea what the real conflict is about. Before our eyes the situation climaxes in an outbreak of pride and animosity disguised as play, a permitted breach in the practiced affability of the day.

Goupil paid Bargue 30,000 francs for *The Chess Players,* and sold it to W. H. Vanderbilt of New York for 75,000 francs. This was not pure profit for Goupil: there was an intermediary, Samuel Putnam Avery.

A final, unfinished chess game by Bargue—probably his last painting—is *Bashi-Bazouks Playing Chess (Bachi-Bouzouks jouant aux échecs)* (painting 53) in the collection of the Malden Public Library, Malden, Mass. This time the setting is the Near East. One recognizes at once, in the foreground, a literal transcription of the Bashi-Bazouk figure from an earlier work (painting 33). In the background is another Bashi-Bazouk, who appears in a fine *ébauche* now in the Art Gallery of Hamilton, Ontario (Canada) (painting 49), a study for this work. Bargue himself insisted on seeing and drawing the contours of the human body in straight lines up to the penultimate moment of painting the picture.

The Bashi-Bazouk in the background wears a headdress known from Gérôme's works; indeed, there are sketches by Gérôme of the same model in the same costume (fig. 43)! This is conclusive evidence that the two artists actually worked together in the same studio, sharing models, properties, and even ideas. Moreover, affixed to the back of the panel is a letter of authentication in Gérôme's hand dated 1 June 1888: "I, the undersigned, declare that the picture representing Bashi-Bazouks playing chess, measuring 0.90 in height by 0.70 in width, is by M. Bargue. I can, moreover, even testify that I saw him do it, and that I loaned him some costumes and headdresses for its execution. J.-L. Gérôme, Member of the Institute."

Bargue may have been placed in the hospital due to his final illness, while the work was under way. There are unfinished passages, such as the standing musician to the right. The figure in the white turban to the left, wearing a vest from Gérôme's costume wardrobe, seems, upon closer inspection, to have been painted or finished by Gérôme himself, who tried valiantly to paint the turban with a soft, feathery brushstroke, as Bargue would have done. (I have been unable to ascertain precisely when Gérôme finished the central figure.) The important move the Arab is making takes place in much calmer circumstances than the Rococo version. While still a splendid picture, one wonders what sumptuous color harmonies might have been achieved by Bargue had he been able to finish it himself. The panel may have been in Gérôme's studio when Bargue died, thereby escaping the Bargue sale, and may have remained there until Gérôme sold it in 1888.

Bargue died in 1883, leaving behind in his studio many drawings, oil sketches, and *ébauches* in various states of finish. They were auctioned off in Paris by a M. Couturier, *commisseur-priseur,* on 31 May 1883. Although there is no recorded catalogue for the sale, nineteen items that Goupil & Cie bought at the sale are entered in the Goupil stock books.[70]

Fig. 43.
Jean-Léon Gérôme.
Bashi-Bazouk.
(Bachi-Bouzouk.)
1882.
Pencil on paper.
Private collection.

A second auction of his drawings took place in the United States a decade later, in 1894. It was the S. A. Coale (of Saint Louis, Mo.) sale held at the American Art Association. A gossipy note in *The Collector* explained: "One feature of the sale will be a collection of sketches and drawings by Bargue. It appears that when Bargue wound his last debauch up by going to a hospital he owed his landlord a considerable bill for rent and the latter seized upon the contents of his studio, among which were the sketches. Mr. Coale bought them in a lot and most of them he framed and kept hanging at his house until his death. The family seems to be clearing out everything in this sale."[71]

Bargue's Death

An account of Bargue's last months must be reconstructed from some meager medical documents, plus a few later, less credible accounts. The first indication of his fatal illness is contained in a letter dated 15 February 1883, without an addressee or signature, from Goupil & Cie in Paris to Knoedler & Co. in New York: "As for Bargue, it's impossible for him to work. He had a stroke and is not recovering. Either he will not live or he will be completely senile. He left behind a painting [painting 37] that could be considered finished, although if he had kept his health he could have pushed it even further. We'll show it to you when you are in Paris."[72]

The clinical record of his illness in the *Entry Register of Psychiatric Hospitals of the Department of the Seine* is succinct and precise but not very probing. (Actually, the Goupil-Knoedler letter gives more information about his condition.)

> *Entry Register of Psychiatric Hospitals of the Department of the Seine, 1883:* Charles Bargue, no. 41321, entered 31 March 1883, 56 years old. Son of Jacques. Painter. Address, 37, rue de Laval. Bachelor. Transferred from Saint Anthony's Hospital to Saint Anne's on 31 March 1883.
> *Medical notes, 31 March 1883:* general paralysis of an apoplectic type; disturbing the repose of the patients in the room.
> *Medical notes, 1 April 1883:* weakening of the mental faculties, with some confusion in his ideas; incapable of taking care of himself. Muscular weakness.
> Died 6 April 1883.[73]

The stroke was probably the result of a thrombo-embolic accident, that is, a stroke caused by a clot in the brain. At fifty-six, Bargue was approaching the age when such strokes are common. His condition between the stroke and his entry into Saint Anthony's Psychiatric Hospital is not known. He may have been bedridden and helpless from the start; the expectation of the writer of the letter that he would be "senile" if he recovered suggests he was probably severely incapacitated mentally by the stroke, without the early recovery of cognition often seen in the first week or so after a stroke. The first medical record notes a general paralysis of an apoplectic type upon entry. In modern French medical terminology *paralysie générale* means a "progressive" paralysis; what it meant at the Saint Anne's Clinic in 1883 is uncertain. The next day, "muscular weakness" is noted, an observation that seems preempted by the report of paralysis the day before. We do not know when he entered Saint Anthony's. The medical note following his transfer to Saint Anne's Insane Asylum is dated at least six weeks following the stroke. One could regard the second notice as just a rewrite of the first. The initial seriousness of the damage to his system and his death within approximately two months of the stroke would not be an uncommon clinical course. His actual death may have been the result of another thrombo-embolic stroke or, as was common, of pneumonia, secondary to weakness and immobility.

Why was the victim of a stroke assigned to psychiatric clinics? The various physiological causes of stroke were not recognized and categorized until the twentieth century. The insane were considered degenerates with an innate, fatal flaw: an inherited inclination for madness lurking in their systems from birth; a tendency waiting to be unleashed by some traumatic event; or the progress of some "degenerative" habit—such as alcoholism or sexual habits or practices—triggering a progression from seemingly normal life into insanity. The symptoms of mental derangement—the aftermath of many types of stroke—were consequently seen as a development of the patient's latent madness. Getting it backward, as they did, doctors did not treat demented stroke patients for the stroke but rather for their madness—if they treated them at all. In most cases demented patients were locked up for observation in the hope of furthering both the scientific categorization of the various types of insanity and comprehension of the environmental or personal factors that caused the innate madness to emerge and develop into full-blown insanity.

A famous resident at Saint Anne's was the psychiatrist Valentin Magnan (1835–1916), who actually lived in the clinic for forty-five years, studying the patients and writing about them.[74] Bargue's condition was probably too advanced—he was incapable of coherent speech—to interest Magnan as a subject for study. He probably would have diagnosed Bargue's case as developed *dementia praecox* (inherent insanity). [The portraits of mad patients by Théodore Géricault (1791–1824), undertaken for a Doctor Georget at the Salpetrière insane asylum in Paris, can also be understood in this medical context as attempts to identify the physiognomic features of different types of insanity. The same can be said for the musings about family history and madness in the novels of Émile Zola, as in his Rougon-Macquart series.]

The only obituary published about Bargue was a paragraph in an English-language magazine, *The American Registrar,* published in Paris: "The artist, Bargue, who painted little gems of pictures, some of them worth thousands of pounds sterling, and mostly belonging to Mr. Wm. H. Vanderbilt and Miss C. Wolfe of New York, died last week at the Saint Anne's Lunatic Hospital in this city and was buried last Sunday. Several of his best works are exhibited at Messrs Arnold and Tripp's Fine Art Rooms, No. 8, rue Saint-Georges."[75]

Almost two years after Bargue's death a newspaper obituary for Albert Goupil, Gérôme's brother-in-law, states: "The story goes the rounds that [Goupil & Cie] made a contract with Bargue for 60,000 francs a year. Bargue was a clever artist who executed, in lithography, a very beautiful drawing course based on Holbein. Once he had the contract in his pocket, Bargue stopped delivery and went crazy. Thus, one can see that art dealers can be taken in as well as the others."[76]

Several years later, in her discussion of the students of Gérôme, the usually well informed Mrs. C. H. Stranahan related an anecdote about Bargue's last days: "One pupil and devoted follower of Gérôme died of want. His short life left but few productions, choice and of exquisite finish, too elaborate to secure for him remunerative prices; and after being refused when in ill health an allowance by a dealer who had profited greatly by his works, he fell in a fit at his door and was removed to a charitable institution to die."[77]

The myths involving Bargue's impecuniousness, eccentric behavior, and poor relations with his dealer Goupil seem to have become established within a few years after his death. Such retrospective explanations of his character could well have been congruent with the then current idea that his terminal "madness" had been latent. Another explanation may have to do with the popular mistrust of art dealers.[78] Then again, they may have been based on actual events whose true circumstances we may never be able to ascertain. Clearly, some were pure embellishments, such as the repeated assertion that Bargue died young when, in fact, he was actually fifty-six at the time of his death. Nevertheless these myths have become "common knowledge" among art dealers and critics, being repeated reflexively at the mere mention of his name.

The pitiful conditions surrounding Bargue's illness and death are made even sadder when one considers that he had just achieved artistic and financial success: his genre paintings had begun to develop a new psychological depth and decent prices were finally being paid for his work.

A PRELIMINARY CATALOGUE
OF BARGUE'S PAINTINGS

A catalogue of the drawings reproduced starts on p. 312.

Ptg 1

Painting 1. *Caught Napping. (La Partie de chat.)* 1847
Lost; known only from a lithograph
Notes: The lithograph is in the Cabinet des Estampes, Bibliothèque nationale, Paris; cote DC282, vol. 1, f. 53. The two earliest recorded paintings by Bargue are known through two lithographs by H. Massard. The title in English and French plus the following inscription are printed on the mat: "Peint par Bargue. Litho par H. Massard. La Galerie sans fin. London, Owen Baily, Palgrave Place, Strand." The English titles are odd translations.

Ptg 2

Painting 2. *Addition and Subtraction. (Addition et soustraction.)* 1847
Lost; known only from a lithograph
Notes: The lithograph is in the Cabinet des Estampes, Bibliothèque nationale, Paris; cote DC 282, vol. 1, f. 54. The two earliest recorded paintings by Bargue are known through two lithographs by H. Massard. The title in English and French plus the following inscription is printed on the mat: "Peint par Bargue. Litho par H. Massard. La Galerie sans fin. London, Owen Baily, Palgrave Place, Strand."

Ptg 3

Painting 3. *The Hush of Nature. (Le Silence.)* **1850**

Lost; known only from a lithograph

Inscriptions: The following is printed on the margin of the picture: "Peint d'après nature et lithographié par C. Bargue. Les Sylphides, III." [The titles.] "Imprimé Bergeret et Frère, Paris. Paris F. Sinnet, Rotonde Colbert."

Notes: The lithograph is in the Cabinet des Estampes, Bibliothèque nationale, Paris; cote DC282, vol. 1, f. 11. There is a coy eroticism in the "innocents" watching butterflies mate.

Ptg 4

Painting 4. *The Echo. (L'Écho.)* **1850**

Lost; known only from a lithograph

Inscriptions: For mat inscriptions other than the titles, see the comments for painting 3.

Notes: The print is in the Cabinet des Estampes, Bibliothèque nationale, Paris; cote DC282, vol. 1, f. 12. *Les Sylphides,* IV.

Ptg 5

Painting 5. *The Water's Edge. (Au bord de l'étang.)* **1850**

Lost; known only from a lithograph

Notes: The lithograph is in the Cabinet des Estampes, Bibliothèque nationale, Paris; cote DC282, vol. 1, f. 13. *Les Sylphides,* V. For mat inscriptions other than the titles, see the entry for painting 3.

Ptg 6

Painting 6. *The Fountain's Edge. (Au bord de la fontaine.)*
1850
Lost; known only from a lithograph
Notes: The lithograph is in the Cabinet des Estampes in the Bibliothèque nationale in Paris, cote DC282, vol. 1, f. 14. *Les Sylphides,* VI. For mat inscriptions other than the titles, see the entry for painting 3. Bird's nests and excited birds are traditional erotic symbols.

Ptg 7

Painting 7. *The Conversation. (La Conversation.)* **1850**
Lost; known only from a lithograph
Provenance: Known only from a halftone reproduction in a page from an undated and unidentified twentieth-century sales catalogue; a clipping in the documentation of the Musée d'Orsay has been used to illustrate the work.
Notes: Les Sylphides, X.

Ptg 8

Painting 8. *The Swing. (L'Escarpolette.)* **1851**

Lost; known only from a lithograph

Inscriptions: For mat inscriptions other than the titles, see comments for painting 3.

Notes: The lithograph is in the Cabinet des Estampes, Bibliothèque nationale, Paris; cote DC282, vol. 1, f. 15. *Les Sylphides,* XI.

Ptg 9

Painting 9. *Mexican Maids. (Le Hamac.)* **1851**

Lost; known only from a lithograph

Inscriptions: For mat inscriptions other than the titles, see comments for painting 3.

Notes: The lithograph is in the Cabinet des Estampes, Bibliothèque nationale, Paris; cote DC282, vol. 1, f. 16. *Les Sylphides,* XII.

Painting 10. *Caught in the Fact.* [*sic*] *(Prise et surprise.)* **1851**

Lost; known only from a lithograph

Inscriptions: On the borders of the print: "Peint et lithographié par. C. Bargue. Lith. De Becqueret Frères, rue des Maçons sorbonnes 5 Paris. Publié par F. Sinnet, 10, Rotonde Colbert. Paris. Pub. by E. Gambart & Cie. 28 Berners St. 5 Oxford St."

Notes: The print is in Cabinet des Estampes, Bibliothèque nationale, Paris; cote DC282, vol. 1, f. 17. Bargue's compositional grouping of two figures has improved in this and the next picture. His new skill in juxtaposing bodies is no doubt the result of the exercise of designing the plates of *Les Sylphides.*

Painting 11. *A Bachelor's Home.* *(Un Ménage de vieux garçon.)* **1851**

Lost; known only from a lithograph

Inscriptions: On print margin, *"Peint et lithographié par C. Bargue."*

Notes: Lithograph in Cabinet des Estampes, Bibliothèque nationale, Paris; cote DC282, vol. 1, f. 18.

Painting 12. *The Last New Novel. (Un Roman du cœur.)* **1851**

Lost; known only from a lithograph

Inscriptions: On print margin: "Peint et lithographié par C. Bargue. Lith. De Becqueret Frerès. Paris. Publié par F. Sinnet, 10, Rotonde Colbert. Paris. Pub. by E. Gambart & Cie."

Notes: Lithograph in Cabinet des Estampes, Bibliothèque nationale, Paris; cote DC282, vol. 2, f. 23.

Painting 13. *Castles in Spain. (Châteaux en Espagne.)* **1851**

Lost; known only from a lithograph

Inscriptions: On print margin: *Peint et lithographié par Ch. Bargue.*

Notes: Lithograph in Cabinet des Estampes, Bibliothèque nationale, Paris; cote DC282, vol. 2, f. 22.

Painting 14. *Letting Out the Fact. (Une Confidence.)* **1855**

Lost; known only from a lithograph

Inscriptions: "Peint et litho. Par C. Bargue. *Les Sylphides,* série II, no. 21. Imp. Lemercier Frères. Paris, publié par F. Sinnet Éditeur, Galerie Colbert."

Notes: The lithograph is in the Cabinet des Estampes, Bibliothèque nationale, Paris; cote DC282, vol. 1, f. 36. The first series of *Les Sylphides* was evidently successful commercially since it comprised a total of twenty plates. The second series, launched with great expectations, probably never surpassed the three known plates. Since it was against the law to display nudes in a shop window, the new series had a title page that could be put in the window. It was coyly phrased so that shoppers would know what was in the plates: "*Les Sylphides,* the second series, starting with no. 21. A collection of graceful subjects after nature to serve for the study of women. Composed and lithographed by Charles Bargue."

Ptg 15

Painting 15. *An Hour of Rest. (L'Heure de la sieste.)* 1855
Lost; known only from a lithograph
Notes: Les Sylphides, série II, no. 22. See comments for painting 14. Lithograph in Cabinet des Estampes, Bibliothèque nationale, Paris; cote DC282, vol. 1, f. 37.

Ptg 16

Painting 16. *Items of the same stalk. (Les Deux Cousines.)* 1855
Lost; known only from a lithograph
Notes: Les Sylphides, série II, no. 23. See comments for painting 14. Lithograph in Cabinet des Estampes, Bibliothèque nationale, Paris; cote DC282, vol. 1, f. 38.

Painting 17. *Napoleon III.* Grisaille.
***(Sa Majesté, l'Empereur des Français. Grisaille.)* 1860**
Lost; known only from a Goupil oval photograph
Inscriptions: On the mount of the photograph: "Peint par Bargue. Photographié par Ballard. Berlin, Verlag von Goupil & Cie. Publié par Goupil & Cie, London. New York. Published by M. Knoedler."
Provenance: Goupil stock books, vol. 1, p. 122. Bargue to Goupil 1860 (Goupil framed it for 41.49 francs and put it in stock); sold by Goupil (stock books, vol. 2, p. 230) at the hôtel des Ventes, 20 May 1863, for 41.49 francs.
Notes: Photograph in Cabinet des Estampes, Bibliothèque nationale, Paris; cote DC282, vol. 1, f. 55; also in the Goupil Museum in Bordeaux. A grisaille, painted as a model for an engraver. Bargue was probably paid for the painting as a model. After it was used as a model for two prints, Goupil framed it and put it in stock. No one, evidently, was interested in a grisaille portrait of the emperor by an unknown artist; after a while the painting was put up at auction for the price of the frame. The model was used by Goupil & Cie for (1) an oval aquatint by Abel Lurat, 1862, and (2) a photograph by Ballard.

Painting 18. *The Smoker. (Breton fumant.)* **1871**
Edward T. Wilson, Fund for Fine Arts, Inc., Bethesda, Maryland
Oil on panel. 13.3 x 8.9 cm. (5.25 x 3.5 in.) Signed, lower right: "C. BARGVE '71"
Provenance: Goupil stock book, vol. 5, p. 132, no. 5514: Bargue to Goupil 29 February 1871, from Everard; sold to Mr. Fox, a dealer in Manchester, England, 11 July 1871, for 1,500 francs; returned by Fox (through Everard?) April 1872; sold by Goupil to Mr. Waring 13 July 1872 for 2,000 francs; Sotheby's New York, 5 May 1999, sale 7300, no. 258; bought by Edward T. Wilson, Fund for Fine Arts, Inc., Chevy Chase, Maryland.
Notes: See the discussion on p. 265 above.

Ptg 19

Painting 19. *Seated Breton. (Breton assis.)* **1871**
Private collection
Oil on paper. 26 x 20.5 cm. (10.25 x 8 in.) Spurious signature and date, lower left, 1865
Provenance: Sotheby's, London, 2 December 1998, no. 142.
Notes: This was described in the Sotheby's sales catalogue as a "Study for *Les Vendéens,*" a painting otherwise unknown and unrecorded. The added signature and date do not help place it, but it must have been painted around the same time as the *Breton fumant.*

Painting 20A. *Seated Young Man from Behind, Bare Back,* **study. (Jeune Homme assis, le dos nu, étude.)**
Edward T. Wilson, Fund for Fine Arts, Inc., Bethesda, Maryland
Oil on canvas. 26.5 x 24.25 cm. (10.5 x 9.5 in.)
Provenance: Sotheby's, New York, 5 May 1999, sale 7300, included in lot 256, without being listed in the catalogue.

Painting 20B. *Seated Young Man from Behind,* **study. (Jeune homme de dos, étude.)**
Edward T. Wilson, Fund for Fine Arts, Inc., Bethesda, Maryland
Oil on canvas. 25.5 x 25.4 cm. (10 x 9.25 in.)
Provenance: Sotheby's, London, 2 December 1998, no. 143; Sotheby's, New York, 5 May 1999, sale 7300, lot 256.
Notes: Sold in a group with the previous painting and painting 51. This fine study might be related to the peasant groups, although the style seems much later.

Ptg 20A

Ptg 20B

Painting 21. *Seated Negro (The Sentinel). (Nègre assis.)* **1871**

Private collection

Oil on panel. 25.5 x 19.8 cm. (10 x 7.75 in.) Signed and dated, lower left, "C. BARGUE '72." On reverse there are stickers for Wallis & Sons, London, and Fearon Gallery, New York (1926).

Provenance: Goupil Stock book, vol. 5, p. 214, no. 6371: Bargue to Goupil 16 April 1872; sold to Mr. Fox, a dealer in Manchester, England, 11 May 1872, for 5,000 francs; Wallis & Sons, London; the Cincinnati Museum Association (the founding organization of the Cincinnati Art Museum) by 1876. The tag on the back of the canvas reads "F. G. no. 28. N62," which probably means that it was included in an exhibition of Bargue's paintings and drawings at the Fearon Gallery, New York, in 1926; it was loaned to the gallery by the Cincinnati Art Museum. Later the painting was deaccessioned by the museum and sold at Parke-Bernet, New York, in 1944; bought by Mr. Louis Daniel of Cincinnati, Ohio; to Mrs. Deborah Long by descent; sale at Main Auction Galleries, Cincinnati, J. L. Karp and Jonas Karp auctioneers, 3 December 2001; bought by Edward T. Wilson, Fund for Fine Arts, Inc., Bethesda, Maryland; consigned to Schiller & Bodo Galleries, New York, 2002. *Notes:* See the discussion of the date of the painting in the text, above, p. 266.

Painting 22. *Smoking Arab. (Fumeur arabe.)* **1871**

Lost

Oil on panel. 35.5 x 24.8 cm. (14 x 9.75 in.) Signed and dated 1871

Provenance: Parke-Bernet, New York, January 1944, lot no. 21–22, $100.

Notes: Known only from the sales record. Image not known. May be one of several Bashi-Bazouks, Arnauts, sentinels, or single Arabs with a hookah or pipe in hand listed in the Goupil stock books without dimensions. The exact titles of the single figures were often mixed up or arbitrarily applied. The studio sketch of two Arabs leaning against a wall (drawing 3), in a private collection, may be related to this work since one figure is meant to hold the pipe drawn next to him.

Ptg 21

Dwg 3

Ptg 23

Painting 23. *A Footman Sleeping. (Valet de pied, dormant.)*
1871

The Metropolitan Museum of Art, New York

Oil on canvas. 34.9 x 26 cm. (13.75 x 10.25 in.) Inscribed, lower right: "C. BARGVE '71"

Provenance: Goupil stock books, vol. 5, pp. 141 and 158, no. 5616: *Domestique endormi,* from Bargue 24 June 1871; sold to Mr. Stebbins 28 June 1871; returned by Stebbins 10 October 1871; sold to Mr. Stephen Whitney Phoenix 19 October 1871, who bequeathed it to the museum in 1881 (81-1-656).

Notes: There is virulent *craquelure anglaise* in the wainscoting and the left knee of the footman. The crackle was already visible in the late 1960s; see the illustration in Charles Sterling and Margaretta Salinger, *French Paintings in the Metropolitan Museum of Art* (New York: Metropolitan Museum of Art, 1966), vol. 2, pp. 175–76. The crackle is probably the result of Bargue's painting over some nondrying base pigment. For more on this painting see Eric Zafran, *Cavaliers and Cardinals: Nineteenth-Century French Anecdotal Paintings* (Washington, D.C.: Corcoran Gallery of Art, 1992), p. 32, no. 1.

Painting 24. *The Sentinel. The Guardian.*
(Une Sentinelle. Le Gardien.) **1871**

Lost

[Medium and support not known], 19 x 12.7 cm. (7.5 x 5 in.)

Provenance: Goupil stock books, vol. 6, p. 132, no. 7348: *Sentinelle, costume jaune & noir,* from Bargue 29 November 1872, 3,000 francs; sold to Oppenheim 6 December 1872 for 7,500 francs; bought by Goupil & Cie at Oppenheim sale, London, 23 May 1877; sold to J. Morris Grant 12 June 1877 for 10,595 francs; bought by Wallis (French Gallery) at Morris sale, Christie's, London, 23 April 1898, for 378 pounds sterling.

Painting 25. *An Algerian Guard. (Sentinelle algérienne.)*
1872

Lost

Watercolor, 32.4 x 21.6 cm. (12.75 x 8.5 in.) Inscribed, upper left: "Bargue '72"

Provenance: Collection of J. Abnee Harper (Vanderbilt collection?), 1880; on loan to the Metropolitan Museum of Art, 1886–1903; Mrs. Cornelius Vanderbilt sale, Parke-Bernet, New York , 18–19 April 1945, no. 28.

Notes: "An Algerian Guard. A Bashi-Bazouk in native costume with blue embroidered jacket and high scarlet and yellow turban, standing with his back to the observer, his face in profile, resting his right hand on his rifle, which is slung over his back." J. Stranahan, *A History of French Painting* (New York: Scribner's, 1888), p. 321.

Painting 26. *The Sentinel. The Guardian.* Sketch.
(*Une Sentinelle. Le Gardien. Ébauche*) 1873
Private collection

Oil on canvas. 32.7 x 22.2 cm (12.75 x 8.75 in.) Signed, lower right, with a spurious signature: "J. L. Gérôme"

Provenance: (Christie's, London, 22 May 1892: F. W. Armytage, *The Algerian Guard*, 1873, 12.5 x 8.5 in; sold to Wallis); Madeleine J. B. Charcot, Gérôme's niece, by descent to Madame R. Allart-Charcot; sold as a work by Gérôme at Knoedler's, New York; Hammer Gallery, New York, 1982; Christie's, New York, 15 February 1985, no. 33, as by Bargue.

Notes: In the first decades of the twentieth century the Gérôme family is recorded as actively buying paintings by Gérôme that came on the market, as well as selling others from the family collections. Perhaps an heir bought this picture from Wallis, honestly thinking it was a painting by Gérôme.

This figure in this painting is too finished for either an *ébauche* or an *esquisse;* the canvas seems to be an earlier version of painting 27; both figures were drawn from the same tracing (see drawing 4).

Ptg 26

Painting 27. *The Sentinel. The Guardian.*
(*Une Sentinelle. Le Gardien.*) 1873
Private collection

Oil on panel. 27.5 x 22.3 cm. (13.75 x 9.75 in.) Signed, lower left: "BARGVE '73"

Provenance: Goupil stock books, vol. 6, p. 155, no. 7585: *La Sentinelle,* replica with changes of 7348. Julius Oehme, a New York dealer, sold to John J. Emery; bequest of John J. Emery to the Cincinnati Art Museum, 1910; deaccessioned (from a "Midwestern Educational Institution") at Parke-Bernet, New York, 18 October 1945, lot 16, illustrated, $450; bought at that sale by Leo Lindeman; Hammer Gallery, New York, 1957; Sotheby's, New York, 12 February 1997, lot 49A.

Notes: The guard is a jailor. It looks af if two ugly iron hooks pointing upward on the wall over the right shoulder of the guard (visible in painting 26, the earlier version) were painted in and then covered much later by a pigment that once matched its surroundings but has since lightened. The hooks were intended to discourage any prisoner thinking of escaping through a window above.

Ptg 27

Dwg 4

Ptg 28

This painting is the result of Bargue's first serious (and successful) tussle with ambient, natural sunlight, making it the first Orientalist subject with a believable atmosphere; although the soldier's pose smacks a bit of the studio, his yellow jacket does not. The brightness of the light and its reflections in North Africa might have impressed Bargue on a purported visit in the winter of 1871–72. A tracing for this figure is in the Art Institute of Chicago (drawing 4). The figure is also the subject of an engraving by Damman entitled "La Sentinelle," which was printed by A. Salmon in Paris and measures 20 x 14 cm.

Painting 28. *The Prayer to Allah.* Sketch. (*En adoration. Ébauche.*) 1874

Private collection

Oil on canvas. 46 x 33 cm (18.5 x 13 in.)

Provenance: A. A. Munger collection; on loan to the Art Institute of Chicago 1890–1901; bequeathed to the latter 1901; deaccessioned 1935 and sold to Charles W. Martin of Omaha, Nebraska; to Francis T. B. Martin by descent in 1940; to present owner by descent ca. 1952.

Notes: Although this oil sketch lacks a signature or date, the brush technique and the background resemble those in the previous entry.

Ptg 29

Painting 29. *The Opinion of the Model. (L'Avis du modèle.)* 1874

Lost

Probably oil on panel. Dimensions a bit larger than 28.3. x 21.6 cm (11 x 8.5 in.), the size of the cartoon (Dwg 6), which is trimmed on all sides, especially on top.

Signed, lower left, on portfolio: "BARGVE"

Provenance: Bargue to Goupil, from whence to Wallis (French Gallery), London, 12 October 1874 for 20,000 francs; present whereabouts unknown.

Notes: Bargue is now in full stride; even from the black and white photograph this is recognizable as a consummate painting. The pose of the model, as she gathers her skirt and peers into the painting, expresses the sweetness of her disposition and her concentration without showing her face. This work is listed in the Goupil stock book (vol. 7, p. 173, no. 9309) as *L'Opinion du modèle,* a fact forgotten when the caption "The Artist and His Model" was put under the colored photogravure published later by Goupil (see fig. 42). Do not confuse this painting with *The Artist and His Model* (painting 43).

Painting 30. *The Artist's Model. The Opinion of the Model.* **Sketch.** *(L'Avis du modèle. Ébauche.)* **1874**

National Gallery of Wales, Cardiff

Oil on panel. 23.6 x 16.4 cm. (9.25 x 6.5 in.) Inscribed on verso: "This oil painting is an original sketch by Bargue. Arnold & Tripp."

Provenance: Alexander Young, Blackheath (Wales); sold at Christie's, London, 30 June 1910 (lot 137); bought by the French Gallery for 378 pounds sterling on behalf of Goupil, who sold it to Margaret Davies of Gregynog, Newton, Wales, 1 July 1910; she bequeathed it to the gallery in 1963.

Notes: The artist is depicted with a touch of satire. Mr. Young, the first known owner of the *ébauche,* also

Dwg 5

Dwg 7

Dwg 6

Ptg 30

Ptg 31

Ptg 32

had several drawings and studies for the painting; they were sold together with the *ébauche* at his sale at Christie's, London, in 1910. Catalogue pages illustrating Mr. Young's collection of Bargue's drawings are in the Witt Library at the Courtauld Institute in London.

Painting 31. *The Painter.* Sketch. *(Le Peintre. Ébauche.)* 1874
Mrs. Noah L. Butkin
Oil on canvas. 25.1 x 16 cm. (9.75 x 6.25 in.) Tag on stretcher reads: "Study by C. Bargue, deceased."
Provenance: Parke-Bernet, New York, 1942, *L'Artiste*, 24.5 x 16.5 cm. (9 x 6.5 in.); Shepherd Gallery, *French and Other Continental Drawings and Watercolors* (New York, 1979), no. 2, illustrated.
Notes: This is a study for *The Opinion of the Model.*

Painting 32. *Lady at a Table. At Table. Breakfast.* Oil sketch. *(Déjeuner. Ébauche.)* 1874–75
Glasgow Museums: The Burrell Collection, Scotland
Oil on canvas. 40.6 x 32.4 cm. (16 x 12.75 in.)
Provenance: William Burrell, Esquire, by 1901; bequeathed to the gallery by Sir William in 1944.
Notes: This is certainly an *ébauche,* but we do not know whether a finished version exists. Although the brushwork and the satirical portrait of the servant would group it with works of the late 1870s, the dog is the same as the one in *The Chess Players* of 1882 (see painting 52).

Painting 33. *Bashi-Bazouk. (Bachi-Bouzouk.)* 1875
The Metropolitan Museum of Art, New York
Oil on canvas. 47.6 x 33.3 cm. (18.25 x 13 in.) Signed, lower right: "BARGVE '75"
Provenance: Goupil stock books, vol. 8, p. 205; Bargue to Goupil; Goupil to Mlle Wolfe, 12 July 1875, for 21,600 francs; bequest of Catharine Lorillard Wolfe to the museum 1887.
Notes: See Charles Sterling and Margaretta Salinger, *French Paintings in the Metropolitan Museum of Art* (New York:

Metropolitan Museum of Art, 1966), vol. 2, p. 176. Two copies of this painting were on the market around the turn of the present century: (1) Christie's, New York, 14 October 1993, lot 255: o/c, 51.4 x 37.8 cm (20.25 x 14.75 in.); (2) Sotheby's, London, 1 May 2002, lot 330: o/c, 47 x 32.5 cm (18.5 x 12.25 in.); unclear signature read as C*** Baird and sold under that name. A pencil study for the model's right arm is in the Museum of Fine Arts in Boston, acquisition no. 27.492, Walter Gay bequest.

Painting 34. *Albanian Soldier. (Soldat albanais.)* **1876**
Private collection
Oil on panel. 27.9 x 21cm. (11 x 8.25 in.) Signed, center right: "BARGVE '76"
Provenance: John W. Wilson sale, Paris, 14–16 March 1881, lot 130, illustrated, 28,000 francs; Mrs. Mary J. Morgan sale, American Art Association, New York, 3–5 and 8–15 March 1886, lot 164, 61,000 francs; John T. Martin sale, Mendelssohn Hall, New York, 15–16 April 1909, lot 80, $9,600; C. K. J. Billings, Fort Tryon, New York (entered and illustrated in a luxurious catalogue entitled *Fort Tryon Hall: The Residency of C. K. J. Billings, Esquire* [New York: American Art Association, 1911], n.p., no cat. nos.); by descent to seller at Christie's, New York, 24 October 1990, lot 93, $66,000; Edward T. Wilson, Fund for Fine Arts, Inc., Chevy Chase, Maryland; Sotheby's, New York, 23 May 1997, sale 6993, lot 110; $112,500; Jerome Davis, Greenwich, Conn., until 2002.
Notes: This painting cannot be found in the Goupil stock books. A work entitled *An Albanian Soldier (Soldat albanais)* is listed bearing the date 1883, but with different dimensions; several other sentinels are listed, but none can be matched with this entry.

Ptg 33

Dwg 8

Ptg 34

Painting 35. *Head of a Young Man,* **study.**
***(Tête d'un jeune homme, étude.)* 1876**
Nationalmuseum of Sweden, Stockholm
Oil on canvas. 21 x 21 cm. (8.25 x 8.25 in.)
Provenance: Goupil stock books, vol. 11, p. 122, no. 17301, and p. 127, no. 17387: Goupil from Donatis, Paris, to Groves, Paris, 1885; Goupil to Heilbourne [*sic*], Marseilles, 1885; bequest to the museum by Consul O. Ph. Heilborn, 1902.

Painting 36. *A Turkish Sentinel. (Une Sentinelle turque.)*
1877
Museum of Fine Arts, Boston
Oil on panel. 28 x 21 cm. (11 x 8.25 in.) Signed, lower right: "BARGVE '77"
Provenance: A. Donatis, 1877; Donatis sale, 1898, bought by Arnold and Tripp, Paris; sold to Susan Cornelia Warren of Boston; Warren sale, American Art Association, New York, 3 January 1903, no. 19, illustrated; bought by the museum with money bequeathed by Mrs. Warren to the museum for the purchase of items from her sale (03.601.)
Notes: The title is probably not Bargue's original title: the soldier is not guarding anything, just lounging around; furthermore, he's not even a Turk since he wears an Albanian skirt.

Painting 37. *Greek Soldier, Pink and White Outfit.*
(Soldat grec, costume rose et blanc.) **1877**
Lost
Oil on panel. 27.3 x 19 cm. (10.75 x 7.75 in.) No inscriptions;
unfinished.
Provenance: Goupil stock books, vol. 11, p. 73, no. 16571:
Bought by Goupil 28 April 1883 from Bargue's apartment
after he had been committed. Goupil may have paid
Bargue's landlord, who had appropriated some of Bargue's
studio stock in lieu of unpaid rent (see p. 276 above.) Sold
to a Mrs. Cornelius Hertz of England, 22 December 1884,
for 11,000 francs; Hertz sale, Christie's, London, 15 April
1899, no. 16; bought by Tooth & Co. (described in Tooth
stock books: London, 15 April, as "Greek soldier in pink
and white dress, 11 x 8 in, bought at Christie's London for
220 pounds sterling"); The Art Institute of Chicago, 1940;
deaccessioned and sold as *Arab Soldier* at Parke-Bernet, New
York, 4 May 1944, no. 12, illustrated (see p. 280 above.)

Dwg 9

Painting 38. *Arab Merchant Among His Antiques. (Marchand arabe parmi ses antiquités.)* 1877
Private collection
Oil on panel. 33 x 24.4 cm. (13 x 9.5 in.)
Signed, lower right: "BARGVE '77"
Provenance: Karl Loevenich, New York, ca. 1926; Walter Chrysler, New York; Edward Pawlin, New York; Robert Isaacson Collection, New York; Isaacson sale, Christie's, New York, sale 9152, 6 May 1999, lot 2.

Painting 39. *Oriental Merchant. (Marchand oriental.)* 1877
Lost
Oil. Signed, lower right: "BARGVE '77"
Provenance: Julius Weitzner, dealer, New York.
Notes: This work is known only from old photographs. One, in the Getty Museum archives, has an interesting verso: a stamp "From the Julius Weitzner File" plus a handwritten note to someone at Gumps Department Store in San Francisco, California, which reads: "'The Oriental Antique Vendor' by Charles Bargue. Less than 20 paintings known by this most exquisite highly finished artist who died so young. This is a must! For windows—[it] ties up nicely with Gumps general atmosphere. Put in window with similar art objects, jades, etc." This might be read as a dealer

(Weitzner) trying to sell the painting to Gumps, or it might be construed as an internal memo from one Gumps staff member to another on the use of the painting in a window display. The store's archives were destroyed in a fire in 1974. There is no record that Gumps ever owned the painting.

Painting 40. *An Oriental Coffeehouse.*
(*Dans un café oriental.*) 1877
Private collection
Watercolor on paper. 29.8 x 21.6 cm. (11.75 x 8.5 in.)
Signed at right, on bench: "BARGVE '77"
Provenance: Sordoni collection, Wilkes-Barre, Pa., in the 1960s; Sotheby's, New York, 23 October 1990, sale 6076, lot 39.
Notes: This is an astonishing watercolor. The great skill evident is an indication that there must exist other Bargue watercolors of high finish; however, only a few watercolor sketches are known by Bargue other than this one and paintings 25 and 41. Perhaps some of the fine watercolors ascribed to Gérôme (but not characteristic of his style) are really by Bargue.

Ptg 41

Painting 41. *The Greek Singer.* **(*Chanteur grec.*) ca. 1877**
Private collection
Watercolor on paper. 36.2 x 26.7 cm. (14.25 x 10.5 in.)
Spurious signature, lower left: "J. L. GÉRÔME"
Notes: At Colnaghi's, New York, 1983. Despite the added signature, the watercolor has all the characteristics of Bargue's work around 1877 and very few traits characteristic of Gérôme's style other than the subject.

Ptg 42

Dwg 10

Painting 42. *The Warrior. (The Guard. The Sentinel. Keeper of the Harem.) (Guerrier. La Sentinelle.)* 1877?

Paine Art Center and Gardens, Oshkosh, Wisconsin

Oil on honeycombed aluminum (transferred from panel in 1986.) 35.6 x 24 cm. (14 x 9.5 in.) Added signature and date. The use of the capital C. for Charles and the U instead of a Roman "V" are both atypical among Bargue's signatures of this time, as is the irregularity of the lettering.

Provenance: Goupil stock books, vol. 11, p. 77, no. 16640, lists a *Guerrier* measuring 35 x 24 cm. that was bought at the Bargue sale on 31 May 1883 and sold to Noyes and Blakeslee, Boston, in July 1884. This must have been one of the three paintings in the Bargue exhibition held at the C. Fearon Gallery, New York, in 1926. John Levey Galleries sold it to Nathan Paine in 1926, who bequeathed it to the center.

Notes: The dense, close composition along with the pile of accessories to the left of the heavily draped model place this work within a series of single-figured subjects from 1877. There are large islands of *craquelure anglaise* in the light areas, and small systems of normal craquelure in the dark areas. There are several questions about this picture, not one of which challenges its authenticity. First the uncertainty of the signature, as noted above. Since it is a factually accurate inscription, it might be a replacement of a signature lost in a cleaning. Next, why did it stay in Bargue's studio unsold until his death for twelve years? Goupil bought it at Bargue's estate sale. Then, where was it between 1884 and 1926–that is, for forty-two years? This lacuna is not a great problem, although one would like to know where it was and how well it was taken care of during that time. Finally the round, light-reflecting mouth of the scabbard of the drawn sword seems, in the photos and our reproduction, looks like a hole in the surface of the soldier's chest. This somewhat disconcerting effect is the same in a photo of 1928. Was the area left unfinished, or had an unrecorded cleaning before 1928 —perhaps before the exhibition at the Fearon Gallery in New York City and the sale to Paine—changed the values in this area, or is it a natural phenomenon observed and recorded by Bargue? In 1986 the panel support was shrinking because of moisture or humidity. The surface became wavy, and pushed the painted surface up. Furthermore, the painting was covered with several layers of thick and discolored varnish, perhaps in an effort to hold it together. It was necessary to change the support. The fact that the painting now still looks as it did in the early photograph testifies to the care taken in the transfer of the painting from a wooden to an aluminum support and the removal of the several layers of varnish by the Chicago Conservation Center in1986. These problems, although of interest to art-historians, will not bother the public who will enjoy the bold composition, and marvel at Bargue's mastery of textures and fineness of detail.

Documentation: Conservation reports of the Chicago Conservation Center, signed by Bob Bauman in the registrar's files in the center (15 July 1986 and 11 May 2003.)

Painting 43. *The Artist and His Model.*
(L'Artiste et son modèle.) **1878**
Mrs. Noah L. Butkin
Oil on panel. 27.3 x 19.7 cm. (10.75 x 7.75 in.) Signed, lower right: "BARGVE '78"
Provenance: Bargue to Goupil 1878; sold, through the New York office, to William H. Vanderbilt in 1878 for 32,500 francs; by inheritance, in turn, to George W. Vanderbilt, Brig. Gen. Cornelius Vanderbilt, Mrs. Cornelius Vanderbilt sale, Parke-Bernet, New York, 18–19 April 1945, lot 39; Robert Lehman, New York; Herbert Roman, Inc., 1979; Shepherd Gallery, New York.

Notes: In this painting Bargue has produced a composition unified in color, what Roger de Piles would call a *tout ensemble* (see note 66). This work should not be confused with *The Opinion of the Model (L'Avis du modèle)* (painting 29). On loan to the Metropolitan Museum of Art, New York, 1902–20. See Eric Zafran, *Cavaliers and Cardinals: Nineteenth-Century French Anecdotal Paintings* (Washington D.C.: Corcoran Gallery of Art, 1992), p. 34, no. 2.

Ptg 43

Painting 44. *The Artist at His Easel. Sketch. (L'Artiste à son chevalet. Ébauche.)* **1878**
Private collection
Oil on panel. 23.8 x 15.2 cm. (9.5 x 6 in.) Signed, lower left, in longhand: "Bargue"—an atypical signature.
Provenance: Goupil stock books, vol. 11, p. 83, no. 16723: bought by Goupil at the Bargue sale 31 May 1883 (24 x 15.5 cm); sold to Amassoff 27 February 1884, Parke-Bernet, New York, 17 October 1942, sold as *L'Artiste* (9 x 6.5 in.) for $100; Sordoni collection, Wilkes-Barre, Pa., until 1975; Christie's, New York, 25 May 1984, lot 76.

Ptg 44

Ptg 45

Painting 45. *The Almeh.* (*L'Almée.*) 1879

Private collection

Oil on panel. 41.6 x 24.5 cm. (16.5 x 9.5 in.) Signed, lower right: "Bargue '79"

Provenance: Goupil stock books, vol. 9, p. 224, no. 13688: Bargue to Goupil, June 1879; commissioned by William H. Vanderbilt (through Samuel Avery, 32,000 francs, 1879); by inheritance, in turn, to George W. Vanderbilt, Brig. Gen. Cornelius Vanderbilt, Mrs. Cornelius Vanderbilt sale, Parke-Bernet, 18–19 April 1945, lot 110; private collection until 1986; Shepherd Gallery, New York; Edward T. Wilson, Fund for Fine Arts, Inc., Chevy Chase, Maryland; sold at Christie's, New York, 2 November 1995, lot 46, for $96,000.

Notes: This work was on loan to the Metropolitan Museum of Art, New York, from 1886 to 1903. The figure was much studied in a series of drawings in various collections (see drawings 11–13). A smaller painting with the same title, measuring 26 x 14 cm. (10.25 x 5.5 in.) was bought by Goupil from Angelino Verrachia in 1883 for 1,250 francs and sold to Mrs. Cornelius Hertz two years later for 2,500 francs. The price is modest; this item may be an *esquisse* of this entry or of another version, but it is certainly not highly finished.

Dwg 11

Dwg 12

Dwg 13

Painting 46. *Arabs at Prayer.* Grisaille. (*En Prière. Grisaille.*) **1875–81**

Lost

Oil. 59.7 x 49.5 cm. (23.5 x 19.5 in.)

Provenance: Perhaps this is the entry in the Goupil stock books, vol. 11, p. 77, no. 16629: "*En prière,* 62 x 49.5 cm.," bought by Goupil at the Bargue sale on 31 May 1883; sold to Defossés July 1884; reentered in same volume, p. 128, no. 17389, as *Intérieur de mosquée, grisaille,* 61 x 50 cm.; bought from Defossés April 1885; sold to Grevet (Grove?) July 1885; Wallis sale, London, 6 February 1909, sold as *Arabs at Prayer,* 23.5 x 19.25; in the yearbook of Barbizon House (a commercial gallery), London, perhaps 1919.

Notes: The image is known only from a small illustration, probably clipped from one of the annual catalogues (perhaps 1919; I have examined every issue of the Barbizon House yearbook except for 1919) of important sales of the year held at Barbizon House, London. The undated clipping is in the Witt Library of the Courtauld Institute of Art in London (it is reproduced here). The composition, an angular view of the interior of an old mosque, presents an elaborate group of worshippers standing in various positions of prayer just to the right of the Mihrab, with the Minbar in full view. This grisaille may have been the model for a book or magazine illustration.

Ptg 46

Dwg 14

Dwg 15

Dwg 16

Dwg 17

Among the group at prayer is a bare-chested Santon—a local holy man or hermit—who is featured in several of the mosque scenes by Gérôme. There are many preparatory sketches in oil and in pencil for this composition (see painting 47 and drawings 14–17). The fact that there are so many pencil sketches and a splendid preparatory oil sketch of high quality for this composition makes one think that they were all done not for a grisaille but for a major colored composition. The lost painting *En Prière* (having almost the same dimensions as the grisaille) bought at the Bargue sale by Goupil might be the unfinished oil version.

Painting 47. *Muslims at Prayer*. Sketch. (*Musulmans prosternés. Ébauche.*) 1875–80
Art Gallery of Hamilton, Ontario (Canada)
Oil on canvas. 35.6 x 27.3 cm. (14 x 10.75 in.)
Provenance: Goupil stock books, vol. 11, p. 77, no. 16641: "Musulmans prosternés, 35 x 26.7 cm.," bought by Goupil at the Bargue sale 31 May 1883; sold to Richard & Co., New York; Sir Wm. Van Horne collection, sold at Parke-Bernet, New York, 24 January 1946, for $700; Schweitzer Gallery, New York; Tanenbaum collection, Toronto, sold at Sotheby's, New York, 23 October 1997, lot 60; Sotheby's, New York, 5 May 1999, lot 230; Tanenbaum Donation to the art gallery, 2003.
Notes: This is most likely a study for painting 46.

Painting 48. *At His Devotion*. Sketch. (*En adoration. Ébauche.*) 1870–80
Arnot Art Museum, Elmira, New York
Oil on panel. 50.2 x 30 cm. (19.75 x 11.75 in.)
Provenance: Goupil stock books, vol. 11, p. 77, no. 16634: bought by Goupil at Bargue sale 31 May 1883; sold to Noyes and Blakeslee, Boston, July 1905, who probably sold it to Matthias H. Arnot; Matthias H. Arnot, who bequeathed it to the museum in 1910.
Notes: See the catalogue *A Collector's Vision* (Elmira, NY: Arnot Art Museum, 1989), p. 78, no. 18.

Painting 49. *Bashi-Bazouk, seated.* **Sketch.**
(Bachi-Bouzouk, assis. Ébauche.) **1880s**
Art Gallery of Hamilton, Ontario (Canada)
Oil on canvas. 46.4 x 33 cm. (18.25 x 13 in.) No inscription.
Provenance: Perhaps this is the painting *An Arab Smoker* (17.5 x 12.5 in.) sold to Boss at Christie's, London, on 14 March 1908 for twenty-one pounds sterling, or perhaps it is the work at the Ullman sale, Associated American Artists, New York, 17 November 1938, identified as "attributed to Bargue . . . 18.5 x 13 in" (it might have been tagged "attributed to" because it is a sketch, not a finished work, or it might have been one of the copies of an earlier Bashi-Bazouk sold at Sotheby's, London, 1 May 2002, lot 330; see painting 33); Schweitzer Gallery, New York, until May 1972; Tanenbaum collection, Toronto, offered at Sotheby's, New York, 23 October 1997, sale 7028, lot 61, bought in; Sotheby's, New York, 5 May 1999, sale 7300, lot 229, bought in; Tanenbaum Donation to the art gallery, 2003.
Notes: Three Bashi-Bazouks of about the same size were bought by Goupil at the Bargue sale in 1883, following which they were touched up, framed, and sold. It is hard to trace them after their first owners: one to Hertz, another to Defossés, and a third to Wallis—probably all dealers. This figure study, which is probably one of the three, with the same dimensions as two of the Bashi-Bazouks bought by Goupil, but without the Bargue sale stamp, is used in the background of Bargue's last painting entitled *Bashi-Bazouks Playing Chess* (painting 53). The model, a favorite of Gérôme, was probably sketched in Gérôme's studio. There is a drawing of the model in the same costume by Gérôme made at about the same time as Bargue's oil sketch (see fig. 43), which provides good evidence that the two worked and sketched together.

Painting 50. *Seated Arab,* **study.** *(Arabe assis, étude).*
1870s
Mark Murray Fine Paintings, New York
Oil on canvas. 20.4 x 15.4 cm. (8 x 6 in.) Dubious signature, lower left.
Provenance: Private collection, Kansas City, Mo.; Sotheby's London, 2 December 1998, no. 143, as one of *Two Studies of Male Figures;* Sotheby's, New York, 5 May 1999, sale 7300, lot 256.

Ptg 49

Ptg 50

Ptg 52

Painting 51. *The Flute Player. (Joueur de flûte.)* **1880**
Private collection
Oil on panel. 28.3 x 19.1 cm. (11 x 7.5 in.) Signed, lower right: "BARGVE"
Provenance: Goupil stock books, vol. 10, p. 127, no. 14809: Bargue to Goupil, August 1880, for 22,500 francs; sold to John W. Wilson for 40,000 francs; Wilson sale, London, 1880, sold for 28,000 francs to William Rockefeller, New York; Emma Rockefeller McAlpin estate sale, American Art Association, New York, 1 November 1935, lot 21; Skinner Auction House, Boston, 5 November 1993, sale 1546, lot 21; Sotheby's, New York, 26 May 1994, sale 6569, lot 139, bought by Edward T. Wilson, Fund for Fine Arts, Inc., Chevy Chase, Maryland, until 1999; Hirschl & Adler Galleries, New York, to present owner.

Painting 52. *The Chess Players. (Joueurs d'échecs.)* **1882**
Private collection
Oil on panel. 28.6 x 43.8 cm. (11.25 x 17.25 in.) Signed, lower left: "C. BARGVE"
Provenance: Goupil stock books, vol. 9, p. 221, and vol. 11, p. 191, no. 16191: Bargue to Goupil, 20 July 1982, for 30,000 francs; Goupil to Avery for William H. Vanderbilt, delivered 1883, for 75,000 francs; by inheritance, in turn, to George W. Vanderbilt, Brig. Gen. Cornelius Vanderbilt, Mrs. Cornelius Vanderbilt sale, Parke-Bernet, New York, 18–19 August 1945, lot 133, to Peikin Galleries, Inc., for 61,000 francs; Sordoni collection, Wilkes-Barre, Pa., Sotheby's, New York, 23 May 1997, sale 6693, lot 162, to Jerome Davis, Greenwich, Conn., for $127,500; Hirschl & Adler, New York, 2002 to present owner.

Painting 53. *Bashi-Bazouks Playing Chess.*
(Bachi-Bouzouks jouant aux échecs.) **1882–83**
Malden Public Library, Malden, Massachusetts
Oil on panel. 88.25 x 68.5 cm. (34.75 x 27 in.) Unfinished and without inscriptions.
Provenance: Evidently this work was left unfinished in Gérôme's studio upon Bargue's death in 1883. Jean-Léon Gérôme's collection, Paris, until 1883 (Gérôme probably sold the painting in 1888); Vos Galleries, Boston, 1944, in which year it was sold to the library for $2,400.
Notes: Some areas appear to have been finished by Gérôme, before he sold the picture. The head, turban and vest on the back of the chess player to the left are in a noticeably tighter style than the rest even though Gérôme has tried to imitate Bargue's feathery touch. The Bashi-Bazouk in the middle background (after painting 49) and the man playing the oud to the right are unfinished. The letter by Gérôme attached to the back attests that the work is by Bargue and that Gérôme lent him costumes for it and watched him work on it. (For the text of the letter see p. 278 above.)

Painting 54. *Seated Moroccan Tailor.* **Cartoon**
(Tailleur marocain assis. Carton.)
Private collection
Pencil on paper. 29.2 x 23 cm. (11.5 x 9.25 in.) "Vente Bargue" stamp.
Provenance: The Drawing Shop, New York, 1962.
Notes: This is a drawing on transparent onion skin paper, ready for transfer to a canvas. I do not know whether an *ébauche* or a finished oil exists of this subject, but this is an advanced stage of picture production. The marginal dimensions of the painting may be larger than the cartoon, but the figure would be the same size.

PAINTINGS LACKING AN IMAGE OR A DATE

Painting 55. *Peasant Boy of the Apennines.*
(Jeune Paysan des Apennins.)
Lost
Medium unknown. 56 x 47 cm. (22 x 18.5 in.) Signed, lower left: "Bargue". The size is a bit large for a head by Bargue.
Provenance: Sold at American Art Galleries, New York, 21 February 1916, no. 31; not illustrated. Catalogue description: "Half-length head of a little lad whose back is towards the spectator, with head turned to look over his right shoulder. The wide-brimmed hat which shields his face is decorated with flowers."

Painting 56. *The Alms Gatherer. (La Quêteuse.)*

Painting 57. *The Holy Water Fount. (L'Eau bénite.)*
Notes: Both paintings are lost. They are known only from lithographs by Bargue. *The Alms Gatherer* is inscribed: "Painted by C. Bargue. Lith. by C. Bargue" ("Peint par C. Bargue. Lith. par C. Bargue"). Well-dressed women in church were a popular theme in the second half of the nineteenth century. These early works by Bargue show a precocious ability to paint drapery; perhaps he was trained in the family workshop as a fabric specialist.

Ptg 56   Ptg 57

Drawing 1. *Arabs Observed at a Distance.* *(Feuille d'études de figures arabes.)*
Private collection
Pencil on paper. 16 x 17.4 cm. (6.25 x 6.75 in.) "Vente Bargue" stamp.
Provenance: Bargue sale, Paris, 31 May 1883; Hazlitt, Gooden & Fox, *Nineteenth-Century French Drawings* (London, 1977), no. 56; Robert Isaacson Collection.
Notes: The immediacy and probable employment of sight-size technique suggests that this drawing was made on the spot during an unrecorded trip to North Africa by Bargue. This may be the only evidence that Bargue visited the Near East except, perhaps, for drawings 2 and 18.

Drawing 2. *Seated Arab. (Arabe assis.)*
The Art Museum, Princeton University
Pencil and watercolor on paper. 26.6 x 19.8 cm. (10.5 x 7.75 in.) "Vente Bargue" stamp. Inscription, lower left: "dessin par Charles Bargue".
Provenance: Bargue sale, Paris, 31 May 1883; Dan Fellows Platt collection; Platt bequest to the museum, class of 1895.
Notes: There is something haphazard about the proportions; the view from above and the uncertainty of the pose makes this seem like a drawing made on the spot rather than the recording of a studio pose. See also drawing 18, which also has an *in situ* aspect.

Drawing 3. *Two Arabs Leaning against a Wall.* *(Deux Arabes appuyés contre un mur.)*
Private collection
Black crayon and some red watercolor on paper. 32.7 x 25.4 cm. (13 x 10 in.) "Vente Bargue" stamp.
Provenance: Bargue sale, Paris, 31 May 1883; Shepherd Gallery, *Ingres & Delacroix Through Puvis de Chavannes* (New York, 1975), no.115; Robert Isaacson Collection.
Notes: The hand of the figure on the left is drawn to hold the pipe sketched to his side. Because the model is sketched twice in almost the identical pose, this drawing can reasonably be taken as a study for a lost work (see painting 22) for which no reproduction has been found.

Drawing 4. *Armed Arab Leaning Against a Wall (Standing Sentinel.) (Arabe armé s'appuyant contre un mur.)*
The Art Institute of Chicago
Graphite on tracing paper, laid down on ivory wove paper. 22.2 x 11.8 cm. (8.75 x 4.5 in.) "Vente Bargue" stamp.
Provenance: Charles Deering collection.
Notes: This tracing was used for both versions of *The Sentinel* (see paintings 26 and 27).

Drawing 5. *The Opinion of the Model. (L'Avis du modèle.)* **1874**
Fitzwilliam Museum, Cambridge, England
Black crayon on paper. 24 x 16.5 cm. (9.5 x 6.5 in.) "Vente Bargue" stamp.
Provenance: Bargue sale, Paris, 31 May 1883; Alexander Young collection sale, Christie's, London, 1 July 1910; C. G. Clarke, who bequeathed it to the museum in 1960.
Notes: This is a compositional sketch for painting 29. It is not an idea sketch; models have already been used, and the composition is too set for an idea sketch. It is probably a study for the cartoon that follows.

Drawing 6. *The Opinion of the Model.* Cartoon. *(L'Avis du modèle. Carton.)* **1874**
Mrs. Noah L. Butkin
Pencil and faint red crayon on tracing paper. 28.3 x 21.6 cm. (11.25 x 8.5 in.)
Provenance: Shepherd Gallery, *Non-Dissenters* (New York, 1976), no. 4.
Notes: This is a cartoon ready for transfer to panel for painting 29.

Drawing 7. Study for *The Opinion of the Model.* **(Étude pour** *Le Peintre et son modèle,* **ou** *L'Avis du modèle.)*
The Walters Art Museum, Baltimore, Maryland
Pencil on paper. 24.8 x 16.5 cm. (9.75 x 6 .5 in.)
Notes: There is wit in the accurate depiction of the left leg and foot.

**Drawing 8. Study for *An Albanian Soldier*.
(Étude pour *Un Soldat albanais*.)**
Private collection
Pencil on paper. 25.4 x 15.2 cm. (10 x 6 in.) "Vente Bargue" stamp.
Provenance: Bargue sale, Paris, 31 May 1883; Jill Newhouse Drawings, *Fall Catalogue* (New York, 1986), no. 8; Martin Reymart collection, New York.
Notes: This study seems to be basic to paintings 34 and 36.

Drawing 9. Study for *Greek Soldier*. (Étude pour *Soldat grec*.)
Private collection
Pencil on paper. 26.6 x 20.2 cm. (10.5 x 8 in.) "Vente Bargue" stamp.
Provenance: Bargue sale, Paris, 31 May 1883; Christie's, New York, 24 October 1990, no. 94.
Notes: The slender, rather sweet young boy in the drawing is transformed into a husky adult for the lost *Greek Soldier* (see painting 37). The head, arms, and shoulders of a mature model have been appended to the boy's legs, with some discomfort caused to the *contrapposto*. Bargue has elsewhere mixed body halves, with similar anatomical disjunction (see painting 41).

Drawing 10. *The Artist at His Easel*. (*L'Artiste à son chevalet*.) 1878
Private collection
Pencil on paper. 19 x 14.2 cm. (7.5 x 5.5 in.) Signed, lower left: "Bargue."
Provenance: Bargue to Samuel Putnam Avery. The Avery family by descent. Private collection 1975.
Notes: This is a study for painting 44.

Drawing 11. Study for *The Almeh*. (Étude pour *L'Almée*.) 1879
The Metropolitan Museum of Art, New York
Black graphite on paper. 22 x 10.3 cm. (8.75 x 4 in.) "Vente Bargue" stamp.
Provenance: Bargue sale, Paris, 31 May 1883; Albert Gallatin gave it to the museum in 1920.
Notes: This is a careful drawing on tracing paper. The costume is the same as in painting 45, but neither the model nor her pose were used.

Drawing 12. Study for *The Almeh*. (Étude pour *L'Almée*.) 1879
Private collection
Pencil on paper. 28 x 17.9 cm. (11 x 7 in.) "Vente Bargue" stamp.
Provenance: Bargue sale, Paris, 31 May 1883; Knoedler's, New York; The Antiquarian, Tulsa, Okla.; Richard Townsend, Tulsa, Okla.; Edward T. Wilson, Fund for Fine Arts, Inc., Chevy Chase, Maryland; sale at Christie's, New York, 1 November 1995, no. 46.
Notes: This is a study for painting 45.

Drawing 13. Study for *The Almeh*. (Étude pour *L'Almée*.) 1879
Private collection
Watercolor and pencil. 26.7 x 18.4 cm. (10.5 x 7.25 in.) "Vente Bargue" stamp.
Provenance: Bargue sale, Paris, 31 May 1883; Sotheby's, New York, 23 October 1997, sale no. 7028, lot 248.
Notes: This is a study for painting 45. An undaunted realist, Bargue is susceptible to the mood of his model. A similar drawing (not illustrated) and of slightly smaller size (24.7 x 18.5 cm./ 10.5 x 7.25 in.) with a catalogue description that could fit this drawing was sold at Christie's, South Kensington, on 25 July 2001 (lot 224).

**Drawing 14. *Arab Kneeling in Prayer*.
(*Arabe agenouillé en prière*.)**
The Walters Art Museum, Baltimore, Maryland
Crayon on paper. 24 x 19 cm. (9.5 x 7.5 in.) Signed, lower right: "C. Bargue"
Notes: This and the next three drawings may all be studies for a lost painting or for an illustration known only as a grisaille (see painting 46). Two of the poses seem to start out seminude and then get clothed.

Drawing 15. *Moslem at Prayer*. (*Musulman en prière*.)
The Walters Art Museum, Baltimore, Maryland
Crayon on paper. 23.9 x 18.8 cm. (9.5 x 7.5 in.) Signed, lower right: "C. Bargue"

Drawing 16. *Moslem Prostrating Himself on Prayer Rug. (Musulman se prosternant en prière.)*
The Walters Art Museum, Baltimore, Maryland
Crayon on paper. 24 x 29.7 cm. (9.5 x 11.75 in.)

Drawing 17. *Moslem at Prayer. (Musulman en prière.)*
The Walters Art Museum, Baltimore, Maryland
Conté crayon on paper. 16.7 x 25.2 cm. (6.5 x 10 in.) Inscribed, lower right: "C. Bargue"

Dwg 18

Drawing 18. *Seated Arab. (Arabe assis.)*
The Art Institute of Chicago
Pencil and watercolor on paper. 30.8 x 18.6 cm. (12 x 7.25 in.)
Provenance: Bargue sale, Paris, 31 May 1883. Charles Deering collection.
Like drawing 2, this also has the air of having been sketched on location in North Africa.

Dwg 19

Drawing 19. *Man Reading in a Rococo Room. (Homme lisant dans un décor rococo.)* 1880
The Art Institute of Chicago
Black crayon on paper. 25.2 x 17.8 cm. (10 x 7 in.) "Vente Bargue" stamp.
Provenance: Bargue sale, Paris, 31 May 1883; Charles Deering collection.
Notes: In this rare finished drawing by Bargue not only is an environment present but all construction lines are gone. The closeness of the subject to that of Meissonier reveals another of Bargue's strong affinities.

Drawing 20. *Italian Peasant Woman.*
(Paysanne italienne ["La Cervarolle"].)
Edward T. Wilson, Fund for Fine Arts, Inc., Bethesda, Maryland
Graphite on paper. 26.4 x 16.5 cm. (10.25 x 6.5 in.) "Vente
Bargue" stamp.
Provenance: Bargue sale, Paris, 31 May 1883; Shepherd Gallery,
New York.
Notes: This is probably a study for an unrealized oil or *ébauche*
bought by Goupil at the Bargue sale that is listed in the Goupil
stock books (vol. 2, p. 77, no. 16632) as *"Italiens montant un
escalier,* huile" (45.5 x 37 cm./25 x 14.5 in.) According to the
Goupil records, the painting was retouched before being sold to
Richards & Co. of New York in July 1884 for just 300 francs. Its
execution could not have been very advanced at that price.

Dwg 20

Note: There are other drawings in appendix 3.

APPENDIX 1:
The Goupil Brochure: On Models for Drawing Classes[79]

. . . These primary tools for teaching must be rigorously reformed.
—M. Guillaume, sculptor, Member of the Institute, etc.

The question of what models to use (in elementary drawing classes) has always been the preoccupation of those who are concerned with the teaching of drawing; various ministers of public education have repeatedly studied reports on this topic; special commissions were created to outline study plans, which were greeted with lavish encouragement of all kinds. Sadly, one must conclude—from the great competitive exhibition of 1865 organized by the Central Union of Applied Fine Arts—that all this toil, all this concern, has been fruitless.

M. Ernest Chesneau reviewed this exhibition in a series of articles published by *Le Constitutionnel* at the end of 1865.[80]

> A great experiment has just been made. The drawing schools of Paris and of the departments, the drawing schools of the lycées, of the colleges, of the normal schools for primary teachers, to the number of *two hundred and thirty-nine,* sent to an exhibition (put on at the Palace of Industry by the Central Union) of more than eight thousand drawings, clay models, and scale models executed according to their special areas of study. . . . Practically all of France, one could say, is represented in the halls of the palace. . . . The great benefit of this exhibition will be its having opened the most obstinately closed eyes, of forcing the opinion of a few to become the general opinion, of leading, we hope, to a complete reorganization of the teaching of drawing. Radical reform in this sense is—I cannot deny it—very difficult to achieve; but it has become absolutely necessary after the lamentable spectacle that was offered us by a run of over a thousand meters at the Palace of Industry, on walls embellished from top to bottom—under the pretext of drawing—with everything that black and white combined could create in terms of inept, ridiculous, and poverty-stricken forms—with practically no exceptions—deprived not only of any of the feelings of art but also far distant from any resemblance, from any shadow of the principles of the science of drawing: correctness, precision, movement, life, beauty. In the presence of such a display of monstrosities in charcoal, Conté crayon, lead pencil, watercolor, etc., one is justifiably astonished to see, at the annual salons, so many artists of honest talent who have passed through and undergone such deplorable instruction. One can only imagine the unbelievable efforts they must have made to unlearn what they were taught. One is full of admiration for those who succeeded. "There are no good models!" That is the predominant cry among the complaints provoked by an examination of the exhibition.

A few days later, at the solemn ceremony for the distribution of prizes awarded after the exhibition, the present director of the École des Beaux-Arts, M. [Eugène] Guillaume, sculptor, Member of the Institute, delivered a remarkable speech in which he explained that he was speaking on behalf of the Jury of the Schools. This is how he expressed himself:

> The main ingredient of art is taste. On this account, *we are afflicted by the weakness of the models* that are called upon to develop it. To place before the eyes of beginners in our schools examples devoid of any elevated sentiment, to have them copy engravings and lithographs in a false style, incorrectly drawn, and executed by routine procedures—this [amounts to] the corruption of the taste of the nation; it renders impossible the development of vocations. *These primary tools of education must be rigorously reformed.* All the books that are used in the teaching of grammar and literature in France are submitted for official approval: as its sworn duty, the Jury calls for the creation of a commission charged by the administration with selecting the most suitable works for the teaching of [the] art [of drawing].

In compliance with the proposition advanced by the vice-president of the Jury of the Schools, a commission was charged by his excellency the Minister of Public Instruction to set up a list of works most suitable for the teaching of [the] art [of drawing]. All known models and pattern books were passed in review; but these models, for the most part, were precisely those that M. Guillaume had just denounced as *corrupters of taste,* as a result of which the work of the Commission could only be one of elimination and its catalogue a list of works as insipid as they were offensive. And so we end up once again affirming the lack of good models. And there is where the role of the administration must of necessity stop.

Thus, it was left to individual initiative to solve the problem. Men of taste and learning—true artists—applied themselves and a handful of excellent models have already been published.

The firm of Goupil & Cie could not remain indifferent to efforts having as their goal the solution to a problem that concerns contemporary art to such a high degree. It, too, set itself to work, and with the aid of some practical men it designed a program whose execution has been entrusted to several distinguished artists.

M. Charles Bargue, with the assistance of M. Gérôme, Member of the Institute, took upon himself responsibility for the models for drawing the figure. His effort, taken as a whole, will present a complete course divided into two parts. The first part, consisting solely of drawings after casts, comprises in and of itself an elementary, progressive course having as its goal to prepare students to draw an entire academic figure. In the choice and execution of these models no concession was made to the pretty or the pleasant; their severity will doubtlessly discourage false vocations. They will certainly be rejected by those who think of drawing merely as an accessory study, *a pleasant pastime*; thus, it is not to such students that these are offered but to those who seriously wish to be artists.

The second part will consist of a collection of drawings after masters of all periods and all schools, comprising *facsimiles* of original studies and of *interpretations* of finished works. These models are intended to develop in the minds of the students a feeling and a taste for the beautiful by acquainting them with creations of a pure and elevated style and, at the same time, with healthy and vigorous transcriptions from nature.

Seventy plates of models taken from casts have already appeared; three sections of the second part—each containing ten drawings after diverse masters—are already in press. The public will therefore be able to judge for itself the manner in which Goupil & Cie has fulfilled the first part of its program.

Very flattering reactions already presage a favorable judgment; in fact, some of these plates were exhibited by M. Bargue and won him a medal at each of the Salons of 1867 and 1868.[81]

Furthermore, the publishers have assigned these same plates a place of importance among their publications at the World's Fair on the Champs de Mars in 1867; and they won a first-class gold medal in their division.

Finally, hardly had the first plates of the course been finished when the city of Paris ordered a special printing for the public schools; and in England the course was adapted by the numerous institutions supervised by the South Kensington Museum.

COURS DE DESSIN

PAR

CH. BARGUE

AVEC LE CONCOURS DE

J.-L. GÉROME

MEMBRE DE L'INSTITUT, PROFESSEUR A L'ÉCOLE DES BEAUX-ARTS DE PARIS, ETC., ETC.

PREMIÈRE PARTIE

MODÈLES D'APRÈS LA BOSSE

70 PLANCHES SUR RAISIN INGRES, TEINTE

Prix de chaque planche : 2 francs.

FRAGMENTS DE TÊTES.

Pl. 1. *Yeux.*
2. *Bouches.*
3. *Nez.*
4. *Oreilles.*

PIEDS.

5. *Pied de profil.*
6. *Pieds (talons).*
7. *Pied du Gladiateur.*
8. *Pied de la Vénus de Médicis.*
9. *Plante de pied.*
10. *Pied du Germanicus.*

MAINS.

11. *Mains de profil.*
12. *Main fermée & main appuyée.*
13. *Main de Voltaire.*
14. *Main de faucheur.*
15. *Main d'une femme pressant son sein.*
16. *Main de femme.*

APPENDIX 2: The Sight-Size Technique

An Experienced Artist and Teacher Defines the Sight-Size Technique

In the course of a letter exchange about the sight-size technique, Peter Bougie, who has been teaching the procedure to his students in his Minneapolis, Minnesota, atelier for years, sent me this fine explanation of the technique:

> The sight-size method of measurement was a common method of working for both students and accomplished artists prior to the twentieth century, during which it fell into disuse in most art education settings. The term "sight-size" refers to making a drawing the size it would be if projected onto a plane extending left or right from your drawing board and intersecting your line of sight. This enables the artist to look at the subject and the drawing from a chosen vantage point and see them side by side—and appearing to be the same size. A plumb line [see glossary] is established for measuring widths on the subject from an established point, and a hand-held plumb line is used to line up features of the subject with the corresponding features of the drawing. This enables the artist to make very objective, virtually absolute, comparisons of shape and proportion. It is a superlative learning tool because it helps the student see objectively how what he or she has done compares to nature; that is, is the knee too high or too low? Has the width measurement to the end of the nose been placed too far from the vertical plumb line or too near to it? If you want the answer to either question, pick up the plumb line and see for yourself. The technique is an excellent tool because it establishes a common vantage point, an objective point of view, between student and teacher. There is no place for arguments about relative point of view, for the teacher and the student look at the subject from the same point of view, and the teacher is able to point out errors and incorrect observations objectively, and so help the student to see and understand what is really there, instead of offering vague generalities about whether or not something feels right or wrong. Finally, it is an excellent working method for any artist who wishes to use it in working directly from life in a controlled setting, because once you have mastered it you are able to fix solid reference points on a drawing or painting quickly, and save yourself a lot of misapplied effort. . . . Sight-size is a well known and proven method for taking measurements in a setting where the model is posed, or the subject is stationary. It's a tool. It is no more theoretical than a pencil or a paintbrush. It's useful when it's used in the right way. Above all, the sight-size method is used to help students develop and improve their "eye" and, as they advance, their problem-solving skills.

Using Sight-Size to Copy the Bargue Plates

The use of sight-size technique is recommended in all three parts of the course. It is basically a method of drawing in which the image produced has the same dimensions on paper as the apparent dimensions of the subject. There are several advantages to this technique when it is followed correctly. It produces an accurate transcription of the subject in the same size in which it is perceived. This permits continuous comparison of the drawing with the model. Once students have become proficient in the use of sight-size, they can easily correct their own work. The practice of the sight-size technique also increases a student's ability to estimate accurately the apparent measurements of the subject and transfer them correctly to paper. This talent soon becomes instinctive; it is the greatest gift of practicing sight-size. Both abilities—being able to correct oneself and being able to estimate measurements—give the beginning student a sense of confidence. For beginners, the advantages of the sight-size technique are so great that it is recommended here, especially for students working alone. Although intended for drawing from nature, that is, from three-dimensional objects, it is easily adapted to the copying of drawings. Using sight-size technique would standardize the approach to all three tasks presented in the course (viz. working from casts, copying drawings, and drawing *académies)* and, in general, would be a proper preparation for the first drawing from live models using the technique.

How Old is the Technique?

There is endless debate among the practitioners about how old the technique is and about who practiced it. Some adherents have attempted to resurrect an ennobling lineage of artists who used the method, much like Renaissance dukes and popes extending their family trees back to Hercules. As a methodical studio practice it seems to be a late nineteenth-century development. Although there are many instances where one unself-consciously uses it not as a method but as a natural approach—say, in portraiture or capturing figures at a distance—it is best as an atelier practice. The examination of many etchings, drawings, paintings, and photographs of early ateliers in session—some as far back as the Renaissance—depict none of the upright easels necessary for the practice of sight-size. In many other depictions of older ateliers, one constantly sees younger students seated on the ground, with their drawing boards in their laps.[82]

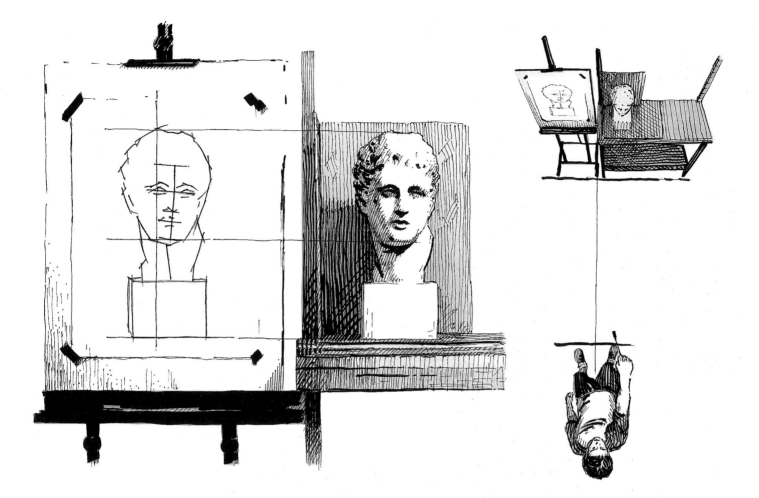

Necessary Conditions for Sight-Size Practice

First, the object drawn and the paper upon which the object's appearance is transcribed must remain stable. Also, the drawing board on the easel must be precisely upright and the easel stable—in the same position on the floor—for the entire time the drawing takes to complete, which may be several weeks. The light upon the object should always be a stable, directional, light or, if coming from a window, always from the same northern exposure. This means that the space or room must maintain the same setup until the drawing is finished.

Second, the observing position of the artist as he or she studies the object and the drawing must always be the same. The observing position is usually at a comfortable distance from the setup and the easel, say, three times the largest dimension of the drawing (to reduce the angle of distortion) and at a spot where the drawing paper and the subject are visually side by side.

Mark the position of your feet on the floor with tape, indicating the position of each foot. The feet are best planted at shoulder-width distance from each other; this increases your steadiness. Plant your feet in position, lock your knees, and stand up straight each

Fig. 44.
The Shadow Box.
<u>Left</u>: the setup of the box with a cast.
<u>Right</u>: floor plan of setup indicating the marked, working foot position.
Drawing: Graydon Parrish

319

time you step back to observe the subject or the drawing. Wear the same shoes throughout the drawing process. Even the slightest change of view—such as higher or lower heels—can affect your view and your judgment.

Note: Never draw the object while looking directly at it; always study it from the same place and distance, and draw from memory, aided by your measured marks.

Excursus: Shadow Boxes

A shadow box is usually used for cast drawings. You will be copying from drawings already made from a cast. Even so, it is good to know how these cast drawings were made since this will help you when you switch from the Bargue cast drawings to actual casts.

The shadow box used for the cast setup is a small, three-sided box with a bottom but no top, and two adjacent vertical sides. It can be built from scratch or reconstructed from a wooden box (see fig. 44). The box, of course, rests on a solid stand or table that elevates it to easel height, so that when you stand in position you are looking at the center of the object. Line the box with black paper or cloth to absorb light and thereby lessen reflected shadows on the cast. (Some users prefer a middle-gray toned paper or cloth to lessen the depth of the shadows.) Light from a northern window or a lamp should create the best effect for the draftsman: clarity of form, outline, and a sense of drama are to be sought after. While working on the plates in part I you will find examples of various ways to manage lights.

To repeat, all these arrangements must remain absolutely stable throughout the drawing process. Slight changes in the position of the light or the cast can make it impossible to continue a drawing already in progress. Trace the outline of the base of the cast on the bottom of the shadow box just in case the cast gets moved.

Using sticks fastened to the sides of the box, hang a plumb line in front of the cast. Position it so that it cuts through the cast somewhere in the middle and crosses through some important reference or angle points. This real plumb line will be the same as the plumb line (vertical reference line) around which your drawing will be organized. It may take some time to set the cast up in the shadow box.

In drawing from a cast, that is, making a life-size transcription of the cast, the drawing paper on its easel will be placed alongside and just slightly ahead of the subject in the shadow box. If the subject is a cast or a still life, it should be in a setup, either on a stand or in a shadow box. When drawing a live model, the model should be positioned behind the easel, at some distance from which both could easily be seen, so that the apparent height of the model would fit upon the sheet of the drawing paper.

Drawing After a Cast: Positioning the Drawing

After the cast has been set up in the shadow box, the light adjusted, and the easel placed with the drawing board and paper on it set properly next to the shadow box, the drawing process can start. The placement of the paper at the edge of the drawing board (on the model's side) and the drawing board at the easel edge (close to the view of the model) will make it easier to make measurements from the subject and to make visual comparisons of your work and the cast (fig. 45).

Step 1: Draw two horizontals across the paper that define the height of the cast. Since you need a plumb line while drawing the figure, the string of the plumb line is the handiest tool for this step.[83] Use your thumbnails to mark the visible distance on the taut string.

Stretch the string between two hands horizontally across the peak of the head of the model and over the drawing paper. Memorize the path of the line of the string across the paper; step forward and mark the path—one or two marks will suffice.

Step back and use the string of your plumb line to check the mark for accuracy; then lower the string and repeat the process for the lowest point of the feet; do not lower your head for this measurement, just your eyes.

Stand back again and check the marks by holding up the string across the drawing and the cast again. Draw a horizontal through each of the marks, top and bottom.

Step 2: Decide on the placement of the cast's image upon the paper by estimating its width using the taught string or your eye.

Measure the width of the cast at its widest point from your set standing position. Move the extended string over to the paper; decide where it fits most comfortably, but not too far from the edge of the paper nearest the cast. Mark both ends on the paper. Check your measurements.

Step 3: Draw a plumb line (a vertical reference line) from the top line to the bottom line. It should be drawn well enough inside the width limits you have previously set up.

Use the string of the plumb line again to check the width of the figure and its placement on the paper before you draw the plumb line on the paper. You must first pick out the plumb line you want on the subject, a line, say, following the center of balance, preferably one that passes through many or several

useful points on the cast. This can be found and preserved by dropping another plumb line in front of the cast from a stick fastened to the shadow box. Judge where to hang the line from your foot position.

Return to the location of the broadest width that you used earlier when deciding where to place your drawing on the paper. Find by measurement where the actual plumb line on the cast is within that measured width and find the same spot on your drawing by measuring again with your string. Draw the perpendicular through that spot, making sure that it is square with the top and bottom horizontal lines.

As you continue, you must always look at the figure or subject from the same vantage point and with the same stance—feet in position, legs and arms locked and steady, as you hold out the measuring string or needle. With your head always in the same position, look with one eye—always the same eye. You want the middle of the drawing to be straight in front of you. When you look down at the model's feet, for instance, don't drop your head, just your eye. These small practices will soon become habitual and will save you much aggravation.

Fig. 45.
Sight-Size Technique.
<u>Left</u>: measuring apparent distances.
<u>Right</u>: finding an appropriate plumb line (vertical reference line); or checking for vertical elements and angle alignments. Both figures are meant to be working from the same marked foot position on the floor.
Drawing: Graydon Parrish

Drawing After a Cast:
Measuring Apparent Distances

Before beginning, measure the model from the plumb line to the widest and lowest points. (1) Look for an important angle, concave or convex, on the contour of the model. (2) From your marked floor position, hold up your plumb line string and make sure that you are holding it horizontally by comparing it with the top and bottom horizontals on the drawing paper. (3) Pick an important point that will help define the shape of the image. Start with the extremities and extended limbs. Move the string—still held horizontally—over the point you wish to record. (4) Make a mark on the plumb line where the horizontal string passes through it and the angle on the cast. Take the length of string (held tightly between the two fingers of your extended hands) and measure the distance from the angle on the cast between your thumbnails and the plumb line hanging before the cast. (5) Keeping your arms extended and the string taut, move the string over the drawing paper; one end of the string should be over the mark on the drawn plumb line, while the other will be over the paper where the contour mark should be. Memorize that spot. Step forward and mark it lightly. Step back and check the accuracy of its placement with the extended plumb line.

Work this way around the figure until you have the shape circumscribed by dots; when you are certain they are all correctly measured and placed, you may connect the dots with straight lines. You can make lines through the plumb line for the slant of the shoulders, hips, or other features. Adding another horizontal or perpendicular vertical may help you deal with some difficult areas. The measuring, placing, and correcting of dots is cumbersome at first, but as you learn the method you will be able to pick out fewer and better points on the contours to work from and to estimate distances more quickly—sometimes with your eye alone. Since there is a lot of stepping back to measure and forward to mark or erase a spot, you should have in your hand at all times the pencil or charcoal, the plumb line, and the eraser so that you can switch instruments without losing your concentration.

Be sure to make these first connection lines straight. The curves can be worked out later. The greater the amplitude of the curve, the more straight lines—connected by points—you will need to outline the curve. One fundamental of Bargue's method is the simplification of complex curves into straights; if one starts drawing a curve, one tends to draw an arc, and it is hard to know where to stop. (As your eye gets experienced, you will be able to connect some of the dots by curves.)

Once a full contour is drawn, it should be carefully checked—through measurement and study all the way around—before features on the inside of the form are put in. Studying your drawing or comparing it with the model in a mirror will help you uncover errors. (A mirror should always be kept handy for checking your drawing.) Refine the outline several times before filling in the curves, putting lines in for the major shadow; then revise the outline again. Once you fill in the major shadow shape, you will see that the contour needs further adjustment.

Keep your dimensions accurate and tight: if the figure spreads just a bit, you will have difficulty fitting the features into the outline and you may even lose the sense of an organic whole. Where it is hard to measure visually, you can resort to a tool for measurements again. Remember that a slightly wider, inaccurate neck may change a young boy into a mature man.

Drawing After Flat Models:
Bargue's Plates

The Bargue plates in parts I and III were drawn from the fixed point of view of a stable model; they might have been drawn with sight-size technique or a version of it. One of the main benefits of working in sight-size—besides the production of an accurate image—is the training it gives the eye in measuring visual dimensions. Both to prepare yourself to work from casts and models in sight-size and to benefit from this training of the eye, it is wise to adapt as much of the sight-size technique as possible to the copying of the plates.

Place the plate and the drawing paper side by side on a drawing board, an upright easel, or preferably on a well-lit wall. Locate a good plumb line on the drawing. (You can tape a piece of string in position over the image for the plumb line and for the top and bottom horizontals.) Transfer them to the drawing. Set up comfortable foot positions centered on a line perpendicular to the juncture of the plate and the paper. Using the foot positions will get you used to judging measurements from a distance with a plumb line, memorizing them, stepping forward to record them, and stepping back to correct them. Try to do as much of your work as possible in this manner. At times copying details close up will be necessary, but always step back to judge your work. Stepping back also keeps you conscious of the effect of the whole, which you can further ascertain using a mirror. Check your shadow masses in a black mirror.

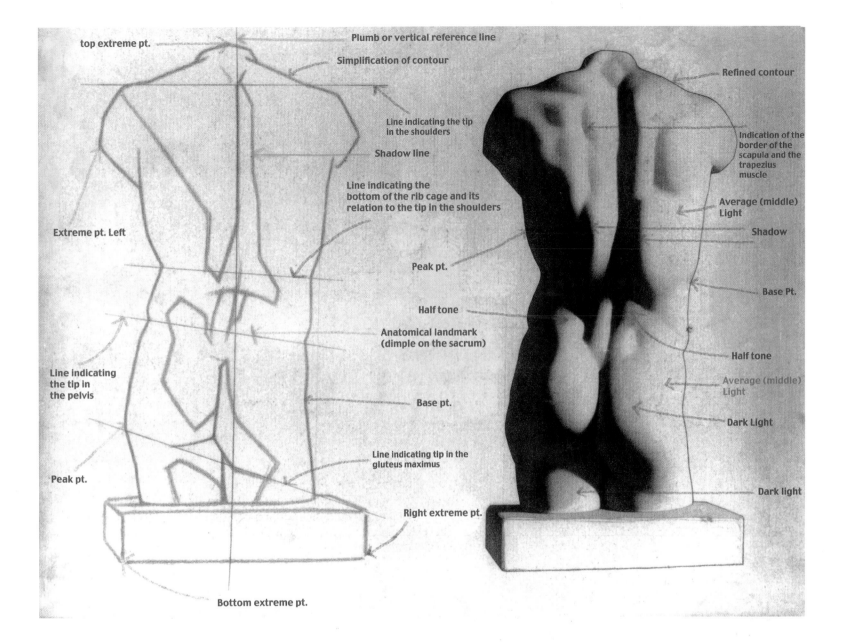

Labels on left figure (line drawing):
- top extreme pt.
- Plumb or vertical reference line
- Simplification of contour
- Line indicating the tip in the shoulders
- Shadow line
- Line indicating the bottom of the rib cage and its relation to the tip in the shoulders
- Extreme pt. Left
- Peak pt.
- Half tone
- Anatomical landmark (dimple on the sacrum)
- Line indicating the tip in the pelvis
- Base pt.
- Peak pt.
- Line indicating tip in the gluteus maximus
- Right extreme pt.
- Bottom extreme pt.

Labels on right figure (photograph of cast):
- Refined contour
- Indication of the border of the scapula and the trapezius muscle
- Average (middle) Light
- Shadow
- Base Pt.
- Half tone
- Average (middle) Light
- Dark Light
- Dark light

Pros and Cons Concerning the Sight-Size Technique: A Dialogue

Using sight-size as the only way of drawing might make practitioners model-bound and interfere with their depiction of objects from memory. Since models are incapable of holding dynamic poses for more than a few minutes, it may delay learning the elements that give motion to a drawing. In addition to increasing the student's dependence upon the model, it also creates a dependence upon ideal conditions—typically those encountered in a studio—such as a controlled light source, an uncluttered and neutral background, and a model trained to hold long poses on a raised platform. However, it does not hinder the depiction of subjects larger or smaller than life size because there are several easy mechanical means of enlarging or diminishing drawn images.

Fig. 46. *Terminology and Concerns in Working from a Cast or Live Model.* The example is taken from the Polykleitan male torso, back view (see plate I, 56). *Annotations:* Graydon Parrish

323

Peter Bougie, the artist responsible for the fine definition of the sight-size technique at the beginning of this appendix, discussed the merits and disadvantages of the practice with me in an exchange of letters in 2001, from which several excerpts follow. In response to my comment about the innumerable times one wanted to draw something when a sight-size setup (particularly an upright easel) was not feasible, he replied:

"On the slant of the easel, I'll only put in this two cents' worth: a vertical easel is necessary for two reasons. One is so you can step back and look at the subject and draw (with both the subject and drawing in view) side by side without moving your head up and down or left and right. Two, since you're working from a fixed vantage point and measuring, your drawing becomes distorted the more your easel tips away from the vertical, because the top of the drawing is closer to the subject than the bottom.

"Sight-size is very useful in many ways but has definite limitations. It's a good teaching tool and we insist that everyone use it because it sharpens the beginner's eye for proportion relatively quickly and provides an objective context in which to work. It's good for use in the studio in a controlled setting, but it's impractical for landscape painting (not theoretically, but in practical terms) or making studies from life on the fly.[84] I've also noticed that for some students who are naïve (in their drawing experience), or of a strong logical mindset, sight-size gets in the way of seeing when they reach a certain point in their development. They will use the plumb line too much and their eye not enough. I've always thought that sight-size gets you close to where you want to go, in terms of seeing nature correctly, but if you don't step back and compare what you've done to what you see, it can trip you up. In an *académie* study, if you have a head that's 1/32 or 2/32 too big and a width across the shoulders that is about that much too narrow, the head will look quite large, and you can stand there with your plumb line for an hour and be unable to measure those small fractions with any confidence. You'll just think the head looks big and you won't know why unless you interrelate the parts. So you have to look and compare; that's what it comes down to. And any artist worth his salt ought to regularly practice sitting down with a pad on his lap, or some flat surface, to develop a capacity for gathering information that way, if for no other reason than that situations often call for it.

"I hope I haven't been too didactic. Finally, it's whatever works. But, in my opinion, that 'whatever' has to be grounded in some solid method, or it sounds a lot like the kind of vague instruction people pay for in so many of the art programs out there these days."

"You cut the Gordian knot for me," I replied. "The knot was in my head." Then I continued:

"Sight-size is great for teaching observation and precision. It is also wonderful in teaching because the correction can be precise. I find a problem in sight-size: if carried on too long, the students become model-bound and limited to the poses they can set before them. This keeps them from attempting motion, some expressions, interactions between personages, etc. They just draw and paint models sitting, lying, or standing around. (Gérôme complained that he often couldn't get the good charcoal renderers out of the life class and into painting.) But, still, if you want to be an exacting realist, sight-size shows you the way.

"The Florence Academy of Art (under Daniel Graves) has evening free drawing sessions where the students draw after models with their drawing boards on their laps, a slanted or a straight easel, whatever. These freewheeling sessions occur two or three nights a week, with poses of fifteen minutes to an hour. You stand or sit where you can. I did not realize that this exercise was a natural corrective to the habits of the sight-size technique that were picked up in the daytime sessions at the school.

"The Bargue course, with its mixture of casts and *académies,* is set up like the private ateliers of the French academy. In Paris the students drew alternately from casts of antiquities and from models, three weeks for each in turn. In Florence students draw from the cast for half a day and from models for the other half. Consequently one could personally move toward realism or idealism in one's personal style. Usually one stopped somewhere in between. Being a purist in either direction could put your style in a straightjacket. Bargue gives you both casts of perfect bodies and parts in the first section and a variety of body types—including the nonideal, aged body—in the third part.

"I am not against other methods nor a partisan of any (although I do naturally prefer and understand best what I was taught, but must protect myself from being dogmatic about it); I think that different methods of drawing from life should just be called methods, none the 'one way,' and that the principles should be recognized as part of the method that organizes work and observation, not as absolutes. The payoff will always be the results.

To which Mr. Bougie replied: "You're right about the shortcomings of sight-size—it's strictly for working in controlled situations, and it does breed a dependence on the model. I'm going to try having students do more work from flat copy of expressive figures, figures in motion, and so on, to try to bridge the gap between the study of nature and its application to making pictures. In doing that, I'm going to compare the two and try to show people how they differ. The trick will be to keep them on track with both the observation and the learning about convention without having the limitations of each method pollute the other, that is, become shortcuts, excuses, or mannerisms in the hands of the inexperienced."

APPENDIX 3: A 1926 Article on Bargue's Drawings (in facsimile)

The following pages are a facsimile of an article published in the art magazine *International Studio* in May 1926. As the text explains, it was published in connection with an exhibition of paintings and drawings by Bargue at the now defunct Fearon Galleries in New York. This is the only known twentieth-century publication on Bargue. The second drawing depicted—of a *Turkish Soldier, bent over*—was in a Los Angeles collection in 1992; its present location is not known. None of the other drawings have been located. The self-portrait is, of course, of interest.

INTERNATIONAL STUDIO

All drawings courtesy of the Fearon Galleries

"THE FLUTE PLAYER" ILLUSTRATES CHARLES BARGUE'S DELICACY OF LINE AND SEARCH FOR PERFECTION

A GROUP OF DRAWINGS BY CHARLES BARGUE

Of Charles Bargue it may be said with a certain note of pathos that his life is recorded only in his pictures. He lived in Paris (these are his only known dates) from 1867 to 1883; won medals as a lithographer in 1867 and 1868; was a pupil and devoted follower of Gerome with whom he had been engaged in the preparation of "A Course of Designs for Schools"; painted about twenty canvases between 1870 and 1883; and died, presumably, in the last-named year. In spite of the fact that his few paintings have always attracted extraordinary interest and admiration, and have brought high prices, no one has ever made the effort to investigate French official records as to further facts concerning his life, possibly because his work has not sufficient commercial value to warrant creating a Bargue legend. Twelve of his paintings are in the United States: two in the Metropolitan Museum of Art; one in the Boston Museum; one in the Chicago Art Institute; one in the Cincinnati Museum; three in the Cornelius Vanderbilt collection; one in the C. K. G. Billings collection; and three, owned by a dealer, were recently exhibited in the Fearon Galleries in New York City. The group of his drawings presented here have hitherto been unknown in this country

DRAWINGS IN APPENDIX 3
Study of the flutist for *The Flute Player*. *(Joueur de flûte.)* (painting 51). Lost
Study of a *Turkish Soldier, bent over*. *(Soldat turc, penché en avant.)* In a Los Angeles collection in 1992; present whereabouts unknown
Study of Female Figures. *(Étude de femmes.)* Lost
Market Scene. *(Scène de marché.)* Lost
Study of an Oriental. *(Étude d'un Oriental.)* Lost
Self-Portrait [?] ***(Autoportrait.)*** Lost
Gathering Firewood. *(Le Ramassage du bois mort.)* Lost

SET DOWN IN BOLD STROKES OF HIS PENCIL, THIS STUDY OF A "TURKISH SOLDIER" IS A COMPLETE DOCUMENT ON THE METHOD AND PRACTICE OF CHARLES BARGUE. THE SKETCH WAS MADE FROM LIFE, AND SHOWS HIS PERFECTIONS IN NOTING THE HUMAN OUTLINE, AND THE PLAY OF MUSCLES

ALTHOUGH WOMEN OF THE MODE OF THIS WATER COLOR, "STUDY OF FEMALE FIGURES," ARE STRANGE TO BARGUE'S PAINTINGS, THE DRAWING HAS ITS DOUBLE APPEAL OF CHARM OF SUBJECT AND HANDLING OF THE MEDIUM, AND ITS ADDITIONAL REVELATION OF HIS INTEREST IN THE HUMAN FIGURE

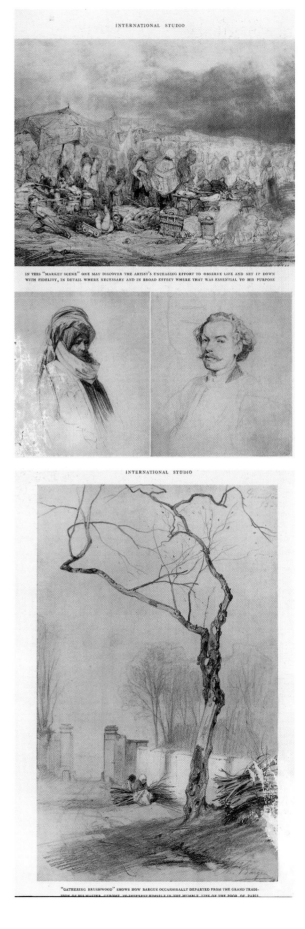

IN THIS "MARKET SCENE" ONE MAY DISCOVER THE ARTIST'S UNCEASING EFFORT TO OBSERVE LIFE AND SET IT DOWN WITH FIDELITY, IN DETAIL WHERE NECESSARY AND IN BROAD EFFECT WHERE THAT WAS ESSENTIAL TO HIS PURPOSE

"GATHERING BRUSHWOOD" SHOWS HOW BARGUE OCCASIONALLY DEPARTED FROM THE GRAND TRADITION OF HIS MASTER, GEROME, TO INTEREST HIMSELF IN THE HUMBLE LIFE OF THE POOR OF PARIS

Glossary of Technical Terms

académie: Besides the more general meaning in French of an official organization of learned men and schools devoted to specific subjects, the more specialized meaning refers to the most common product of academic drawing courses, a finished drawing after a carefully posed nude studio model; strictly speaking, the model should be male, but drawings of female nudes are now often referred to as *académies*. It is usually on a full sheet of paper and executed in charcoal.

axis: an imaginary straight line around which a body rotates; **axial,** the adjectival form, describes an extension, line, or plane perpendicular to the axis.

black mirror: see **mirrors**

chiaroscuro: an Italian word (lit. "light/dark") used to describe the use of a wide range of values, from light to dark, in a painting or drawing. Rembrandt is the most famous practitioner of chiaroscuro.

concours: a French term for contest or competition. The École des Beaux-Arts in Paris held many contests, some within the various studios and others for wider segments of the student body. The most prestigious was the annual Grand Prix, or Prix de Rome, as it was commonly called. As part of a weeding-out process, painters were put through several preliminary tests. Those few who survived had to produce a history painting on a theme selected by the school. The winner received a pensioned stay in Rome, with lodging at the Villa Medici. *Tête d'expression* contests were also held, with sculptors fashioning busts and painters making drawings of heads that expressed or signified specific emotions.

construction line: an actual or imaginary straight line drawn through two or more points in a drawing that aids in establishing the proportions and contours of the object being drawn.

contrapposto: an Italian term describing the turning or twisting of the body on its own axis or, put differently, an arrangement of the body in which the arms and shoulder positions contrast with that of the hips and legs.

craquelure, crackle: the term used for small cracks on the surface of a painting. When the crackle forms a mosaiclike system of tiny irregular islands on the surface, it is considered a natural state—the result of the drying and shrinking of the oil pigments over time—and not damage. *Craquelure* can also be the result of accidents. Some types of crackle are produced by faulty craftsmanship (see next entry).

craquelure anglaise, English crackle: a term describing a series of cracks, of varying widths, on the painting surface that surrounds large flakes of paint, usually induced by slow-drying underpainting.

drawing: *drawing from nature* is the term for drawing from objects, natural and man-made, in the real or natural world; *drawing from memory* is the term for drawing such natural objects as nudes, vases, houses, trees, and flowers accurately, without recourse to models, using what one has learned from studying actual models; *drawing from practice* is a step down from drawing from memory since it involves using learned, predetermined, unvaried ways of presenting objects or parts of objects without further reference to nature, resulting in a personal style or manner; *drawing from fantasy (drawing from the imagination)* involves the depiction of fanciful creatures and human beings bearing unnatural features—as in certain decorations (grotesques) or the paintings of Hieronymus Bosch. This was the lowest or least respected practice, according to academic theory, because the image distorted the truth.

ébauche: technically defined as a preparatory compositional sketch in oil on canvas, wood, or paper, with the underpainting rubbed in to establish general values and colors; sometimes a few areas are finished rather carefully (see also **sketch; study**).

esquisse: see **sketch**

ethos: the essential character of a person—his or her moral nature or guiding beliefs—based on principles or truths and resistant to change from external events (see also **pathos**).

étude: see **study**

expression: in traditional art theory the term referred to the emotional and intellectual content of the subject in a painting or sculpture (the "expression of the subject") as well as to the intellectual or emotional meanings conveyed by the poses, gestures, and faces of characters in a painting or sculpture (the "expression of emotions"). Expressions were thought to be reactions to "movements of the soul" or internal emotional and intellectual states. The emotions were thought to be absolute, distinct, and differentiated—hence with standard effects in terms of facial features and, as a result, recognizable. Students consequently studied and learned a set of defined facial features that represented certain emotions and could be precisely interpreted when carefully depicted. Around 1880 the term took on the connotation of *self-expression,* which is the general meaning today.

foreshortening: a term used in drawing for the act of transcribing the apparent (rather than the actual) lengths of objects not parallel to the picture plane; the apparent length appears shorter the more perpendicular the object is to the picture plane.

good taste, or *le grand goût,* reflects a style based on classical art. In the nineteenth century classical art included the art of antiquity and the works of the High Renaissance in Italy, particularly the paintings of Raphael. The combination of good taste with the exact imitation of nature resulted in *le beau idéal,* or *la belle nature,* the rendition of nature in its most perfect manifestation or form; this ideal also involved many mannerisms, including the simplification of forms as in antique statuary.

Grand Prix: see **concours**

halftones: see **value**

hatching: a technique of building up shadows with parallel lines; when a second set of lines crosses the first, it is called *cross-hatching.*

history painting: works that depict an important event in biblical or ancient history from which a moral lesson could be drawn or a truth inculcated. In the nineteenth century modern subject matter—that is, events after the fall of the Roman Empire—gradually worked their way into the repertoire. Paintings that depicted events from everyday life—with or without high morality—were called genre pictures. At the École des Beaux-Arts in Paris the training of painters was designed to turn them into history painters: the state expected these state-trained artists to glorify its accomplishments and back the doctrines of the official religion.

humors or **temperaments:** an ancient but long-surviving division of human beings into four temperaments (sanguine, phlegmatic, choleric, melancholic) based upon the predominance of the associated fluid in their bodies. The fluid that dominated determined the person's constitution and character, which could be mitigated by the amount of the other three humors. Adam and Eve had a perfect balance of the four humors until the Fall; as a result, all human beings are mortal because of imbalances among their humors. Each humor produced a certain physical type. Artists could use one of the four physical types to stress the emotion associated with the type. For instance, the melancholic temperament, characterized by a predominance of black bile, produced a stocky, heavy body. Examples of melancholics are Hercules, Samson, and King David, who are often shown in a depressed state (seated, with hand to chin or cheek). Sanguine types, with a predominance of blood in their system, are frequently depicted as cheerful.

in situ: (lit. "in the original site"), a Latin term used for works of art made for a specific setting or site that have never been moved or relocated from that site, such as The Statue of Liberty.

interpretation: in Goupil's special terminology one of the firm's published model drawings after a "realized" or finished work of art; in the *Drawing Course* it is used to describe drawings after paintings.

local color: the actual color of an object or a color devoid of halftones, shadows, or reflected light.

mirrors: small but not too tiny rectangular mirrors were recommended by Leonardo da Vinci in the fifteenth century as a tool to check the accuracy of one's drawings. **Black mirrors** are used to simplify the dark masses on the subject, helping one to see and transcribe shadows correctly. They can be bought commercially as smoked glass (*verre fumé*) or made by painting one side of a rectangle of clear plastic black (bind edges with masking tape to protect them and your hands).

Neoplatonism: a term describing a philosophical system of the Renaissance ultimately based on ancient interpretations and systematizations of philosophers of late antiquity. Building upon the theories of Plato, Neoplatonists believed that not only material objects were based on forms or *ideas* in heaven or in God's mind at the time of the Creation, but also abstract ideas such as truth, justice, goodness, harmony, and beauty. Since beauty was a quality of art as well as an idea itself, contemplating a beautiful work of art could lead to the understanding of the *idea* of *true beauty* and open a path to the comprehension of other heavenly forms or *ideas,* ultimately leading to enlightenment and virtue.

pathos: a Greek term for the reactions and emotions evoked in the soul by external events in the world, such as pity, fear, or lust (see also ***ethos***).

plumb line: (1) a drawn line that is absolutely straight up and down, used both to show the direction of gravity and, in a drawing, as a reference line for measuring apparent distances of the model on the paper (see **vertical reference line**); (2) a simple, ancient tool for discerning straight up and down, consisting of a balanced weight on a piece of string.

Prix de Rome: see ***concours***

repoussoir: a French term for a figure, tree, or other object that frames the central event of a history painting, much like a theatrical side flat; the typical classical repoussoir figure is a muscular man (often a river god), whose back is to the viewer as he looks into the scene from a lower corner of the painting.

schema, schemata (pl.): a simplified yet accurate sketch of the outline of an object used as the plan for a finished drawing.

self-expression: see **expression**

shadow box: a three-sided box in which to pose casts as models for drawing. The box is lined with black or gray material to simplify the reflected lights and solidify the shadows on the cast. The position of the box, the cast, and the light source must remain stable throughout the drawing. See Fig. 44.

sketch, *esquisse*: a quick, unfinished, generalized drawing or painting usually based on the artist's imagination and usually made in preparation for a finished work. Often these are simple notations of things seen or imagined (see also *ébauche*).

stop modeling: instead of modeling every square inch of the surface of a subject in a drawing or a painting, the artist can decide to "stop" at a point where the detail and values produce a sufficient effect.

study: a finished painting or drawing of a model, object, or setting without a unifying, elevating, or animating idea; either executed in preparation for a larger composition or to learn about the subject.

têtes d'expression*, expressive heads:** see ***concours

tonality: the predominant harmonious colors and values of a composition or the interrelation of these colors and values.

tone: see **value**

value: the lightness or darkness of a color. Black is the absence of light, with shadows being values of light. The values of shadows between darkness and light are referred to as *halftones,* without any mathematical precision e.g., there can be several graduated halftones next to one another between the darkest and lightest value.

vertical reference line: a term occasionally used for the plumb line to distinguish the line drawn by the tool from the tool itself, and at other times to indicate extra vertical lines, supplemental to the plumb line, that help organize a drawing.

Notes

1. Individual plates were sold separately at one franc fifty centimes starting in 1868, and once the printing of the three parts was completed in 1871, each of the three parts was sold in a separate portfolio (*en portefeuille*) for around seventy-five francs. Title pages for each part are included in the copy at the National Art Library of the Victoria and Albert Museum, London—the only complete commercial copy known, preserved intact because the plates were all mounted separately on cardboard sheets and then bound in three separate volumes.

2. The two complete sets in the Goupil Museum consist of a master proof copy without printed legends *(avant la lettre)*, used for reference in the printing room, and a copy with titles. Plates from both of these two sets were selected for this edition. Some of the proof sets have the models completely nude; in some cases drapery was applied before the commercial sets were printed. The present editor let the quality of the impression, not prudery, be his guide in determining which plate to reproduce.

3. In England and the United States this was the general point of view, but the various private and municipal drawing schools, being more independent and less autocratic, were not able to discourage the practice of using live models. Eventually, life-drawing sessions surreptitiously entered the official curriculum of most late nineteenth-century art schools. General dissatisfaction with the teaching in decorative and industrial art schools had been mounting for a long time. See Pierre-Lin Renié, "Goupil & Cie et l'ère industrielle," *État des lieux* 1 (1994): 92–93. For an enlightening discussion of the problem in England, see Quentin Bell, *The Schools of Design* (London: Routledge & Kegan Paul, 1973).

An important teacher who dissented from academic theory in figure drawing was Horace Lecoq de Boisbaudran (1802–1897), drawing master at the École des Gobelins, an arts and crafts school. He encouraged his students to draw from memory; see his *Training of the Memory in Art* (London: Macmillan, 1911) (*L'Éducation de la mémoire pittoresque et la formation de l'artiste,* Paris, 1848). Not to be overlooked are two more masters of independent painting ateliers, Thomas Couture (1815–1879) and Émile Auguste Carolus-Duran (1838–1917). Couture's method is described in his *Conversations on Art Methods* (New York: Putnam, 1879) (*Méthodes et entretiens d'atelier,* Paris, 1869), whereas Carolus-Duran's teachings are known only from the unsatisfactory recollections of his students; see R. A. M. Stevenson, "J. S. Sargent," *Art Journal,* March 1888; and J. Carroll Beckwith, "Carolus-Duran," in John C. Van Dyke, *Modern French Painters*, New York, 1896. You can also mine the bibliography in the exhibition catalogue *Carolus Duran. 1837-1917,* Lille: Palais des Beaux-Arts, 2003.

4. There are numerous references to the course in *The Complete Letters of Vincent van Gogh*, 3 vols. (London: Thames & Hudson, 1958);

see also Vincent van Gogh, *Correspondance complète*, 3 vols. (Paris: Gallimard, 1990).

5. See Irving Lavin, *Past–Present* (Berkeley: University of California Press, 1993), pp. 203–213; see also Marilyn McCulley, *Picasso: The Early Years* (Washington, D.C.: National Gallery of Art/Abrams, 1997).

6. In the mid-1960s Daniel Mendelowitz (1905–1980) and I drove from Stanford, California—where we were both members of the university's art department faculty—north to Sacramento to visit the studio of Wayne Thiebaud (1920–). Mendelowitz studied at the Art Students League in New York, where he learned an already modernized but still somewhat academically based figurative tradition. His textbook, *Drawing,* was published in 1967 and is still in print. Wayne Thiebaud had recently begun a series of life-sized figures, clothed and nude, that we were inspecting for an exhibition at the Stanford Art Museum, Stanford, Calif. (*Thiebaud Figures,* Stanford Art Museum, 1966).

Thiebaud's figures in the paintings we saw in his brightly lit studio were, in almost every case, neither animated nor posed but simply positioned before a white wall, arms at their sides, facing the artist but unaware of him. The two painters started the normal studio shop talk concerning materials, lighting, the difficulties with models, and so on. I, an art historian, stood to one side, listening. In the course of the discussion, Thiebaud complained about how much work the wrists on one figure had caused him, and that despite his efforts they still did not look right. Mendelowitz volunteered gently, "Don't you know, Wayne, there are two sets of bones in the wrist." Picking up a small pad and a pencil from a table in the studio, he carefully drew, in summary form, an outline of the wrist, and then the two sets of three bones each within it. This once common anatomical information had dropped out of art school teaching between the training of the two men.

7. Renaissance Neoplatonism introduced and developed the idea that the beauty of art could teach moral lessons and inspire virtue. This doctrine still persists today in the convictions of some artists, critics, and theorists that the decline of representational art in the twentieth century was part of a moral and social decline, and its return would foster (or herald) a moral revival and a renewal of political order. See also note 47.

8. Anon., *Des modèles de dessin* (Paris: Goupil & Cie, 1886), 12-page brochure. See appendix 1 for the complete text.

9. *Le Constitutionnel,* 5, 12, and 20 December 1865; cited in *Des modèles de dessin,* pp. 3–5.

10. The French word in the original text is *le joli,* which simply means pretty; the passage can in no way be construed as a defense of realism or an attack on beauty.

11. Anon., *Des modèles de dessin* (Paris: Goupil & Cie, 1886). Goupil could well be proud of the work in progress. At the Salon of 1867 Bargue had won a medal for ten lithographs under one number (4166)—plates

47. Some late eighteenth-century authors expanded this idea into a political or social philosophy. Thomas Crow, a modern art historian, has paraphrased their thinking as follows: "The ideological background to this perception must be sought in the changing significance (in the eighteenth century) of antiquity as a source of ethical and aesthetic ideals. . . . A corrupt state, it was said, produced corrupted bodies, imperfect flesh. . . . The perfection of ancient sculpture was a small window left to modern humanity through which a lost, better form of community might be glimpsed." Thomas Crow, *Emulation* (New Haven: Yale Univ. Press, 1995), pp. 26–27; see also p. 306, n. 71. See also note 7.

48. Cited in Heather Hawkins, *The Nude in French Art and Culture, 1870–1910* (New York: Cambridge University Press, 2002), p. 48.

49. Charles Bargue, *Vingt scènes enfantines d'après H. de Montaut*, in J. Laran et J. Adhémar, *Graveurs après 1800* [Cabinet des Estampes, Bibliothèque nationale, Inventaire des Fonds français, vol. 1] (Paris: Chartrain, 1930–33), pp. 319–23. One hundred and forty-eight lithographs are attributed to Bargue in this inventory. However, the Bargue collection in the Cabinet des Estampes of the Bibliothèque nationale, Paris, contains many more prints by Bargue than are recorded in this tome.

50. For a transcript of the document, see the section entitled "Bargue's Death" in the present study.

51. The pun in *La Partie de chat* is fairly simple. However, the only dialect of English in which *Caught Napping* might sound like "cat napping" would be Lycée Oxford.

52. Among the various publishers of Bargue's lithographic work were Lazerges, Janin et Cie, Benoist, and (later) Goupil et Cie, occasionally with Gambart or Knoedler as international distributors. For a summary of the history of Goupil & Cie see Gérard Monnier, *L'Art et ses institutions en France. De la Révolution à nos jours*. Paris: Gallimard, 1995; pp.154-182 *passim*. and for more specific information see the exhibition catalogue *Gérôme & Goupil. Art and Enterprise*. New York: Dahesh Museum of Art, 2000.

53. See Hélène Lafont-Couturier, "La Maison Goupil ou la notion d'œuvre remise en question," *Revue de l'Art* 112 (1996–2): pp. 59–69; see also Patricia Mainardi, "Copies, Variations, Replicas: Nineteenth-Century Studio Practice," *Visual Resources* 15 (1999): pp. 123–47. For more about Goupil & Cie see note 52.

54. See Ackerman, *Gérôme*, cat. nos. 15, 15.2, and 15.3.

55. According to Pierre-Lin Renié, Delaroche's works were the most reproduced in prints by Goupil & Cie and hence probably the most copied in reductions. See his essay "Œuvres de Paul Delaroche reproduites et éditées par la maison Goupil," in *Paul Delaroche, un peintre dans l'Histoire*, exhib. cat. (Nantes: musée des Beaux-Arts; Montpellier: musée Fabre, 2000), pp. 200–221; see also Stephen

Duffy, *Paul Delaroche, 1797–1856: Paintings in the Wallace Collection* (London: Trustees of the Wallace Collection, 1997).

56. Fanny Field Hering, *Gérôme* (New York: Cassel, 1892), p. 201.

57. Guy de Montgailhard, *Lecomte du Nouÿ* (Paris: A. Lahure, 1906), p. 114.

58. Roger Diederen, *Telling Tales I: Classical Images from the Dahesh Museum of Art* (New York: Dahesh Museum of Art, 2001), pp. 10–11.

59. There is another gap in Bargue's sales to Goupil, from 29 September 1872 to 12 October 1874—more than a year—but the time was probably taken up with the complex composition *The Opinion of the Model* (*L'Avis du modèle*) (painting 29).

60. See Hering, *Gérôme*, p. 215.

61. I prefer to retain the title *The Opinion of the Model* (*L'Avis du modèle*) for painting 29 to prevent it from being confused with painting 43, properly called *The Artist and His Model* (*L'Artiste et son modèle*).

62. For a reproduction of Jean Bart, see Ackerman, *Gérôme*, cat. no. 140.

63. *French and Other Continental Drawings and Watercolors, Oil Sketches* (New York: Shepherd Gallery, 1979), no. 2.

64. In painting 37 one can verify that the bifurcated ivory handle poking out of several belt holsters in other paintings belongs to a dagger and not a pistol.

65. See *The Greek Singer* (*Chanteur grec*) (painting 41) and perhaps *A Beggar Asking for Alms in a Mosque* (*Mendiant demandant l'aumône dans une mosquée*), reproduced in Ackerman, *Gérôme*, cat. no. A5; although the beggar is a model used by Gérôme, he is too strange anatomically for either artist.

66. The term is that of Roger de Piles (1635–1709), the great French art theorist, who explains the principle of compositional unity through color as follows: "The harmony of the colors of nature comes from the fact that things relate to each other through reflections. For there is absolutely no light that does not touch something, nor is there any illuminated body that does not simultaneously pass on both its light and its color, according to the vivacity of the light and the strength of its color. This participation of reflections in light and in color creates the unity and the harmony of nature that the painter should imitate: and from which it follows that white and black are rarely used in reflections". Roger de Piles, *Cours de peinture par principes* (Paris, 1708), pp. 353–54.

67. It appears as a small reproduction in a catalogue clipping from the now defunct Barbizon House gallery in London.

68. This moment may have been inspired by Gérôme's *Bashi-Bazouk Singing* of 1868, now in the Walters Art Museum, Baltimore, Maryland; see Ackerman, *Gérôme*, cat. no. 185.

69. Gérôme's use of Bargue as an assistant seems quite probable, for at this period Gérôme was still immensely popular as a painter. He had begun a series of several ambitious and expensive sculptures; thus, he may have been finishing off—with Bargue's help—many incomplete paintings lying around his studio in order to raise funds for the sculpture as much as to get the paintings out of the way.

70. Goupil stock books, vol. 11, pp. 77–78. The stock books are in the collection of the J. Paul Getty Research Center, Los Angeles, California.

71. Alfred Trimble, "Springtime Sundries," *The Collector* 5, no. 11, 1 April 1894, p. 168. I wish to thank Eric Zafran for bringing this item to my attention.

72. The letter is in the Roland Balay Archives. I wish to thank DeCourcy E. McIntosh for informing me of this letter.

73. My thanks to Judith Schub for locating Bargue's medical records. I also wish to thank Robert Spencer, M.D., and Johan van Damme, M.D., for their help in interpreting these records.

74. See Theodore Zeldin, *France, 1848–1945* (Oxford: Clarendon Press, 1977), vol. 2, pp. 834–35. Zeldin provides a short list of Magnan's publications.

75. Anon., "Art Notes," *The American Registrar* 15, no. 784, 14 April 1883. Thanks to Madeleine Beaufort for locating this item for me.

76. "Bloc Notes Parisien: Autour d'une Tombe," *Le Gaulois*, 18 October 1884. I wish to thank Hélène Lafont-Couturier at the Goupil Museum in Bordeaux for sending me this notice.

77. J. Stranahan, *A History of French Painting* (New York: Scribner's, 1888), p. 321.

78. On the ambiguous position of art dealers—as both promoters and exploiters—see Jacques Lethève, *The Life of French Artists in the Nineteenth Century* (London: Allen and Unwin, 1972), pp. 142–45; he draws attention to the unattractive dealer père Malgras in Emile Zola's 1886 novel *The Masterpiece (L'Œuvre)*. See also Zeldin, *France*, vol. 2, pp. 464–67.

79. This is the full text of the unsigned brochure describing the publication of the *Drawing Course*. It was published in Paris in 1868 by Goupil et Cie, Éditeurs, rue Chaptal, 9, as a twelve-page brochure. The text is followed by a partial list of plates for the first two parts of the course (up to and including drawing 30 of part II) and an advertisement for a forthcoming *Cours d'Ornement* by Édouard Lièvre.

80. Ernest Chesneau, *Le Constitutionnel*, 5, 12 and 20 December 1865.

81. At the Salon of 1867 Bargue exhibited ten lithographs after Angelo Gaddi, Masaccio, Andrea del Sarto, Hans Holbein the Younger, Hippolyte Flandrin, Jean-Léon Gérôme, Jean-Jacques Henner, and Paul Dubois; at the Salon of 1868 he exhibited another ten after Michelangelo, Raphael, Holbein, Flandrin, Gérôme, Bonnat, and Gleyre.

82. Of course, many of the Renaissance and eighteenth-century methods and machines for drawing that establish a large-squared screen before the subject (sometimes the screen is a net or a plate of glass), an equally squared drawing paper, and a fixed head position are more or less duplicating features of the sight-size technique. So are portrait painters like Velasquez and Sargent, who place their sitters alongside the canvas and stand back to view them. The Boston painter Ives Gammell (1893–1981) taught the technique at his various ateliers, and his students and even their students continue to use and teach it. Gammell had learned it from William Paxton (1869–1941), who had studied with Gérôme and Dennis Miller Bunker (1861–1890), an American student of Gérôme. I do not know where Paxton learned the technique.

83. You will be using the plumb line constantly as you draw, particularly at the beginning. Later, when you are more practiced in the technique, you may prefer a steel knitting needle for some quick estimates. Make your measurements from the point to your thumbnail. Either tool—plumb line or knitting needle—can be used to check the vertical relationships of features of the subject, both externally and internally, and the relationship of one bodily feature to another, say, the lineup of the big toe and the chin, or the distance from a shoulder to a hip or to the navel, and so forth.

84. A film by Victor Erice entitled *Dream of Light* (1990) chronicles the attempt by the Spanish painter Antonio Garcia Lopez to paint a quince tree using the sight-size technique. Although the technique is not named or explained, it is easily recognized as Lopez (in his backyard in Madrid) attempts to prepare a canvas on which to depict the tree with autumnal morning light filtering through its leaves. It takes him a long time to decide where to put his canvas. He establishes foot positions, marks them, and takes elaborate sight measurements using strings. He establishes a position for his feet, always standing in the same spot and wearing the same shoes throughout. An unexpected early rain forces him to have a small shelter built to protect his position marks and his workspace. As the light and weather change, he stops painting and draws on the canvas. After six weeks, as the quinces begin to fall, he gives up. I wish to thank Chris Westenson for bringing this film to my attention.

Ptg 43

Photographic credits

Ackerman collection, pp. 272, 279, 284, 291, 299, 300, 301, 303. Arnot Art Museum. Bequest of Matthias H. Arnot, 1910, p. 306. The Art Institute of Chicago, pp. 293, 314. Artothek/Hans Hinz, Weilheim, p. 169. Bibliothèque nationale de France, Paris, pp. 16, 253, 254, 256, 258, 259, 260, 261, 262, 264, 273, 282, 283, 284, 285, 286, 287, 288, 289, 294, 311. The British Museum, London, p. 123. Christie's, London, pp. 290. Christie's, New York, pp. 293, 299, 300, 304. The Cleveland Museum of Art, Cleveland, Ohio, pp. 295, 296, 303, 335. Courtesy of Annette Lesueur, pp. 14, 15. Courtesy of Daniel Graves, p. 17. Courtesy of Hazlitt, Gooden & Fox, London, p. 266. Courtesy of Jill Newhouse Drawings, New York, p. 297. Courtesy of the owner, p. 268, 294. Ecole nationale supérieure des Beaux-Arts, Paris, p. 19. Fine Arts Museums of San Francisco, p. 21. Fitzwilliam Museum, University of Cambridge, p. 295. Edward T. Wilson, Fund for Fine Arts, Bethesda, pp. 289, 290, 315. Glasgow Museums, p. 296. Göteborgs Konstmuseum/Carlsson, Ebbe, p. 111. Malden Public Library, Malden 310. The Metropolitan Museum of Art, Bequest of Stephen Whitney Phoenix, 1881. (81.1.656) Photograph (© 1994 The Metropolitan Museum of Art, p. 292. The Metropolitan Museum of Art, Catharine Lorillard Wolfe Collection, Bequest of Catharine Lorillard Wolfe, 1887. Photograph (© 1997 The Metropolitan Museum of Art, pp. 269, 297. The Metropolitan Museum of Art, Samuel D. Lee Fund, 1940. (40.11.1a), p. 112. The Metropolitan Museum of Art, Gift of Albert Gallatin, 1920. (20.166.2), p. 304 (drawing 11). Musée Goupil, Bordeaux, p. 262. Musée Goupil, Bordeaux/B. Fontanel, pp. 17, 28-97, 134-167, 186-239. The Museum of Fine Arts, Boston (© 2003), pp. 270, 298. The Museum of Fine Arts, Boston, p. 117. National Museums and Galleries of Wales, p. 295. Nationalmuseum, Stockholm, p. 298. Öffentliche Kunstsammlung Basel, Kufperstichkabinett/Martin Bühler, Bâle, p. 179. Paine Art Center and Gardens, Oshkosh, Wisc., p. 302. Private collection, pp. 319, 321, 323. RMN, Paris, p. 125. RMN, Paris/C. Jean, p. 121. RMN, Paris/Hervé Lewandowski, pp. 100, 103, 126. RMN, Paris/R.G. Ojeda, p. 108. Saskia Ltd, Littleton, p. 101 (right). Scala Picture Library, Florence, pp. 101 (left), 107, 116, 119. Shepherd & Derom Galleries, New York, pp. 291, 310. Sotheby's, London, pp. 307. Sotheby's, New York, pp. 271, 293, 297, 301, 304, 306, 307, 308, 309. Trustees of Princeton University (c 2002), p. 267. Wadsworth Atheneum, Hartford, Conn., p. 302. The Wallace Collection, Londres, p. 255. The Walters Art Museum, Baltimore, Md., pp. 5, 295, 305. Witt Library, Courtauld Institute of Art, London, p. 305.